The Buccaneer Of Nemaris

The Buccaneer of NEMARIS

Andy + Mary
Enjoy the Adventure!

J. D. Delzer

ISBN 10: 159298-318-9
ISBN 13: 978-1-59298-318-6

Library of Congress Control Number: 2009941625
Printed in the United States of America
First Printing: 2009
13   12   11   10   09   5   4   3   2   1

Cover illustration by Katie DeSousa
Illustration on page 122 by Kristina Zidon
Chapter illustration on pages 1, 60, 90, 139, 185, 220, 283, 333, 365, 395, and 435 by Christine Ponce
Map illustrations by the author
Book design by Ryan Scheife, Mayfly Design

BEAVER'S POND
PRESS

Beaver's Pond Press, Inc.
7104 Ohms Lane, Suite 101
Edina, MN 55439-2129
(952) 829-8818
www.BeaversPondPress.com

To order, visit www.BookHouseFulfillment.com
or call (800) 901-3480. Reseller discounts available.

For Gail

"We found the islands hospitable
... our prison was a paradise."

—Cpt. Terrance K. Scyhathen
                    C.S. Nemaris
                January 15th, 1583

Contents

One   ✳   A New Cabin Boy *1*

Two   ✳   Embarking on the Centra Sea *18*

Three   ✳   The Kingdom of Cimmordia *35*

Four   ✳   Lost in Paradise *60*

Five   ✳   Magic and Mysteries *70*

Six   ✳   Acadia *90*

Seven   ✳   Great Hosts *96*

Eight   ✳   A Visitor From the Sea *109*

Nine   ✳   Visions of Destiny *117*

Ten   ✳   Trepidation and Trust *126*

Eleven   ✳   Marshall *139*

Twelve   ✳   Legends and Lies *147*

Thirteen   ✳   Above the Surface *166*

Fourteen   ✳   Fear on the Rocks *174*

Fifteen   ✳   The Burning Seas *181*

Sixteen   ✳   Cimmordian Tea *185*

Seventeen ✳ Demonic Dossier 187

Eighteen ✳ Young Love 200

Nineteen ✳ A Dolphin's Lament 207

Twenty ✳ Greed and Betrayal 222

Twenty-One ✳ A Fish For A Fool 245

Twenty-Two ✳ Kidnapping for a Kidnapping 272

Twenty-Three ✳ Beneath the Mist of Sirens 283

Twenty-Four ✳ Nyguard's Word 298

Twenty-Five ✳ Echo of the Winds 306

Twenty-Six ✳ Calm Seas in Crystal Bay 321

Twenty-Seven ✳ Twilight Reunion 333

Twenty-Eight ✳ A Change of Colors 346

Twenty-Nine ✳ Raiders of Rhydar 355

Thirty ✳ Beyond Time 363

Thirty-One ✳ Greed's Manifest 377

Thirty-Two ✳ A Demon in the Den 381

Thirty-Three ✳ The Wizard of Nemaris 395

Thirty-Four ✳ Triumphant Return 417

Epilogue 435

Prologue

The word "buccaneer" was originally used to describe a person who made preserved meat—often beef jerky or dried pork. When the Caribbean Sea was first inhabited by the Spanish in the 1600s, French seamen and English traders often tried to take claim of the Spanish Main. During trips across the Atlantic, they would leave animals on islands to provide them with meat through "island hopping" stops along the way.

These buccaneers often had their animals slaughtered by the Spanish for attempting to claim lands granted by the Pope to the nation of Spain. So, in search of other forms of food or payment, these buccaneers became mercenaries, often intent on attacking Spanish ships. They were also known as "privateers" or even outright "pirates." While many dictionaries and encyclopedias will state that a buccaneer is no different than a pirate, I beg to differ. For there were many times when a gentleman, civil and just, would resort to actions more becoming of a lesser man to accomplish a vital goal.

The famous Captain Morgan was one of these mercenaries. Working with the approval of the United Kingdom, he successfully attacked Portobello, a major port on the Spanish Main. Like many buccaneers of the era, Morgan was a ruthless fighter and tactician, but he was also a gentleman who carried himself with honor and civility.

Unlike buccaneers, pirates are first and foremost thieves. Their goals are wealth and the supplies or technology needed to gain that wealth. A pirate crew has nothing to lose and everything to gain; they will drown, cut down, or shoot any who stand in their way.

Classically, a pirate did not have the resources to simply call together a few friends and sail on a six-week excursion in hopes of finding a few gold bars. He would find himself a crew of men who shared his passion, and then they would steal a ship and command it as their own. After finding another ship, they would attack it—head on with full strength, as the men had nothing to lose—and they would claim whatever they could find, usually ship stores, lantern oil, and grain supplies. Surprise and fear were their greatest weapons. Almost never would they find gold and riches ... unless they happened across a treasure galleon en route to Spain or elsewhere.

Treasure maps were never used, and burying booty ashore was unheard of. Treasure, when found, was divided up at once. A system of collective trust was used aboard ship, but if you got killed in your sleep, your treasure was gone. And that would be that.

Pirate guilds, much like thieves' guilds, were simply larger organizations of pirates who teamed up to stage larger raids. In this novel, one such group is named the Ranthath Cult. It formed in much the same way as the privateers did; trade was in high spirits, and those who did not have other means of livelihood fell back to the old patterns of taking what belonged to others. The Centra Sea, a region open to the currents of the seas but not unlike the Caribbean, was also ripe with this trade.

In the world of the Centra Sea, however, there were men who were honest, honorable, and moral who also sailed the seas. They sought adventure and stability, and learning what lay beyond the next wave. Did they fight? Yes, to defend what they had found, but not because they coveted the next fortune. They took care of their own and stood by their word. These were the buccaneers of the Centra Sea, hoping to capitalize on cargo and grain exchanges to better the world around them and maintain their daily adventures.

Taking the differences between pirates and buccaneers a step further, the three ship captains in the book represent three views of greed. One captain is the buccaneer—the gentleman, the traveler, the journeyman. Another is the villain—the heartless, the thief, the kidnapper. And finally, the third seeks revenge, through brutality and remorseless death ... revenge for his fate and his toils in life. He lives with fear in his heart and greed in his soul.

None of it would have happened without a fourth captain, Terrance K. Scyhathen. The renowned adventurer had a passion for sailing and received a commission from the king of Xavier in hopes of charting the world with his own pen. He later achieved this goal with his own boat, sailing by his own rules. First he traveled north to Kynniayck, finding it a large and well-developed continent. Scyhathen next sailed east across the Eastrell Ocean to the exotic continent of Eastrell to open trade with the other nations of the world. Then he sailed west to Tabia's Qui-Kinneas and the land of the endless deserts.

Finally, Scyhathen aspired to complete the compass rose and head south to the frozen continent of Phrynn and its hidden nations ... but Scyhathen failed in this endeavor, only to be shipwrecked upon uncharted islands.

Scyhathen did not seek treasure. He was funded by the nation of Xavier and the port of Elna City and earned that funding because of his talent as both a diplomat and his skill as a swordsman. He would become the best-known buccaneer in the world, for he not only was a world-traveled explorer but also returned any treasure he was given. Scyhathen had neither want nor use of such artifacts, and refused most offers.

The islands that ended Scyhathen's legacy now bear the name of his galleon. These fabled and feared islands were home to another buccaneer of sorts, one who did his dueling differently—not with swords, but magic. Hoping to reprimand those who chose the way of the pirate instead of the way of the buccaneer, this wizard brought them to his islands and placed their treasure in with his own while punishing the roguish lifestyle. Once satisfied, he would return that treasure to its worthy owners....

But that's another story.

For many of Gaia's citizens, stories are just as valuable as fresh water and the most treasured jewels. Scyhathen charted many ports and touched countless people ... and everyone has a story to tell of their encounter with the great captain. Enjoy these stories, and pass them along as the treasures that they are. For what are stories if they are kept hidden and forgotten?

The Lands of the Centra

Two continents, each with its own stories and adventures to tell. To the east lies the continent of Crellan, home to regal Cimmordia, cosmopolitan Dieteria and agricultrual Xavier. The western continent of Tabia holds industrial Tallebeck, the arid dunes of Qui-Kinneas and the uncharted lands of the King's Forest and the Faate Mountains.

The era is one of exploration and expanding commerce, when tales of adventure and grandeur can buy a weary traveler a cot and a warm cup of stew, for magical beasts and fantastic castles are not the stuff of dreams but part of the fabric of reality.

It is here, upon the lands of Crellan and Tabia, where the Buccaneer of Nemaris first left his home port on a journey of exploration and under-standing. His efforts transformed a few dots on a chart to represent more than simply distance and time, but a chance for people of different lands to know one another.

Tabin River
Derrisburg
Grand Point
Blyster Bay
of
TABIA
Teraske Highlands
Dens Forest
Derris Road
Shenna Shallows
Valiavista Island
Teraske
Crystal Bay
South Centra Sea
Cyeal Point
Nemaris Islands

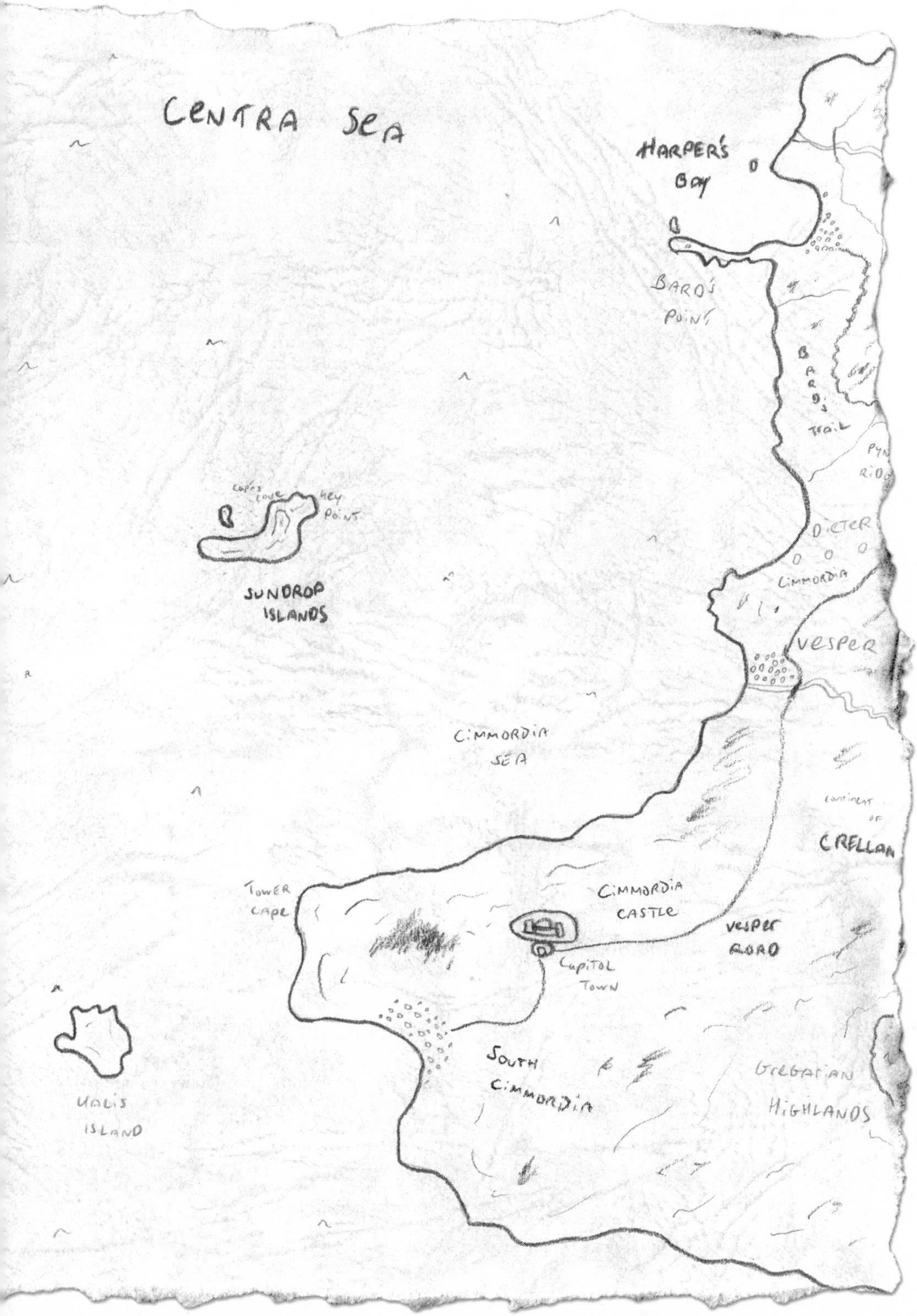
CENTRA SEA
HARPER'S BAY
BARD'S POINT
BARD'S TRAIL
DIETER
CIMMORDIA
VESPER
Key Point
SUNDROP ISLANDS
CIMMORDIA SEA
continent of
CRELLAN
TOWER CAPE
CIMMORDIA CASTLE
VESPER ROAD
Capitol Town
SOUTH CIMMORDIA
GREGARIAN HIGHLANDS
VALIS ISLAND

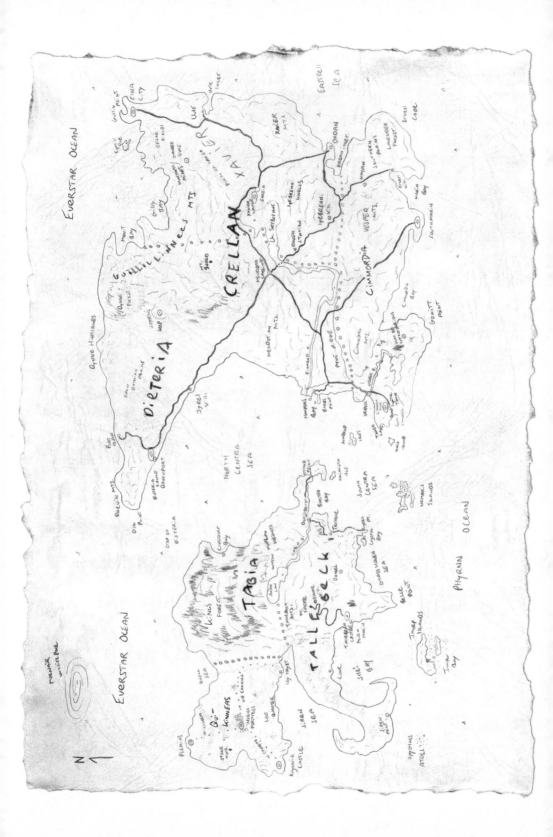

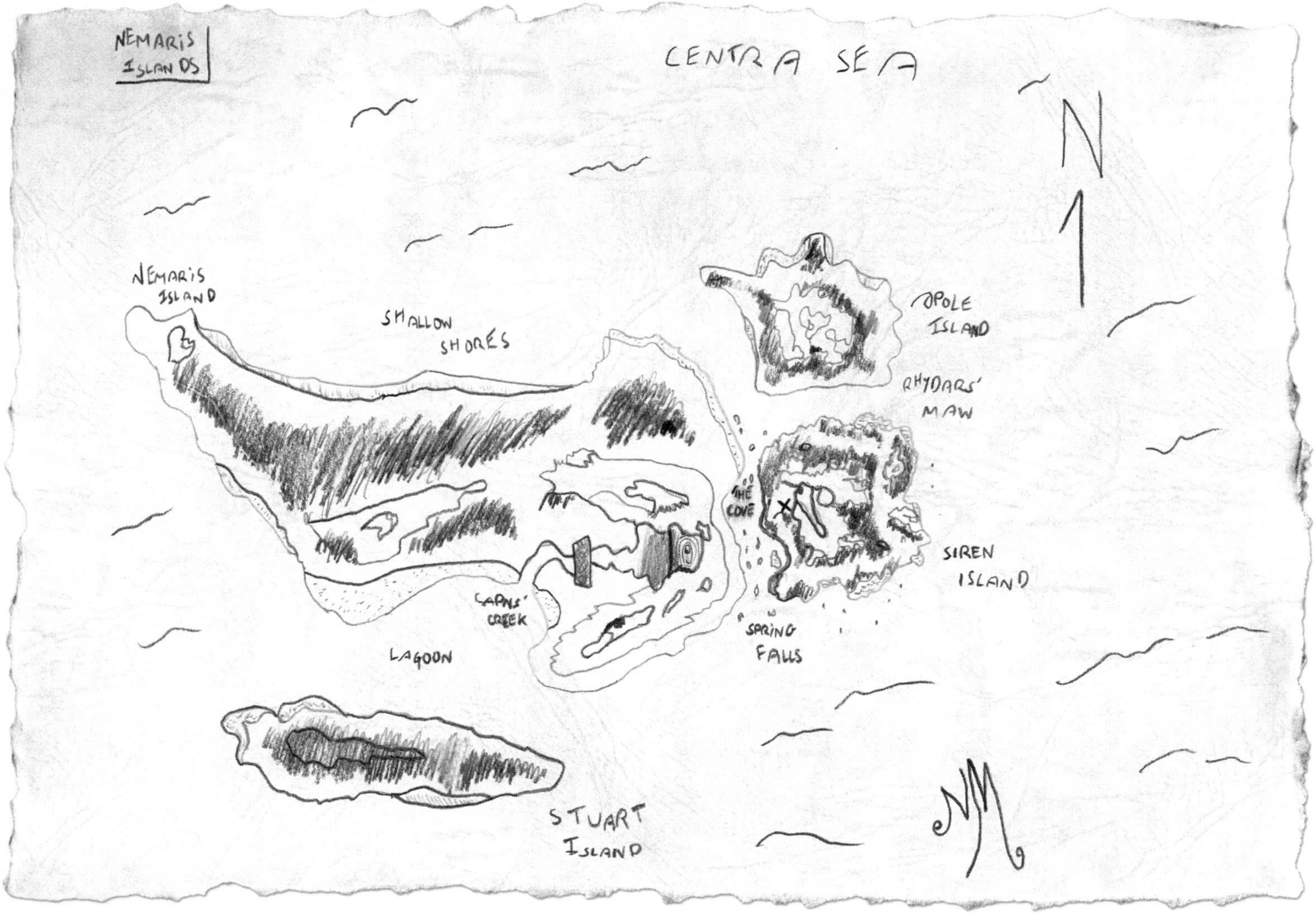

NEMARIS ISLANDS
CENTRA SEA
N
NEMARIS ISLAND
SHALLOW SHORES
OPOLE ISLAND
RHYDARS' MAW
THE COVE
SIREN ISLAND
CAPNS' CREEK
SPRING FALLS
LAGOON
STUART ISLAND

*I*t was a time of adventure, pirates, and magical mysteries. At the southern reaches of the Centra Sea lay islands rumored to be full of vast riches and demonic ills. Mystical and beautiful as these islands were, they remained isolated and untouched, due to the tales of horrible evils and fantastic creatures said to dwell both upon and beneath their shores.

The Nemaris Islands were named after the vessel commanded by Captain Terrence K. Scyhathen, a sailor who attempted to discover the island chain's many secrets. Scyhathen became famous throughout the world of Gaia for his legendary exploits, but his legacy was defined by his last expedition. It was then he met his greatest foe, a terrible pirate known simply as Epoth.

Encountered during Scyhathen's charting of the Nemaris Islands, the evil entity Epoth attacked by means of terror and secrecy. As the days passed and the attacks increased, the good captain and crew struggled to survive as Epoth's shadowy form filled the men with a dark, all-encompassing fear.

It was said Scyhathen solved his battles with words, seldom needing nor employing his famous longsword in battle. Yet according to his last writings, Scyhathen thought it a wonder that he and Epoth had never crossed swords, and he regretted never meeting his opponent face to face.

Captain Scyhathen's fate is a mystery, for he never returned from this final journey. Some suspected the dastardly Ranthath Cult, a well-known clan of pirates, had claimed the islands for use as a hidden base. Others claimed Scyhathen had simply became part of the Centra Sea's most taboo legend. The wreck of the *Nemaris* remains lost, believed to be entombed at the bottom of the Centra Sea, and with it all evidence of her crew.

Many years after Scyhathen disappeared, a clue finally materialized when a map of the Nemaris Islands surfaced in the nation of Dieteria. Few could decipher the map's many secrets, and stories of the final fate of the *Nemaris* began to emerge again.

Old rumors of fantastic demons and terrors again discouraged all but the hardiest of treasure hunters; the very thought of the Nemaris Islands would incur dread. Eventually, the islands faded into obscurity, and the chain's existence was accepted as nothing more than fantasy. For this reason, all sanctioned expeditions to the mysterious isles were cancelled ... but that did not stop those who coveted the vast riches purported to be hidden within their depths.

The legend of the Nemaris Islands would remain forgotten until young Thomas DeLeuit made an unexpected find some forty years after the famous captain's fateful expedition. Although he had visions of cruising the seven seas in search of fame and fortune, Thomas lived modestly with his mother in Harper's Bay. Life in the small port town had always been peaceful and uneventful, but shortly after a discovery in his father's study, Thomas's world would change forever.

A New Cabin Boy

*T*t was as calm and picturesque a morning as there could ever be. The sound of gentle waves upon the beach blended with the scent of freshly baked bread from the DeLeuit's home in Harper's Bay.

The mid-morning sun was full in the sky, and the breeze gently ruffled the unkempt, light brown hair of the fourteen-year-old boy who always came to Diamond Falls to pass the time between tasks. Soft sand lay beneath his feet as the sun beamed down on his jerkin and vest. Thomas was near the beach carving into a rock and watching a ship sail by when he heard his mother's call. Their modest house, once a tavern on the northern edge of town, had a grand view of the ocean. Years ago, a sailing ship in the distance meant business that night, but now, there was other work to be done.

"Thomas!"

"Coming, Mother!" Thomas quickly jumped to his feet and ran to the house.

Inside, his mother was wrapping a half-dozen loaves of bread in a large basket. They had just come out of the oven, and the wonderful aroma of grains and yeast filled the house.

"Yes, Mother?"

"Bring this to Captain Janes. His crew is waiting for it at the docks."

Marianne DeLeuit wasn't a stern woman. Her love was sometimes difficult to see, but Thomas knew that he was everything to her. Caring for her son alone meant requiring him to bring deliveries to the docks and attend to other tasks—nothing interesting, let alone dangerous. Thomas was often amazed he got away at all because of her tight watch on him. But no matter how hard she pushed him, she showed her love for her son that much more.

"Of course, Mother." Thomas carried the basket onto the path leading to the docks.

"And hurry, Dear! The captain got cold bread last time!"

"I will!" Heeding his mother's words, Thomas ran south as quickly as he could for about a quarter-mile toward the port.

Although Thomas often dreamed of other places, Harper's Bay had always been his home. He never thought of the city as a destination, but a rest stop for Dieteria's merchant sailors to the ports of Cimmordia. Originally founded by bards and poets, the city began as a small camp until shipping traffic began to increase near the rocky shoals along the coastline. Several lighthouses would be built, and much to the shagrin of the city's founders, a port soon followed. A market for artisan bakers and spices from the local woods came next, and before long Harper's Bay was a full-fledged city.

Well aware that the bread was starting to cool, Thomas stopped before reaching the docks when Bobby Lewis halted him in his tracks. Of the families in Harper's Bay, Bobby was one of the handful of boys Thomas's age, but that wasn't the only reason they were the best of friends.

"Hey Tommy, where you going this time?"

Bobby Lewis also had an unusual family. He lived with the town elder, Master Harrion, who had taken Bobby in when the boy was left on his doorstep as an infant. Bobby respected his elder and took heed of his teachings. In fact, with his elder's expert assistance, Bobby had learned how to decode the languages of the Centra Sea and its nearby nations, including texts written in regards to the Nemaris Islands.

"Making deliveries for mother." Thomas stopped for a moment.

"Are you free after dinner tonight?" Bobby's tone was nonchalant. "I wonder if you would chance a look at some of my maps with me."

"Elder Harrion's maps? Does he let you look at them now?" Thomas knew maps were a treasured resource.

"Not exactly, but he will be at the town meeting tonight, and we will be free to take a gander!"

"I look forward to it! But I must go for now." Thomas hastened back to his chore.

"Just meet me before the church bell sounds eight, okay?"

"Right, see you then!"

Thomas continued on, knowing that his delivery might get cold from the breeze that flowed off the sea.

"Until then!" Bobby waved after him.

Thomas rushed past the sprawling Mermaid's Rest Tavern and the stone façade of the town hall to arrive at the docks. Spotting Captain Christopher Janes' blue and black flag among the bobbing masts, he made his way to the *Valiant*. First mate Seriam Ward greeted the boy as he scampered up the gangplank with the breadbasket.

"Hey Tommy, got the bread there?"

Thomas handed Mr. Ward the basket. "Fresh bread here, sir."

"Hmm! Got it here warm yet! Here's something for your mother—there's a bit extra for being so prompt." Ward passed him a handful of coins.

Thomas pocketed the money. "Thank you, sir."

"Tommy! Is that you?" Captain Janes called from the deck.

Captain Christopher Janes had been on the ocean all of his life, having joined a merchant's galleon when he was six. He earned the right to captain a ship at the ripe age of thirty-eight and had been in command of the *Valiant* ever since. In addition to stops on either side of the Centra Sea, he visited Harper's Bay at least once a month. Sometimes he would visit Mrs. DeLeuit's homestead for dinner. The two were old friends and always shared conversations about the ports he'd last visited. Every time his crew docked, they'd purchase a basket of bread. Janes had taken a shine to young Thomas; he saw much in the boy that he'd once seen in himself.

"Hello, Captain Janes!"

Captain Janes shook Thomas's hand firmly. "Ahoy there, boy! You keeping to your mother?"

Thomas nodded. "Yes sir, all the time."

"Would ye mind taking me to her? Need to ask her something."

"Sure can sir. Follow me." Thomas took point, and they headed up the hill.

"You're a good boy, Tommy. You're too much like me, but a good boy." He took Thomas's hand as they walked north to the DeLeuit homestead.

Captain Janes appeared at the upper half of the open Dutch door at the back of the house. "Excuse me, Madam, may I come in?"

"Oh!" Mrs. DeLeuit looked up from her sewing. "Good day, Captain. Yes, of course you may! Please, come and rest your legs."

Following behind the captain, Thomas emptied the coins into his mother's hands. "Here's the money from Mr. Ward, Mother."

She placed the currency inside an apron pocket. "Yes, thank you dear. How are you today, captain?"

"Quite well, thank you. I do hope I am not intruding." Janes sat himself at the kitchen table.

"Nonsense, you are always welcome here. Where have your adventures brought you safe from today?" Marianne asked.

"A distant port known as Derrisburg. I'm sure I've spoken of it before. It's a tad larger than this one, but there be one thing that port doesn't have."

"What is that, sir?" Thomas asked.

"Why, the both of you, of course." Janes patted the boy on the shoulder.

Mrs. DeLeuit smiled at the pleasant gesture. "Go on, Thomas, get the captain some ale."

"Come now, Marianne, you know me. I'm not the drinking sort. Although I do admire your tea—nobody else makes it like you do." Janes's expression was hopeful.

"Oh yes, of course … I always forget." She laughed. "I'm so used to the days we ran a tavern here, you know that."

"Yes, and those were good times."

"We have a jug of tea cooling in the cellar, sir." Thomas headed to the stairs to fetch it.

"Marianne, have I ever mentioned you have a wonderful boy?"

"I am certain you have, Christopher, but it is always appreciated." Marianne finished the cuff she was hemming and set her sewing aside. "Yes, he is a hard-working young man. Just like his father."

"Indeed … a shame I never was able to meet him.…" Janes looked down at his calloused hands a moment before returning his gaze to her. "Forgive me, Marianne, but I come with a bit of a predicament. Fallon, the cabin boy who's been with us since we last journeyed from the north, has come to a tad bit of trouble, I'm afraid. We had to leave him at Derrisburg because of a mysterious illness."

Marianne gave a concerned look that only a mother could make. "The poor boy … is he in good care?"

"Yes, and the doctor has high hopes for his recovery." He glanced at his hands again then smiled. "But, in the meantime, we'll need a replacement, and you and I both know that young Thomas is well trained in the arts of sailing and can handle himself with a sword quite well."

"He has followed your training to the letter, Chris."

A beaming smile crossed the captain's face. "He's got the blood of a buccaneer, Marianne. If he were to come with us, I could further his skills ... provided he did a few chores for us around the ship, earn his keep if you will."

Marianne regained her motherly concerns, suddenly worried she might lose her son. "You are suggesting he live as you do?"

Thomas returned from the cellar. "Here is your tea, sir. It should be cold—the cellar is usually quite cool." He gave the captain a mug filled with the draught.

Janes accepted the tea with a smile. "Thank you, Tommy. It's greatly appreciated."

"Mother, shall I begin dinner?"

"It is nearly finished, Thomas. You may go about your business for awhile—but do not stray too far, hear?"

"As you wish, mother." Thomas headed outside, unaware of the tension between his mother and guest.

"Of course, I'd pay the boy well," Janes continued. "A fair day's pay for a cabin boy, provided he earn it—three Dictares a week."

"That seems reasonable, and the income would certainly be welcome ... but I'm not sure." Marianne turned from Janes a moment, reaching for a poker by the hearth.

"I seem to recall your telling me that Thomas's father was a cabin boy in his youth, yes?"

Marianne nodded, her attention on the cooking fire. "Yes, but Gregory never spoke about that time. I have often wondered what Thomas could have learned from him."

"He's a good boy, Marianne."

Marianne looked back at him with a critical gleam in her eyes. "True, he is. And a hard worker ... this is sudden, though. Let me think about it, captain. I'll give you an answer tonight." Turning away, she set aside the poker and stirred the stew.

"Yes, I agree it is sudden to thrust this upon you, but I've thought it over for some time now, and I believe he's ready." Janes spoke with conviction.

"I know ... and he does need a path in life, but..." Marianne began.

"If you refuse I shan't think any less of you." His voice softened. "I understand how important he is to you."

"Tell me, would you care to stay for dinner tonight?" Marianne asked, changing the subject.

"I'd be delighted!" After all, the captain had been craving the cooking since he arrived, and he could not refuse.

Although Thomas didn't usually wander too far when dinnertime came near, he would occassionally travel just to the north to the Diamond River to listen to a serene waterfall at the delta. Of all the places in town, Thomas decided, this place had always been his favorite.

It was a warm April day, and with wildflowers beginning to bloom among the rocks along the river, everything was in a state of beauty. Thomas looked out to sea, where a schooner was sailing by from Harper's Bay to the distant capitol of Dieteria in the north. He did not know the name of the city, but longed to visit such a place, even if only for a day. Thomas knew the castle was always there, as Harper's Bay was governed by it, but his mother would never allow him to travel so far away.

Thomas would often sit by the waterfall to collect his thoughts and dream that someone would come to take him to see the world, but he was convinced that such a thing would probably never happen.

Thomas enjoyed the falls not only for their peaceful beauty but also because they held a special secret—it was a place of visions. When he was very young, Thomas had been drawn to the falls on a foggy day. As soon as he'd arrived, the fog dissipated and a ship appeared beyond the point to the south. A few moments later, the ship vanished, but then he heard a voice.

"Thomas ... be good to your mother, and I shall be good to you...."

This experience remained somewhat of a mystery until a later vision proved that the voice was indeed his father's. The second vision was of a horrible shipwreck on an island west of Cimmordia Castle. The voice cried out his father's name, a voice that often reminded Thomas of fear itself. It was unclear if his father was speaking from beyond the grave, but Thomas knew that his father was trying to tell him something....

Now there was no fog or mystery, and Thomas relaxed blissfully as the afternoon wore on. The scene was indeed amazing, as the skies were crystal blue, the wind was calm, and the rhythm of the gentle waves was very soothing. Thomas slowly began to drift asleep when suddenly the skies grew gray.

He opened his eyes. "A storm?"

The winds increased. Clouds rapidly blocked out the sunlight, and the ocean groaned as its waves grew wild. Lightning struck as a deep voice began to shudder inside of Thomas's mind....

... You shall feel my wrath, my creator....

"Thomas!"

Thomas was startled as his mother's voice brought him swiftly back to reality. All was as it had been before ... as if he had dreamed it all. But violent waves broke the ocean's surface several yards from shore. There was a shadow in the sea, and Thomas stood up to investigate.

"Thomas! Come home for dinner!"

Quickly, Thomas glanced into the nearby surf, and whatever he thought he had seen was gone. Ignoring the apparition, he rose to his feet and ran toward the house. If he had indeed dreamed the voice, or that image in the water, both could wait to be explored later.

"Thomas!" Mrs. DeLeuit called from her back door.

Captain Janes stood behind her, squinting into the distance. "Does the lad often wander off?"

"He likes to sit on the beach just north of here, so I'm not worried. He should be along soon."

Janes sat down at the supper table. Thomas arrived a moment later, cleaned himself up, and joined the captain at the table. "Good evening, sir."

"Not yet Thomas—make up the table," Mrs. DeLeuit ordered. Thomas went to work.

"Allow me," Janes said, getting up to help.

"That's not necessary, Captain." Mrs. DeLeuit handed Thomas bowls and spoons.

"I don't mind, actually." Janes fetched a hot mitt and carried the stew to the table.

With the meal spread out on the table, they sat down and enjoyed Marianne's creation. After everything had been cleaned up, Thomas went off to meet Bobby. That left Captain Janes and Marianne together in the parlor to share a cup of after-dinner tea.

"Sailing south to Vesper, and further south from there."

"It depends on what materials you carry for your next port, yes?"

"Indeed." With his free hand, Janes gestured as though pointing to spots on a map. "We usually run a circle route—from here to Vesper, to South Cimmordia, beyond the Nemaris Islands to Teraske, north to Derrisburg or Grand Point, and then start over again here in Harper's Bay."

"Nemaris Islands? That sounds like a place I have heard of before."

"Quite an infamous locale, Marianne." The captain's brow furrowed slightly. "We keep our distance, but the islands are not far from our route. They're uninhabited as far as I know ... and far to the south of here."

"Yes, now I remember. I've heard they're enchanted."

He shrugged. "That's the common word among most sailors on the Centra. The crew and I have a general rule that there is little reason to head there, and we make a point to avoid them as much as possible. That we sail by them so close is often too much for the men to bear."

"What stories have you heard?" Her tone was conversational, expressing neither curiosity nor concern, and Janes appreciated the question wasn't asked lightly.

"Very few—mostly rumors that the islands once belonged to a sorcerer and he had amassed some treasure. Others say it was the headquarters of a pirate clan that hid from the royal armada after pillaging several nations. They're out of our way, and that's that."

"How are conditions on board?"

"They are probably best when we are not out to sea for more than a few days. We dock quite regularly, the only exception when we sail between South Cimmordia and Teraske. There is plenty of food, enough jars of fruit to last a week at a time, and ample space for every hand. I have my own quarters in the stern, but aside from more living space it is very much like what the men share."

Marianne took a drink of her tea. "You are headed for Vesper next, yes?"

"Correct."

"Well, I should think to tell Thomas to gather his things into the trunk, then," Marianne said softly.

"You will let him come with us?"

Marianne nodded. "I trust you'll take good care of him, Christopher. You and I both know it'll be good for him. He will discover what it means to live on the sea, learn a thing or two about sailing, and will get some exercise working daily tasks. He learned how to swim from you, how to defend himself, how to tie his shoes … every time you've come ashore he's learned so much—you're almost like a father to him."

"Yes, yes. A shame that Gregory couldn't be here to teach his son."

"Yes." She gazed toward a chair in the front corner of the room. "I fondly remember him, Christopher, sitting there in his chair. We were married in King Roland's court … and then before I knew it he was gone."

Janes had never heard that detail of the story. "Right away? Before Tommy was born?"

Marianne nodded again. "There was no question of our love, of course. And we had been together for so long.…"

Janes took a drink from his own cup. "If I've learned anything from my days of sailing, Marianne, it's that the Centra Sea has her own agenda. She doesn't care who you are, where you come from. If she wants someone … well, that's just her nature."

Marianne sipped her tea, wiping a tear from her face. "The seas can be dangerous… but I trust he'll be safe on your ship. My only reservation is that Thomas comes home every month."

"You have my word. You will see your son every month as long as Thomas is learning and enjoying himself. I trust you've discussed a chance like this before, yes?"

"I haven't, but I expect he'll be quite happy to go. When are you due to leave?"

"Tomorrow morning. Will that be enough time for him to prepare?"

"I'll help him get ready. Tomorrow, then?"

Janes set down his cup and started for the door. "Tomorrow. Good eve, and thank you again for the dinner."

Marianne smiled. "Anytime, Christopher."

While the captain and Mrs. DeLeuit prepared for the future, Thomas and Bobby focused on the past. They were looking at some of Elder Harrion's charts of the Centra Sea, several of which were as old as sailing itself.

Harrion's home had been made from a converted lighthouse, no longer needed once the new ones had been built upon rocky Bard's Point. The lantern room had been made into a den, although much of it was used for storage of Harrion's historical archives, and for some of his old friend

Gregory DeLeuit's as well. It was one of the elder's favorite games to quote foreign lands and forgotten locations, a trait that Bobby had inherited.

"So where are we?" Thomas asked, looking over a chart of the local area.

"Right here. That's the town, there's the Diamond River, the falls, and Bard's Point is right out there," Bobby explained, pointing out the various locations on the chart.

"Then, this harbor down here must be Vesper, and further beyond that is South Cimmordia and Kalis Island, right?"

Bobby nodded. "That's right, but it's very far. About three day's sail, I believe."

Thomas pointed to a small group of four islands that lay south of Grand Point. "What about those islands down there?"

This turned Thomas's expression to one more quizzical. "I thought you knew everything about those, considering your father served with the great captain."

"Which great captain?" Thomas didn't remember hearing about this from his mother.

"Come, on Tommy, the captain!" Bobby spread his hands wide to express the enormity of the name. "Captain Scyhathen—the explorer who discovered those islands and charted them out. Surely you've heard of the Nemaris Islands."

"Maybe in a bedtime story. Are they very close to here? I always thought they were in some distant land."

"Well, they are nearly a week's sail, but that's not important, because nobody goes there." He gave Thomas a knowing look. "Unless, of course, they're looking for trouble."

"I was told those islands are enchanted."

"Enchanted, yes! Safe, no." Bobby shook his head for emphasis. "One man's fantasy is another man's terror. It's said the place is full of traps and horrors unimaginable. Some people say just going ashore is bad for one's health!"

"You're just playing me for a fool." Thomas huffed. "Nothing can be that bad."

"Suit yerself. All I know is that you'll never find me within sight of that place. And woe to those who get lost there." He reached for another chart.

While Bobby moved onto the next chart, Thomas took a closer look at the Nemaris Islands. Although the map wasn't as detailed as he would've liked, he was able to determine that the chain contained four islands. The first was small and very rocky, a second consisted of forests and a few steep hills, a third was the largest and the most uncharted of the group, and the fourth was rather small and narrow with a few sparse trees. Three of the four were crescent shaped, except for a few variations along the coastline. The largest island appeared to have an inlet to a lagoon that wasn't clearly marked. Although the map was incomplete, Thomas could visibly imagine the island chain's allure.

"Hey, look at this," Bobby said, showing him a painting of a young woman. Even at first glance, Thomas could clearly tell the woman had an air of mystery about her.

"Who's that?"

"I don't know, but I'd sure love to find out." He passed over the portrait to look at some old navigation equipment.

Thomas took a more careful look at the painting. The woman appeared to be deep in thought. Her face and long hair were lovely, but it was her blue eyes that caught his attention. She had no tears in her eyes, although their deep hue and gaze told of sorrow. Thomas's gaze next followed glistening hair, gracefully draped across her shoulders. Her hair was a rich shade of amber that reminded him of tall, mighty oaks growing in the forest. Her skin was pale and soft, without blemishes or impurities. Her expression was innocent and displayed a deep wisdom, as if the history of countless generations filled her thoughts. However, the sadness of her look convinced Thomas that she had other thoughts on her mind when the portrait was made.

Noticing his friend's interest, Bobby laughed. "You looking to court her or something?"

Thomas frowned. "Just trying to understand her expression. I wonder what was on her mind."

"It's only a portrait, Thomas! If it was a real person, she'd probably be bored waiting for the painter to finish."

"I guess that could be the case." Reluctantly, Thomas set the portrait aside.

Bobby handed him a chart displaying a large continent. "Here, take a look at this."

At that moment, Harrion returned home. "Bobby boy, I'm back," the Elder announced as he closed the door behind him.

Elder Harrion had been the town historian for many years and had become an authority of the region's history and folklore. His main interests were literature and cartography, which had resulted in the great collection of books and maps that lay in his upstairs den. He had known Gregory DeLeuit very well before he disappeared, and had hoped to make a library with the materials they had both amassed. Although he had adopted Bobby shortly after Thomas was born and cared deeply for his adopted son, the elder restricted access to much of his literature. It was Harrion's belief that such business should be kept by elders, not young men.

"He's home! Put these charts away while I go distract him!" Bobby cried. Thomas quickly began putting everything back where they'd found it.

"Bobby? Where are you, lad?"

"I'm here, sir." Bobby came down the stairs into the main room as calmly as he could.

"Were you upstairs in my den, lad?" Harrion's brow furrowed.

"Just putting your magnifying lens back where it belonged. I borrowed it for a moment." It was a believable and reasonable explanation, one that should keep Harrion from climbing the stairs to investigate.

"I see. As long as you were careful, I can overlook it, I suppose." Harrion headed into his chambers.

"Come on, hurry up!" Bobby whispered to Thomas. After quietly slipping the last chart onto its shelf, Thomas rushed down the steps and outside before Harrion could return.

Oblivious, Harrion grumbled in his chamber as he exchanged his jacket for his evening robe. "I tell you, boy, the townsfolk get stranger every day, preaching and fussing about expanding the town and creating a ruckus with the castle, oy." He shuffled back to the main room and made his way toward his favorite chair. "They say we're too isolated from the rest of the nation and want more help from the capitol. Largest city in the world, the capital city of Davenport … so far away and yet so powerful even here."

"I recall you said you prefer our isolation, sir." Bobby was careful not to rile his guardian too much on this subject, for he had always known about Harrion's thoughts on politics.

"Isolation and intercooperation, Bobby, are both necessary and exclusive. Remember that!" With a huff, he sat. "These townfolk, well … they want aid, but they don't want to have people telling them what to do or pay additional taxes to the king."

"I hope to never get involved in such matters, sir," Bobby said sagely.

"You're telling me—you're educated, boy ... these people ... I tell you! Humph." Shaking his head, Harrion reached for his pipe.

Thomas returned home to see Captain Janes leaving.

"Hello, Tommy," Janes patted him on the shoulder.

"Good evening, sir."

"I think there's something your mother wants to ask you." With a smile, he walked off.

Somewhat confused, Thomas went inside. His mother was finishing a cup of tea.

"Mother, the captain mentioned that you needed me for something?"

She placed the empty cup on her kitchen counter. "Yes, Thomas. I was talking with the captain, and he's looking for a cabin boy. Someone to swab the deck, perform a few chores, and assist the crew. Important job, he said."

Thomas perked up. "Would I stay with him on the ship, then?"

"Of course." She busied herself tidying the kitchen. "You'd see the ocean, visit distant lands, maybe help with the ship rigging. He also said that he'd teach you sword skills, the way of the ocean, and pay you quite fairly as well. Maybe you'll even learn about some things your father did."

It was like a dream come true. "Wow! That'd be wonderful!"

Mrs. DeLeuit turned to him and smiled. "You'd like to go along with him, then?"

"If I may? Please?" There was no hiding his enthusiasm.

"I had a feeling you'd be all for it, so I already told the captain you'd join him."

"Wonderful! Thank you, mother!" Thomas threw his arms around her.

She hugged him back tightly, knowing that she wouldn't see her son for a month at a time at least. "Before you go, you need to prepare for your journey. The trunk is in the attic."

"Yes, mother." After a final hug, Thomas headed for the stairs.

"Thomas, wait. There's one more thing that you should bring along … something that you might find useful should you find yourself with free time."

Thomas turned toward his mother, who picked up a dusty book from the bookshelf. She wiped the dust clean before handing it to him. A glint of light struck the brass medallion sewn onto the book's cracked leather cover. Intrigued, Thomas held the book with shaky hands.

"Go on, open it." She nodded to him. "Careful, it's a very old book."

Thomas did so, opening it to the first page. Inside was a handwritten signature and its full title, From Grand Point to Phrynn: The Journal of Captain Scyhathen.

"Captain Scyhathen?" Thomas asked curiously. He remembered hearing the name from Bobby.

"He was a great explorer from Elna City, where I grew up. But he was not born there … he was said to come from a place on the Mynnac Sea," Marianne explained.

Thomas nodded, flipping through the first several pages.

"This book was among your father's things … who knows, you may find it interesting. Don't read it now … you have a lot to do before tomorrow. But take care of it … your father treasured it, and so should you."

Thomas closed the book. "Yes, mother. May I go now?"

She nodded, sighing as he left.

Thomas went up to the attic, which was his bedroom. While Thomas slept in a small room with a grand view of the ocean, a second room was used solely for storage. Aside from those items kept safe by Elder Harrion, the rest of Gregory DeLeuit's possessions were here. Although he was discouraged from digging through this room, once in awhile Thomas would wander around inside. He didn't have to search hard for the trunk, as it wasn't buried nor very heavy, even with the items that remained inside. After moving a few other things aside, he pulled the trunk into his room.

Once there, he opened up the trunk and removed a number of old sheets and coats, one of which fit him quite well. Underneath that were several books, charts, and a few tablets of paper that were largely unused. There was a bracelet with some ornamental beads on it, a small rag that could be used to polish rocks, a few small tools, and some other miscellaneous items.

His mind quickly returned to Captain Scyhathen's journal, and Thomas took a moment to again page through the book. As he scanned through the journal's entries, Thomas read tales of islands and adventure, exciting events, and daily travel logs. The majority of the journal was unfinished, while sections of pages had been torn out and were missing. He was about to begin reading when he heard his mother climbing the stairs, and he put the book at the bottom of the trunk underneath some sheets.

"How are you coming, Thomas?" Mrs. DeLeuit asked as she came into the room.

"I'm not certain what I should pack, Mother."

"Well, anything you want really, but you should at least pack your clothes," she answered with a smile.

Thomas nodded, pulling things from his wardrobe. "Yes, thank you Mother."

His mother chuckled quietly. "Don't worry about a thing, Thomas. The captain'll take good care of you."

As he removed clothes from hangers, it occurred to him his mother would be alone. What if something happened and he wasn't there to help her? The thought made him shiver. "I guess I'm just a little scared, Mother."

She kissed his forehead. "You worry too much, dear. You'll see me once a month, you know that. We both know that. Once you get underway, you'll be seeing new places, meeting new faces, and you'll be having such a good time with Captain Janes that you won't have time to think about what's going on here at home."

Thomas nodded slowly.

"Here, this should help." Mrs. DeLeuit reached into her apron pocket and pulled out a small cobalt orb about two inches in diameter. It was made of glass, and as the dim light passed through, it left a small blue circle on her hand.

"What is that?"

"It's something special my mother gave me. Something that she gave me before I met your father."

Thomas watched the light reflect within the orb.

"She told me one thing before I left home, and it was this. She told me, 'Marianne, whenever you're far from home, and you're too far to see it with your eyes, just look into this orb and it'll help your heart see where your home is.'"

Thomas took the orb from her hand and looked into it. "All I see is blue glass, mother."

"Okay, so it is only glass." She rumpled his hair like she used to when he sassed her as a little boy. "But when you're out there in the world, it'll work for you, trust me."

Thomas nodded.

"Now then. Let's get you packed and ready. You do know how to wash your clothes, right?"

"Of course." He sighed. "I've done it since I was eight."

"Good, cause if you don't, I'm sure the shipmates won't like you much after a few days." She began sorting through his things. "Let's see, you'll need some shirts, this coat will be good on the windy days...."

"Mother, you mentioned that Captain Scyhathen was an explorer?"

"Yes, he charted the distant lands of Eastrell," she explained. "The far eastern nation of Sysia ... the vast northern continent of Kynniayck ... the western desert nations of Qui-Kinneas. Scyhathen was quite a great man, Thomas."

"If Scyhathen went east, north and west, what about south?"

Mrs. DeLeuit paused to look out his window. "He had a great dream to chart all four points on the compass."

"Did he ever make it?" Thomas asked intently.

"Nobody knows for sure." With a blink, she returned to the task at hand. "But don't worry about that right now, dear. I would suggest you ask Harrion or Captain Janes sometime. Here, try this coat on." She picked it up and handed it to him.

Thomas tried it on, finding it to be a perfect fit.

"Wonderful! Now then, what else do we have? Let's see...."

They continued to pack until well after sunset, when they had to light the lanterns to finish filling the trunk. Aside from clothes and the orb, he also brought personal items, including a bag of polished rocks he picked out from Diamond Falls, a few books, and other necessities regarding hygiene and cleanliness. As soon as everything was packed, he closed the trunk and went to bed.

The excitement of new ports and the open sea kept his thoughts in motion, and he dreamed of the wonders to come. Yet another thought entered his mind.

His family had always been him and his mother, without a thought of his father's whereabouts. Perhaps sometimes he envied the other families in Harper's Bay, and he longed for that sense of household love.

Occasionally the thought would surface, but every time reality would set in and he would again accept things as they are. Tonight was different, in that he was about to experience the sailing life ... the life that separated Gregory DeLeuit from Harper's Bay.

For a time, he would be separated from his mother. He would have to remember her gift whenever he grew homesick.

Embarking on the Centra Sea

*T*he following morning, Thomas descended the stairs to the main floor and was immediately greeted by Mr. Ward.

As a man with saltwater in his veins and a sailing history as wide as the horizon, Seriam Ward knew the seas. He was the mate aboard the *Valiant*, and Captain Janes's best friend.

"Morning lad. Cap'n tells me you're to be our cabin boy."

"That's correct, sir." Thomas rubbed his eyes awake.

"You'll be needing to be up by now, keep that in mind," Ward counseled.

Mrs. DeLeuit refilled his cup of tea. "Now Seriam, he's not on board your ship just yet."

"Don't worry, madam, we'll take good care of your boy. Just making sure he can handle it, dat's all." The sailor chugged his tea, setting the cup down with a nod of thanks.

Thomas took some biscuits his mother had made and buttered them for his breakfast. He noticed Ward was getting impatient.

"We're shoving off soon 'ere, so try to keep it moving." Ward was heading for the door.

"Seriam, would you be so kind as to bring Thomas's trunk for me? It's quite heavy, and I'm not sure he can carry it himself." She gave the man a look that suggested it wasn't a request.

"I suppose I can do that fer ye. Just so long he gets some muscles while he's with on ship." With a nod, Ward turned for the stairs.

"That's okay, Mother. I can handle it," Thomas said between bites.

"Nonsense, Thomas. You're no good to the captain if you're stuck with a bad back." Mrs. DeLeuit absently straightened Thomas's collar.

He gave her a knowing grin. "You would much rather I stay, wouldn't you, Mother?"

"Well, of course I would because you're all that I have left." Smiling, she tucked a stray lock behind his ear. "Sure, the money is a good incentive, but here's how I see it, Thomas. Your father was a man of the sea, and so you should be. The experience will be good for you. There's only one way to learn, and this is the best way."

"I understand, Mother, thank you."

She hugged her son tightly. He finished his biscuit. "Now put on your coat, Thomas. I'm sure the captain is waiting." Mrs. DeLeuit hesitated to remove him from her arms. He rushed to put on his coat and was halfway out the door before he stopped to say one last thing.

"Don't worry, Mother. I shall see you in a month."

She smiled. "Work hard, focus on the tasks at hand, and be good to the captain. I'll be here when you return."

"I will, Mother." He put his hat on and walked toward the docks.

A tear left his mother's eye. She returned to her projects for the day. A moment later, Ward came down the stairs with the trunk, surprising her slightly.

"Oh! Seriam, I forgot you were up there."

"You didn't tell me where it was, madam," Ward replied gruffly.

She laughed. "My apologies. Thomas has already left for the docks."

"Yes … after all, the boy shouldn't arrive 'fore his luggage does," Ward muttered, carrying the trunk out the door.

"Thanks again, and please tell the captain good-bye for me."

"Aye ma'am." He set off with the trunk to the harbor.

She watched him leave. "Take care of my boy."

Thomas hurried down the hill past the tavern and the town hall. He slowed his pace as he passed through the tiny marketplace where the fishermen were already peddling their morning catch. Outside Harrion's home, he stopped to see Bobby before reaching the docks.

"Thomas? Why you all dressed up? What is all this?" Bobby eyed him curiously.

"I'm joining the crew of the *Valiant*, Bobby!" He hadn't planned to say it quiet so loudly but couldn't help himself. "They're making me cabin boy."

"Cabin boy?" His friend's mouth hung open for a moment before transforming into a wistful grin. "Starting just like your father, then? Such a lucky one!"

"Yes … too bad you cannot come, too." Thomas would miss Bobby but was too excited to feel down about it.

"Someone's gotta look after the old librarian … but wow! You're an expert with the maps now, right? I'm sure you'll be fine, just beware of those accursed islands … you know what I mean," Bobby cautioned.

"The captain knows what he's doing. We've got nothing to worry about. I'll send you a letter if I can, and you'll see me in a month, I promise!" With a wave, Thomas turned and continued on down to the docks.

"Just make sure you return, instead of disappearing like your father did, Thomas," Bobby said quietly to himself, heading inside.

A moment later, Thomas arrived at the dock where Captain Janes' *Valiant* was still preparing to depart.

The *Valiant* had been commanded by Captain Janes for nearly a decade. She was structurally sound, and rarely encountered any problems at sea. By no means a small ship, she was 60' long with a 20' beam and 10' draft. Thomas had always admired her two powerful mainsails that towered high above the main deck, square in shape and crowned by a flag displaying five stripes each of black and blue, emblazoned with a white dove across the field. Multiple jibs and gallants fitted out the rest of her topsails.

On either side of the main deck were a pair of rowboats, each secured and operated by way of a crane to hoist and lower them to the water below. A mermaid bust adorned the bow, while the quarterdeck in the rear was home to the ship's bridge and compass.

Below deck the ship was equipped with unique features not seen in older ships on the Centra, including a large freshwater tank for drinking water, a refuse bin, an expansive cargo hold, and a system of stabilizers designed to keep the vessel level in rough seas. The *Valiant* was a magnificent vessel any captain would be proud of, and Thomas had always paid attention to the captain's instructional description.

"Ahoy, Tommy!" Captain Janes met the boy at the foot of the gangplank.

"Good day, sir!"

"Is Mr. Ward behind you?"

Tommy blinked in confusion. "Mr. Ward? I thought he was already here."

"I say, he did go to your house, yes?"

"Why yes, I thought that ... oh." Just then Thomas heard Ward behind him, grunting under the heavy wooden trunk.

Thomas watched the first mate struggle with the cumbersome trunk. "Should I help, sir?"

"Nah, Tommy, I's got it," Ward replied.

"Get the crane, lads!" Janes knew that his best crewman wouldn't be able to get the trunk up the gangplank without help.

While Thomas scurried up the gangplank, the men picked up the trunk with the crane and hoisted it aboard the ship. "Right then! Gather at attention!"

All the men had been checking on various parts of the ship, making inspections and securing ropes for the upcoming voyage. As soon as Ward came aboard, however, the six crewmen quickly reported to duty and filed into a line. While it was clear that they were not as orderly as his mother's tales of military units would suggest, Thomas was impressed.

Ward came aboard and stood with the men. "Your orders cap'n?"

"First thing's first. Lads, this is Thomas DeLeuit, our new cabin boy. Tommy, these are the men: Harvey Jennings, Roland Benson, Jared Roberts, Barry Gritzol, James Lewinston, and Perry," Janes explained, pointing out each man from left to right. "And you already know Mr. Ward, my first mate."

Thomas took a good look at the rest of the crew. Mr. Jennings was a man of average build. He wore a worn striped shirt, short hair, and a disagreeable look upon his face. To his right stood Mr. Benson, a tall, limber and refined fellow. He carried a book in his coat pocket and a brass compass in his hand. Next stood Mr. Roberts, who was younger than the rest, his light brown hair hung in a ponytail and a fife made of nickel dangling from his belt. Standing next in line was Mr. Gritzol, an older fellow with graying hair and beard, and with battle scars upon his muscular arms. Mr. Lewinston was quiet and stood isolated from the rest of the crew, but he kept his clothes and hat clean. There was a skull and crossbones tattoo upon his left arm in plain sight. Lastly, Mr. Perry was a large, dark-skinned man who wore a vest and dark pants, but kept his chest exposed. He also wore a gold earring, like a gypsy would wear.

Thomas had seen or met most of the men at one time or another, and he knew them to be of good character. He directed his attention back to Captain Janes and Ward.

"Now I know that seems like a lot of luggage, but I'm certain the boy is here to work, not play. He's industrious, and I'm sure you'll all get to know 'im in no time. Tommy, I'll show you your sleeping quarters. Meantime, Mr. Ward, let's unmoor the ship and get 'er ready for sea!" the captain ordered.

The first mate stepped forward and called out the orders. "Benson, free the riggings. Jennings, the topsail; Perry, you hoist anchor, Lewinston, you free the moors, Gritzol, you set the jibs, and Roberts, you set the mainsail. Let's get at it!"

"Aye sir!" the men chorused.

The captain took the front end of Thomas's trunk. Thomas took the back handle.

"Right this way, lad, and watch the steps."

"Aye sir." Thomas carefully navigated the narrow staircase. They went down the first hall past the mess room and the galley, then past another cabin and the barracks. They passed by a large clock at the end of the hall, as well as several lanterns that lit the interior of the ship. Then they descended down another deck that had cargo stores on either side. At the front of the room near the bow of the ship, they came to a stop.

"Here we are, lad, your new home." The captain set his end of the trunk just inside a doorway covered by a curtain. Unlike the barracks and mess hall above, there wasn't a porthole in this room, as this was the bow where water could rush in the easiest. It was not completely dark, however, as there was a lantern in the corner. The room was sparsely decorated with a cot and several pegs along the wall to hang a sword and a few personal effects but little else. There also was a chamber pot, and Thomas knew well enough to empty that whenever necessary.

"It's ... nice, sir."

Janes chuckled. "Not really, but trust me, you'll get used to it in no time. At least here you've got your own space. In the barracks, you would only get a locker and a bed, so be thankful. Before you settle in, have ye got any questions?"

"How does one handle seasickness?"

Janes laughed deeply. "Well, just like most things you'll learn on the ship, if it isn't worth keepin', it goes over the rail."

"Does that include … what I think it does?" Thomas gave the chamber pot a meaningful look.

"You'll learn pretty quickly why the poop deck is so named, my boy." Janes turned to leave.

"Sir, a moment."

"What is it, lad?"

Thomas put his coat and hat on the nearest peg. "Would it be okay if I got settled before coming up?"

The captain shook his head. "You'll have plenty of time for that later. There's things that need to be done. Besides, I'm sure you'll want one last look at home 'fore we get too far out. Come along then."

"Aye sir." Thomas followed the captain through the depths of the ship and back to the deck. By then, the *Valiant* was already a few hundred feet out. Harper's Bay was fading into the distance.

"Ship's ready for sea, captain," Mr. Ward reported.

Janes nodded. "Well done. We'll be heading for Vesper as soon as the sails are up."

"I'll prepare the men." Ward turned to do his job.

"Leave me Roberts, Mr. Ward. I've a task for him."

"Aye," Ward left to inform the crew of the captain's wishes.

"Mr. Roberts!" Janes called.

"Aye sir," Roberts jogged to the captain.

"Tommy, this is Jared Roberts. He'll show you the ropes and explain what a cabin boy is expected to do."

"Yes sir." Thomas replied. The captain left toward the stern.

Jared's tan showed off his easy smile, which Thomas's mother said all the girls in town admired. The matrons in Harper's Bay shared this affection, as Thomas had observed Jared's gentlemanly manners were favored over average unkempt sailor talk. Roberts was younger than the rest of the men under Janes's command. From bits of conversation with Captain Janes, Thomas had learned Jared had been aboard ship since childhood. He had to be a capable seaman to be on Janes's crew at such a young age—Jared didn't look more than 25.

"How old are ye, Tommy?"

"Fourteen, sir."

"Sir?" Roberts laughed. "Try again."

Thomas has always been taught to call his elders "sir"; this wasn't an aspect of ship life he'd considered. "Fourteen."

"Aye, that's better. I'm no sir. Save that fer the captain and the mate." Roberts leaned casually against the rail. "You and I, we don't need to be so formal."

"Okay...." Thomas leaned against the rail, too. "What exactly do I do?"

"You're the 'get it now guy' on board, and you'll be doing a variety of jobs, but there's three main things the cabin boy does each day." The sailor held up three fingers, ticking off the tasks as he went. "He swabs the deck when she needs it, or just when the captain's watching. He keeps the cook happy with his supplies and wares, and he fetches rum for the men when they ask for it."

"Only three jobs? I thought there'd be more than that."

"I never said it wasn't, but here's the trick, Tommy." Roberts tapped the side of his nose. "If something needs to be tended to, do it before you're ordered to. It'll keep the captain and the men happy, and you'll have more time for other things. You might get yelled at once or twice, but don't take it too personally or you may regret it. Least until you can handle a fencing blade proficiently."

"Are there ever fights on board?"

"Not with Captain Janes in command. But someday, when you least expect it—clash!" Roberts abruptly slammed his fist into his palm. "Some men'll fight at the drop of a hat, others just because they like it so much. I warn ye, though, some'll just forget they carry a sword and beat ye to a pulp with their knuckles, so I'd encourage working hard or you'll just be soft the rest of your days."

"Aye." Thomas straightened against the rail.

"That's the lingo! But let me be honest with ye ... these fellows are all good men, true. This crew be more civil than most, and I think you'll find yerself a good niche here in no time flat. But for now, the mop and bucket's over there. Remember, always use the sea for mopping water." He pointed to a small storage area in the aft of the ship. "Go on, get started."

The mainsails caught the wind as soon as Roberts was finished instructing; it wouldn't be long before Harper's Bay was just a memory. Soon Thomas was mopping the deck from bow to stern, just as Jared had ordered.

After he had mopped for what seemed like an eternity, Thomas took a moment to look off to the port side of the ship toward the rocky coastline. Harper's Bay was behind him; there was no going back. As he cleaned up the last spot of dirt, Mr. Ward walked over to him.

"Hey Tommy, ye swab like a pro!" Ward knocked him to the deck with a friendly slap to the back.

The boy picked himself up with a grin. "Thank you, sir."

"Shouldn't be too long 'til the lunch bell rings. See if cookie needs any help below."

"Aye sir." After dumping the dirty water overboard, Thomas put the mop and bucket away then headed to the galley. There was an iron stove bolted to the floor and a work table in the middle of the room with vegetables and pork already cut up on it. Stores of dried food and fruit were kept in sealed wooden crates and barrels near the back and sides of the room. The rest of the galley was mostly clean, aside from an open sack of potatoes on the floor.

"You the new cabin boy?" The cook's voice was so raspy and deep it almost made Thomas shiver.

"Aye sir. Thomas DeLeuit." Thomas extended his hand.

The cook held up his hand, which was covered in pig blood and smelled of raw fish. Thomas took his hand back quickly.

"Name's Ellis, and don't you forget it. Good timing, lad. Peel up about a dozen of 'em taters and put 'em in this pan." Ellis pointed to the pot then turned to the pig carcass.

"Could I have a knife, sir?"

The cook grumbled angrily, which made Thomas cringe.

"Ain't you got yer own? Well, here!" Ellis barked, throwing a knife toward Thomas. He dodged it as the knife stuck into the floor. "Make sure you know where it is 'til you get one!"

Thomas pulled the knife free, wiped it off on his shirt, and began peeling potatoes.

"Clean up them skins when yer done! Already got too much vermin on this boat!" Thomas cut a potato in half accidentally, narrowly missing his own fingers in the process. "Aye sir." Still shaking from the strike, he took extra care and made certain not to cross Ellis' path as he worked.

Meanwhile, Captain Janes and Mr. Ward were meeting privately in the captain's quarters, located in the stern of the ship below the bridge.

"The cargo list checks out as usual, cap'n. Lumber heading to Vesper, more heading to South Cimmordia; cotton heading to Derrisburg, and ore to Vesper." Mr. Ward flipped a page in the small ledger he held. "When we arrive at Vesper, they'll probably 'ave a shipment of grain to send to Teraske."

"And when we arrive at Teraske, there'll be a shipment of copper to Harper's Bay," Janes replied unenthusiastically.

"Does this seem like a rut to you, captain?"

"It sure does, Seriam. When I was a lad, 'round Tommy's age, I reckon, I had visions of a lifestyle similar to those of the buccaneer." Janes held up his hands as though contemplating a pleasant painting. "The adventurer, saber-wielding jack-of-all trades seeking treasure and whatever else he could find." He let his hands fall to his desk. "Here, all these years later, I'm stuck in a merchant trade running me in circles."

"Aye." The first mate nodded. "And although she's a profitable lot, she's quite dull."

"Aye." Janes sighed.

"You know, I've myself a friend in Davenport. Lou is a fine collector of maps, and if you need adventure and excitement he can provide a map leading right to it."

"Yes, I know your friend Mr. Westyln." The captain waved the prospect aside. "But we'll have to empty this ship of wares before we can go chasing after any treasure. Besides, some of those treasures are being hunted by those dastardly pirates. A wonder that we've been lucky enough not to run into any of 'em."

"Maybe after this circle route we otta try it," Seriam suggested.

"Aye, maybe we should." After a thoughtful moment, Janes shrugged. "Depends on if the crew's up to it, I suppose. We'll wait a few ports before asking such a thing, though. We've been with these men a long time, and many would prefer routine over risk and rigor. I can't have ourselves digging up a new crew when they hear news like that."

The dinner bell rang.

"Bell time." Mr. Ward stood to go but paused when his captain huffed.

"That'd be the other thing getting old around here."

"What's that?"

"The same old food." Without enthusiasm, the captain got to his feet. "Perhaps a more varied menu rotation is in order. I wonder what Mr. Ellis's version of pork and spuds'll be today?"

The rest of the crew gathered in the mess hall. There was no Captain's Mess on the ship; Janes ate with his men. Only once in awhile he would retreat to his quarters while eating, and that was usually when there was something on his mind that couldn't be shared with the crew.

Thomas had been thankful to get out of the kitchen before Mr. Ellis was finished, because the cook gave Thomas the shivers. There was always one person on a crew to avoid, he decided.

The dinner was broiled pork and vegetables with potatoes and gravy. Although Thomas thought the meal was pretty good despite Ellis's personality, he couldn't help noticing the grumbling of some of the men.

"I tell ye, Jim, this stuff seems the same as what we had Thursday," Mr. Jennings said to Mr. Lewinston.

"I can barely remember what that stuff was." Lewinston shook his head. "But I's still deciding whether it should be called food or not, Harv."

"It was some sort of pork dish, probably these exact same ingredients but with different spices, and served in a casserole instead," Mr. Gritzol replied in a lower voice than the other men.

The captain turned to his newest crewman. "What do you think, Tommy? How's the food?"

"It actually tastes pretty good, and the gravy goes well with the potatoes."

"Really? You sure, kid?" Jennings asked.

"Well, I guess if I'd been eating it for the past week, it might get a tad old," Thomas answered quickly.

"Aye, that's fer sure." Ward nodded.

"Okay, boys. Don't forget Horatio is in the galley yet. That man deserves our respect," Janes said.

"Especially since he's making the food," Jennings added.

"I'd hate to get on his bad side, probably poison it," Lewinston said somewhat under his breath.

Ellis came into the mess hall and picked up an empty pan. In a low grumble, he addressed his fellow crewmen. "Someone not like the grub around here?"

"Not at all, Ell. You do a good job," Lewinston replied in a normal level.

"Great job," Jennings added.

"All right, all right. You don't like pork and veggies, do ye? Catch me some fish, I'll make ye fish. Kill a gull, I'll make ye gull. Dig up a bunch of maggots, I'll make ye maggots! It's all what you guys give me to work with." Ellis turned back to the galley, slamming the door.

They were quiet for a moment, then Janes cleared his throat. "He's right, boys. We'll pick up some beef in Vesper. Til then no more critical comments concerning the food, hear?"

"Aye, cap'n," the men all echoed, including Thomas.

"As soon as you finish, it's back to the deck. We're on a deadline here—but I promise ye, someday we won't be," Janes said, leaving the mess for his quarters.

All the men watched him leave before returning to their food, finishing quickly and returning to their posts. Roberts followed Thomas as he went out.

"How're you doing so far, Tommy?"

"Just fine, Mr. Roberts."

The sailor chuckled. "The name's Jared. Not formal, remember? Say, if I'm gonna be calling ye Tommy, you be calling me Jared. Deal?"

"Aye, Jared." It felt strange but a bit exciting to call a man by his first name.

"Yeah, we's got this thing going … you and me, Tommy." Jared absently flicked his ponytail over his shoulder. "You're a good kid. How'd you like for me to show ye a thing or two about sailing and riggings?"

"Maybe it could wait for a bit? I was hoping to get settled in my cabin."

"Aye, that could wait I s'pect. If I was you, I'd feel a bit more comfortable once my lodgings were settled first, too. Provided, of course, there's nothing else ye should be doing. Keeping busy—that's one of the rules, lest there be nothing to be busy about."

"Aye, I'll be back in a bit." Thomas nodded and left for his cabin.

When Thomas got to his room, he lit the lantern and opened up the chest. He first looked for his bag of smooth rocks. He knew that putting them along a shelf would be pointless due to the movement of the ship, so he picked a peg along the wall where it would be easily seen from the cot. The coat and hat were hung in a similar fashion, reserving a pair of the hooks for drying his clothes if they got wet or were washed. He dug a bit further into the chest and found Captain Scyhathen's journal and began to read.

> *June 16th, 1582. We're docked at the south harbor of Grand Point, where I have been provided a useful note of information. I met with a man who had served with Sir Martin Kalis of Cimmordia who spoke of a group of islands southeast of Cyeel Point. Although I am not familiar with these islands, they are within a few day's sail and likely along our route toward the Phrynn Continent. The explorer went on to describe the islands as a dangerous locale that must be avoided. I did not prod the man for details on the forest castle in the rainy forest of the northlands. Kalis's death remains a tragic loss in my mind yet to this day. An explorer's final days, and the story of a man. But I digress.*

> *My curiosity is enthused. However, are these the islands that every sailor claims to really be the shores of Davy Jones? Perhaps the Nemaris and I are the only ones who shall really ever find out. I plan to discuss the matter with my first mate Smitty before we sail at dawn.*

So the journal began before Captain Scyhathen had found the Nemaris Islands! Thomas wanted to read further, but could only get to a few paragraphs before he had trouble keeping his eyelids open. He managed to blow out the lantern before he fell asleep.

It wasn't long until Thomas was roused by a visitor.

At an impressive 6'2", Mr. Perry towered over Thomas. He had no hair on his head, and merely a trace of it anywhere else on his massive frame. His gold earring gleamed even in the dark, and there was something about him that made Thomas wonder if he was truly of this world. When he spoke, his voice was deep, mystical, and poetic, with a true maritime accent.

"Captain wishes to see you in his cabin."

Thomas nodded, and quickly followed Perry upstairs.

At the top of the stairs and inside the ship's quarterdeck, a small hallway shared the staircase leading to the lower decks.

Mr. Perry left Thomas at Captain Janes's door. "Go on in. He expects you."

Thomas entered and was awed by the fine space Captain Janes had for a cabin. It was large, encompassing the rear quarter of the ship. Windows covered three of the walls, and artwork was displayed on the remaining wall space. Along the stern of the ship was centered the captain's bed, flanked by two matching sets of drawers that were built into the room. The rest of the space was a parlor area. Along the starboard wall, a table and a collection of navigation charts and equipment were stored along with three chairs. Across the room, a couch and a large easy chair sat across from one another. A moderately sized wardrobe stood along the wall nearby. To offset the balance of the ship, a small iron stove and fire box for coal sat across from the wardrobe. On the wall facing the bow, there was a tapestry with a crimson and gray insignia, while a rug under the bed matched the blue curtains on the windows.

Sitting at the table, Janes spread his hands to encompass the room. "A fine place for a captain, do you agree?"

Thomas found his mouth was slightly agape. "Aye sir. It's amazing."

"Perhaps someday you'll have a place like it yourself, lad. Over here, I wanted to show you these charts." Janes unrolled a chart of the Centra Sea.

Thomas found Harper's Bay easily. He then followed the coast south to find Vesper, Cimmordia Castle, and South Cimmordia beyond that. As he was familiar with the charts that belonged to Elder Harrion, Thomas found his way on the map without trouble.

"You seem to know this area quite well, Tommy. Are you sure you haven't been out here before?" Janes chuckled.

"Quite sure, sir, but I've seen similar charts belonging to the town elder."

"Aye, then. Can you show me where we are?"

Thomas was at a loss. He knew the *Valiant* was currently between Harper's Bay and Vesper, but he wasn't sure where. After all, it was difficult to pinpoint their location without seeing the shore, especially since he had fallen asleep after lunch.

"No, I'm not sure, sir," Thomas confessed.

Instantly, Janes pointed to a spot on the map a short distance from the shore, just short of halfway between Harper's Bay and Vesper. "Right here."

"Is that correct, sir?"

Janes went to the wall and took a spyglass off of a set of hooks, and handed it to Thomas. "Go to the window Tommy, and take a look." He pointed to the portside window.

Thomas looked through the spyglass and could easily see the shore in the distance. "Of course, it's so close."

"I've gotten adept at navigation, Tommy. In the open ocean, it can be difficult to find your location. You almost have to go by instinct, but with practice it'll come to you naturally."

Returning the glass to his captain, Thomas studied the map again. "According to this, then, we're only a day away from Vesper, correct?"

Nodding, Janes replaced the glass on its hooks. "That's right. You catch on quickly, excellent!"

"Thank you, sir."

"I have some business to do. In fact, the evening meal shouldn't be too long from now, so you might see if Mr. Ellis needs anything from you," Janes suggested.

"Aye sir, I'll check with him." Thomas didn't let his opinion of the cook affect the tone of his response.

"Run along then." Once Thomas left, Janes considered the map again—perhaps his new cabin boy had the makings of a navigator.

Thomas entered the galley to find Mr. Ellis chopping at yet another slab of pork.

"Mr. Ellis, sir, do you need any assistance?" Thomas asked hesitantly.

Ellis looked up slowly. "Do I *need* assistance?"

"Well, do you?"

Ellis didn't shift his gaze from the wall. "Do I need assistance? Are you saying that without your help, I can't complete my task? Or would you rather I suffer because your expert help will make or break this meal?" Ellis grumbled sarcastically.

"The captain asked me to check with you, sir, to see if you needed any help," Thomas said quietly as he backed away slowly.

Ellis took a few breaths of air and returned to his chopping. "Nah, I don't need any assistance," Ellis replied in a lighter tone. It seemed to Thomas that since the captain made the order that Ellis wouldn't make a big deal about it.

"Aye, sir."

"Get out of here, 'fore you get splattered with blood," Ellis muttered.

Thomas did not hesitate for a moment and left wondering if Ellis hated kids. With no specific job, he sought Mr. Roberts and found him on deck working with some ropes.

"Jared, can I ask you something?"

"Sure, Tommy, but give me a hand with this first." The sailor passed a rope to Thomas. "Hold this while I secure it." With a loop and a twist over a sturdy cleat, they tied down the last blunt line of a topsail with a hitch knot.

"Aye, that's it. Now then, what can I do for ye?" Jared settled himself on a large spool of rope.

"I was wondering about Mr. Ellis, actually." Thomas thought for a moment about what to say. "He seems somewhat distraught ... I just met the man, and yet he gets upset when I offer to help."

"Distraught sounds like a good word 'fer it. I may not be the best expert on Ellis' situation, but then not even the cap'n is, more likely than not." Jared shrugged. "All I know 'bout him is that he joined us after our last cook drowned. Ellis isn't much of a conversationalist and keeps mostly to 'imself. In fact, he usually sleeps in a chamber just behind the food locker where he can be alone. He's a very private man."

"Does that explain his attitude toward the crew, too?" It didn't seem like an adequate answer to Thomas's question.

"Ellis's not a bad guy, Tommy. Some people are just that way." After a thoughtful chin scratch, Jared added, "The way I sees it, it's best not to try to pry. I stay out of Ellis's mess me self, and you should probably be doing the same."

"I suppose you're right." Thomas turned to head to his cabin.

"Tommy, hold up a moment."

"Yes?" Thomas looked back to see Jared pointing upward.

"Remember I was going to tell ye a few things about riggings?"

"Oh, of course. That would be great." There were so many ropes Thomas could hardly hope to figure them all out on his own.

"All right! First off, if you look up there, that sail there is called the mainsail...."

As Thomas learned the basics of sailing, the sun began to set in the west. The breeze slowed for the night, bringing the ship to a crawl. The men lowered the sails and weighed anchor. They had sailed closer to shore to take advantage of calmer waters. The men gathered in the mess hall to enjoy another pork meal. This time, the meal consisted of pork chops, brown gravy and mashed potatoes with the skin still on; Mr. Ellis did not peel the potatoes for this meal.

"Pork again," Mr. Gritzol muttered as he dished up.

"At least the gravy was for the meat this time," Mr. Jennings added.

"Are you sure? It seems to go better with the potatoes," Mr. Lewinston quipped.

"It goes good with both, boys, didn't your mamas teach you that one?" Mr. Ward's stern gaze was enough to break up the little argument.

"I don't reckon it couldn't go by itself, actually. It's good brown gravy," Mr. Roberts replied.

"What is it with you, Jared? You never comment on the food unless it's gravy. It's always about gravy," Lewinston observed.

"I happen to be a connoisseur of gravy, if you must know," Roberts replied proudly.

Thomas laughed.

"So then, you eat gravy by itself, too?" Lewinston asked.

"If it earns the seal of approval, aye," Roberts replied.

The men laughed out loud at his statement. Janes calmed the men.

The captain sat at the head of the table. "You sure love your gravy, Jared. On another note, Mr. Ellis has done well again tonight, and we owe 'im our thanks."

"Aye," the men muttered.

It seemed Ellis either didn't hear the conversation or didn't care to respond to the praise. The door to the galley was closed tight and didn't budge.

After dinner, most of the men went into the barracks. Some stayed in the mess hall, passing the time doing personal activities or talking with the other crewmates. Thomas swabbed the deck a second time before going below. He might've liked to have stayed up doing odd things around his cabin or reading a few more entries in Captain Scyhathen's book, but having earned a good night's sleep he instead rolled over in the cot at once.

Although he would've liked to be able to see the stars from his cabin, he saw them in his mind as he drifted off to sleep.

The Kingdom of Cimmordia

In the morning, Thomas awoke to the sounds of water rushing past the ship. It became apparent that the men had been awake for a good while. He quickly put on a clean set of clothes and headed on deck. However, he didn't quite make it, halted by the scent of sausage and eggs as he passed by the mess hall.

"Tommy! Come here, lad. You're missing the morning meal," Mr. Ward called.

"Sorry I slept so late, sir," Thomas replied as he went to dish up.

"Get yourself some breakfast lad, gotta fuel up 'fore working too hard." Ward pushed him toward the spread of food on a table at the bow end of the hall. Thomas dished up some grub as most of the men bussed their plates and returned to deck.

Jared was still eating. Thomas joined him as Ward left to go to deck.

"Morning late riser."

"Good morning, Jared. How does the morning find you?"

Rubbing his eyes, Jared yawned. "The sunbeam usually penetrates my eyes. You'll want to rise a bit earlier if you like warm food."

He was right—the food was cold.

"It's okay." Thomas forked another mouthful of eggs. "I'd rather eat it cold than trouble Mr. Ellis to warm it."

"Did you sleep okay in that cabin? Not very hospitable, is it now?"

Thomas shrugged. "Well, I really was quite tired last night."

"Aye, hard work's the best thing for a good night's sleep. But here's the real secret … instead of treating it as work, ye pretend you're having fun. So are ye having fun?"

Thomas took a bite of sausage. "Yes, I am … really having fun."

Jared smiled. "Good to hear it, Tommy. Don't rush now—as long as you start rising at a normal hour. See you on deck." Jared left Thomas alone to finish his meal.

Thomas wasn't so certain if fun involved mopping a deck that never seemed to get clean, especially while attempting to keep the bucket from falling overboard. Then again, he hadn't felt sick once, nor had he yet traversed rough seas. Perhaps he was having fun after all.

While Thomas ate, Ellis came into the mess hall and picked up the remaining food, what little there was, and dumped it into a small metal container. Ellis took a long look at Thomas, who had stopped to watch him.

"Something wrong?" muttered Ellis.

"No, sir. Good morning, sir." Thomas offered him a sincere smile.

"Food's cold, isn't it?" Ellis's wrinkled brow creased.

"It doesn't bother me, sir. I came late, so I guess I got what I deserved."

"You've got that right. Humph." Ellis tromped back to the galley.

"If you don't hurry you'll be cleaning yer own mess!" Ellis called, encouraging Thomas to gulp down the last few bites. Quickly, Thomas bussed his plate and headed for the deck.

When Thomas arrived on deck he immediately collected the mop and bucket. As he scrubbed, he overheard Mr. Ward speaking with Captain Janes. Behind them on the navigation deck, Mr. Perry manned the wheel.

"Can you see Vesper yet?"

Lowering the spyglass, Ward shook his head. "No sir, but we should arrive by midday."

"Right. But that's not my main concern. See out there?" Janes pointed starboard.

There were dark clouds on the horizon, and the rest of the sky seemed somewhat hazy as well.

"Seems like a storm brewing."

"Indeed." Janes gave a speculative hum. "If luck is in our corner, we'll make it to port before it gets near us."

"Aye. Can't be that big a storm though." The first mate spoke with the confidence of experience.

"Perhaps, but one never knows how far it goes beyond what we see."

They watched the dark clouds for a moment or two before Perry spoke out in his deep mystical voice, catching both men off guard.

"I agree with Mr. Ward, cap'n. Storm be not that great of concern," Perry replied.

Captain Janes nodded. "You're a man of few words, Perry, but those words always speak the truth." He turned to Ward. "I'll be in my quarters, Seriam. Let me know when we arrive."

"Aye sir." Ward left to check on the other crewmen. Thomas continued to swab the deck. As the mate passed by, he brushed his hand through Thomas's hair. Thomas straightened it out and continued swabbing.

A few hours passed, and it had cooled off on deck. A cold breeze grew stronger and rain clouds drew closer. The normally mild spring weather grew uncomfortably chilly. Fortunately, Thomas had already completed swabbing the deck. He brought his bucket inside to work in the mess hall, which was in great need of cleaning. It was good timing, as a light rain shower had begun.

Thomas worked diligently. He had to wring out the mop out the window so that any food particles that had been trapped in it wouldn't get his already dirty water more soiled. After awhile, Mr. Ellis came through the mess hall and headed toward the deck, without as much as a word to Thomas.

Ignoring Ellis's presence, Thomas continued to mop away. He mopped past a set of tables, then wrung the mop outside the window and collected a drink of water from the spigot in the back of the room.

Thomas had heard about the water tank many times. It was well sized, able to hold enough water to last for a week and a half. Janes had decided that storing fresh water there instead of in barrels, known for being too small, made life on the *Valiant* much more suited for long-distance travel than traditional ships. The captain had directed the unique addition, modifying a space in the rear of the ship. Formerly used for additional fresh food storage, it was a space that would have been too close to the nearby refuse bin for comfort. The refuse bin was only cleaned occasionally, filled with spoiled food and all the garbage that collected during a standard voyage.

Of course, Thomas heard the captain say that most everything went over the rail … perhaps Captain Janes preferred not to leave a trail of garbage behind his ship.

Another thought crossed Thomas's mind. If indeed Ellis was correct that there were already too many vermin on the ship, the refuse bin was probably where they lived.

As Thomas finished up the mopping, Ellis returned. He stopped, startling Thomas.

"Rain a' coming ... where you tossing that wastewater, boy?"

"Er, outside, sir," Thomas replied quickly.

"Good. And whatever ye do, keep that bin door closed! Mark my words, you set foot into that room, you're trousers'll be stinking worse than a hog's sty for weeks!" Ellis laughed to himself and headed to his cabin beyond the galley.

Thomas again tossed the contents of the bucket out into the ocean, shuddering. He focused on the task at hand, not letting Ellis's presence bother him.

He proceeded to put the bucket away before going down to the cargo deck to look at the stores they were carrying. Most of the storage space was taken up by lumber. Aside from bags of cotton and boxes of ore there was little else for merchant trade, although there were a few small barrels of spice and dried tea leaves. Thomas decided these belonged to the captain or were leftover from another shipment. Across from the ore were ship stores, including a few dozen bags of flour, a supply of whale oil for lanterns, and emergency supplies for riggings and sail repair.

Thomas explored the lowest deck further, discovering a second room close to the stern. Here, a wooden tub was complete with laundry materials and soap, and stores of other dry goods. The area also was used for storing the crew's weapons. Thomas knew that the captain's sword was in his quarters. Mr. Ward probably kept his in his quarters as well, as mostly rapiers and cutlasses hung from the wall.

Two blades stood out among them. One was large and ornate, which Thomas assumed belonged to Mr. Perry. He slid aside the leather sheath of the second sword to find a broad, curved blade of tempered steel. A second blade was a scimitar, lightweight and narrower than the others. It was a blade that he himself had been trained with by Janes personally. Thomas admired all the weapons in the room, and his curiosity got the better of him.

Picking up a rapier and leaving its sheath on the floor, Thomas fenced an imaginary opponent with it, mimicking a battle he'd read about in Captain Scyhathen's journal.

July 18th, 1581. A miracle has happened that I may continue to write today. A dastardly crew of scabs, certainly from the Ranthath Cult, attempted to disturb our southward journey. My men and I were strong enough in both numbers and wits to fend them off, but not before one of my men was injured. Thankfully, Mr. Rhudel Corvair's wounds were nothing serious. However, they will slow him down. Corvair is my riggings expert, and while he heals our mission to the southlands of Phrynn and its territories will take that much longer.

I'm confident in our rapiers and skill, yet I sympathize for such men who keep such greed in their hearts, rather than with might and main. I just hope the leader of such a disillusioned band considers what his mother feels about how his life turned out.

Something else troubles me, however. I continue to wonder about the islands of which the explorer spoke, and what might happen should we come within their shores. Perhaps this skirmish was a cautionary measure from some higher power; perchance my dreams should not be allowed to materialize. But if such is the case, that we shall find out upon our arrival; we've come too far to return without a rock of proof of their existence.

Thomas continued to fence his imaginary opponent until Mr. Benson came below deck, looking for him. "Tommy, here you are. Have you any experience with one of those?"

Thomas lowered the blade quickly. "I'm sorry, I'll not touch it again."

"It's no trouble, lad. Seems to me you're just playing with swords. I thought the captain gave you some training? Well, nothing against what you're doing, but if you're going to be a swordsman, you must first hold the blade properly." Picking up another rapier, Benson demonstrated how to grip it. "Like this, see? This is a rapier, a stabbing weapon. It's a matter of stick and move, using your other hand mostly for leverage. May I?"

Thomas stepped aside, and Benson took on Thomas's invisible opponent easily, even making a final thrust to stab the opponent through.

"So that's how it works." Thomas understood the difference between his play and Benson's practice.

Benson placed the rapiers back into the weapon's rack. "A rapier is elegant and cunning, but a bit advanced. See along the wall there? You might try a cutlass, or the scimitar instead."

"Scimitar, sir?"

"The one with the tempered steel, here. Perhaps later I'll work you through some exercises, seeing as you already have the basics."

Thomas pointed toward the large, ornate sword next to the scimitar. "What is that one called?"

Benson smiled, using both hands to remove it from its mount. "This is Perry's sword ... he calls it the Kah Lunaseif, meaning the 'axe of the moon' in his language. Very few have the strength to wield anything like it."

Thomas admired the blade, seeing that it indeed resembled a crescent moon. It was nearly five feet long and about four inches wide. Thomas marveled at its size and strength.

Benson returned the large sword to the rack. "I'll tell you more, but later. The rain's let up and the cap'n wants to show you something."

"Aye sir." Thomas trailed Benson to the deck.

Janes was standing atop the forecastle as Thomas arrived. "Tommy, there you are, lad. Something I thought you might want to see. Look out there."

Thomas looked over the starboard bow to see a pair of dolphins jumping along in the *Valiant*'s wake. He smiled, as they kept up with the ship easily.

"They look so playful."

"Indeed, that they are. Dolphins are interesting creatures, and mysterious as well. I've learned that one doesn't want to get too friendly with marine life, but I suppose I've heard too many terrible tales myself. One more thing. Look that way." Janes turned him toward the port side.

Off in the distance, about a half-mile or so, was Vesper. Larger than Harper's Bay, it boasted textile merchants and artisans. In the fertile valleys of the nearby Vesper River, farmers produced grain and corn, as well as cattle and other livestock. There was a sawmill that could transform raw timber into planks and carpenters who used it to create fine pieces of furniture, homes or ships. Although it wasn't home for Thomas, it was good to see a city again, especially one that he'd never been to.

"Aye, that's Vesper. We'll be pulling into port shortly. Tommy, if you would assist Mr. Perry in bringing the lumber up from below that would be most helpful." Janes turned to his first mate. "Mr. Ward, ready the ship for arrival."

"Aye sir," Ward replied. Thomas followed Perry below to haul some lumber.

Perry and Thomas began loading up what they could carry. The lumber had been cut into six foot by five inch boards, each weighing around twenty-five pounds. While Perry managed to bring several lengths a load balancing a few in each arm, Thomas could only carry two—period.

"Mr. Perry, how strong are you?"

The dark head tilted to one side. "See them boxes of ore there? Fifty pounds each. I carry them two at a time. Can carry four, but they be hard to get through the ship."

"Wow … and the lumber doesn't hurt your arms either?" The wood was splintery and Perry was only wearing a vest.

"It doesn't anymore." Perry grinned. He then hauled more lumber upstairs.

Thomas decided right then and there that it was better for him to have Perry on his side. He'd hate to anger the big man. Thomas noticed that Perry always was quiet and kept to himself. He wasn't outgoing or friendly, nor grumpy or violent, but then he wasn't the kind of man who appeared to be looking for any trouble. Thomas decided that for the moment it was best not to think about it.

As he carried what he could on deck, Thomas found out that they had already come within a few hundred yards of port. He placed the lumber onto the pile Perry had started and returned to the cargo hold. Thomas again had to avoid Perry, who was carrying another load of six lengths. Working together, they soon got most of the lumber on deck. Since there was no way Thomas could possibly carry the boxes of ore, Perry worked on those as Thomas finished with the lumber. It was hard work, and the ship was already docked and moored before Thomas had all the lumber stacked.

As Mr. Ward went ashore to inform the customers of their arriving shipments, Jared joined Thomas on deck.

"See that storm coming, lad? You ought to cover that lumber with a tarp 'fore it rains," Jared suggested.

"Is there one around?"

"I'll help ye; it's over here." Jared showed him to one of two storage rooms on the portside of the quarterdeck and returned with a tarp. It was made from a thick canvas material similar to the ponchos the crew had for rough weather. Using small ropes to keep the tarp from flying in the wind, they covered the lumber just as the rain started to fall again.

"Aye, 'n' not a moment too soon." Jared patted Thomas's back lightly.

"Is there anything else the captain needed us to do? What happens now?"

"He's in his cabin, but I wouldn't bother him. Also, Jennings and Gritzol said they'd deliver everything, so we're free. Mr. Ward is going ashore to contact those waiting for this stuff." Jared pointed to the lumber with a thumb. "As far as I know he won't mind if we take a quick look around town. I've been here before, so I'll take ye."

"But it's raining."

"Ahh, it's only water. You're not afraid of water, are ye?"

Thomas replied quickly. "No, of course not."

"I didn't think so. Come on then. We may not get as much time as we like." Jared headed down the gangplank with Thomas in tow.

The town of Vesper was centered around the port. The first few blocks of town along the waterfront contained most of the downtown area, similar to Harper's Bay. A sawmill and woodshop were located on the south edge near the Vesper River. There were three or four taverns, complete with inn rooms and bars that catered to the traveling sailor, as well as a warehouse for the sawmill and other local craftsmen. Beyond that was the commercial district, with a modest marketplace for grain and farming goods. Outside of town lay extensive woods, but these woods were protected by the king of Cimmordia and harvested sparingly.

It became clear that Vesper was much more active than Harper's Bay. They saw more young children running around than the ten or so in Thomas's hometown, and there were many teenagers as well.

Thomas and Jared came to a small farm along the east edge of town, where, as luck would have it, Thomas noticed a young girl about his age who was struggling to carry a bag of flour into her home.

"Jared, don't go too far. I'll be right back."

Realizing Thomas's intent, Jared couldn't help grinning. "Oh my goodness." Anticipating a long wait, Jared sat on the porch in front of a nearby tavern and began to play his fife.

Not wanting to startle the girl, Thomas cleared his throat. "Excuse me." The girl turned to Thomas. She had long brown hair, blue eyes, and a lovely smile. "Would you like a hand?"

The girl replied in a soft, gentle voice. "Oh! Yes, that would be most helpful."

"It's no trouble." Thomas tried to pick up the bag of flour by himself, but it was rather heavy and took the both of them to lift it. The rain picked up just as the sack was brought into the house's pantry.

"Thank you very much. That was much larger than I thought!" She dusted off her hands on her skirt and smiled. "Would you like to come inside for tea? After all, it would be quite rude of me to send you into the rain right away."

"That's very kind of you." Thomas followed her into a modest kitchen with a new iron stove.

"I've not seen you around town before. Are you visiting from the countryside?"

"Visiting yes, but not from the countryside." After she gestured that he should, Thomas sat at the kitchen table. "I live up north in Harper's Bay."

"Harper's Bay?" She paused to look back at him. "That's a long way to travel on foot. You didn't come this way by yourself, did you?"

"Actually, I'm a cabin boy aboard the *Valiant*." Although he tried, he couldn't contain the hint of pride in his voice.

"A cabin boy? Perhaps you've seen many places, then?" The girl put a kettle on to boil. Something in the pot next to the kettle smelled pretty good—probably the girl's dinner.

"I'm afraid not. This is my first voyage."

"Oh, I see." She spooned tea leaves into a teapot and brought it to the table.

"We haven't been introduced yet. My name is Thomas DeLeuit."

The girl shied away a moment. "Where are my manners? It's a pleasure to meet you, Thomas. I am Miranda Bennedict."

"A pleasure, indeed." After several days of listening to sailors, Thomas appreciated how well spoken she was. "Are your parents farmers?"

"Yes, my father is a wheat farmer, and we have a few cows in the barn. He's out in the fields right now. I believe he'll be along shortly." After stoking the coals in the stove, she brought some cups to the table.

"And your mother?"

Miranda hesitated, shaking her head sadly.

Thomas nodded in understanding. "I didn't mean to offend."

"My mother passed away when I was very young. It's just Father and me, and although our farm is small there's always something to be done." Grabbing a mitt, she carried the kettle to the table and filled the teapot. "Do you live with both of your parents?"

Thomas shook his head. "Only my mother ... I have never met my father. I am not even certain he is alive."

"I'm very sorry." After setting out a creamer and honey jar, she sat across from him. "What does your mother do?"

"She spends most of her time either sewing or baking goods for crews, but once in awhile if a sailor needs a bed for the night, she'll rent it to him."

"She must be a wonderful person." Apparently satisfied the tea had steeped long enough, Miranda poured it into the cups, adding a dollop of honey to hers.

Thomas sipped a bit of tea. Although it was refreshing, he knew his mother's tea was superior. They sat in silence a moment as the patter of rain came to a stop.

"See those woods out beyond the fields, Thomas?" She pointed out the window. "There are lots of trees there ... Father says they once covered the entire nation of Cimmordia, all the way to the farthest eastern shores."

Thomas nodded with interest, but with his thoughts drifted toward his crew. He began to wonder if Jared was looking for him.

Miranda looked outside with a smile. "I think the rain has lightened up a little bit. Would you like to see the cows?"

"I don't want to get in the way of your chores."

Miranda laughed. "Nonsense, they enjoy seeing visitors. Follow me."

She led him out the back door and to a pasture where three cows, as well as a young calf, contentedly munched grass.

Leaning over the top rail of the pasture's fence, Miranda smiled proudly. "Those're my cows. I haven't named the adult ones, but the calf is Sunny."

"Very nice." Thomas did not want to reveal his limited experience with livestock.

Just then, a tall man came through the field. He was carrying a scythe and wearing a large-brimmed hat. "Did you get the flour in 'fore the rain, Miranda?"

"This boy gave me some help with that, Father."

The man leaned his scythe against the fence and looked at Thomas. Because the man was nearly as tall as Perry, Thomas found him intimidating.

"Hello, Mr. Bennedict."

"Hello yourself." He glanced at his daughter. "Miranda, who's your friend?"

"This is Thomas DeLeuit, from Harper's Bay. He's a cabin boy."

Mr. Bennedict smiled. "Ahh, from the port, no less. That's nice of you to help out. DeLeuit, eh? I should know that name … I'm Beauford Bennedict, but my friends call me Bo." Mr. Bennedict offered his hand, shaking Thomas's with authority.

"Nice to meet you, Mr. Bennedict."

"Did you try some of our tea? Miranda here makes quite a cup."

Glancing at Miranda, Thomas nodded in agreement. "We already shared some, actually."

She laughed. "I gave him some as thanks for helping with the flour, Father."

"That so?" Mr. Bennedict gave Thomas a big grin. "What a gentleman. Have you time to stay for dinner, lad?"

"I'd like to stay, but I should go find the crewmate who came with me. I told him I wouldn't be long."

"You're not with those pirates, are you, boy?" Bo asked sternly.

"Pirates? No sir," Thomas replied quickly.

"All right then." Hefting his scythe, Mr. Bennedict made his way to the barn. "Bring your friend with. We've got plenty enough stew for ye both."

Thinking about the crew grumbling about pork, Thomas asked, "What kind of stew?"

"Stew, you know. Beef, potatoes, carrots, onions, and broth." He paused to face Thomas. "How do you folks make stew up north?"

Thomas laughed. "The same way, sir. I'll go find my shipmate."

"Hurry back!" Miranda said.

Thomas rushed to find Jared, who was still at the tavern.

"There ye are, Tommy. Who's your friend?"

"Her name's Miranda. She's a farmer's daughter."

"Aye, she's a cute one. " Jared winked. "Shall we be off?"

"Actually, her father invited the two of us for dinner. They're having beef stew."

Jared jumped up from his seat. "Beef? Why didn't ye say so?"

"Um ... I didn't realize I should have."

"Take me to them, then. Come on now," Jared begged. The prospect of a meal consisting of anything other than pork really appealed to him. They went back to the farmhouse to share the meal with the Bennedicts.

Meanwhile, Mr. Ward had returned from his customers and reported to the captain. Mr. Jennings and Mr. Gritzol were finishing the deliveries.

"The load for 'ere is all clear, cap'n," Ward said as he came onto the deck.

"Aye, good work. Before we go, pick up some beef, apples, and vegetables from the marketplace, as well as a hundred feet of rope if you would."

"Aye, beef, apples, veggies, and rope." Ward turned to the gangplank.

"Hold a moment, one more thing."

"Aye cap'n?"

Janes whispered something into Ward's ear, and he nodded.

"Aye, a good idea. Won't be long, cap'n." Ward headed to the marketplace. As for Captain Janes, he went to the mess hall to dine on the pork Mr. Ellis had prepared for those still on board.

Following the feast of stew at the Bennedicts, Jared and Thomas felt it appropriate for them to thank their hosts.

"I say, good sir, that was by far some of the best stew I have ever eaten," Jared said elegantly.

"Yes indeed," Thomas added.

Bo chuckled. "It must beat the food on board your ship, then?"

"Well, Mr. Ellis is a good cook, mind you, but when one's been eating pork every day for the past month, it gets to be a tad uninteresting," Jared confessed.

Miranda tried to stifle a grin. "I can see how that'd be a problem."

"You seem to be a good man, Mr. Roberts." Bo gave him a pat on the shoulder. "Perhaps you would like to take some meat with you? I've butchered a cow, and there's always too much to eat ourselves. It seems everyone in town's selling it lately ... what do you say?"

"I would be honored to." Jared beamed. "But I should check with my cap'n first, to be sure."

"Of course. The offer stands whenever he decides, then." He rose from the table. "I don't mean to be rude, but I've got work to do 'fore the rain picks up too much again."

"We understand, sir." Jared stood to shake the man's hand. "Tommy and I should be getting back ourselves."

"Aye, it's appreciated," Thomas said.

Jared tugged on Thomas's arm. "Good day!" He took Thomas and headed for the door.

Miranda curtly smiled as the men left. As thunder sounded in the distance, Mr. Bennedict made his way to the barn. Again he wondered if he hadn't heard the name DeLeuit before.

"You're making friends, I see," Jared said as they walked back to the port.

"She's a sweet girl."

"Aye indeed." Jared chuckled. "But the captain's waiting for us; I'm sure."

Thomas remained silent most of the walk back, his thoughts focused on Miranda. In fact, given Thomas's level of distraction, Jared was quite surprised the boy didn't fall or trip.

"I think you like her, don't ye?" Jared observed as they passed by the marketplace.

"Huh?"

"Aye, you're blushing, Tommy!" Jared exclaimed jovially.

"You don't really think that, do you?" Thomas couldn't help but deny it.

Jared laughed out loud as they climbed the gangplank onto the deck of the *Valiant*.

Mr. Jennings overheard the laughter. "What's going on?"

"Our cabin boy found his first affection!" Jared replied.

Jennings laughed richly. "Aye, good for you lad! When're you going to marry 'er?" he teased. The other men broke out in hysterics.

"There's more. We possibly found some beef, too!"

"Hey, this story gets better and better!" Jennings replied.

Thomas continued below deck, away from the taunts of the crew. Hopefully a few days at sea would distract their focus from his love life.

Mr. Ward returned from the marketplace a half-hour or so later, with Mr. Benson and Mr. Gritzol helping load the remainder of their supplies. Within the hour, the *Valiant* was sea bound and heading along the coast toward South Cimmordia, the port town for Cimmordia Castle.

Although they would pass by the castle first, their next destination was the port of South Cimmordia. On the south end of Tower Point and behind Kalis Island, a small, well-defined harbor consisting of sheltering currents and light winds. Though they wouldn't arrive until the following afternoon, it would be their last stop before heading across the sea, past the Nemaris Islands, to Teraske; a five-day sail provided the wind was good and the sea cooperated.

The afternoon passed uneventfully, as the threat of rain was minimal and the sails were full, leaving the crew with little to do. Benson and Jennings made sure everything stayed normal. Perry slept; Gritzol read a book; Lewinston worked on some projects below deck, and Ward and the captain tended to their business in the cabin.

Roberts, on the other hand, spent his time with his fife. He sat on the stern, just playing whatever came to mind. Although the other men had come not to mind the music, Jennings didn't care for it.

"Every time, Jared, you play that fife, and it's always out at sea, too!" Jennings muttered.

"And every time you protest; every time I continue to play, yet nothing happens," Jared replied, putting the fife down for a moment.

"That's 'cause they've been following us, and haven't caught up yet," Jennings said.

With no tasks at hand, Thomas had come to the deck after hearing the fife, but now that it had stopped he only saw Jennings and Jared arguing.

"Who would be following us?" Jared barely repressed a laugh. "Nothing."

"How you know that? They swim underwater, ye know," Jennings said. He turned away from the wheel for a moment.

"Who does?" Thomas asked.

"Sirens," Jennings said.

"Oh here we go again…." Benson muttered.

"What are sirens?" Thomas inquired.

"You know, mermaids! They follow sailors and drag 'em down with 'em to the depths below!" He reached a grasping hand toward Thomas to demonstrate. "Me own grandfather met such a fate."

Benson made a dismissive noise. "Don't you know anything, sailor? Sirens and mermaids are completely different."

Jennings sneered. "That doesn't change the fact."

"I suppose they slept with him first, too," Jared said.

Swinging his attention back to Jared, Jennings shook a fist at the young sailor. "That's enough! That fife of yours draws 'em closer! Their pet dolphins scout the area ahead of them … they just love music."

Benson chuckled.

"Ahh, you keep out'a this, Roland," Jennings scoffed at him.

Jared turned to Thomas. "Tommy, you're a bright lad. Tell me, do mermaids exist?"

Thomas shook his head. "Of course not. That's just superstition."

"How do you know they don't?" snapped Jennings. "Have you ever seen one?"

"Well, no, have you?" Thomas shot back.

Before Jennings could think of a response, Ward came out of the cabin. "Hey, what's all the yelling up here?"

"Just another fantasy trip on Jennings's part, sir," Jared called.

"More of those mermaids, right?" Ward huffed. "Well, nonsense. The cap'n was enjoying the music."

"You'll be hearing from me if we ever see one." Grumbling, Jennings turned his attention to the ship's wheel as Ward went back below.

"Do you play your fife often, Jared?"

"Not as often as I'd like, but when I need to pass the time."

"Too often," Jennings griped.

"Music critic," Jared mumbled.

Remembering the tunes folks played back home, Thomas thought it might be nice to hear Jared play. "What songs do you know?"

"Songs?" With a shrug, Jared grinned. "I don't really know any songs, I just make up a melody as I go."

"I'd like to listen." Thomas sat down beside him.

"Aye then." With a wink, Jared put the fife to his mouth. He wet his lips once, and then started to play. Jennings shook his head as Jared invented a quick jig.

Thomas applauded. "That was marvelous, and you say you're not much of a musician?"

"Well … ye know, I don't like to brag."

"That's fer sure," Jennings mumbled.

Thomas decided that the deck should be swabbed again after the rain they'd had earlier that morning. Much to Jennings' dismay, Jared continued to play without interruptions for the rest of the afternoon.

The midday sun soon faded into evening, and a beef dinner brought peace to the sailors. Before the crew lowered the sails for the night, Thomas watched the sunset off the starboard side of the ship. It was a bit chilly, but beacuse the wind had died down it didn't bother him much.

As Thomas rested his arms on the edge of the ship, it occurred to him that he was no longer in his mother's care. Although the men were easy to get along with, he wondered if this serene sea life would always be as easy as it had seemed the past two days.

While he pondered, Ward came out onto deck, puffing on a cigar. "Tommy, whatcha looking at lad?"

"Just looking, sir." Thomas turned to the first mate.

"You don't have to be at attention." He took another drag at his cigar. "Tell me, how are ye liking things so far?"

Thomas looked out to sea again, before he replied. "I'm sure that once things become a bit more routine, sir, I'll feel right at home."

Ward smiled. "Won't be long. Ye might want to go below deck, though. Lots to do tomorrow."

Thomas nodded. "Goodnight, sir."

"Rest well, lad." Ward watched over the ship as his cigar burned down to a stub. Soon, the crewmen were all asleep.

In the morning, while the other men were setting sail, Thomas was in the galley assisting Mr. Ellis with the eggs and bacon that would be served with biscuits.

"Boy, take them biscuits out of the stove 'fore they burn," Ellis muttered as he scrambled some eggs.

"Do you have a cloth or something so I don't get burned?"

"Here." Ellis threw a wet rag at him. Moving fast, Thomas took hold of the metal sheet they were on and nearly spilled them onto the work table, as the rag didn't offer much protection from the heat.

"Don't drop 'em!" Ellis growled, making Thomas jump.

"Sorry sir, they were hot, sir."

"Get out of here! I don't need yer help anymore!" Ellis growled. Thomas made for the exit before Ellis could throw anything else at him.

"Kids...." Ellis grumbled to nobody in particular.

While the crewmen were busying themselves with other tasks, Thomas went to work with the mop. Mr. Lewinston was the only other crewman on deck.

"Tommy, what's new?" Lewinston asked from behind the wheel.

"That Ellis ... it's nothing, sir." Thomas tried to calm himself down.

Lewinston chuckled. "Ahh, Ellis's not a bad guy. Just a rough fellow, that's all. You get to know him a bit, eh? You'll see."

Thomas nodded. "I hope you're right."

Adjusting his sleeve, Lewinston briefly exposed his skull and cross-bones tattoo.

"Sir ... may I ask about your tattoo?"

Lewinston shook his head. "I'm not proud of it, Tommy ... I'd rather not talk about it. Hey, look toward the shore, up on the bluffs."

Thomas looked over the bow and to the crest of the hills ahead. In the distance a dark crag of stone capped the bluffs. There, surrounded by trees and a massive stone wall lay the towers of Cimmordia Castle. Easily the largest freestanding structure that Thomas had ever seen, it was as magnificent as it was large.

"Largest wall, and longest for that matter, of all the nations on the Centra." The sailor sighed in admiration. "Supposed to be quite a place on the inside, too. Sure would like to see sometime."

"Maybe ... it doesn't look all that large from here, though." Gauging distance and size on the sea was still very new to Thomas.

Lewinston laughed. "Well, no ... but keep in mind we're a good distance from it yet! We'll pass by, and then you'll get a feel for the size. Quite a place, Cimmordia Castle."

"Aye." Thomas returned to his mop.

Thomas found swabbing the deck both peaceful and tranquil, especially after Mr. Ellis's outburst. He made an effort to pretend he was a worker in the castle, and the task was completed in no time.

Later that evening, the *Valiant* did pass closer to the castle. And true to Lewinston's word, the castle was large. In fact, Thomas never lost sight of it as they rounded Tower Cape.

The rest of the day was uneventful and passed quickly as they sailed around the rocky coastline leading to South Cimmordia. Just as the sun was setting, the bay came into view.

A port much larger than Vesper, South Cimmordia maintained a population consisting mostly of mill workers, fishermen, and textile workers. There were fewer trees in this region, and lumber was a valuable item to those who lived there. Much of the materials received or produced here went directly to Cimmordia Castle and its Capitol Town, located on the plateau a short distance inland. The royal family boasted a beautiful and well-defended castle with a garden covering more than 10 acres.

South Cimmordia was also Cimmordia's second largest city, with a population of just over 70,000. Second only in population to the port of Southmarin to the east, it was also the nation's busiest port. With Kalis Island nearby to control the ocean currents, Kalis Harbor was busy even as the sun melted the gentle waters to a bright golden orange.

Thomas had never seen a city so large. He was again reminded of his dream to visit the large city of Davenport to the north. Maybe this is what visiting a castle city was like!

With the sun quickly setting, the men lowered the sails and rode the momentum into port, mooring at the docks a few moments later. Their customers would be anxious to receive their supplies after the dawn.

Thomas woke up the next morning, made ready for the day, and headed toward the stairs. He didn't get past the cargo hold. Mr. Gritzol and Mr. Perry were already hauling several lengths of finished lumber atop deck.

"This load goes to Lasselton's Mill, Barry," Mr. Ward observed. "He'll have some raw lumber to deliver to Derrisberg on your return, so make sure to get the order right."

Gritzol nodded. "Why that man keeps ordering raw timber from all the way across the sea is beyond me."

"Can't get lumber from the King's Forest. He's got his reasons."

"Aye."

Hoping to avoid hauling lumber again, Thomas walked past Ward to make his exit, but Gritzol pulled Thomas aside.

"Hey Tommy, you're here just in time. The rest of this lumber needs to go into town. Grab hold of some boards and give us a hand." It was not a request.

"Okay, right away." Thomas took a hold of three lengths. As usual, Perry was carrying a bunch at a time, while Gritzol only carried six or so. Thomas, on the other hand, still struggled with the load that he had, small as it might be.

Eventually, all of it was brought on deck. They used the crane to lift the boards onto a cart so it could be delivered to customers.

"Thanks for the help, Tommy!" Gritzol called as he and Ward carted the lumber away.

"No problem, sir!" Thomas waved to them then took the mop and bucket from their storage area.

There wasn't anyone to stop him from swabbing the deck, so he proceeded to work near the steering wheel before his other chores. Not long after he finished, Jared exited the captain's cabin and met up with Thomas.

"Hey, I just worked it out with the cap'n ... would you like to see this town, Tommy?"

"Sure." He sighed as he appreciated his handiwork. "But you could've asked me a half hour ago."

"Don't ye like swabbing the deck?"

"Well...." Thomas began.

The sailor gave him a confidential look. "Yes?"

"I guess it would've been easier not to do it."

"Aye, that's true, Tommy, that's true." Jared's ponytail bobbed in time with his nodding. "Needed to be done, though, didn't it?"

"It did, yes."

"So why argue it then? Come now, there aren't too many things 'ere left to do on the ship." Jared started down the gangplank.

After a moment's consideration, Thomas couldn't think of any pressing chores. "Coming!" He caught up to Jared, and they went into town.

Thomas and Jared walked toward the marketplace. They noticed two suspicious men who were talking just outside of a tavern. Each had a tankard of ale. One wore a red coat, while the other man smelled of rum and wore a sheathed cutlass on his belt.

Jared pulled Thomas aside. "Shh … keep quiet."

"So it's settled then. Me old man knew the place was rich with treasure, and he drags his boat there," the man in the coat said.

"Yeah, you told me all that. Where did it come from, anyways?" the rummy asked. He turned over a worn, rolled scroll in his hand.

"From a map collector in Davenport. It was all they took … one worn, scribbled map that must be 40 years old."

The rummy spat onto the cobblestoned street. "Aye, and a cursed a map it be. I tells ye, some of the men and I don't feel right going out there, ye know."

"Curses be a bunch of rubbish," the man in the red coat scoffed, keeping focused on his drink. He adjusted his red overcoat upon his shoulders.

"Maybe, but none of them fools never came back alive either," the second man added.

"That's superstition, old news. And besides, Marshall wants it; it's not our lot."

"Don't use his name!" the rummy gasped.

The man wearing the coat looked around the square. "There's nobody around who knows who he is."

"We're in his hometown; he'll have our heads if we talk about him like that! We don't need that kind of attention, and I won't be the one to walk the wake of blood." His eyes darted around the square as well. "Besides, we have to make the drop soon. We don't need the castle guards sniffing around here."

The man wearing the coat nodded. "We should vanish soon. His man'll be coming by any time, and we can't be blowing our cover."

"Right, right … remember what happened last time someone broke a deal with these dastards," the rummy said, getting up.

He adjusted his coat again and finished his ale. "I'd rather sell it to 'em than have it taken from me with a sword at my neck," he added.

Both men glanced toward a bell tower at the far end of the square. "Shush! It's almost time … you remember the plan?" the rummy asked.

The man with the coat nodded. "We make the drop at the bell tower and pick up the gold at the market in Capitol Town."

"Right. Let's go ... no talking from here on," the rummy cautioned.

"I'm the captain. I make the orders. No talking!" the man in the coat snapped.

The rummy nodded, taking a last sip of ale as they left the table. Both men then crossed the marketplace, stopping in a corner by a narrow alleyway leading to the bell tower, very near where Thomas and Jared were hiding.

Thomas gave his companion a wide-eyed look. "Who are those men?"

Shaking his head, Jared started for an alley behind the bell tower. "I've seen them before. Just keep quiet."

The two men approached the bell tower. The one wearing the gallant red coat walked with a limp and made his way across the square. The bells began to chime the quarter hour, as the one carrying the cutlass took a nervous look around the square.

The two men stopped near the entrance to an alleyway. The man dressed in the coat dropped some sort of scroll onto the ground near the alley. Without a word, both men quickly left the area and headed east.

"Hey." Thomas watched them leave in confusion. "He dropped something."

"Tommy, no!" Jared had finally realized who the men were. He quickly grabbed the scroll and pushed Thomas further into the alleyway so they couldn't be seen or heard.

"What? He dropped this, Jared."

"Aye, he did, but I remember those men after all." The sailor's expression was uncharacteristically serious. "They's bad company. They're pirates."

"Pirates?"

"Shh!" He covered Thomas's mouth with his hand. "Aye, let's get out of here 'fore they catch us with this." Jared shoved Thomas through the alley to the street on the other side.

"Should we bring this to Captain Janes?" Thomas whispered.

"Aye, right away, too. Come on, quickly now." They hurried back toward the docks. As they approached, Jared recognized the ships at the far end of the port. The first was a ship called the *Stargazer* and parked at its side was a larger ship with red sails called the *Inferno*.

A moment or two later, an older fellow wearing a red-striped shirt and a stocking cap entered the square from the alleyway. He stopped at the entrance and looked around a few times. After lifting his cap and scratching his bald head, he replaced his headgear and continued through the marketplace. He stumbled over some uneven stones in the pavement, but left in a rush as the chimes finished their announcement.

"Do you think he got it?" the man in the red coat asked his co-conspirator.

"Was it the guy in the hat or the tall fellow and the kid?" the second asked.

"It's always the guy in the hat!" the red coat exclaimed.

"I don't know … I couldn't see," the second replied.

"Well, forget about it … if Marshall wanted it that badly, he'd get it himself … we've done our part. Come on." The two then headed toward the outskirts of town.

By then Jared and Thomas had returned to the *Valiant*. They knocked on Captain Janes's doors, and once invited to enter, they found him sitting comfortably inside.

"Ahh, Mr. Roberts and Mr. DeLeuit. What's the good word?" He was sipping some tea.

"Captain, we've got something to show you. Look here." Jared handed him the scroll.

"What's this?" The captain raised an eyebrow at them.

"Some pirates dropped it in the town marketplace," Thomas said.

Slowly Janes set his cup in its saucer. "Pirates?"

"I saw the *Stargazer* in the last moor, right next to the *Inferno*," Jared added.

Janes slowly nodded, apparently quite familiar with both vessels. "Once Mr. Ward returns … we'll want to be out of here within a moment's notice." Janes opened the scroll.

Both Thomas and Jared looked over his shoulder at the scroll as it opened. Inside was a map of four islands—one large one, another smaller and rocky, a third short and narrow with many trees, while a fourth very small. Several landmarks were once marked, but had since been blotted out. Very few trails were marked on any of the islands, but the center of the rocky island was marked with an X.

Thomas wondered if these islands matched one of Bobby's charts.

"Aye, it certainly looks like a treasure map," Janes murmured.

"Indeed." Jared nodded.

Thomas couldn't understand why anyone would drop something so valuable. "Treasure?"

The young sailor sighed. "Aye, but who knows where these islands are?"

"Hmm ... indeed...." Weighing down the corners of the parchment with his teacup and a book, Janes's eyes never left the map. "I haven't seen a chain of four islands in these parts, unless...."

"Sundrop Islands?" Jared offered.

With a wave, Janes dismissed the possibility. "No, that is a chain of only two islands."

Thomas didn't say anything as he looked over the map. This version was not the same as the chart of the Nemaris Islands he had seen in Elder Harrion's study, but the two charts were similar.

Before Thomas could be sure, Janes rolled the map back into the scroll.

"Captain, sir ... who operates the *Stargazer* and the *Inferno*?" Thomas had never seen a ship with red sails before.

"Pirates, Tommy ... dastardly ones, too." A frown crossed Janes's lips as he absently tapped the scroll's edge against his chin. "The *Stargazer* ... they deliver things of interest to the commander. And the *Inferno* ... well, that is the flagship of the Sundrop Cult."

"And they are not to be trifled with," Jared added.

The captain nodded. "Gentlemen, we don't mention any of this until we are beyond Kalis Island."

"Aye," Jared said.

"Tommy?" There was an almost tangible weight to Janes's gaze.

"I won't mention it, sir."

"Aye, you won't." Janes turned his focus to Jared. "Mr. Roberts, let the men know we'll be leaving soon, but don't do anything 'til Mr. Ward returns."

"Aye sir, we'll be ready." Jared headed onto the deck.

"Thomas, you help too. In the meantime, we'll hide this away." Janes took the scroll to a small safe at the bottom of his wardrobe and stowed it safely.

"Aye cap'n." Thomas returned to deck to be with the rest of the crew.

Roberts approached what crew remained on deck. "What's the word?" Jennings asked.

"Cap'n says we're to be prepared for shipping out."

Benson scratched his head. "Why for? We're told by Ward that we'd be staying a day."

Jared shrugged. "Those're captain's orders."

"Okay, but I'd like a better reason personally," Jennings muttered.

"All right, if you must know, there be some pirates in port." The younger sailor hitched a thumb in the direction of the ship with red sails. "The *Inferno*—Captain Marshall, if I remember correctly."

The three men muttered to themselves.

"Aye, Roberts, we be ready. When's the word?" Gritzol asked.

"As soon as Ward gets back from town, we act. Work fast, but don't look like we're in a hurry." To emphasize his words, Jared gave a lazy stretch.

"Aye." The three men went about preparing to leave.

"Tommy, come here and help me with these ropes," Jennings called from the mainmast as soon as he spotted the boy.

"Aye." Thomas climbed carefully to meet him.

"Hand me that thick one," Jennings instructed, and Thomas handed him a rope that was tied onto a pulley.

"Hand me t'other one," Jennings said, and Thomas handed it to him. Jennings then carried it up to the upper part of the mainsail and tied it in place.

"Okay, climb back down then. Ye shouldn't have to worry when … oh, there he is now," Jennings said, seeing Ward arrive with supplies.

As soon as the mate waltzed aboard, the crew went to work. "To work lads," Gritzol called as they began making the preparations. Perry raised the anchor as Lewinston raised the gangplank. Benson raised the gaff sail. Jennings raised the mainsail, and Gritzol manned the jib. Roberts then ran back to the ship's wheel and steered the craft out of the harbor while Mr. Ward tried to make sense of it all.

"What the?" The first mate called aloud to no one in particular. "Why we leaving in such a rush?" Grumbling, he lent the crew a hand.

Captain Janes stepped out of his cabin after they had made some distance. "Seriam, come here."

"Captain, what's going on?" Ward asked as the sails caught the wind, giving them a good burst of speed.

"Come here," Janes repeated, returning to his cabin. A confused Ward followed.

"What's the deal?" Ward asked again.

"Look there." Janes pointed toward the last moor on the north end of the port.

Ward looked out with the spyglass, seeing the mighty galleon known as the *Inferno* through the lens.

"Gosh, why didn't ye tell me? I had no idea them low lives were in town." Ward returned the spyglass to its place and sat down at the table.

"Neither did we. They must've arrived this morning. But I've no intention of staying nearby because the last time we ran into 'em. Remember that little adventure of ours?" Outside, Kalis Island slowly slipped by.

"What's up about now?" Ward asked.

Unlocking the safe, Janes withdrew the scroll. "Look here." He unfurled the map.

Ward looked it over then rolled it up and handed it back to Janes, who returned to the safe.

"You wouldn't really want to do that, would ye?" Ward asked.

"No, not right away." Shaking his head, Janes sat himself across from his first mate. "Not until our second pass through the circle—and besides, I'm not sure exactly where these isles are. I've not seen them on any charts."

"Aye, me neither. Perhaps my friend in Davenport would know?" Ward asked.

The captain chanced the suggestion. "Maybe ... Davenport would certainly be out of the way, however."

"Chris, I suggest we just keep it and forget about it. These islands are not worth our time."

"I say, I believe you're correct." Janes nodded. "After all, we've got deliveries to make."

Lost in Paradise

After their departure from South Cimmordia, the *Valiant* experienced smooth sailing. For the rest of the day and into the next, all went well. Because the *Valiant* was much smaller and faster than the *Inferno*, they had enough of a head start that left the *Inferno* a day behind, even if it had left within an hour of the *Valiant*'s departure. That is, of course, if they knew that the map was missing and where it had gone.

The next day started out with Thomas again swabbing the deck. Captain Janes and the other men gathered around him shortly after breakfast.

"Is there something I can do, sirs?" Thomas asked curiously, putting the mop down a moment.

"No, you're doing fine, Tommy." The captain gave a conspiratorial grin. "In fact, we've got a little surprise for you."

Thomas panicked, thinking he might be in trouble. "Whatever it was I did, I'm sorry about it."

Janes and the other men laughed.

Mr. Ward slapped the boy's back, nearly sending him to the deck. "Tommy, you've been doing great here! I heard Mr. Ellis mumbling, and the other men and I agreed that if you're to learn the ways of the sea, you need a good tool. And the best tool you'll ever use is a good sharp knife."

Captain Janes took out of his coat a knife in a black leather sheath, about nine inches long from the handle to the tip.

"A knife ... for me?" Thomas asked. Janes handed it to him.

"I'm confident you'll be careful with it, but since you've done so well thus far, we decided that the sooner you got to using it, the better off you'd be."

Thomas took the knife out of its sheath. Along with a sturdy handle and a sharp edge, the blade had a sea snake carved into the hilt on one side. It was a very beautiful knife—and brand new!

"Wow … it's so shiny … thank you, all." Reverently, Thomas replaced it in its protective sheath.

"All right men, back to work!" Ward said. The men congratulated Thomas and went about their business.

Mr. Benson took Thomas's hand. "Say, you ready to learn how to handle riggings? Come on up, Tommy. I'll show you what you need to know."

Thomas nodded and followed Benson as he climbed the mainmast.

"Keep up the good work, lad, and worry not about the deck today," Janes called.

"Aye sir," Thomas said, as he took lessons from Mr. Benson.

As the day came to an end, the seas calmed. Thomas had learned a lot about riggings from Mr. Benson, and found his new tool quite useful. Even though the seas were calm, in the skies above a different story began to unfold. Dark clouds loomed on the western horizon and hues of crimson and magenta filled the night sky.

As Thomas relaxed in his cabin, he could see no evening colors and instead focused on another entry from the book of Scyhathen.

I'm no longer sure what day it is, as our calendar keeper Mr. Banes has grown seasick and too ill to make his daily reports. He knows the Dieterian calendar well, and I am not worried about him giving me a full report in due time. I be sure of this, though—a sudden storm has tossed my ship well off course, and forced us aground near the shores of four uncharted islands. To our fortune, the Nemaris is intact. Our next task is to discover where we have landed. This task is one I am certain will prove a challenge.

I know not of these islands' exact location, and neither does my navigator Mr. Mandalay. What we do know is our last position was east of Cyeel Point and south of Grand Point. Sadly, storms have a way of dashing all history of one's previous course across the seaboard. Nonetheless, I am captivated by the islands that lay before us. Smitty and I went ashore to find luscious flora, ripe fruits, and fertile soil. There is a large ridge on the main island, from which one could view all points of the island chain. The intermittent sound of falling water mixed with the chirps of birds, monkeys, and all manner of blooming flowers, lush fruit trees, and tropical grass; all this against the backdrop of crashing waves makes the crew and myself very calm indeed.

Perhaps these islands are the four the explorer spoke of; regardless, our journey to Phrynn has most certainly been delayed. When tomorrow comes, I hope to journey further inland.

Thomas had hoped to read further, but then he heard the sound of Jared's fife, a lighthearted melody that floated undaunted across the calm sea. Putting the book inside the chest, he went atop deck and listened.

Thomas immediately noticed that the men were uneasy tonight. Apparently, the darkening sky did not bode well with the crew.

"I don't think you should be playing right now, Jared." Jennings said.

Jared put down the fife. "Are you going to give me your speech again?"

"Look at them clouds out there." Jennings pointed at the spreading gloom. "Something tells me that we ought to either keep going as much as we can or prepare for the worst."

"Aye, storm coming strong," Gritzol said.

"Aye … storm indeed." With a grin, Jared shrugged. "That, and be keeping in mind we can't weigh anchor tonight, we're too far out. If you're that worried, tell the captain."

Jennings nodded and was just getting up when Mr. Ward and Captain Janes came on deck. The men stood up at attention. Jared returned his fife to his belt.

"Captain on deck," Ward said.

Janes stood before the men. "It looks like there is a storm coming, lads. We'll need volunteers to keep watch tonight."

Jared raised his hand. "We are too far out for anchor, yes?"

"Aye, too far indeed," Ward answered.

"The storm looks to be heading somewhat to the north of us, but storms are unpredictable, so anything may happen." The captain scanned across his crew. "Any volunteers?"

The crew rarely failed to volunteer for everyday assignments, but all agreed that the storm clouds appeared anything but friendly.

"Perhaps shifts are a good idea, Captain," Ward suggested.

"Aye, indeed. Who wishes to go first?"

Jared and Perry put their hands up.

"Good, thank you Jared, Perry. Second shift?"

Gritzol and Lewinston volunteered.

"Wonderful! That leaves two more then."

Ward cleared his throat. "Jennings, you and I will do the third shift."

Jennings grumbled something, and then replied, "Aye."

Janes clapped his hands together with a smile that didn't reach his eyes. "That should cover it. If morning comes and the storm has managed to pass us, you six will be allowed to sleep in. Meantime, the rest of us should rest up in the event the storm gets too much for two people."

"Aye," the men replied.

"Good. Well, goodnight all." With a nod, Janes returned to his cabin.

"Okay then." With his gaze shifting, Ward addressed each team. "First shift 'til midnight, second 'til three and third 'til dawn. Check the clock in the hall if you're not sure."

"What about getting up?" Lewinston asked.

"The team before will inform you—and any trouble'll wake the captain or myself, mind you." Ward left for his quarters.

"Aye," the men said. With their plans agreed upon, Perry, Roberts, and Thomas remained on deck while the other men headed for the barracks. Perry sat down on the deck and leaned against the port rail. Jared returned to his spot along the stern.

"You don't object to my music, do you, Perry?" Jared asked.

The man quietly shook his head.

"Do you mind if I listen?" Thomas asked.

"Please do." Jared wet his lips and put the fife to his mouth. He began to play a melody similar to the one he'd played earlier, except that it sounded like there was harmony to his music. He stopped playing quickly. "Do you hear that?"

"Hear what?" Thomas asked.

Lowering his fife to his lap, Jared looked around in confusion. "I could've swore I heard someone singing."

"I didn't hear anything. Mr. Perry?"

Perry shook his head slowly. He kept his eyes closed and did not respond further.

"How odd." With a shrug, Jared continued to play. As before, there was harmony with the melody, except this time much clearer and more audible. Jared stopped playing once he heard the second tune, and the singing continued for a few bars until it stopped suddenly.

"Very mysterious ... and perhaps even fishy," Perry spoke up.

Jared turned to Thomas. "You must've heard it that time."

Thomas nodded. "It sounds like someone is echoing your melody."

"Let's see what happens when I do this." He played only a few notes on the fife. The mystery soprano voice continued a few moments before realizing that it was the only one making music. "That sounded like a girl's voice!"

"Wait, remember what Mr. Jennings said about sirens? Mermaids?" Thomas gazed across the water, though he wasn't sure what he should be looking for.

"Be sensible, Tommy. The increasing clouds must have an echo effect, I believe." Despite his words, Jared's expression seemed uncertain.

"If there are mermaids around, they're probably just enjoying the music like I am." Thomas gave his friend a hopeful grin. "Play, and I'm sure they'll listen."

"Perhaps I should stop playing for tonight, Tommy. You should go to sleep, too. The storm is fear enough for me—not that I'm afraid of mermaids, mind you, but you must get your rest, like cap'n said," Jared suggested.

"You're scared, aren't you?" Thomas asked. A splash, perhaps the sound of a fish jumping, broke the tension.

"Uh ... no, don't be ridiculous! I am the embodiment of, er, courage."

Thomas chuckled to himself, although he was unsure who or what, if anyone, had made the voice.

"Go on now; get some sleep. You may need your strength tonight, Tommy." Jared all but pushed Thomas into the hallway.

"Good night," Thomas said.

"Rest well, Tommy," Perry said.

"Aye, goodnight," Jared said. Thomas went downstairs.

Perry opened his eyes. "I assure you I do not sing soprano, Jared."

Jared nodded. "No, I did not suspect you did, Perry ... but we had best keep our wits about us this evening."

While Thomas slept well, he could have swore he heard voices in the night. Yes, there was activity on deck, but the voice he continued to hear was too soprano to belong to any of the men on board. It reminded him of children's voices back home.

Although much of what was said was drowned out by the sound of the waves, a few words kept coming through, as if the melody Jared had played continued in the background.

The voice almost seemed to ask, "I am lonely, will you spend some time with me?"

It got to the point where Thomas would sit up in the cot and try to focus on what the voice was saying, but when he did that the voice stopped.

Perhaps he had been dreaming it all, spurred on by the imaginations of Jennings and Roberts. Thinking the voice might be a dream based on the melody that Jared had played, he turned to the glass orb that was hanging inside a small bag upon the wall.

Thomas picked up the orb and held it to the light, but saw nothing but a blue hue. He must not have been homesick enough.

Replacing the orb on its hook, he focused on his bedroom back in Harper's Bay and fell into a deep sleep. So deep, in fact, that not even the arrival of a raging storm woke him. On deck, the story was much different.

"Get the others up! Oh, mercy, this is not good!" Jared called to Perry, who took off below deck to gather the troops as Jared did what he could to trim sails that had come loose in the torrential winds. The smell of salt water waved across the deck like a fog as rain fell in sheets.

Wearing all-covering ponchos, the others arrived quickly, including Ellis. They worked as fast as they could to lower all the sails, even the jib—anything that could fly loose and injure someone was tied fast. Ward manned the ship's wheel and fought to maintain the course; the struggle was difficult and the waves were winning.

"Lower them sails! Secure the riggings! She's a mean one!" Ward called as he fought to control the rudder. It soon became too much for him alone, but Perry gave him a hand and Captain Janes came to aid as well.

"Ellis! Give a hand with these stabilizers!" Janes called. Ellis did so, avoiding his preferred post atop the crow's nest.

"Aye!" he grumbled, as the thunder made an unbearable noise.

"Hold tight! Wave incoming!" Gritzol cried. A large wave exploded into the ship from the starboard side. Fortunately, nobody was washed overboard. A seasoned crew, this one knew storms quite well.

"Get that last sail secured! Quickly now!" Lewinston cried as Roberts and Jennings did their best.

"Another wave advancing!" Ward cried. Another large wave approached again from starboard.

"Hold tight!" Janes called. The men each took hold of whatever they could as the wave rocked the *Valiant*, thrusting the boat into a sharp left turn. Although Perry and Ward held the wheel tightly, there was no forcing the ship back to the right, and control over the ship was no longer a concern.

"One more coming in!"

"Brace!" Janes called again. This wave hit hard on the stern, causing Ward to lose not only his grip but also his footing.

"Aaagh!" Ward cried, as Perry let loose the wheel to grab onto Ward's foot before his head rammed into the railing.

"Someone hold the wheel! We've lost control!" Perry cried. Only Ellis could get to it. He got there quickly, but before they could get the ship back under control, it had turned almost entirely about.

Another splash of cold water wrenched against the bow, spraying across the railings.

Roberts called to Jennings, who had finished securing his side of the mainsail. "Harv! We've got to get down from here! It's too windy!"

"One of us should get to the crow's nest and double knot the riggings!"

"Too risky!" Janes called up. "Get on those stabilizers, everyone!"

"Aye!" both men said, taking care to climb down carefully. As they began their decent, a fourth wave approached from portside.

"Wait! Hang on!" Lewinston called, seeing the approaching wave.

"From the bow! Hold tight!" Gritzol called, increasing the amount of rope he had toward his stabilizer. As he pulled, a two-pound counterweight nestled amid the bilge at the bottom of the ship shifted. When each stabilizer was in position, even massive waves would be less likely to direct the ship off course.

Unfortunately, these waves appeared to have a mind of their own and were relentless.

The next massive wave crashed with a tremendous impact, hurling a wall of water onto the deck and upward toward the yard right into Roberts and Jennings. Although both men managed to hold on, the fife on Roberts' belt did not. It flew into the sea, with only the echo of air blowing through its holes.

"No! My fife!" Jared cried. He struggled to hold onto the main beam.

"Come on! Forget about it!" With a curse Jennings shook the dripping hair out of his eyes. "Your life is more important!" He climbed down. Robert's eyes darted toward the approaching waves.

"Jared Roberts! Come to your senses!" Jennings shouted as he completed his descent. Jared followed and eventually took hold of the stabilizer on the starboard bow. With the use of these stabilizers, they managed to reduce the sharp turns the craft made. But even with the stabilizers active and three men on the wheel, their hopes of staying on course were worse than trying to keep an egg on a mad bull's back.

Impossible.

They held to their positions through most of the night; the storm carried them where it wished.

After some time, Janes ordered the men to release the stabilizers. "Stand down. The storm seems to be lightening."

"Are we on course?" Gritzol called.

"We won't be able to find that out until the seas are calm." Ward replied.

"Hold on a minute! Look out there!" Benson called, looking out beyond the starboard bow.

Through flashes of lightning in the distance, they could faintly see some islands on the horizon. In the dim light the island chain appeared inhospitable, but at that point anything besides endless water seemed welcome for the crew.

"Look at that ... land ho!" Lewinston called. Each man observed the approaching islands with a quiet vigil.

"I see 'em there!" Ward shouted back.

However, the storm waves had not ended as yet another leg of the storm to the north had sent more and more waves in their direction, this time from the port side of the craft.

"More waves portside!" Ellis cried.

"Brace with the stabilizers!" Janes shouted. "Hold starboard!" Each man returned to his stabilizer. Wave after wave impacted the craft. Although no structural damage resulted, the waves continued to push the craft further toward the chain of islands. Soon the waves pushed the craft enough so it was on a direct course toward them. Now, the waves pushed from astern rather than to the bow.

"Shall we try the anchor sir?" Lewinston said.

"Not yet! We're too far out!"

"Captain! Look, we're much too shallow!" Ward exclaimed.

"Dear me ... hang on tight!" Janes cried, realizing just how close to the shore they were. So close, in fact, that they had run aground.

A solid blow to the keel of the bow rocked Thomas awake and out of his cot. He went above deck to see what had happened.

Each man returned his stabilizer to its place. Large waves continued to push the craft further onto the sandy bottom.

"Well ... now what do we do?" Ellis asked.

"Aye, what indeed," Janes said.

Thomas came onto deck and looked around in the dim night sky, carrying a lantern with him. "Did we hit something?"

"Aye, we've run aground," Ward said.

"Aground? Where?" Thomas asked.

"I'm afraid we're not sure, lad," Janes said, as the other men stood aside.

"Damage report?" Ward asked.

"Someone check in the cargo hold. Make sure we're not taking on water." Lewinston followed the captain's order and rushed inside.

Gritzol glanced over the side of the bow. "Seems we survived that much ... hull looks fine."

Janes nodded as the rain began to pick up. Winds and waves were no longer a concern, as the storm suddenly changed from wicked and windy to steady raindrops.

"Guess we'll have to do a full check in the morning." The captain and mate went inside.

"That's it?" Thomas asked.

"Aye, that's it," Benson said as he walked past Thomas to go inside.

"Come on lad, before you catch cold," Gritzol said, going inside. All the men went inside except for Jared.

"Aren't you coming too, Jared?"

Jared made a low sigh. "Aye, I suppose so." He passed by Thomas to the cabin door.

"What is it?"

Jared sighed again, said nothing, and slowly walked downstairs.

Once Thomas was inside and had shut the door, Mr. Perry's deep voice echoed quietly in the dim light of the hall. "His fife."

Magic and Mysteries

The rains continued well into the night, but cleared before dawn and became a stark contrast from the storm before. There was a clear view of the stars above. All was calm, blowing the remnants of the storm away with a soft breeze. Waves gently cascaded against the sandy shore.

The night's storm had ended as suddenly as it came, leaving the ship aground with the bow toward the islands. Waves striking the flat hind of the stern had little to no noticeable impact. With the ship wedged deep into the sands, the waves did little more than create a soft noise.

The *Valiant* had landed in a large beach area that stretched out a good half mile or so from the shore. The waters surrounding the ship were some fifteen or twenty feet deep, so the ship sat in the water about the same as it would've while normally at sea.

Captain Janes came out in the early morning, well before the sun brought warmth to the air. With his usual cup of tea in hand, he surveyed the situation. "I say, if one's going to be stranded someplace it may as well be a place of enchanting beauty."

Even in the dim light, he could see majestic palm trees and other tropical fruit plants lined the beach. Beyond that there was a high ridge. The faint sound of a waterfall could be heard beneath the calls of birds in the sky. It was a wondrous scene.

Mr. Ward arrived on deck with navigation tools and charts. "Here we are. It's just a matter of finding our bearing now." He went to work setting up the equipment.

"Look out there, Seriam," Janes said.

Ward gazed at the island, letting the entrancing view sink in.

"I do believe we're in some sort of paradise, aren't we?"

Janes placidly sipped his tea. "Quite a place if I do say so myself. So then, let's find out where this paradise is." He turned to the equipment Ward had set up, which included a compass, a sextant, and a map of known regions. "Let me see that compass."

Ward handed it to him. He held it up, and beneath the light of the lantern, watched the compass find magnetic north. "North's that way," Janes exclaimed.

"Aye," was all Ward said in response. He adjusted the sextant, and after a brief moment looked up from the scope to follow the lines on the map.

"What's the word?" Janes brought the map nearer the lantern.

Ward sighed. "According to these readings, we're here." He pointed to a location just off the bottom edge of the map.

"Well, this is quite a discomforting lot, isn't it now." The captain took another sip from his cup.

"Indeed."

"Seriam, would you keep tabs on the calendar?" Janes rolled up the map. "I think it would be best if we are aware of how late Mr. Grimbeck's lumber is."

"I'll get to work on that later today ... what would you like done in the meantime?"

"Well, while we have some time, I wonder if Mr. Ellis has prepared breakfast." Apparently Janes preferred ignoring the issue of their location for the moment.

"Perhaps not, captain. It isn't even dawn yet."

"Well, no matter. We'll check anyway." Draining his cup, Janes headed inside. Even though they were completely lost and marooned, he would not let the entire situation affect his relaxed mood.

Confused, Ward watched Captain Janes with a shocked look before schooling his expression, collecting the gear, and following the captain inside.

After sunrise, life on board the *Valiant* began to pick up. Ellis began work on the morning meal, and before long, the rest of the crew began to rouse around the ship.

As the men gathered in the mess hall, Janes dished up and took his breakfast into his quarters. After Janes left, Ward sat down with Gritzol and Lewinston.

"Seems the Captain's got something on his mind," Gritzol said.

"Aye, that he does." Ward's tone had an edge that hinted he didn't want to discuss the issue.

Thomas arrived, bringing with him Scyhathen's book. He had been reading since dawn and left it on a table as he dished up some breakfast.

"Morning Tommy," Ward said.

"Hello everyone," Thomas replied, filling his plate.

"What's the book about?" Jennings asked.

"Something my father had." Thomas sat and straightened the book on the table. "A journal that belonged to a Captain Scyhathen."

"Scyhathen?" Ward asked, dropping his fork.

"*The* Scyhathen?" Benson asked, also looking up from his breakfast.

Several other reactions came from the crew and they circled Thomas.

"You've heard of him?" Thomas asked.

"Heard of him? Tommy, everyone's heard of him!" Jared cried.

Ward nodded. "Aye, I even met the gentlemen once. Tall fellow, had a long ponytail, gold tooth. Nicest man you'd ever meet, but if you saw him in action, you'd almost want to not know him. When he was in command, you knew that his ship would always be better off than any other."

"He was only the greatest explorer of our time," Gritzol added.

Benson turned to Ward. "Did you serve under him?"

"No, I only met him the once. It was a rare opportunity to see him in action as his ship sailed away from Grand Point for the south. Of course, I was pretty young back then and didn't know very much of seafaring." Ward's grin was almost youthful. "But I was so captivated, I joined the next ship that passed through."

"When was that, if you don't mind my asking?" Thomas asked.

"Goodness ... heck, it be forty years now that I've spent on these waves," Ward said.

"That would make it 1582 then," Gritzol said.

"Aye indeed ... almost to the day," Ward added.

"The first entry in this book was made July 18th, 1582, sir," Thomas said.

Thomas opened the journal to the first entry, and Ward looked the page over. "Aye, that was the day he left for the south. You've been reading this, then?"

Thomas nodded. "I read that sometime during 1582 the captain ran aground upon some uncharted islands."

"Uncharted islands ... Tommy, let me see that book if I may." Thomas handed it over. Flipping through, Ward soon found the description of isles similar to those the *Valiant* was trapped in. Abandoning his breakfast, Ward stood. "Tommy, come with me a moment."

They hurried to Captain Janes's cabin. Thomas caught up as Ward knocked hastily on the door. "Cap'n, I've got something to show ye."

Janes unlocked the door. Ward brought in the book and showed the description to Janes, who raised an eyebrow at them. "Okay ... and this pertains to what, exactly?"

"Doesn't this description seem awfully familiar compared to what's outside?" With a sweep of his hand, Ward indicated the spectacular view.

Janes took a quick glance out the starboard window toward the shore. He saw the luscious flowers, the many tropical fruits, and the shallow beach where they were grounded, similar to the situation the *Nemaris* had been in.

"If I'm not mistaken, Seriam, that description covers both Scyhathen's islands and ours."

Ward nodded.

Janes approached his safe and used his key to open it, removing the map that Thomas had found. Rolling it across the table, he took his finger and pointed at a spot on the shores along the north side of the main island.

"Thomas, I must know where you found this book." Janes's look was oddly intense.

"My father had it in his materials, sir, but I'm not certain how he obtained it."

"I would've enjoyed meeting your father, Tommy," Janes replied.

"So would I, sir, I never knew my father," Thomas said quietly.

"Indeed ... a shame." After a thoughtful pause, Janes returned his gaze to the journal. "Would you lend me this book of yours?"

"Of course, sir, for a while anyway." When the captain looked back up at him, Thomas shrugged. "I'm still reading it."

"Anytime you need it back, it's yours. Meantime, we've got a little bit of time yet." Janes faced his first mate. "Seriam, I'm looking for two or three volunteers to go ashore. If you'd stay and keep the ship, I'd be thankful."

"Aye, I'd rather stay here besides...." Mr. Ward shuddered. "Especially if they're the islands I think they be."

"Why's that?" Janes asked curiously.

"Just bad rumors about these islands," Ward replied.

Janes turned back to his cabin boy. "Tommy, what do you think? Does a paradise like that give you any chills?"

"I, too, have heard stories about these islands sir," Thomas said.

"Like what?"

"Stories about hidden traps, and that those who entered the inland often received death," Thomas explained.

"Tommy, how could someone write about it if they were killed off?" Janes asked.

Thomas didn't have a reply.

Janes looked toward his silver sword on the wall. "Aye, then. Since you've read some of this journal, I'd like you to come with. That way, we'll both find out how deadly the inland is."

"Aye, sir," Thomas said softly.

"We'll need two more men ... Roberts and Perry, I believe. We'll get a rowboat wet by midday."

"I'll let them know, sir," Thomas replied.

"Tommy, you're a great kid. You know that? A great kid," Janes said to himself as Thomas left the cabin.

"You seem awfully confident about this, Captain," Ward said.

"I'm not one to ignore superstition, Seriam, but if there're any traps we'll find out when we reach them." Janes put on his hat and then removed the sword from the wall.

"What should we do in the meantime?" Ward asked.

"Check on the ship ... check for damage from the storm and how badly we're trapped in the sand. Lewinston mentioned that we were dry in the hold, so I'm not worried. Otherwise, I'll be ashore." Janes headed for the door.

"Aye," Ward replied.

After making necessary preparations, Jared and Perry lifted one of the two rowboats with the crane and lowered it into the water. Then, each man climbed down the ladder to the rowboat. Perry carried the Kah Lunaseif with him, Roberts his rapier, Thomas his knife, and Janes his own longsword. They each had a canteen of water, several pieces of parchment, and a compass to make notes of their findings.

From the deck, Jennings and Benson worked the crane.

"Can't believe they're actually going ashore ... this is a bad idea," Jennings said.

Benson frowned. "How so?"

"Are you daft? Just look at these islands ... doesn't it seem as if you've heard stories of them before? You know ... *those* islands," Jennings said.

"Of course I have, but I don't buy into superstitions. Why should you?"

"Why? *Why?*" Jennings answered nervously.

Benson chuckled. "They're just islands. We'll find out more when they get back."

"If they get back," Jennings muttered.

Once free of the ship, Jared made a note of their situation.

"Strange, the water here seems plenty deep. Wonder why we ran aground," Jared said.

"No, it can only be fifteen feet at the most. That's usually how low we sit in the water," Janes said. Perry started rowing the men into shore.

"What do you think we'll find?" Thomas asked.

"Hopefully my fife," Jared said.

The captain chuckled. "You can't stop thinking about that, can you?"

"I've carried it with me since my mother passed away, Cap'n."

"Aye, I remember your mother, Roberts." His hat's feathers danced as he nodded. "Sweet lady ... and a wonder of an oyster cook."

"How did your mother pass, Jared?" Thomas asked as they approached the beach.

"I'd rather not talk about it now, Tommy. Later." Jared jumped out and pulled the craft far enough up the shore so the tide couldn't carry it away. As an added measure, he tied a small anchor to the bow and tossed it into the beach.

"Tommy." The captain waved at the journal in the boy's hands. "Does it say anywhere in your book the name of this main island?"

"Let me see." Thomas unwrapped the book from its protective oilcloth and scanned through it. After a few entries he found one where Scyhathen had finished exploring the main isle.

I still don't know what day it is, and as Mr. Banes is getting better, it shouldn't be too long till I can put days in the calendar again. In the past week while we've been marooned here, my first mate, Mr. Smitty, and I have journeyed onto the main island. With assistance from Mr. Mandalay, we have completed a rough survey. In area, the main island covered 160 fields. We estimate a length well over 1,400, and a width closer to 800.

We found the islands to be most hospitable. If this is to be where we end up for the time being, at least we shall be comfortable. We are marooned, yes; but our prison is a paradise ... and we shall do our best to survive amongst these golden islands.

Aside from the lush vegetation and colorful wildlife, there was little else that we discovered. Some of the other men suggested this might be the tropical paradise of a sorcerer, although nobody could think of his name, and at this time I predict that these are islands, no more. Since I am certain this is man's first visit to these islands, Smitty and I agreed upon giving them the names that Mr. Mandalay printed on the map he scribed for us. Nemaris Islands they shall be—with Nemaris Island being the largest, Opole Island being the smallest, Siren Island being the rockiest, and Stuart Island being the narrowest.

"Nemaris Island, sir." Thomas closed the book and wrapped it in the oilcloth again.

"Aye, Nemaris Isle then ... Nemaris Island?!" Janes cried.

All the men had heard the legends before, as had Thomas. Perry climbed back into the rowboat.

Janes composed himself, adjusting his coat. "So ... it is the Nemaris Islands that you and Mr. Ward were nervous about, Tommy. It would seem that storm brought us closer than we'd like, men." His gaze grew stern. "On the shore, all of you, now."

Both men, and Thomas, went onto the beach and stood at attention.

"Does anyone see any demons?" Janes gestured at the treeline.

All three shook their heads.

"Or any traps?" Janes asked.

"None yet, boss," Perry replied.

"Aye then. Keep your wits about you, lest you come across any. We're here now, and there's no getting away from it." Turning, the captain headed out with a purposeful stride. "So, let us see what we can see."

The four men started inland through the trees. Perry went first, clearing any brush that would have made travel difficult. The captain followed next, with Jared and Thomas behind.

"Tommy, you seem awfully reserved." Jared held a palm frond aside to let Thomas pass. "Surely you've heard of this place."

Thomas nodded. "Yes, but if there were any demons, they would've found us by now, right?"

Jared gave a reluctant grin. "Right. Keep your eyes open though, aye?"

Thomas nodded, following carefully behind the captain.

They came to a clearing at the base of the ridge and found that there were two obvious directions to travel.

"Seems to be either left or right here, sir. Too steep to climb," Perry said.

"Aye it is." The captain turned to Jared. "Roberts?"

Jared looked both ways. "Should we split up?"

"According to the book, there isn't much on the island, so it should be safe either way," Thomas said.

"At least there were no traps," Perry said.

"Aye, for now. Well then, we split up. Perry, you're with me," Janes said, and they traveled east toward a rocky shore. Jared and Thomas went to the west into the jungle.

Janes and Perry traveled east toward the channel between the islands. There they discovered a long waterway with an offshoot to the east, separating their island from the two eastern islands. The channel running north and south offered little space to maneuver a large ship, but the larger east and west channel was more than able to support the passage of several rowboats traveling side by side. Following the main channel toward the south, rocky cliffs gave way to a region of flat-topped rocks inside a sheltered lagoon. Although it was hard to see within, a rowboat could enter with care.

As for the two islands they could see from their vantage point, one was directly to the east, and a smaller one was off to the north a short distance. The northern one could not be seen very well from their vantage point, but had a definite shoreline with a large rocky ridge in the center.

The south-eastern island was much rockier than the other two, and did not have any beach to speak of. Large flat rocks stuck out of the water, and would make nice places to sit and fish from, provided the tide was low. Atop the high cliffs stretched a plateau, although it was difficult to see inland, the jungle beyond was easily twenty or thirty meters above sea level. The cliffs on their side of the channel reached only half that height. Both cliff walls were comprised of very solid rocks, most of which had shown little wear from the elements. On the plateau, a few palm trees could be seen, but they had not grown nearly as large as the trees on Nemaris Island.

"Which isle would you suppose that is, Captain?" Perry asked.

Janes shook his head. "Pretty rocky, Siren Island by the looks of her. Good thing we didn't sail too close to those cliffs."

Perry peered over the ledge toward the channel below. "Suppose the channel is deep?"

"Hard to say, judging by the size of those rocks. Too narrow for the ship to go through, but we might bring the rowboat later." Removing his hat, the captain wiped the sweat from his brow with a handkerchief then turned from the ledge. "We're walking this island for now, so let's continue."

Jared and Thomas headed left to the west of the ridges. They came out of the forest into a small field compromised of tall grasses, small rocks, and surrounded by tall palm trees. Beyond the field, the island's lush vegetation closed back in, forming a forest along the western point.

"Tommy, I must know why you are so calm here." Scratching his head, the sailor gave Thomas an uncertain smile. "Every story I have heard tells of death and demons."

Thomas nodded. "As have I, but I've also heard things much scarier."

"Is that right?" Jared seemed to pale slightly under his tan.

Given how Jared teased Jennings about superstitions, Thomas considered his words for a moment. "Back home, I've heard strange voices at the base of Diamond Falls, just north of my house. Some were good, others quite bizarre."

Jared nodded with anticipation.

"Just the other day, I had the strangest dream. In my dream, it was a clear day, blue skies … when suddenly it grew stormy and dark. Then, there was a voice that exploded like thunder … and then went away."

"Do you remember what it said?"

It was not something Thomas could forget. "It said … you will feel my wrath, and called me its creator. Strange, no?"

Jared nodded. "No stranger than how we managed to find ourselves here after the storm last night. I'm no expert on dreams, but hopefully it was simply that, a dream."

Thomas nodded.

As they came around the hillside, a creek flowed southwest toward the lagoon between Nemaris Island and Stuart Island. What intrigued both of them, however, was that the creek was fed by a very tall waterfall. It became an instant wonder, as neither of them could explain how a fifty-meter-high waterfall could appear and run constantly without a major source of water. Although this was the widest part of the island, the craggy ridge seemed to grow out of nowhere.

"Tommy, are you familiar with waterfalls?"

"Yes, I don't understand where so much water could come from on such a small island."

"I thought so." Taking a swig from his canteen, Jared contemplated the falls. "Maybe we should climb it and find out."

"Seems like the thing to do."

They headed for the creek. While the pool of water at the base of the waterfall was less than two meters deep, the water in the creek was just deep enough that the two of them had to swim across. The creek would be navigable for the small dinghy if need be, as the creek flowed into a large bay on the south side of the island.

Both crossed the creek quickly and followed it along the water basin, which was some nine meters across and maybe twenty meters long. Along the edge of the pool, a rocky trail followed an upward path. It wasn't steep, but it did take some effort to climb.

As they climbed, they pushed aside long vines that hung down across the cliff's face. The vegetation grew thicker with each step. After nearly thirty minutes, they reached the top of the ledge. From there, they could see Siren Island to the east, Opole Island to the northeast, and the narrower Stuart Island to the southwest. The shores of all three islands were similar to Nemaris, except for Siren Island, which seemed quite rocky along the entire coastline.

Atop the ridge, the start of the creek could clearly be seen. Rather than a massive river feeding the crest of the falls, there was a small pool located about a dozen meters from the edge of the falls. The pool was about a man's height in diameter and a few feet deep at the edge. Aside from a deeper section in the middle it had no apparent source.

Jared made his way to the edge of the pool. "Here's where the water originates, from a spring it would appear."

Kneeling beside him, Thomas cupped his hand and reached in.

"Tommy! Wait, what if it's a trap?" Jared cried.

Thomas gave him a carefree look, bravely taking a sip from the crystal blue water. It was pure as rain, and quite refreshing, too. "Ordinary freshwater, just like Diamond Falls back home."

"Well, perhaps I should refill my flask … that explains the waterfall I suppose." The sailor shrugged and did so. "We may as well head back down."

Meanwhile, Captain Janes and Mr. Perry were journeying the other direction, and came around the ridge to the south shore. Off to the west they could see Stuart Island, a narrow spit of land only forty fields wide, but half as long as Nemaris Island. Besides brush, several coconut and pineapple trees and long grasses, there seemed to be little there.

"Guess we should continue back toward the ship. It should be this way." Janes turned back the way they'd come after they reached the edge of the ridge.

"Aye." Perry followed the captain.

As they made their way down the cliff, Thomas grew tired and stopped to catch his breath.

"Are you coming, Tommy?"

"Just give me a moment." Thomas stopped at a flat spot by some vines along the cliff's face. He leaned back to rest on the vines. They gave way and he fell through into some sort of cave.

"Tommy!" Jared spread the vines aside, and the light revealed a small staircase headed down. With a look they agreed to follow the stairs and discovered a cavern behind the waterfall.

"What is this place?" Keeping his hand on the wall to prevent a fall in the dim light, Thomas entered the chamber. There were no vines or roots, and the walls had been carved from the solid rock. The ground was the same, covered with a layer of dust. The entire cavern was lit by a series of openings about the entrance, sheltered enough to let in light but to keep weather out. With the exception of an opening in the wall where water rushed toward the pool below, there was nothing else. The cave was a mere ten by sixteen feet, and nothing more.

"Some sort of waterfall cave," Jared suggested.

"But there must be more to it than that."

Jared inspected the walls, discovering they were very solid. "There cannot be any more to it, not with walls this thick. Maybe we should head back ... Tommy, look at this!"

Jared had found evidence of carving along the wall. Two names had been scratched over and were no longer decipherable, but a third name clearly had been etched into the wall.

"Tommy ... it's your name!"

Thomas read the etched letters carefully, observing that it clearly spelled out his first name. There was a space, then the letter A ... but anything that was etched afterward had been scratched out.

"Who could've done this?" Thomas asked.

"This is too convenient to be natural ... it ..." Jared paused and blinked groggily at the boy. "I say, Tommy ... how long have we been walking?"

A gentle breeze began to waft into the chamber, and soon both Jared and Thomas found themselves overwhelmed with fatigue.

"Not ... long ... enough to be sleepy." Thomas yawned.

"I think ... a rest ... is in order." Jared slid along the wall and slumped into a more leisurely position.

Thomas nodded, also sitting down on the cool rocky floor. "Okay ... but first, I need to ... sit a moment." He yawned several more times.

"We'll take ... a moment here. See what ... we can ... find ..." Jared said between yawns.

Almost instantly, both Jared and Thomas were sound asleep against the stone floor.

Janes and Perry returned to the rowboat on the north shore across from the ship. Despite the late hour, Jared and Thomas had not yet arrived.

"Where could those lads be?" Using his hat so shade his eyes, the captain scanned the trees. "It's too small an island for them to get lost."

"Shall I look for them?" Perry offered.

"We'll have to get a lantern first, it'll be dark soon."

Perry nodded, squinting at the evening sun.

"Let's give them a few moments." Janes put his hat back on with a decisive flourish. "If we lose too much light, we'll head back and return with a lantern."

"Aye, sir … do you hear something?" There seemed to be music in the distance.

"Maybe Mr. Roberts found his fife." Janes said as he and Perry continued to wait.

Jared and Thomas were fast asleep in the waterfall cavern. The muffled sounds of a fife attempting to be played sounded, waking Thomas.

"Huh? Jared, wake up." Thomas tapped his companion.

"A little longer … unnh …" Jared muttered.

"We fell asleep! Wake up! The captain's probably waiting for us!" Thomas shook him awake. He stood up to discover that, even in the dim light, the etching along the wall was no longer visible. In fact, it looked as though the wall had never been touched.

"Jared … on the wall … we did see something earlier, didn't we?"

"I don't remember anything out of the ordinary … why were we asleep?"

Neither one of them had any memory of the past several hours, and soon it was silent again—except for the muddled sounds of a fife attempting to be played.

"Do you hear that, Jared? It sounds like…."

"My fife! But, that's impossible! It was lost at sea! Come on, lad!" Jared headed for the stairs, and they quickly, but quietly, climbed back down the cliff.

They had failed to notice a third set of footprints inside the cave.

At the bottom of the ridge, the sound of the fife grew louder. There, in the shallows of the waterfall pool, a young girl with long blond hair sat with her back turned toward the two men. She was trying to play the fife, but with little success.

"That is my fife all right ... but who is she?" Jared whispered to Thomas.

"I think she's my age, maybe I should try to talk to her."

He reached out a hand to stop Thomas. "Wait, what if she's a demon? Like that Jennings is always saying?"

"Jared, look at her. Does she look like a demon to you?"

Jared shrugged. "No! Not from this distance ... but if she's no demon, you might scare her."

"She's probably just trying to learn how to play it. It'll be okay." Thomas carefully approached the pool, stopping about ten feet from the girl.

The air around the young girl smelled like sea lilies, and the entire scene had an aura of peace and calm. The girl was in her own little world as she turned the fife over in her hands. The object seemed foreign to her, yet she seemed to know it played music.

She put the fife to her mouth, but not at the end. Rather, she blew into it through one of the holes on the side. The sound of air blowing through it was the result, rather than the steady pitch of the intended note.

Thomas couldn't help but offer assistance. "If you wish, I could show you how that works."

With a soft yelp, the girl slipped underwater, taking the fife with her. She didn't surface again, and with the exception of ripples from where she went under, there wasn't anything else moving except for the waterfall.

"Where'd she go?" Thomas asked, looking into the shallow water. Although he could see the bottom, with the exception of a flat rock slightly submerged where the girl had been sitting, there was nothing else to be found.

"Ye blew it, lad." Jared chuckled.

"I couldn't think of a better way."

"Aye, I guess if I had tried, probably would've happened same way."

Thomas suddenly realized other ramifications of the girl's disappearance. "I don't feel like crossing that creek by getting in the water anymore."

"Aye, me neither," Jared replied.

They both plotted the chances of jumping the creek, but because it was far too wide that option would both get them wet and probably injured.

"Maybe we should build a bridge. Nothing fancy, but take some of the palm trees and just build a short bridge across." Thomas turned to contemplate the nearby trees. "That way, we won't have to try to jump it, and won't have to get wet."

"I agree, but we can't do it tonight. Getting dark out." Jared tilted his head in the direction of the setting sun.

"Aye."

"Tommy ... there was something on the wall in that cave, wasn't there?"

Thomas pondered a moment, then shook his head. "I'm not sure."

"Do you suppose the girl...?" Jared quickly dismissed the thought. "We'll report the cave, but the girl and the etching in the cave ... that stays between us, aye?"

The thought made Thomas uncomfortable. "Shouldn't we tell the captain?"

"Aye we should, but if there's nothing to see, then there's nothing to report, right?"

"Aye."

They searched along the creek, trying to find a better place to make the jump, but after awhile they both gave up about halfway between the bay and the pool and waded across.

They arrived back at the rowboat a good ten minutes later, much to the captain's relief.

"Where have you been?" The captain's expression was a cross between concern and irritation. "We've been worried."

"We fell asleep, actually," confessed Jared.

"In a cave just behind the waterfall," Thomas added.

"Fell asleep? Everything okay?"

"We're fine, sir. I think it was ..." Thomas tried to think of a reasonable excuse. "Because of the climb."

Janes nodded. "You'll have to show me that later."

Thomas got into the rowboat, leaving Jared to shove off. Perry again manned the oars.

"Captain, Thomas and I both feel there should be a bridge across that creek. It is rather wide, and probably can't be crossed without a bit of a swim." Jared made the suggestion sound perfectly practical.

"A bridge?" After a moment's consideration, the captain shrugged. "Certainly, but only if we're unable to leave. We'll see how the other men are doing when we get back."

"If we are to be stuck here, we'll need something to do," Jared replied.

"Aye, and building a bridge will certainly meet that need. We'll see." Janes stood as they arrived at the *Valiant*. Perry held the craft near the ship, the others climbed up and then lowered the crane's hoisting block. Once the rowboat was back on the main deck, they secured it and called it a night.

Gritzol and Ward were out on deck as the shore party returned. Benson had remained topside also, enjoying a breath of night air. As Thomas, Perry, and Jared each retired for the evening, Janes listened to the crew's report on the day's findings.

"How stuck are we, Barry?"

"Quite, sir. Roland and I both agreed that we were a good several meters into the sand," Gritzol replied. Benson nodded. "And it seems to get worse every passing wave."

"Aye. Captain, that wind was something else last night." Ward frowned in frustration. "The storm seemed bound and determined to keep us here for quite some time ... it'll take no less than a wind of equal strength in the opposite direction if we're to have any chance of escape."

"If we had some of that magical black dust, we might be able to blow ourselves out," Gritzol said.

All the men gave him curious looks, except for Roland Benson, who shook his head. "I've actually seen some of that stuff. Blast powder, that's what they call it. It doesn't work underwater, and even if it did, it doesn't exist this side of Tallebeck."

Ward nodded. "Aye, even those crafty pirates don't know where to get any. So that's out."

"What about the sails? Can't we raise the sails?" Gritzol asked.

"Barry, perhaps we shall have to wait it out. The winds aren't as powerful as they were last night, and they certainly aren't as cooperative," Ward explained.

"Take it easy, Barry." Benson gave his shipmate a reassuring pat on the shoulder. "We all want to leave just as much as you do."

Janes nodded. "As unfavorable as our situation may be, you both did your best. Thank you for your efforts."

"Did you find anything interesting on shore, captain?" Gritzol asked.

Janes shook his head. "At least there were no traps."

Later that night, Janes looked through the journal of Scyhathen and found several passages that went further into detail concerning the islands.

Although Mr. Banes is beginning to rouse himself in a better spirit, we still have yet to determine the length of our stay upon these islands, which are now officially named after our marooned craft. We spent the better part of yesterday with our charting gear in hand and have completed the survey of the entire chain.

To restate the survey of Nemaris Island, it is the largest with 162 fields of area, a length of 1,456 yards; and at the widest point 762 yards. It covers land ranging from tropical jungle to vine-crested ridges, the tallest being over forty yards high. A great expanse of shallow beach covers the northern shore, with sandy bottom extending as far out as the eye can see. The cliffs along the eastern shore tower nearly 29 yards, where the mountain above soars almost 100 yards, making for an impressive view. Also, this is the only island that has a pond, with a long creek and a steady current flowing into the southern lagoon from a tall waterfall.

Survey addendum, Stuart Island. Our survey on Stuart Island produced an area of twenty-eight fields. It is a narrow island, being 832 yards long but a mere 270 yards at her widest. It is also a shallow and flat island, scarcely climbing more than a hundred feet above sea level at its wooded, grassy center.

Third survey: Opole Island was discovered to be the smallest of the chain with an area of a little less than twenty-six fields. It is a rather oddly shaped island, but reaches 416 yards in width from north to south, and 554 yards in length. The elevation of this island increases dramatically in the center, reaching a mighty sixty yards tall with sharp and steep cliffs on the southern edge. There is evidence of a cavern beneath the vines of these cliffs, but it is clear that it does not descend deep into the island, and is of little interest to us.

Fourth day and final survey. We discovered a means of climbing ashore the rocky Siren Island, and despite the desire to avoid a narrow mountain region in the western portion, were able to chart an area of thirty fields. It covered a length of 485 yards and a close width of 416 yards. As with Nemaris Island to her west, Siren Island's western cliffs are an impressive thirty yards tall. The island has a very round appearance, but is neither a square nor a circle in shape. The jungle region is shaped similar to a crescent. While ashore this island, I noted that our surroundings seemed very eerie, as if there were something there not welcoming our presence. We completed our survey and quickly returned to the ship.

Overall, these islands are substantial despite their tiny appearance from the sea. If nothing else comes from our stay here, we have done this much to confirm their existence in the Centra Sea. We continue to plan our expedition to Phrynn, but as long as we continue to be marooned in the shallow shores our date of departure is doubtful. In the meantime, we remain hopeful and optimistic.

After reading the final paragraph, Janes bookmarked the page. He was intrigued with the description of the islands they had landed upon. He blew his lantern out and drifted off into sleep as he lay back on his bed.

He thought about the old legends his crew had mentioned and how the stories told of demons and death to all. The passage on Siren Island reflected this the most—that it may have been the source of those tales. Still, Scyhathen's stay had not been with peril, nor any feelings of unease. At least not yet.

But those concerns would have to wait, as the crew still had to survive, even if such legends were in fact true. For now, the evidence suggested otherwise, and that was his final thought before falling fast asleep.

The cool breeze of the clear night brought a soft sound to the open windows of the barracks below, and deeper still the sands beneath the waves continued to settle into a solid seal around the *Valiant's* hull. To an observer, it appeared that the island almost wanted them to stay, tightening its hold on the gallant ship.

Come morning, their situation had not changed for the better. Janes and Ward met early in the cargo hold to discuss the means of their escape.

Ward tapped the side of the hull with his knuckles, listening for changes in the wood. After several taps, he turned to the captain.

"I think we're going to be here awhile, Chris."

Janes nodded. "How do you think Mr. Grimbeck will feel when he discovers we used up his lumber?"

"He is more concerned with the timing than the amount," Ward said.

"We'll just foot the difference … seems the idea of building a bridge will give the men something to do as long as we're here."

Ward nodded. "Aye sir, works fer me."

Jared, Thomas, and Benson went ashore with the dinghy and landed at the same place as the day before. They each brought with them a saw, a coil of rope, and a knife. Perry and Ward came in the second rowboat, carrying with them wedges, hammers, and a dozen planks of the lumber they had picked up in South Cimmordia.

Once they arrived at the creek, they began by cutting six trees down. Some of those were cut into halves, cutting the rest into boards so they would lie flat across the halves. These were used as supports, while the rest of the boards were used to make the bridge itself. With a supply of lumber from the ship, there was enough to make a bridge that was twenty meters long and two meters above the creek. Using the rope to hold it all together, they had built a pretty solid bridge. They even finished well before sunset.

After the men returned to the ship for dinner, Janes went to the island and inspected the work they had done.

"Hmm … you men did good work. That's a fine looking bridge. Let's see if it passes the test." He walked up the short ramp to the bridge deck and made his way across. He also walked back a second time for good measure. There were no rails on it, but they weren't necessary for such a small bridge.

"Thank you, sir," Thomas said.

"Appreciate it, sir," Benson said.

"It was nothing, sir," Jared said.

"As fer getting free from the shallows...." Janes gave them all a serious but confident look. "Mr. Ward tells me that we've settled in a bit deeper into the sand, so we might be here awhile. That bridge will come in handy, I'm sure."

"Are there enough supplies?" Benson asked.

"I see that there'll be enough for a good while, and no worries about water." Nodding, the captain gestured to the lush flora around them. "Tomorrow we'll send a few men out to pick fruit. That'll have to help. Fishing should help, too. We should still have some fishing nets so see what we can pick up to add to the food supply."

"There is grain in the hold too, isn't there?" Thomas asked.

"Aye there is, but that belongs to a customer. We won't tap into that unless it gets to be a necessity."

"Captain, that lumber was a shipment too, right?" Jared asked.

"It was, but I've known Grimbeck for a long time ... now Mr. Henning at the grain mill, on the other hand ... he won't appreciate us using his grain."

"Aye, I hear ye, Captain," Benson replied.

"Meantime, let's head back." The captain made his way to the boats with his men in tow. "Nothing more to do out here."

"Aye, Cap'n," the three men chimed. When they reached the beach, Benson shoved off.

"Do you want to row, Tommy?" Jared asked.

"It'd be good to develop your arms, lad," Janes added.

"Well, okay."

Although he was still tired from his work on the bridge, Thomas sat in the middle of the boat and rowed. They didn't go as fast as when Mr. Perry had rowed the night before, but they soon reached the *Valiant*. The men manning the crane complimented his effort, and with sore arms but a satisfied heart, Thomas retired to his cabin.

Acadia

$\mathcal{L}$ate that evening, well after the sun had gone down and the full moon lit the night sky, Thomas found himself unable to sleep and went up to the deck for some fresh air. It was a cloudless night, with a panorama of stars and constellations across the sky.

Thomas walked to the starboard railing and rested his arms upon it. Looking south toward the isles, he pondered the events of the day. Had it indeed been only fatigue that had caused him and Jared to sleep in the cave? Who's voice had he heard before he left home? Nor had he forgotten the warnings that his friend Bobby had left him with … but were they all really true? He had spent two solid days on the islands, and nothing bad had happened. There had been no traps or anything—just a young girl. But who was she? Why was she sitting on a rock in the pool? And just to where did she go?

As he stared toward the islands, he again heard the faint sound of a fife playing intermittently. On impulse, he unlatched the rowboat, swung it over the water, lowered it, and rowed into shore. After making certain that the craft wouldn't wash away with the tide, he went inland toward the creek, with only moonlight as his guide. The sounds of the fife grew louder as he approached, and again he saw the young girl, sitting on the rock in the pool.

Same as before, the water line obscured her from the waist down, although she was facing toward him rather than away. Thomas hid behind some bushes, so he could see her but she would not be frightened by his presence.

He watched silently as her small hands fumbled with the fife. Apparently, she had not yet discovered how to play it.

He removed his boots and moved closer, making sure to not make too much noise. Even in the dim moonlight, Thomas was captivated by her eyes.

She continued to struggle with the fife. Several notes emerged, but nothing as lyrical as Jared would have played.

Thomas had never been much of a singer, but he could whistle. As the girl made sounds with the fife, Thomas did his best to mimic the notes, but in actual pitch.

She looked up quickly. Thomas got a good look at her face as she searched for the source of the sounds. Her blue eyes were the first thing he noticed. Perhaps she wasn't that young, Thomas thought, as her eyes told a different story, deep blue and mysterious. Her blond hair was long and silky, and captured the moonlight wonderfully. Her nose was cute and petite, a perfect match with the rest of her face. Moving lower, he saw that she was wearing a smooth silken fabric bodice covering an ample bosom. Where she may have found silk was a mystery worth exploring, Thomas decided. Lastly, upon her left wrist she wore a charm made from a scallop shell with a mysterious honey-colored crystalline gem inside. It was supported by string that may once have been part of a fishing net.

Thomas was stricken by her stunning, perfect proportions. Although his view was disrupted by the slowly lapping waves of the creek beneath her, it did not tarnish his impression.

Thomas remained silent as he watched, hoping to not give himself away.

Her eyes returned to the fife. Again, she blew through one of the holes, and again Thomas mimed it.

With a confused expression on her face, she looked up from the fife again. This time, she peered into the treetops. Still unable to identify the source of the sound, she returned her attention to the fife.

Before the girl could suspect birds again, Thomas made the sound himself. He whistled the same melody as before, adding several notes.

This time she was not so naive. In a soft voice with a lyrical accent, she called out to the mystery whistler. "Who's there?"

She hadn't swum away! "My name is Thomas." He did not come out from his hiding spot.

"Is that you whistling?"

"Yes."

The girl held up the fife and attempted to blow through it again.

"I can show you how to play that, if you wish."

The girl lowered the fife. "I cannot see you."

Only then did he move, stepping out from behind a thicket, into her point of view. She didn't flee or cower at all.

"You are young." It was a statement, not a question.

Thomas nodded. "I am fourteen years old."

She held up the fife. "Will you show me?"

"If you tell me your name."

"Your name is Thomas," the girl said.

"That's right. Do you have a name?"

"Acadia."

"You have a very lovely name, Acadia," Thomas replied.

She held up the fife again. "Will you show me how to make this work?"

"I will, but please, don't be afraid."

"You seem gentle...." She gave a regal nod of her head. "You may approach."

He walked slowly toward the pool, kneeling down and sitting with his feet in the water a few yards away from her.

"Hold it like this." Putting one hand atop another, Thomas demonstrated how to hold the fife the way Jared did, contrary to the method Acadia had been using previously.

She held the fife horizontally with the mouthpiece upright.

"Now blow through it."

She raised it toward her lips. With a breath of air, she blew through the fife, making a perfect note. She had played a C, the highest note on the fife.

Acadia held it back and looked at it once more. Then, she again brought it to her mouth, blew through it, and put her fingers over the holes, lowering the notes by steps each time.

"Now you've got it," Thomas said.

That was the first time Thomas had seen her smile, which was warm and friendly. "Thank you." She put the fife down.

"I'm curious, Acadia. Where did you find that?"

She waved her hand to the north. "Somewhere near the beach, stuck in the sand."

"You mean it washed ashore, then?"

With a lift of her chin, she looked away from him. "No, but I found it."

"What if I told you that it belonged to a friend of mine?"

Her gaze swung back around to him. "Did he lose it? Perhaps he didn't want it anymore."

Thomas wasn't sure how to answer her question. He knew that Jared's fife meant a lot to him, and did not want to let it slip away.

Before he could respond, Acadia spoke again. "Is it yours?"

Thomas shook his head. "No, it really does belong to a friend of mine. It belonged to his mother, and he always has it at his side."

"Your friend misses it, then." She examined the fife in her hands with a thoughtful tilt of her head.

Thomas nodded.

Acadia slid off of the rock and swam up to Thomas. Even though the water between him and the rock was only some three or four feet deep, she remained low in the water.

"You should give it back to your friend." She offered him the fife. "It was not mine to take."

From up close, Thomas found it difficult not to notice that she seemed to stop past her waist. He was simply bewildered ... he could almost see a large fish behind her.

"Can you stand up? I would like to show you something."

Acadia shook her head. "I cannot."

"Why?"

It was then the crew's discussions about creatures of the sea actually proved true. Rather than tell Thomas directly, she lifted herself out of the water and sat next to him on the bank, where he discovered what she meant.

True to life, she had no legs with which to stand. Instead of legs and feet, an elegant fish tail replaced them from the waist down. Even in the dim light, her scales shimmered with a profound cerulean blue hue. At the tip her body were two great fins, with a powerful blue and white fin between them.

Thomas could only stare in amazement as it sunk in that Acadia was a mermaid.

"Acadia...." Thomas began.

"You wanted to show me something?"

"It's just that ... um...." Thomas stuttered, unable to finish his sentence.

"What is it? Are you ill?" Acadia asked a second time, confused by his reaction.

"Nothing ... nothing at all."

"You may return this to your friend." She handed him the fife before carefully sliding back into the water.

"Wait, you're not leaving, are you?" Thomas asked, getting up.

"Unless you really did have something to show me."

Thomas hesitated, before blurting out a story quickly. "I do, but I do not have it with me. I can show you tomorrow, perhaps. It is late."

"I understand. Where shall we meet tomorrow?" Acadia asked.

Thomas didn't know the island very well. He did know that the island came to a point.

"The westernmost point on the far end of the island."

Acadia gave another regal nod. "I shall wait for you there. I hope your friend will be happy to have his fife back."

"He will. See you tomorrow, then." Thomas waved farewell.

"Good eve." Acadia ducked under the water.

After Thomas watched her swim downstream toward the bay, he headed back to the dinghy and to the ship. In his excitement, he forgot to secure the craft to the deck.

Thomas went below quickly. Before he went to his cabin, he went inside the barracks where the men were fast asleep. Approaching Jared's locker, he took the leather strap on the fife and hung it from the locker's handle. Quietly as before, he headed toward his cabin.

Lewinston had heard Thomas moving about and stopped him in the hall.

"Tommy? What're you doing up?" he whispered angrily.

Thomas jumped. "Um ... couldn't sleep."

"It sounded like the rowboat moved. Someone on deck?" Lewinston asked.

"No sir. I ... went ashore for awhile."

Lewinston's eyes rounded. "You what?"

"Nothing happened ... everything's fine."

Grimacing, Lewinston calmed down. "Okay ... but next time you want to go anyplace, you tell the captain. I won't say nothing, but you got to promise me. Understand?"

"Yes sir."

"Right. Get some sleep."

"Yes sir."

Thomas rushed downstairs and headed straight for bed, although he was certain it would be difficult to sleep after meeting the young Acadia.

Lewinston watched him leave. "That boy must think this is a vacation … and he's lucky to not get eaten by a demon."

Great Hosts

*I*n the morning, Thomas joined the others in the mess hall.

"Tommy! Ellis just cleaned up," Mr. Gritzol said.

"He didn't," Thomas replied.

With a grim frown, Gritzol nodded. "Aye, he did. Ye should've woke sooner."

"Early bird gets the worm," Mr. Jennings said.

"Oh, well, that's okay." Thomas sat down anyway.

Mr. Ward gave him a stern look. "You up late, boy?"

"Couldn't sleep last night," Thomas replied.

Lewinston gave Thomas a nod, but kept his silence.

Jared then walked in, playing his fife, happy to have it back.

"Must you play that incessantly?" Clearly Jennings was frustrated by the fife's return.

"Aye, I must." Grinning, Jared sat down next to Thomas.

"Say ... I thought that thing went overboard?" Gritzol asked curiously.

"Aye, I thought so too, but I found it on the handle of me locker," Jared replied.

"Well, come on, we've got fruit to pick," Lewinston replied.

"Come on, Thomas," Jared said.

Ward raised a hand to halt them. "Nope—only four guys can fit in the rowboat—'sides, cap'n said you two can stay 'ere today."

"Oh, okay, then," Thomas replied.

"Glad you found your fife, Jared," Ward said, and the four men left.

"Jared, I have to tell you something." Although they were alone, Thomas couldn't help whispering.

"What's that?" Jared whispered back.

"About your fife. I found it last night."

"You found it? Well, yes ... thank you!" Jared's expression changed from elated to puzzled to curious in a matter of moments. "But ... how? You and I both knew it went over the side. That large wave could've taken me, too."

"Remember the girl we saw? Who hid underwater after I spoke to her?"

"Aye, what about her?"

"She had it. I saw her again ... she had the fife."

"I say then, that was most charitable of her. Should you see the miss again, give her my thanks." Jared got up to leave.

Thomas grabbed his sleeve. "Wait, there's more. Think about it! The fife fell overboard, and into the deep waters. How do you suppose she was able to get it?"

After a moment's consideration, Jared shrugged. "I don't know ... washed ashore perhaps."

"No, when she hid underwater, we waited for ten minutes and didn't see her surface. Doesn't that strike you as curious?" Thomas asked, a bit intensely.

Chuckling, Jared patted him on the shoulder. "Thomas, I do believe you're suggesting that the girl was a mermaid."

"That's it! She is! Acadia was able to find it because she's a mermaid!"

"You know her name? Well...." Jared's mouth opened and closed a few times while he gathered his thoughts. "Thomas, perhaps all this was a dream that you shared with ... Acadia ... last night. Sometimes they be real to oneself, but all mermaids are simply dreams."

"You don't understand! I told her I'd meet her on the far side of the island today, and ...." Thomas began, before trailing off.

"Tommy, you know we're buddies, we trust each other ... but mermaids are just fantasy."

"You said you believed they exist."

Jared chuckled. "Aw, that was just to ruffle up Jennings. You're sensible, right?"

"But you saw her."

"If I saw a mermaid, I think I'd know."

Thomas sighed. "That doesn't mean I shouldn't keep a promise."

"There's another boat, you know. If it concerns you that much let the captain know before you take it out. I don't quite accept this nonsense, mind you, but if this Acadia is important to you, do whatever you must."

Jared left for the hall. Thomas also got up then, and started for Captain Janes's quarters.

He knocked at the door. "It's Thomas, sir."

"Come in, Tommy, come right in."

Looking up from a ledger on the table, Janes straightened. "What can I do, lad?"

"Would it be all right if I took the other boat out today?"

"Of course, but for what purpose?" His brows gave a quizzical quirk. "The men are already ashore collecting some fruit, and you don't have to go ashore today."

"I know, sir, but I would like to get a good view of the island from the water." Thomas flexed his arms. "And also work my arms a bit, for some exercise."

"You're not planning on exploring the other islands, are you?"

"No sir."

"Well, all right then. You remember how to swim?"

"Aye sir."

The captain gave him a nod. "Go right ahead then. Just be sure to put the boat back when you return."

"Aye sir, you have my word."

"Don't work too hard…" An odd gleam flashed in Janes's eyes. "And tell me if you find anything interesting."

Thomas nodded. "Thank you sir, I will."

Thomas then left and headed toward the deck. Before launching the second rowboat, he went below and collected the blue orb his mother had given him. Putting it inside a pouch attached to his belt, he returned to the deck to lower the second boat and head westward.

From the water, the island was a paradise. The sandy shore continued along the western end of Nemaris Island. The ocean was not nearly as shallow as where the *Valiant* was grounded. It dropped off much quicker, falling to about forty meters in depth even close to the tidewater. The beach was as equally picturesque as other parts of the island, hugging the shoreline around to the point where trees no longer grew and a rocky outcrop thrust into the water. A grove of banana trees were full of ripe fruit nearby, enveloping the area with a pleasant scent.

Thomas climbed out and pulled the rowboat up onto the beach. In his hunger, he couldn't help but notice a single fallen fruit that had fallen from a large bunch. It was ready to eat and quite a nice treat. Knowing Acadia might be nearby, Thomas quickly finished and tossed the peel into the forest.

After awhile, Thomas was on the verge of drifting off into a late morning nap. Then out in the surf, not far away, Acadia surfaced.

She looked around a moment, and then saw Thomas.

"Acadia?" Thomas asked quietly.

She swam in closer, keeping low in the water. "Thomas, it's good to see you again."

"Can you come ashore?" Thomas asked.

"I don't think I should. There are some men on the shore to the east." She glanced across the shore. "I'd rather they not see me."

"They're my shipmates. They won't hurt you, I swear."

"Perhaps they are your friends, but I feel we need our privacy. We should go to another island."

Recalling his promise to the captain, Thomas hesitated. "Okay, sure. Which one?"

She pointed a delicate hand. "The island right across the lagoon, off the southern shore. If you bring your boat, I'll swim alongside you."

"Sure, one moment." Thomas hauled the boat back into the water. Acadia ducked underwater as he shoved off. After he'd rowed a few strokes she surfaced again.

"Come; follow me." Kicking her tail, Acadia swam swiftly away. Thomas did his best to keep up. Since he was facing the other way he had to continuously look over his shoulder to avoid hitting her. To his surprise, she was always just one length ahead.

They circled around the end of Stuart Island, when Acadia swam up to the rowboat. She leaned onto the edge.

"Was it difficult to follow?"

Thomas shrugged. "A bit, yes. I didn't want to hit you."

She smiled. "Will you help me?"

"Of course, but with what?"

"If you'll take my hand and help me in."

Thomas was more than a little surprised. "Are you sure?"

"Thomas, I trust you. Will you trust me?"

Thomas reached out his hand. She took it, and then with Thomas's help, she was able to flip her tail into the boat and onto the bench across from him.

"There, this should make it easier for both of us," she said with a smile.

"Are you comfortable?"

"Quite, although I've never been in a craft like this before." Experimentally, she put her hands to either side and rocked it a bit. "How exciting!"

"So, where are we going then?"

"How do you steer if you can't see what's in front of you?" Acadia asked as she looked around the craft.

"It's tricky. Where should we go?"

"Go straight for now. I will let you know when to turn left."

Thomas started rowing. He had his eyes on her at all times—not only because she was sitting directly in front of him, but also because of her immense beauty. After several moments, the silence between them seemed deafening.

"My friend Jared was very appreciative of your gift. He asked me to thank you."

"That's wonderful; I'm glad to hear that." After a smile, she pointed. "You may start bearing left now."

Thomas began taking them along the shore of Stuart Island.

"How long have you and your shipmates been here?"

"Just a day or two. The ship is stuck in the sandy bottom offshore."

She tilted her head in a thoughtful manner. "You are marooned here, then?"

"For the moment. But from what we've seen of these islands, it's hard to imagine why anyone would want to leave."

"Is there a place you call home?"

Thomas slowed his rowing. "Yes, but it's pretty far from here. A small port called Harper's Bay, along the continent to the east."

"Your home is near the sea, then?"

"Yes, there is a point with a lighthouse on it, and a waterfall to the north, and I get to see the waves every day."

She closed her eyes, as though envisioning it. "It must be breathtaking."

"Do you have a home?" Thomas asked.

A graceful sweep of her arm encompassed the islands. "These are the closest I have to a home. Aside from the sea."

"But, do you have a room of your own?"

Acadia shook her head. "But, there is no shortage of places to go if I need to be alone."

"It must be wonderful to always be near such beautiful surroundings."

She nodded. "Yes, but I do not go ashore often."

"I can imagine... but it's quite lovely offshore, too."

Smiling, she pointed again. "If you go left here we can go ashore. There is a beach there."

"Aye."

"Did you know that there was another ship marooned here once before?"

She didn't look very old, but he wondered if she knew about the *Nemaris*. "I've read stories. What can you tell me about it?"

They hit bottom in the shallows near the beach.

For a moment, there was a distant look in her eyes. "It was a long time ago, but the ship was impressive. Come to think of it, your ship is very similar."

"Was the name of that ship *Nemaris*?"

Acadia thought a moment as Thomas climbed out and pulled the boat ashore. Acadia remained in the boat before saying, "I do not know."

"Oh ... but, you saw that ship?"

"No, but a friend of mine told me about it. Perhaps she can tell you more someday." She flopped over to the edge of the boat. "I may need your help again."

Thomas attempted to pick her up toward her fin, but she was far heavier than he had expected. He fell to the beach, and she landed on top.

"Oomph," was all he could say as she rolled off of him.

"Are you okay?"

Thomas sat up with a groan. "I'm sorry, that wasn't part of my plan."

She laughed at his misfortune. "Nobody was hurt, but thank you." Rolling over, she straightened, and the waves washed over her tailfin as they sat next to each other.

"You're not like other sailors at all, Thomas."

"Why is that?"

"Your voice is refined, if not elegant. Also, you keep your hair neat and tidy, while some other men would rather catch sand in it."

Thomas laughed at that. "Your hair is very lovely, too. Does it bother you at all, it being so long?"

"Some days it can be a bother, but I like my hair this way ... especially when it blows in the breeze." Acadia combed her fingers through her hair with one hand.

Thomas also combed his hair back into its part. It had gotten wet and sandy when they crashed to the beach.

"What did you want to show me today, Thomas?"

"I hope it didn't break." He reached into his pouch. To his good fortune, the orb was still intact. He pulled out the sphere of blue glass and held it up in the sunlight. As light passed through it, blue light shined onto his hand and onto Acadia.

"It's beautiful. Does it do anything?" She reached out to give it a tentative touch. "Can it see faraway places or talk with distant friends?"

Thomas shook his head. "It's something my mother gave me. To remember her and my home, when I'm far away."

"May I hold it?"

"Sure." Thomas handed it to her, and she held it up to her face.

After a moment she handed it back to him. "It feels like being underwater when I look through it."

"She told me it would help me see my home, but all I ever see is blue."

"How was it made? Or is this a large gem?"

"No, it's called glass. It's actually manmade from sand and other materials, I believe."

"From this?" Acadia took a handful of sand and let it slip through her fingers.

Thomas nodded. "I'm not exactly sure how it's done, but it must be an amazing process to create something so lovely."

"Your people must be sorcerers in order to create such treasures." She seemed truly awed.

"Sorcerers?" Thomas laughed. "No, not that I know of."

She seemed puzzled by his denial. "Are you certain? Long ago, there was a sorcerer on these very islands. His name was Rhydar."

"Rhydar?"

"He was a powerful sorcerer, and used his magic to create these islands as his home." She sighed. "Although I didn't know him for very long, my sisters did."

"Your sisters?"

"Well, we're not directly related, but I think of them as sisters. They would spend time with Rhydar when he came down to the shores. His home was atop the rockiest island." She pointed east. "The one Captain Scyhathen named Siren Island."

"Captain Scyhathen?" Thomas was both shocked and excited that she knew of the legendary seaman. "Acadia, how do you know all this?"

"My friend Cynthia told me all about it." She tilted her head as though unsure of his reaction. "It is true, is it not?"

"Of course it is … in fact, I've got a journal that belonged to the captain."

"Then you've read all about it, I suspect."

He shook his head. "No, not all of it. I've only been reading it for the past week and haven't had much time to devote to it."

"I should introduce you to Cynthia sometime." She nodded as though she'd made a decision. "I'm sure the two of you would have much to discuss."

"Can you tell me more about Rhydar?"

"I do not know much more, I am afraid." Looking away, she absently splashed with her tail. "I was very young at the time … but I do know this. He had amassed many rare and wondrous possessions. I do not know why, but their value would be great to those who sold them in a port. He guarded the collection quite well before he left us."

"Did he die?"

She looked back at him with a slight crease of a brow. "Cynthia said so, but she also believes that he has never really left. His spirit is always here, guarding his treasures from those who would try to claim them."

"He must've been very powerful."

"From what I've heard, he was." Acadia nodded solemnly.

They sat together for much of the day. No topic was taboo, and the day seemed to pass as quickly as their conversation, which flitted like a fish from subject to subject. The sun began to sink lower into the sky, and the waves lapped against the shore. Birds chirped in the trees behind them.

"Would you like a tour of the rest of the islands? Unless there's something more you wish to talk about." Acadia gave a stretch that made Thomas realize being out of water so long might be tiring for her.

"You've given me some valuable information." Using his hand to measure the sun's distance from the horizon, he guessed at the time and how long it would take to return to the *Valiant*. "It'll give me plenty to think about, I'm sure. But, it seems somewhat late in the day for a tour of each island. Not to mention your..." Thomas said, his eyes drifting toward her tailfin.

Acadia smiled. "I meant from the water, actually. Or your rowboat perhaps."

"I'd like that."

"Let's go then."

"Should I try to help again?"

Her eyes squinted in amusement. "Maybe it would best if I did it myself. Not that your help wasn't appreciated."

"Yes, I apologize again for that."

"Please, don't. Any help is appreciated." She edged over to the rowboat and climbed in.

Once she was settled, Thomas pushed the boat out and jumped in then reached for the oars.

They began by heading east. Thomas rowed beyond Stuart Island toward the southern shore of Nemaris Island. The evening sun began to glow. As they passed the tall peak of the waterfall, Thomas glanced towards it.

"I'm sure you're curious about that waterfall," Acadia began.

Thomas nodded. "A little. Jared and I found a large cave inside, and at the top there was only a small spring."

"That spring is actually fed by ocean water, but because of Rhydar's magic, it comes out pure. It's usually quite cool, and is quite refreshing to drink."

"What about the cave?"

"Is there a cave ashore as well?" She casually played with her hair. "I'm afraid I know nothing about the islands beyond the lagoons and the waterfall. However, there is an underwater cave beneath the waterfall that has been occupied by one of us in the past."

They came around the southeast edge of the island, where a narrow channel separated Nemaris and Siren. It was no wider than ten yards and sheltered from the winds. Rocky cliffs rose high on both sides, and the channel was filled with rocks.

"Should I continue straight for awhile?" He wasn't too anxious about entering the sheltered channel.

"If you wish." Raising her hand, she pointed behind him. "By going straight, we can come around Siren Island and see where Rhydar's main dwelling was—although it isn't there anymore. When his flesh body died, the dwelling disappeared, scattering his treasures and personal items across the islands. If you go left, you can see where my friends and I sometimes pass the day."

"It looks like a nice place to swim."

Acadia laughed. "It is, because it is extremely deep—much deeper than it appears. It was there Rhydar would sometimes come and tell us stories of fame and glory. He was a magnificent story teller."

"I think for today I shall go straight so we can spend more time together."

Acadia smiled. "It's so wonderful to spend time with someone other than just the three of us." Her eyes drifted into the narrow channel as they passed by.

"Three? There are three of you, then?"

"Four, actually, but he has not been here for some time." She counted on her fingers. "Myself, Cynthia, Marsha, and Onell."

"Onell is not here anymore? Why?"

"I'm not sure. After Rhydar passed away, he swore to keep an eye on us, but not long after that he swam away." She gave a fluid shrug. "We haven't seen him since. I was very young then."

Although his mother had taught him never to ask a lady about her age, Thomas hoped they were friends enough for him to broach the subject that had been pestering him since he'd first seen her face. "I don't mean to be rude, but how old are you?"

Acadia shook her head. "I'm afraid I don't have much concept of time, as most days are similar to the next. The one thing I remember about Onell is he enjoyed spending time with us girls, but then he left."

"Oh, okay." Thomas rowed onward, directing the rowboat around the southern coast of Siren Island.

Acadia pointed to a clearing atop the ridge. "It may be too high to see from here, but it was on that ridge Rhydar's house sat. While not very big, it was comfortable enough for Rhydar, I have heard."

"And he could climb up from there," Thomas said, pointing to a natural docking area along the nearly all rocky coast. The rocks formed a narrow stairway, and even had several funny shaped stones that resembled cleats that one could tie a rowboat to.

She nodded. "I would think so, as the rest of the cliffs along the island are very steep."

As Siren Island had only a mile of coastline, it didn't take them long to come to the northern shore. They followed the northern coast and entered the straight between Opole Island and Siren Island.

"This was called Rhydar's Maw," Acadia explained.

"Why was it called that?"

"Cynthia told me its name." She tilted her head in thought for a moment. "I think one of Scyhathen's men decided upon it. It is much like the strait to our south, but a little more open. You might call it a gateway to the islands."

Thomas nodded, carefully observing how the two islands formed almost a hallway of sorts. Palm trees covered the edge of the island coastlines like a ceiling, though much of the channel was open to the fading sunset.

The mermaid turned toward the south. "That channel we passed by earlier? Inside that strait is an area we call the Cove. It's very deep, and very special. Cynthia spends most of her time there."

"It certainly looked lovely," Thomas said.

As they rowed between Nemaris Island and Opole Island, Acadia spotted the *Valiant* a short distance to the west.

"I can see your ship just ahead."

"That means you'll want to get off here, then." Thomas slowed his rowing.

She smiled. "Perhaps it would be best."

"Yes, the men might be a bit confused about you."

Acadia moved closer to the side of the rowboat. "Thomas, I'm sure the men you serve with are good people, but I'm a bit wary of meeting them. Perhaps I'll meet this friend of yours someday, but not today."

"I understand. There have always been myths, you understand."

"Myths?" Acadia asked suddenly, a bit bewildered. "Of what sort?"

"Well ... maybe we should talk about it next time."

"I'd like that. But before I go, which direction is Harper's Bay?"

Thomas pointed northeast. "A long way in that direction."

"Next time we meet, we should meet on the smallest island then. To face toward your home."

"Perhaps we should." He finally brought the rowboat to a halt. "We're getting close to the ship ... have a good evening,"

"You as well. I enjoyed our time today. Until we meet again." Acadia leaned backward, flipping her tail over the side as she made a splash.

"Good eve."

The ripples dissipated quickly, and Acadia was gone. The sun had begun to set. Thomas waited until the tide had pulled the boat clear of where Acadia had entered the sea, and then made haste to return to the ship. Arriving at the *Valiant*, he was greeted by Jared, who assisted in hoisting the craft aboard.

"Where ye been all day? I've been wanting to talk to you."

Thomas helped him secure the rowboat. "I've been rowing around the islands. Mostly, I wanted to get an idea of where everything is in case we're stuck here for awhile." After all, he wasn't ready to tell Jared about his special friend, especially if Jared wouldn't believe him.

"About your finding my fife—are you certain that it washed ashore? We were pretty far out when that happened, you know."

"Actually, I never found it ashore. Acadia had it, remember?" Thomas knew the truth—even at this point—was all he had going for him. "We saw her playing it by the falls?"

"What? Oh, the girl ... right." Jared chuckled as though Thomas had told a good joke. "I was thinking about what you said, and whether it could really be true, but then my good sense got to me again. Tell me, really, how did you find my fife?"

Thomas shrugged. He knew that Jared would not believe the truth, so he decided to proceed with the only option that Jared wished to entertain. "You were correct, it did wash ashore. I spent most of the evening cleaning it out and making sure the sand was gone."

"And the girl we saw? How do you explain her, Tommy?"

He sighed. "I cannot."

"Aye, I thought so. Well ... maybe we both dreamed her, since something caused us to sleep so sudden. This islands have been playing tricks on us all. For now, I got the fife back and that is enough. Did ye get something to eat?"

Thomas's stomach gave a sudden growl. "Not really ... I am a bit hungry."

"I think Ellis is getting ready to turn in, but he usually closes his door when he's in there doing whatever it is he does. You could make a cold sandwich if ye need it."

"I'll do that, thanks."

"Keep up the good work lad. Make sure the deck gets swabbed tomorrow." Jared patted his shoulder before heading below deck.

"I will."

"Night lad."

Thomas stayed on deck a moment longer and leaned on the banister looking toward the now dark skies.

"I guess I can't blame him for not accepting the truth ... someday Jared will be able to thank Acadia in person," Thomas said aloud to himself. With one last look at the twilight sky, he made certain the second rowboat was secure and went to his quarters, stopping at the mess hall before calling it a night.

A Visitor From the Sea

That night, Thomas slept with a great weight on his mind. Somehow, Acadia's tales of sorcery and treasure denied him rest.

Perhaps it was similar tales of greed and mystery that Thomas's uncle Ian had once told him that stuck in his mind. Stories of wizards and creatures who patrolled the fields and mountains of the nation of Xavier, and countless desires that gold alone could not satisfy.

No matter the story, the theme was often the same. Treasure was always the cure for greed. From greed came treasure; from treasure came wealth, and with it power and ambition. For it was with power that status came, and the one thing that could either make a man or break him: respect. Ambition brought pain and want, and both often led to chaos. Either he would be respected by his fellow man for that power and wealth, or hated because of his financial superiority. An infinite succession had been created—for greed always came with aggression and blood.

Eventually, Thomas managed to drift off and get some much needed rest.

In the morning, the state of the deck and whether it needed scrubbing had little influence on him, as a desire to further his knowledge of Captain Scyhathen preceded over all else—except breakfast. He caught a warm meal, and then after retrieving his journal from the captain, retreated to his cabin, intent to find out more from the book of Scyhathen.

August 2nd, 1582. Still marooned on the mysterious islands that we have named the Nemaris Islands. Mr. Banes is now in good health, and I am happy for him. Accordingly, he has been able to finally update the crew and me on the calendar.

The abundance of fruit on this island, and the ease of catching fish offshore, has been most helpful for sustaining the men. Although there have been complaints about the variety of food, Cook Jones keeps reminding them about the alternative. And if Barnaby's word wasn't enough, my mate Smitty always keeps things chipper.

However, our worst fears have come true. My vessel is stuck far enough in these sands that even the tide can't shift us loose. We have come to accept our residency here, and, in the meantime, have since increased our efforts on charting the chain of islands in full.

Our tours around the islands have revealed many strange sites. A tall waterfall with no apparent source; a rocky mountain with a high peak, a seemingly endless supply of fruits and supplies, and a constant feeling that we are being watched.

Perhaps Smitty did see a young lady on the beach, perhaps he has been spending too much time in the sun. The man has always had a weakness for the fairer sex.

The crew has been optimistic about our continued stay, but I grow weary as the legends of these islands are starting to return to my mind. I may never be so content, lest we discover a truth to old rumors.

Thomas read carefully, beginning to see the similarities between his crew and Scyhathen's. He continued with the next entry.

August 7th, 1582. No change in situation. As of yesterday, our secondary survey of Nemaris Island, the largest, is complete and being charted by Mr. Mandalay. I look forward to seeing his results.

Of the second largest island, Siren Island, we have discovered an accessible ledge on her eastern coast and are looking into exploring this rockiest of islands.

The trade winds remain calm. There is little hope in sight for our departure—although as our time in this paradise grows, I find myself more reluctant to leave.

Mr. Smitty spoke of yet another odd meeting today, describing fantastic creatures that were half women, half fish that lived below our waters, but I was quick to skepticism. Mer-somethings, the cabin boy called them. Rubbish, that's my response to that little speck of nonsense.

Thomas wondered if Acadia might be descended or even part of this group of mer-somethings of which the captain wrote.

We have plans to journey ashore to the three remaining islands once the tides prove favorable. Meantime, our food and water supplies are holding out well, and survival has been a goal reached without difficulty.

Thomas wondered about further similarities between the crew of the *Nemaris* and his own, but he decided that the deck had been left unattended far too long. He made haste to the mop and bucket before Captain Janes or one of the crew would order him to do so.

By midday, the deck was spotless and Thomas had enjoyed a hearty lunch. With his chores complete, he felt it was time to approach Acadia with his assumptions. The events described in Scyhathen's journal were a mirror of their own ... and it was time to seek her side of the story.

Once he had permission, he lowered the second rowboat to the water and made for the northeast shore of tiny Opole Island.

Rowing along the northern shore, Thomas made an error in projecting his course, wedging the keel of the rowboat's bow into solid sand.

"Ooph, what happened?" He turned around and discovered that he had hit bottom a few feet from the island. Climbing out, he worked the bow back and forth a few times, trying to free it. However, the movement caused the sand to settle around the bow again, making progress difficult.

The sound of his efforts somehow reached Acadia's ears, and a few moments later she arrived.

"Thomas?"

Surprised, Thomas slipped onto his knees in the surf. He quickly stood up, casually leaning onto the side of the rowboat. "Acadia? Hello!"

"Is everything okay? You seem to have a problem."

He continued to fight with the rowboat, which was clearly winning. He refused to allow himself to appear defeated. "No, no, unngh ... everything's okay, mmph!"

Acadia gave him a confused look. "Are you certain?"

"Yes, everything is under control." Thomas leaned on the bow and again tried to push it free from the sand.

"Please, let me help."

"If you can pull, that'd be great."

A girlish grin crossed her lips. "I have a better idea. Just climb back inside, and leave everything to me."

Thomas wasn't quite sure how getting back inside would solve anything, but he decided to trust Acadia. She swam to the bow and took the rope that was tied there then ducked underwater and began to kick her tail. Splashing came from underwater, and soon the boat came free of the sand. She continued toward the eastern shore. Acadia surfaced a moment later, still guiding the boat.

"There now. Is that better?"

Thomas could hardly speak from surprise. "Remarkable ... How'd you do that?"

She responded with a feminine smile. "Come, I brought you something." Acadia moved onto the beach, but only so far that the surf would keep her tail moist. As Thomas joined her, she held up a pewter comb with about sixteen teeth and an ornate flower on top. "Can you show me what this is? I've had it in my things for some time, and I'm not sure how to use it."

"I think you know what that is."

She blinked at him, confused. "Why? Should I?"

"It's a hair comb, that is used to either straighten one's hair or hold it in place. You do comb your hair, right?"

"Like this?" Acadia ran her fingers through her hair.

"Right, but do it with this." He ran the fingers of the comb through her long blond tresses.

Acadia took the comb back, and brushed the tangles out of her flowing locks. Then, taking her hair in one hand, she swirled a ribbon of seaweed, forming her hair into a long ponytail. Lastly, she stuck the comb in to help secure her hair tightly in place.

"Is this right?"

"Perfect ... that's very lovely." Thomas couldn't help admiring her silky hair.

"Thank you. Very comfortable, too." After tilting her head from side to side, trying out her new hairstyle, she turned back to him. "What did you want to talk about today?"

"We were going to talk about myths, but there's something else I would like to ask you about."

"Anything you'd like, Thomas."

"About your friends ... what were their names again?"

She smiled. "You refer to Cynthia and Marsha."

"Yes, Cynthia and Marsha. When did you meet them?"

"A long time ago, when I was very young."

"Do you remember your parents?"

"Parents ..." A slight frown pulled at the corners of her mouth. "You mean my birth family?"

"If you want to call them that, yes."

She waved the frown away. "I cannot remember my parents. Rhydar called me to him when I was very young—still a minnow, if you will. I knew Rhydar for some two or three years after that, but that's when his life ended, as mine was only beginning." Gazing at him intently, she leaned a little closer. "What about you, Thomas? I have told you things about me, but I know very little about you."

"What would you like to know?"

"About your parents. Can you tell me about them?"

"My mother is a very sweet woman. She's raised me from day one all by herself." Just the thought of her brought memories of freshly baked bread and the secure comforts of home. "I have never met my father."

Acadia absently splashed her tail. "You are fortunate to know about one parent, at least. Your father ... what do you know about him?"

"A few things, but not much. He was a man of many interests. They ran a tavern out of our house. When he was away, he traveled at sea in search of rare and exotic finds. Gregory was his name- and from what I've heard from Mother, he would manage to be home often." Thomas gazed across the water; it helped him remember this part of his life. "But one trip was different shortly before I was born. His ship was traveling toward the southwest, in this direction as a matter of fact, and they never returned. There are no paintings, and no records of his existence ... except a few trinkets from his travels that a friend of mine holds onto for safekeeping. I don't even know what my father looked like or if my father is still alive today."

"Then, you joined the crew to search for your father's legacy?" Acadia asked.

"Mainly to seek adventure and see the world, but yes." He nodded. "To find a trail that he left—if any."

"It sounds like he must have been great." She worked a shell out of the sand and examined it with an expert eye before setting it down again. "What else do you like to do? How do you pass the time?"

"I don't have many hobbies, really." He shrugged. "Back home, there are few children my age to play with, but I keep busy. Sometimes I'll go for a walk around the shore, or make carvings on small rocks. Nothing fancy or very good, but something to pass time not spent assisting Mother with other tasks."

Her eyes lit up. "Carvings? What do you carve?"

"Small pebbles, ones like this." Thomas found a small oval stone in the sand. This particular stone was well suited for carving.

"But, what do you usually carve them into?"

Thomas thought a moment. He never really carved them into anything; he just made small markings on them. "I don't know. Whatever strikes my fancy, I suppose."

"Would you carve me something? A necklace, perhaps?"

Thomas swallowed. The thought of actually making something while rock carving seemed challenging, but worthwhile. It would definitely be a good project for him, considering their odds of leaving the islands were quite slim.

"A necklace ... of course. In fact, this stone would work perfectly for such a thing." Thomas tossed it in his palm lightly.

Their gazes turned back to the water, toward the northeast.

"Your home is in that direction, if I remember correctly."

"That's right. I'm sure it hasn't changed much."

She looked over at him. "Do you miss your home?"

"Not really." But as soon as he'd said it, he knew it wasn't completely true. "I do miss my mother, but the town itself is just a place."

"A place, you say? Why is that?" Acadia asked curiously.

"I don't know ..." Thinking about it, he shrugged. "There was no sense of family, of belonging ... and never really much to do."

Acadia sighed softly, spurring Thomas to continue.

"Sometimes I watch people in the street, a father, a mother, and a child." The thought was private, but he needed to express himself. "They take leisurly walks around the waterfront, enjoying each other's company...."

"And you want to walk with your mother, and your father, much in the same way."

Thomas responded with a soft nod as he gazed into the distance.

"Thomas, there are things in this world we cannot always have." She patted her tailfin softly. "Seeing my home from inland, for example. But I can always come ashore and see the trees and the birds, and that is enough. They keep my interest."

"But at home ..." He shrugged. "Nothing is there to keep me interested. Everything is too familiar, perhaps."

"But here, it is not too familiar," Acadia commented.

Thomas nodded. He continued to stare toward the sea.

"Where is your home now, Thomas?"

"On the ship, you mean?"

"Well, of course you stay on the boat." She chuckled. "But are you with the other sailors or do you have a place of your own?"

"I stay in the cabin boy's quarters, located in the lowest point of the bow."

"Are you comfortable there?" Acadia asked.

"Comfortable enough."

"That must be nice, having your own place."

Thomas remembered her mentioning that before, but he hadn't really thought about it in a practical context. "Where do you sleep?"

Acadia opened her mouth to reply, but she faintly heard the sound of rowing and turned to face it. Thomas couldn't hear anything, so he continued to look at her, awaiting a reply.

"Was that question a bit too personal?" Thomas became somewhat wary of what he was asking her.

"Someone is coming."

Thomas got up and went along the coast a bit. Indeed, the other rowboat was coming. Mr. Perry was alone, so his back was to them as he manned the oars.

"Perry's coming. You might want to ... leave." He turned around to discover Acadia was already gone. There wasn't even a trail in the sand.

Thomas shrugged as Perry approached.

Glancing over his shoulder, the big man spotted the cabin boy. "Tommy, there you are." Perry rowed closer to shore, keeping his boat in the water. "Cap'n was wondering where ye were. There be a meeting starting soon."

"All right, I'll be right behind you." Thomas made sure he had the stone Acadia selected for a necklace, quickly picking up a few others in the event that one didn't quite work right.

"Don't be long. Very important." Perry turned the rowboat with a few quick strokes and headed back toward the *Valiant*.

Shoving his rowboat off the beach, Thomas jumped in and made haste to follow Perry to the ship. Unbeknownst to him, Acadia surfaced and watched him for a few moments before diving back under.

Visions of Destiny

*O*nce Thomas and Perry joined the crew in the mess hall, Captain Janes got up from his chair and gestured for the others to sit. "Tommy, there you are. Glad you made it."

"Found him on Opole Island, cap'n," Perry said.

A curious expression crossed Janes's face. "Ah ... You'll have to tell me about the island later. For now, to business." He turned to address the crew. "Mr. Ward and I have been looking for options to get the ship free from the reef. Sadly, our best ideas involve patience and a great deal of luck. Mr. Ward will explain." With a wave to the first mate, he sat back down.

"Here's how it works." Ward used his hands to help him demonstrate. "The keel is sitting a good four to six feet into the sand, as that violent storm wedged us in quite tight. The tides have been changing slightly as the days have been passing, but not enough to help our situation any."

"So we's stuck 'ere, then?" Gritzol asked. Some of the other men moaned quietly.

"Sadly, yes." The captain glanced at the cook. "Mr. Ellis, how are the supplies holding out?"

"Going fast, cap'n. Grain shipment'll have to be tapped into, as our stores are nearly depleted. There's a good supply of jerky, but the longer we can hold onto it the better. Pork's gone, the last of the beef's nearly gone, and unless we get to fishing we'll be finished 'fer shore," Ellis reported in his usual gruff tone.

"Tomorrow we'll get the nets out and see what we can catch. The water here is pretty shallow, so we'll have to head to deeper water. Also, once every two days a few men will gather fruit from the islands. The fruit trees ashore seem to have an abundance, and should be adequate. We'll alternate. "Janes nodded to his first mate. "Myself and Mr. Ward included."

Thomas shuddered slightly when he heard the word "nets." What would become of Acadia and her friends?

"Nets, sir? Isn't there any wildlife on the islands?" Thomas asked.

"There's some. The monkeys are too fast, rabbits are too scarce, birds are too hard to catch, and insects aren't very filling." The captain sighed. "That's all we've seen."

"Aye, no signs of deer or game. Fish or nothing, boys …" Ward gave them all a stern glare. "And I ain't listening to complaints about it."

"Can't we use the sails to pull us out the way we come in?" Jennings spoke up.

"Or use the rowboats to pull us free?" Lewinston asked.

"The sails might work, but we're wedged in pretty tight now. There'd have to be a pretty strong southeastern wind for them to work to their fullest, and even then something would have to give underwater. The rowboats on the other hand…" Ward shook his head. "Even with two men to a boat and two boats, we'd either break the ropes or just tire ourselves out."

"Guess we may as well get used to the place," Jared said.

"Aye," Gritzol added.

Lewinston grumbled. "Aye, but I'm still sleeping with me sword handy."

"Tomorrow, some of us will work on the fishing. From now on, we'll have to go fishing at least every other day." Janes turned back to the cook. "Mr. Ellis, is the dinner prepared?"

"Beef brisket. It'll be a few minutes." Ellis retreated into the galley.

"At least we get beef for a while longer," Lewinston muttered.

"Sure beats pork," Jennings added.

"Gentlemen, consider the alternative." While his tone was light, Mr. Ward's expression was not.

"Aye," both men replied.

That night, Thomas took a scrap of paper that had been inside his trunk and sketched some preliminary ideas for the necklace he was going to carve. As he only dabbled with rocks in spare time, his skill was limited. Working from what he did know, he included a hole for the string to thread through and enough space on either side so the rock wouldn't crack or break. With that in mind, he let his imagination run.

The rock itself was somewhat irregular shaped, like a flattened out egg with one end very round while the other tapered slightly toward a mild curve. On his sketch, he thought that the center of it should be like the moon, pure and bright, while the natural beauty of the stone would be left unaltered except for a rise-and-fall pattern, similar to waves. Instead of a continuous line, however, he'd do two lines in a parallel pattern before stopping and adding a single mark between the two. He would call it the Moon Pendant.

Thomas woke to a rapid knocking. It was always difficult to tell the time in his windowless cabin, but he felt too sleepy for it to be morning. Bewildered, Thomas took his lantern and lit it in the dim light from the hall only to find no one was there. It was still night, and the entire ship was quiet, save for the knocking.

As the knocking sounded again, he followed the sound. It seemed to originate in his cabin. Listening carefully, he realized the knocking seemed to come from the ship. Could it be occurring from outside?

"Acadia?" he asked himself aloud.

There was a steadier knock coming now. It was also much louder.

Wondering if it was her, he collected his lantern, climbed through the ship to the deck, and looked off of the port bow. Directing his lantern toward the water didn't accomplish much, as the light reflected off the surface. Apparently, Acadia spotted him. She surfaced a moment later, a worried expression on her face.

"Acadia! Is everything okay?"

"I must speak to you, Thomas. I fear something might happen," Acadia urgently called out.

"Shh! You'll wake the other men. I'll come down to you."

The rowboat he had used earlier was still on the crane rather than secured on deck. He slowly lowered it and climbed down to sit in the craft, where they could speak at a normal level.

"What's wrong?"

"I had a vision." Acadia's eyes were wide with worry.

"A vision? What kind of vision?"

She frowned. "I do not know, but it was very confusing. Can you come with me?"

"Right now?" Thomas wasn't yet fully awake, but he remembered he'd narrowly escaped trouble from his last midnight outing. "It's very dark."

"You have your light, yes? Please!" She swam to one end of the boat then back, as though pacing. "Cynthia wants to meet with you as well."

It was difficult to say no to an anxious mermaid. Thomas unhooked the rowboat from the crane and pushed off. "Where are we going?"

Acadia quickly climbed in. "To the Cove. Cynthia is waiting for us there."

"The Cove?" Thomas had heard her speak of it before, but in his sleep-deprived state could not remember its location.

"Between the islands, I will show you. Please, we must hurry."

Thomas nodded. "Take the lantern. You'll need it to navigate if we're going through those narrows."

"I can see well in the dark, thank you." She spoke with some of her normal amused charm.

"Really? Well … yes, I suppose you can. But I cannot. Besides, it must be easier with the light, yes?" He handed her the lantern.

"I understand what you mean."

"Don't touch the flame inside." With a huff, he began to row. "Let me know when to turn."

They arrived at the area Acadia called the Cove, a narrow strait between the eastern edge of Nemaris Island and the western cliffs of Siren Island. About ten meters at its widest point, Thomas could see that it was not only private, but that even with ample light it could be difficult to navigate. A dozen or so rocks stuck high out of the water, while several more were flat and close to the surface. These rocks were shaped just perfectly for a mermaid to relax and sunbathe if she so chose. The channel was very deep, perhaps several fathoms, and tall aquatic plants obscured the bottom. Towering cliffs flanked either side, creating a valley between the two islands. There was enough of a gentle breeze to keep the space relatively cool and cause soft waves to dance off the cliff faces. Thanks to the confined space, Thomas's lantern lit the entire area very well.

"We're here. I would encourage remaining in the boat, as the water is very deep," Acadia cautioned.

Thomas glanced over the side. "It doesn't look all that …"

Acadia smiled. "I assure you, it is."

"Is there something I can tie the boat to?"

"I do not think so, but worry not—there are very few currents here." She moved closer to the edge of the boat.

"Are there no currents because Rhydar...?" Thomas began.

He was halted by Acadia's polite wave. She leaned over the rowboat's edge.

Thomas began to grow nervous, as her emotional state was contagious. "What do we do now?"

"Cynthia should be right below us, but she is waiting for me to signal for her." Acadia took a small shell from her hand and dropped it into the water. A few moments later, Cynthia surfaced and sat on a rock.

She appeared to be the same age as Acadia, as she had no blemishes upon her skin. Her tail gleamed from the dim light of the lantern, a rich teal pigment to each individual scale. Upon her chest was a sash of silk similar to Acadia's, but of a deep black that had a touch of yellow to the edges. Her hair was as long as Acadia's, but of a rich amber shade that, while less profound, made for a lovely impression. Her face was also rather simple with a smooth nose and soft lips that were turned down in a melancholy expression. There was something else about her, though. Maybe it was a sense of wisdom in her, or a mysterious compassion that ran deeper than the sea. Or maybe, it was as if Thomas had seen her before.

"Cynthia, I presume?"

Cynthia nodded. "You are the one named Thomas?" She spoke in a deep but sweet voice, again similar to that of Acadia's, but tempered with age and deep wisdom.

"Cynthia, I have found him to be a very friendly person."

"I am not doubtful of your findings, Acadia." She glanced at her sister then turned back to Thomas. "Although I had imagined him to be older. Thomas, I trust Acadia informed you?"

"Briefly. She had a vision that something bad might happen, but that was all."

Acadia sighed. "I do not know what it means, Thomas. I am sorry."

"You should not have to apologize, Acadia. Visions are something that are without single meaning and serve to guide those who experience them." She raised a hand to her chest. "I, too, had a vision this evening, and perhaps it can help. Thomas, am I correct that you know of a man named Captain Terrence Scyhathen?"

Thomas nodded. "I do. I have a journal of his, although I have yet to read all of it."

Cynthia '95

"The visions that Acadia and I shared had him in it. I remember Scyhathen well—a tall man, well fortified and just. Although he carried a weapon at his side, it rarely left his belt. In fact, only once did I hear of him exercising it for a use other than defense," Cynthia began.

Thomas listened carefully.

"Often he would walk the shores and try to understand us. He sought our way of life, our experiences ... our purpose in this world." Her eyes drifted toward the path atop the cliffs to the west. She may have even been watching the gallant captain walk by. "He strove to understand why we were called here and inhabited the surface here, rather than hide our existence for eternity. Never did he discover the answers, since completing such a task was interrupted by another man's arrival."

Hearing Cynthia's words, Thomas suddenly remembered the voice that had spoken to him that day before he boarded the *Valiant*.

"Cynthia ... I once heard a voice, near my home. It was a warning, I think," Thomas began.

"Visions come in many forms, Thomas. What did this voice foretell?"

"Well ... I'm not sure if it was speaking to me directly, but the skies darkened, and the wind stopped ... it said that its creator would feel its wrath," Thomas explained.

Cynthia nodded, understanding. "I too, Thomas, have had such a vision. Often, in fact ... but as in your case, the voice is never speaking to me directly. Caution is always a wise course of action, particularly if one is left with an ominous feeling of things to come."

"If this ... voice ... is seeking its creator, then what does that mean for me?"

Cynthia shook her head. "No single vision will ever answer such questions. But worry not. Scyhathen's personal journal is a valuable tome, Thomas. Inside it lies many clues. Tell me, in your readings, have you ever read of another visitor to these islands?"

"No, I haven't read that far," Thomas confessed.

"It would be advisable to research the journal then. But a visitor did come to these islands ... one most unwelcome, even more than those who stumbled upon these islands carelessly. I implore you to listen carefully," Cynthia began.

Thomas nodded.

"To be prepared is to be fearless. Should you or your crewmates encounter this man, I strongly encourage you to learn as much as possible.

For it is this man who first attempted to claim Master Rhydar's distinguished possessions."

"Of whom are you speaking?"

"The one called ... Epoth," Cynthia spoke the name with hesitant trepidation.

Acadia trembled slightly upon hearing it. The lantern flickered from the passing of a sudden cool breeze.

The name was unfamiliar to him. "I had thought you meant someone else ... who was this Epoth?"

Cynthia shook her head. "I cannot tell you more. Not at this time. I am sorry, but in my vision my instructions were clear. Tell a visitor to these islands to beware of this man, is what my vision said."

"What else can you tell me?"

"For tonight that is enough." She glanced at the sky. "The stars tell me it is late, and I know well enough not to ignore their advice. Acadia, you may guide him back to his vessel."

"That's it?" Thomas asked Cynthia.

Cynthia slid off the rock and, approaching the boat, held his hands tightly. "Thomas, my heart knows of your discomfort. In time, I am certain you will know the answer. Rest this evening and be patient, for questions eventually answer themselves. Explore the journal, and in time we shall meet again." Cynthia let go of his hands and slowly descended into the waters.

"Let's go," Acadia said.

He turned to her as he reached for the oars. "Do you understand any of this?"

Acadia shook her head. "I'm afraid my understanding is as shallow as yours, Thomas. Cynthia is correct, however. I've trusted her advice ever since I was young ... there will be another time."

Thomas felt confused and disoriented by the encounter. But as he began to grow sleepy, he agreed with Acadia's suggestion.

Acadia took a handful of water and dumped it onto her tail as Thomas hesitated. Seeing that she needed to return to the water, he brought the rowboat about and began rowing back toward the ship.

As they approached the *Valiant*, Acadia leaned close to Thomas and held his hand tightly.

"Thomas, I must ask of you a sacred vow," Acadia asked.

"Anything, Acadia. Name it."

"Ever since Rhydar has been gone and with Onell's return questionable, life has been routine. When your ship arrived, Cynthia became very worried. Now, I am starting to share her fears, but I'm not certain why." She held his hand tighter. "I know that your vessel carries weapons of defense, especially swords. All ships do, Cynthia told me. Thomas, I must be assured of one thing...." Acadia drew a deep breath as though steeling herself and spoke slowly, carefully. "Promise me that you'll always be there for me."

Her request startled him. How could she think he might harm her? "You're safe with me, Acadia. I swear to you. Nothing will ever change that." He held her hand tightly in his own.

She continued to hold his hand for a few moments longer. The stars shimmered in the night sky. One of the stars flew by with a long tail behind it, almost appearing to shoot beyond the moon. There the two sat together for what seemed to be an endless time, but when morning arrived the rowboat was secured on deck, Thomas was in his cabin, and Acadia safely beneath the waves.

Trepidation and Trust

W hile most of the men were fresh at sunrise, Thomas didn't stir until much later. Jared was sent to check on him.

"Tommy? Ye up lad?" Jared asked from the hall.

"Ugh ... Jared?"

"Time to get up, lad." This time, Jared knocked loudly.

Thomas rolled over and sat up on his cot. "I'm up, I'm up."

Opening his door without invitation, Jared looked him over. "Have a rough night?"

Thomas shook his head. "Late perhaps, but no, not rough. It was, however, interesting."

"Interesting, do ye say?" Leaning against the doorframe, Jared cocked a brow. "How so?"

Thomas thought about what he might say, and then decided to go ahead and inform Jared of what happened between him and Cynthia. "You may not believe me, but I met a second mermaid last night."

Jared took a deep breath. "You seem awfully convinced about the existence of such creatures. I hope this isn't going anywhere deep." He sat down on the trunk.

"Jared, you're my friend." Rubbing the sleep from his eyes, Thomas sighed. "Ever since I came aboard, we've been getting along great together. You've got to believe me."

"Let's hear it, Tommy." Jared waved him on. "You seem so set on this, after all. Chances are there's nothing left to tell except the truth."

Thomas recounted his encounters with Acadia and Cynthia. He mentioned how Acadia found Jared's fife, how Thomas showed her his glass globe, including the short but vital conversation with Cynthia concerning Epoth and Rhydar.

"Aye, that's quite a drink of water, it is." Jared nodded solemnly, but his thoughtful expression didn't last long. "This Acadia girl … she seems to be attached to you, then?"

Thomas nodded. "Last night she asked me to protect her from whatever might happen."

"Aye, then protect her you must." The older sailor slapped his knee for emphasis. "A gentleman never breaks his word, Thomas. Not even on his life."

"But I don't know how to use a sword that well," Thomas admitted.

"Hasn't Roland given you some pointers on swordplay?"

"A little, but not to the point of proficiency."

Standing up, Jared patted the boy's shoulder. "We'll have to fix that, then. But first, the cap'n wanted us to help with the fishing."

"Fishing?" Thomas had forgotten to warn Acadia about the nets.

"If we catch your friend, we'll let her go, aye?"

"Hopefully she won't be nearby." Thomas rummaged through his trunk for a clean shirt.

"I'll be on deck. Don't keep me waitin'!" Humming to himself, Jared headed down the hall.

After a moment's thought, Thomas called after him. "Jared, can we keep this between us? I trust you will not tell the others."

Jared turned and winked, his smile bright in the gloom of the hold. "Aye, for the moment. Maybe once we've got some proof they'll believe us. Or at least more information on the matter."

"Okay then. I'll be right up."

Quickly getting dressed, Thomas joined Jared on deck. The men were lowering both of the rowboats into the water. A few nets were rolled up inside.

"Tommy!" Mr. Ward gave him a tooth-rattling slap on the back. "About time you came around."

"Sorry sir, I had a rough night."

"I guess that's true for most of us, lad. After all, nobody thought we'd be staying here this long. Say, go below there and get in the boat, case it floats away on us," Ward ordered as Lewinston finished lowering it.

"Aye sir," Thomas climbed down along the edge of the ship and into the rowboat. He held onto the ladder so Ward could get inside. Then, with three nets along, they rowed out toward the west end of Nemaris Island. Once both rowboats were a fair distance apart, each man pulled out an anchor so they wouldn't drift.

"Okay, you remember how to net fish, don't ye?" Ward called to the other boat.

"Aye," Jared and Lewinston chorused.

"Can't say I've done this before, sir," Thomas replied.

"No matter. I'll show ye." Ward turned back to the others. "You fellows go ahead ... see that ye don't get tangled."

They nodded and cast their nets out in different directions as Ward and Thomas went to work in their own rowboat.

"'Ere's how it works, lad. Ye hold it like this, so that it'll spread out when you hurl it," Ward began, holding the net between his hands. "Then, you hold this strand in your teeth so it won't get away from ye, and throw it out like this." He lobbed the net into the water. With a flick of his wrist, the net spread out to its fullest size and slowly began to sink.

"Then what?" Thomas asked.

"Let it sit, and it'll sink toward the bottom. After a few moments, pull it in. If you're lucky, you'll fish out a few things—maybe some shrimp, nothing too big, probably. If you get anything you get should be thankful."

"Seems simple enough." Thomas accepted a net from Ward. Holding the lead string in his mouth, he took the net with both hands, pitched the net outward into the water and let it sink. Then, he held the lead rope tightly, letting out string with his free hand.

"That's a good toss. The further out you can get from the boat, the better. Now let it sit a few minutes."

"Does net fishing work better than using a pole, sir?" Thomas asked.

"For what we're doing, yes. Of course, it helps if there's a lot of fish around. Okay, let's see how we did." Ward pulled his net into the rowboat. Inside there was a good-sized crab, although that was the extent of the catch.

"Avast! Frisky critter, aren't ye?" Ward said, being careful with the crab so it wouldn't clip the net too much.

"Umm ... now what?" Thomas asked.

Ward took out his knife and, in a quick motion, stabbed the crab right in the head. "That's what you do if you catch a crab. Otherwise, just toss it in a pile and make sure it doesn't try to get away from ye." Ward tossed the crab behind him onto the bottom of the boat.

"Won't they try and get away?" Thomas asked.

"Well, sure … but we're both wearing boots, and we'll clean the boats out afterward, so it's fine. You might pull your net in now."

Thomas pulled in the net a moment later. He didn't find a crab, but he did find some shrimp.

"Not a bad start … we may even get a crab bake out of it if we're lucky! That's not a bad idea … we'll let the net sink a bit before we try again."

"Should I keep going, sir?'

Ward nodded. "We'll keep going for awhile. No need to go quickly, there's plenty of time."

Thomas continued to work the net, although his catch never was as large as the others.

Later on, Jared seemed to be having some trouble with the net.

"Hmm … seems I've got something big 'ere," he muttered. Whatever it was in the net tried to break free.

"Mr. Ward, I think Jared needs help," Thomas said.

Lewinston and Ward both pulled in their catch, as Thomas rowed their boat closer.

"Something big, Jared?" Lewinston asked.

"It's a tough one, give me a hand here," Jared said. The two men struggled with it some more. Soon, however, it was broke the surface, and Thomas knew exactly what it was … by her comb.

"Acadia!?" Thomas cried slightly under his breath.

"Tommy?" Jared asked, as she hadn't entirely surfaced.

"Is that … a girl?" Lewinston asked.

"What in the world?" Ward asked.

Acadia heard Thomas's voice and knew it was him, so she surfaced with the net over her head, as her comb had been caught in the net.

"Thomas…." Acadia began sadly.

Jared looked on in amazement the moment she surfaced, but Thomas immediately reached out and began freeing her from the net.

"Jared! Help me out here." Thomas quickly pulled netting off of Acadia, and in doing so removed her comb. Jared eventually helped out, and soon she was free of the net. She quickly swam away, leaving her comb with Thomas.

"Well … I guess we caught her and let her go, just like I said we would," Jared managed to say.

"I must be seeing things …" Shaking his head, the first mate huffed. "A blond fish."

"Can someone explain this?" Lewinston asked.

"I'm afraid I can't," Jared said.

"What's that you have there, Tommy?" Ward asked.

About to put the comb inside his pocket, Thomas started to find an explanation. Ward took the comb from him before he was able.

"Well I'll be a mermaid's uncle …" Ward said with a smile.

"I let her go, sir," Thomas said.

"Tommy, how could you?" Lewinston cried.

"Let her go?" Ward's gaze shifted from the comb back to Thomas. "Did you say anything to her? Did she say anything to you?"

"Well … actually sir, I know her quite well," Thomas said softly.

Ward had a puzzled look on his face. "You know her, like a friend?"

"Yes sir," Thomas replied.

"We'll need to discuss this with the captain." Grabbing the oars, Ward called out. "I think we've got our catch for today, lads. Lewinston, start bagging up the catch…. Thomas, we'll talk when we get back."

"Aye." Roberts and Lewinston stowed the rest of their gear and followed Ward back to the *Valiant*.

Once both boats were back, Jared and Lewinston were left to clean up the catch while Ward and Thomas headed for the captain's cabin. Mr. Ward went into Captain Janes's cabin first and explained to him what had happened. Thomas waited outside, unsure of what might happen next.

After about an hour, Captain Janes called Thomas in and closed the door behind him. Acadia's comb was sitting on the table.

There was a big smile on Janes's face. "Tommy, Seriam here tells me you've made a friend."

"I couldn't let her be caught, sir."

The captain shook his head. "Of course you couldn't. It's not good form, capturing someone against their will. Especially in such a crude method. Tell me about this friend of yours."

"Did Mr. Ward tell you her situation?" Thomas asked.

"Her 'situation'?" He said the word in an amused tone. "By that, you must mean her fins?"

"Right, sir."

"Yes, he told me. What I don't know is who she is." Janes twirled his hand in a way that indicated he expected Thomas to tell him more. "What's she like?"

Thomas thought a moment about the words he wanted to use, then gave his reply. "A good friend of mine, sir."

"Does she have a name?"

"Acadia, sir."

Janes smiled, intrigued. "Lovely name... what else?"

"We met about a few days ago, near the waterfall. She had recovered Jared's fife and was trying to play it. I managed to get near her and show her how to play it, and that's when I noticed her...." Thomas still felt odd saying it aloud. "Her situation."

Idly, Janes fingered the comb. "And you've seen her since then?"

Thomas hadn't been sure what to expect, but he was glad the captain seemed to be taking it all calmly. It made him feel less reluctant to share his secrets. "Right, sir, when I've taken the rowboat. She and I have had some lengthy conversations."

"Conversations?" Janes looked up from the comb. "What have you been talking about?"

Thomas shrugged. "About each other mostly. She asked where my home was, my parents, that sort of thing. She also knows about Captain Scyhathen."

Ward and Janes's eyes lit up. "She does, now? Can you elaborate on that?" Janes asked.

Thomas nodded. "Of course. It gets a little complicated."

"Go ahead, lad," Ward said.

Thomas repeated to the captain and the first mate what he had told Jared earlier. Both men were intrigued at what they were hearing, especially concerning Scyhathen.

"Hmm...." Janes leaned back in his chair. "I've read through some of that journal of yours, Tommy, and it sounds like Acadia was there the same time Scyhathen was."

"Acadia said she was very young at the time. I spoke with Cynthia yesterday, and it sounded like she knew him better than anyone. Even down to his physical description," Thomas explained.

Janes thought a moment. "You've been very helpful telling me all of this, Thomas."

"Do you need me any longer, Captain? I would like to go find her, and give her this back." Thomas reached for the comb.

"Yes, that would be the proper thing to do. Do me one favor though." Janes took a piece of parchment from a small stack.

"Sir?" Thomas asked.

"Before you go, if you could lend me your journal again, I'd be appreciative."

"Of course. I'll bring it right away."

As Thomas left to get it, Janes brought out a quill and inkpot and wrote a note for Acadia.

Thomas quickly returned to Captain Janes's cabin and placed Scyhathen's journal on the table. Janes's completed letter lay beside it, tri-folded and sealed in blue wax with Janes' signet ring.

"Thank you, Thomas. And when you find your maid friend, please give her this letter." Janes handed him the note. "It should mend some rifts in your relationship."

"Yes, thank you sir." Confused and curious, Thomas took it.

"I'm sure she's waiting for you now, so don't dawdle." Janes made a shooing motion.

"Aye sir." Thomas turned to leave.

"Remember, don't be gone too late."

"Yes sir," Thomas replied, closing the door.

"You don't suppose this Acadia is one of them sirens, do you, Chris?" Ward asked.

Janes shook his head. "If a siren wanted this crew, Seriam, she'd have taken care of us by now. I just hope these aren't the demons that those old legends were speaking of."

Jared and Lewinston had already cleaned up by the time Thomas stepped out of the captain's cabin.

"Tommy, what happened?" Jared asked.

"Nothing really. The captain just asked me what I knew about Acadia, and then asked me to give this note to her." He held it up.

Jared noted the wax seal on the back of the letter. "Hmm … with his personal seal, I see. You head'n out then?"

"Right away, yes."

"Would you object to some company to help you look?" Jared's casual tone did a poor job of hiding his interest.

"I am unsure if that'd be the thing to do right away. If she sees you with me, she might not come," Thomas said.

"Hmm … yes, I hope I didn't frighten the girl too much. But let her know that I am deeply sorry for what has happened." Jared helped lower the rowboat.

"I'll do that. I'll even ask her if you can come with next time," Thomas said.

"I'd appreciate that. Good luck, lad." Jared waved as Thomas climbed down and into the rowboat.

"Thanks Jared." He unlatched the moors and shoved off, then turned the rowboat about and headed for the Cove.

Along the way, Thomas didn't see much of anything except a few sea birds and some other shore creatures. He looked over his shoulder and maneuvered the rowboat into the strait, navigating the rocky cliffs carefully.

Once inside the cove, he slowed the rowboat and approached the largest flat rock. He spotted a rock fragment that was sticking up, and tied the rowboat tightly to it. Then, he climbed off the bench and sat in the front of the boat and waited.

And waited.

And waited.

The afternoon eventually passed. The sun had moved from the center of the sky to a point where it was blocked by the top of the waterfall, making the cove much darker as day became evening.

Thomas continued to wait, however. He wished he had brought the necklace along so he could continue to carve at it and pass the time. Instead, he took a deep breath and continued to wait.

Another hour ticked by. The bugs came out, making it uncomfortable to sit in the bottom of the boat. He had also gotten a bit hungry, remembering the prospect of a seafood dinner. Thomas did not leave, however, because he had to speak with Acadia.

Sunset approached quickly. Since he didn't bring a lantern with him, it wouldn't be long until he had to turn back.

Crimson skies loomed overhead as evening came to a close. Thomas knew that the time to return to the ship had arrived. He sat up and climbed onto the bench with the oars, and untied the rope from the rock. With one final look around and no sign of Acadia anywhere, he took the oars in hand and began rowing back towards the ship.

However, he didn't go anywhere. In fact, one of his oars was stuck in the water.

Acadia surfaced, holding onto the oar. "Wait, don't leave yet."

"Acadia, I'm sorry. Jared's sorry, everyone's sorry." Thomas pulled the free oar inside the boat.

"Thomas, I don't know what to say. I had hoped that I could trust you." Acadia let go of the second oar.

He felt shame burn his cheeks. "You can! What happened back there was just an accident. Our crew's supplies are running short, Acadia." Thomas pulled the other oar in. "You were just in the wrong place at the wrong time."

Acadia looked away. "I want to trust you, Thomas, I do."

"Acadia … please, nobody meant for that to happen, I swear it. How can I regain your trust?"

She looked up, pushing her hair away from her face.

Thomas could see that she was waiting for him. Remembering the letter from the captain, he fumbled in his pocket for it. "Please, sit on the rock there. I've got something from the captain that you should read."

Acadia emerged from the water and sat on the large rock. She took a hold of the edge of his rowboat and pulled it closer, so Thomas could again tie the boat up.

When he offered her the note, she sighed. "You have been waiting here all day for me to come, after all." After unsealing it she paused. "Shall I read it aloud?"

"Er ... do you know how to read?" It never occurred to him she had had the opportunity.

Acadia nodded and turned to the letter. "'To Miss Acadia. First and foremost, my crew and I are deeply apologetic about the scene today. I understand an item of yours was caught in one of my crewmen's nets, but I am hopeful there was no permanent damage to either your person or the item." She paused to brush her hair aside. "If there is, please let Thomas know and I will offer my services to you. I understand that a friend of yours has met Captain Scyhathen. Perhaps after this matter is resolved your companion and I could discuss the good captain over tea sometime. Again, if we have caused any discomfort please let Thomas know. My sincere apologies, Captain Christopher Janes.'"

She read through it again to herself carefully. Then, she looked up at Thomas.

"Do you have something to write with?" Acadia asked.

"Not with me ... can you write also?" Thomas asked.

"Yes, Cynthia taught me. Hmm...." Acadia handed him the note before slipping off the rock. "I'll be right back." With barely a ripple, she was gone.

It began to occur to him how Cynthia might have learned how to read and write. If there were no visitors to the island, was it Rhydar or someone else?

Several minutes later, Acadia returned with two items, a small shell and a strange writing tool. She placed them on the rock and then again sat upon it.

"Could I see the parchment again, please?" Acadia asked.

"Of course." Thomas handed it to her and watched curiously as she flipped the note over and began writing below the captain's seal. Using what looked like a pen, she scribed a few lines. She then dropped the item into the water and handed the note back to Thomas.

"There you are." She nodded gravely. "Give this to your captain, it should resolve everything."

"Do you mind if I read it first?" Thomas asked.

"Please do," Acadia said in a lighter tone.

It read as follows: "To Captain Janes—Thank you for the letter. I appreciate your concern, and am informing you that any assistance regarding this matter is not necessary, as I am undamaged. I would, however, like to set up a meeting between yourself and Cynthia if she agrees. I hope to meet you someday soon. Yours, Acadia."

Thomas was surprised at how well written the letter was, even with the mysterious writing tool that left a clean mark.

"I'll make sure he gets this." Thomas placed the note on the bench so the ink could dry.

"Of course. There is one more thing," Acadia said.

Thomas nodded.

She held up the small shell. It resembled a tiny conch, starting at a small tip and spiraling and opening up into a bell shape similar to a horn, even though it was only two inches long.

"Please, take this. It should eliminate further problems like today's." She placed it firmly in his hand. "Try blowing through it."

"From this end?" Thomas pointed to the bell end.

Acadia smiled. "From the other one," she said, remembering their previous encounter with Jared's fife.

Thomas put the tiny shell up to his lips and blew through it. No sound was produced.

"Blow as hard as you can," Acadia said, and Thomas did so.

"I don't hear anything."

"The sound of this shell can only be heard underwater. It also travels very far. If you ever wish to talk to me, blow through this shell and I will come as fast as I can. However, if you want me to be cautious of what is going on at the surface, like with your nets, blow it three times of equal length. Then I will know to keep clear. However, if you blow it again for a long time, I will come just as before. Do you understand?"

Thomas held up the shell, and then placed it into his pocket. "Yes, I understand perfectly."

Acadia smiled again. "I am confident we can move on. It has gotten very late, hasn't it?"

"Yes, it has. Actually, I wasn't sure you would come after what happened earlier."

"One small accident can't break us apart that easily. Come on, you worry too much!" Acadia said with a smile, making Thomas laugh slightly.

"I'm glad we were able to work that out. Oh, I nearly forgot. Here's your comb." He dug into his other pocket and handed it back to her.

Acadia took it and immediately used it in her hair. "Thanks so much. Come here a moment."

"What is it?" Thomas asked.

"I want to whisper something to you."

Thomas wasn't sure what she wanted. "There's only the two of us here."

"Come here!" Acadia teased.

Thomas leaned closer, and then Acadia pulled him into the water and laughed.

Suddenly drenched, Thomas was able to surface and looked at her with a surprised expression. "What are you trying to do?" he asked in a light tone, although he was trying very hard to be serious about it.

"Have some fun!" Jumping off of the rock and behind Thomas, she swam around him and splashed him a few times.

"We'll see about that," he laughed, and splashed her back.

"Come on! Is that your best?" Acadia teased, and they splashed each other for a few moments before Thomas snagged her and took her into his arms.

"I've got you!"

"Wrong, it is I who have you!" Acadia retorted. She put her arms around his neck.

Suddenly, everything stopped. The sun had almost entirely set; the stars had begun to reveal themselves, and it was just the two of them alone in the water. In slow movements, they approached each other and were about an inch or so away when Acadia put her lips to his.

It was Thomas's first kiss. They made a beautiful scene in the evening twilight. As they held onto one another, all the terrible things that had happened earlier in the day became a memory. Even the waves grew silent as they embraced.

In reality the kiss only lasted a few seconds. Yet, it felt like an eternity to them, having shared such a lovely moment.

"That was amazing."

Acadia blinked, both surprised and amused. "I've never experienced that before."

"Was it magic?"

She put a hand to his lips. "Have you ever ... done that before?"

"Never." Now that he had, he fully understood the appeal.

"We should try it again sometime," Acadia said.

"How about now?"

Acadia laughed slightly and shied away. Then, she kissed him again-but only a quick one this time.

Despite the tropical latitude, the combination of evening air and the water moving through the strait was beginning to chill him. "You know what? I should really head back before it gets too dark."

"Will I see you tomorrow?"

"Of course." Thomas climbed onto the rock and then stepped into the middle of the rowboat so it wouldn't tip over. He sat down and settled himself as Acadia untied the rope for him.

"Would you like a guide?" Acadia asked.

"If it is no trouble."

"It is not." Acadia climbed in. While Thomas balanced the boat, she took a seat across from him and pulled the loose rope from the water.

"You have your letter, yes?" Acadia asked.

"It's right here." Thomas picked it up and, after testing the ink, slipped it in hip pocket.

"Let us go then." Her girlish grin belied her regal tone.

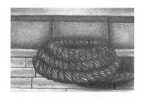

Marshall

The sounds of the night played a soft chorus as Thomas rowed onward. Acadia watched the rocks go by as they returned to the ship. Even though it was getting darker by the minute, Thomas could always see her face, and the worried look that slowly replaced her smile.

"Why are you worried?"

Acadia looked at him. "Worried? Do I look worried to you?"

"A little."

"Every once in awhile, I wonder what Onell is doing." Acadia sighed.

"What is he like?"

"Very quiet. He always waited for the right moment to say something. Or, the right moment for taking action." She gave a little shrug. "I guess that one moment came when he left us."

"There must've been a good reason."

"I'm sure your father had one, as well." She tilted her head in that inquisitive way of hers. "Do you think about him sometimes?"

"Once in awhile, I try to picture him. He may look something like me, or like a person I met one day, but it's usually dark and I can't see his face."

"Do you believe he is still looking for you?"

Although thinking of his father muddied his feelings, he smiled. "As long as I am looking for him."

Acadia nodded her head. She continued to look away as they rowed onward. After a few moments, they approached the starboard side of the *Valiant*. Thomas stopped his rowing some fifteen or twenty yards out.

"Here we are then."

Acadia lifted her chin. "Go ahead and approach your ship. I want to stay with you a little longer."

"Okay, certainly." He rowed to the side of the hull. Acadia could see someone looking out the window of the captain's cabin, but not well enough to make him out, so she chose to ignore it.

It was Mr. Ward who noticed Acadia sitting with Thomas.

"Looks like your letter worked," Ward said to Captain Janes, who was sitting at the table looking over the map of the islands.

"Why is that?"

"Come see for yourself." Ward hitched a thumb at the window.

The captain got up to find Thomas and Acadia coming in closer to the ship.

"My, she is a lovely one...." When the rowboat got alongside the hull, he turned to Ward. "He's not going to bring her aboard, is he?"

"We should go make sure," Ward suggested.

"I'll check on it. Meantime, put the map away, if you will."

"Aye." Ward did as he was ordered while Janes put on his dress coat and went on deck.

Thomas and Acadia rowed close to the starboard hull of the ship. Thomas brought the oars in.

"This is it," Thomas said.

Acadia looked up toward the deck. "Seems much larger up close."

Thomas arranged the crane hooks to put the rowboat into position. "Sure does. Could you move your fin a moment, please?" He took hold of one of the crane's hooks, which had been dangling from the rigging above. She moved aside, and Thomas put the latch onto one of the two large steel hooks in the bottom of the boat.

"Time for me to go, then."

Thomas latched on the other hook. "I suppose so. I will see you tomorrow, then."

Janes called from above. "Tommy!"

"Captain?" Thomas asked, looking up. Acadia also looked up.

"Good evening ... do you have a moment, my dear?" Janes asked.

Acadia looked at Thomas, a bit unsure.

Thomas turned to her. "You don't mind meeting the captain, do you? It's okay."

"As long as I can stay in this rowboat," Acadia said to Thomas.

"Of course. Can you pull us up, sir?"

"One moment." Janes turned the crank and pulled them up to the level of the railing, but let the boat hang over the edge. Then, he locked the crank in place and leaned on the rail of the *Valiant*, next to the rowboat.

"Captain Janes, I'd like you to meet Miss Acadia," Thomas said.

"Captain Christopher Janes." With a flourish, he took off his hat and bowed as elegantly as possible.

Acadia nodded her head in respect as well. "It's an honor to meet you."

"I trust everything is well. You did read my note, yes?"

"Yes, I did. In fact...." She turned to Thomas. "Could you give him my note, Thomas?"

Janes was instantly curious. "Note?"

Thomas took the note from the bench and handed it to Janes.

Janes looked over the paper, astonished. "My, you have excellent penmanship."

"You don't have to read it right away if you don't want to. In fact, I hope to meet with you again, Captain." She yawned. "It is late, after all."

Janes adjusted his coat. "Yes, yes you are correct. Shall I lower the boat again?"

"No, that won't be necessary. Perhaps we shall meet over tea tomorrow, but ashore." A wave of her hand encompassed the *Valiant*. "I'm a bit uncomfortable on your boat, I'm afraid."

"Of course, whatever you wish." Janes bowed again. "A pleasure meeting you."

"You too. Until tomorrow, Thomas." After flashing a gleaming smile, she climbed over the edge of the rowboat and dropped into the water, swimming off. Despite the manner of her departure, she moved with the utmost grace.

"A lovely friend you have there." Janes was still gazing after Acadia.

"She's more than that to me, sir." Thomas climbed onto the deck.

"Yes, of course." He started back to his cabin with the note.

"Shall I mop up before I turn in, sir?"

His attention on the note, the captain blithely waved Thomas's concern away. "You've done enough swabbing, Tommy. Pass it off unless it needs it."

"Aye sir." Thomas raised the winch so he could bring the boat back over the deck of the *Valiant*. Then, with a quick glance at the now almost dark sky, he made a stop by the mess hall, having missed yet another meal.

Thomas was fortunate to have discovered a covered bowl of fresh cut pineapple and a sandwich that Jared had left specifically for him on the table. A note suggested that Jared had felt awful for what happened earlier.

His strength renewed, Thomas went down to his cabin to call it a night.

Mr. Ward spoke with Captain Janes before he retired to his own cabin.

"How is she?" Ward asked.

"I don't believe my own old sea eyes, Seriam. Quite a sight, she is." Janes removed his dress clothes, returning them to the wardrobe. "I daresay she is no older than Tommy, but very lovely just the same."

"Aye, I suppose so. Those mermaids are born beautiful, live beautifully, and never seem to age until they're older than ye think," Ward said.

"That's the common perception, I've heard. The lady gave me my note back, though." The captain tossed the note on his table as he readied for bed. "Quite a surprise, she can write exceptionally well."

Ward looked it over, admiring the elegant handwriting. "Aye, she sure knows her calligraphy."

"I invited her aboard, but she's uncomfortable around the ship." Janes sighed at the inconvenience.

"As she should be. Aye, we're not going anywhere, but how does she know our intentions might not be to capture her?" Ward asked.

"A good reason to be concerned. No, capture isn't in our blood. Only a man like Captain Marshall would drop to that level...." Mention of the pirate brought to mind how they'd come across the treasure map that lay next to the note. "I wonder what happened to that rascal."

Ward walked over to the window, looking toward the northeast. "A ship as large as the *Inferno* would be a bit slower than us."

Janes nodded. "But that doesn't mean they know where we are, assuming they suspect us of anything."

Ward chuckled. "Aye, especially after we foiled them last time."

"Wasn't that entertaining? Yes, the fact that Marshall still has men is quite a surprise." Janes laughed softly.

"He probably collects men quickly, through whatever method he might choose. But when you burned his sails with the reading lens...." Ward's grin was wicked. "That was genius."

"Aye, the sciences always produce the best weapons available—and are often the least known about, too."

Ward started toward the door. "Well, this note is made out to you, so I won't read it. In fact, I's be getting a tad sleepy besides."

"Aye, I suppose ye are. Well, we shall call it a night then ourselves."

"Good night, Chris," Ward said as he left.

"Good eve, Seriam."

Somewhere in the Centra Sea, northwest of Cimmordia Castle, the massive *Inferno* rested in the shark-infested waters of the Sundrop Islands. Its despicable yet refined commander, Captain Marshall, had yet to discover the whereabouts of his treasure map.

A larger and broader vessel than the *Valiant*, the *Inferno* was a mammoth among ships. With a mainsail nearly seventy feet wide and a hull nearly two hundred feet long, she was impressive. The canvas of her sails had been made in the distant nation of Qui-Kinneas. Because of the sail's yellow and reddish hue, the *Inferno* had a moniker as the "Ship of the Burning Seas." Marshall's reputation as the chief of the Sundrop Guild, the resident pirate clan on the Centra, was well known by sailors who sailed the region. Yet in South Cimmordia, Marshall kept a prim edge. A former naval commander, he was both refined and evil.

After departing South Cimmordia, Marshall had sailed the *Inferno* to his hideaway in the Sundrop Islands. Once the home of the dreaded Ranthath Cult, an infamous pirate guild, Marshall continued his own operations from these island headquarters.

Captain Marshall was in his cabin, counting the money in his safe as his second-in-command, Leo Nyguard, entered.

Marshall drew his sword as Nyguard opened the door.

"Just me, boss."

"Dammit, Leo, knock when you enter a man's room," Marshall muttered. He placed the sword on his counting table as he dropped several gold coins into a pouch, returning them to the safe.

"Sorry, sir. I's just been talking to the men, they're wondering where our next target will be."

"Target? Leo, honestly, we don't 'target' places. We liberate them. The lands and wealth that once belonged to the unworthy will someday go to charitable causes." Marshall gave him an insincere smile. "You understand."

"Charitable causes, boss?"

"Aye charitable. To the children," Marshall said.

"You don't have any children, do you, boss?" Nyguard poured some ale for the captain.

"Me? Children? None I know of—most the ladies I court usually fail the nightly exam," Marshall said with a smile.

Nyguard put a cup of ale on the table for the captain. "You are surely the charmer, boss." He set down a cup for himself.

"Aye a charmer I be. And as for charitable causes, know that we all be somebody's children, aye?" Marshall asked with a laugh.

"Aye boss, aye," Nyguard smiled. Marshall drank some ale out of Nyguard's cup.

There was a knock at the door.

"Who bothers?" Marshall bellowed.

"Gretty, sir."

Marshall quickly put away his riches and locked the safe. "Enter."

Gretty entered, holding his hat tightly. "Sorry to bother ye, boss, but I've heard word that the map hasn't quite been recovered yet."

Marshall leapt from his chair. "What?! Hasn't been recovered yet? An entire fortnight later, and I only now hear of this? That blithering idiot Nicalis said one of you losers picked it up before we left South Cimmordia!"

Gretty cowered, but continued to deliver his report. "He ... er, that is, the men, boss ... they're afraid to tell ye."

"As they should be. Know this much, Gretty, he who tells me sooner than later may keep his limbs intact," Marshall warned.

Gretty shook nervously, nodding quietly.

"Do they know what happened to it?" Nyguard asked, reaching for his cup of ale. Much to his dismay, he found it empty. He did not, however, touch the captain's. He knew better.

"They thought they saw some kid pick it up," Gretty said hesitantly.

"A little kid ... very well. Nyguard, you said the men wanted to know where our next destination was. Where did the *Stargazer* head onto?" Marshall asked.

"You sent them north to Dieterian waters, sir.""

Marshall grumbled. "So I did ... the mystical treasure of Rhydar will be claimed someday, and it'll be by my hand, not somebody else's!" Marshall pounded his fist on the counting table, causing the cups to hop.

Gretty winced, crushing his hat a second time. Not yet dismissed, he waited to be given clearance to leave. He wasn't about to turn his back to Marshall.

"So we are returning to South Cimmordia?" Nyguard asked.

Marshall nodded.

"I'll summon the men, boss. Gretty, get gone," Nyguard ordered.

Gretty didn't need to be told twice.

"Hold, Gretty, who be the man who held out?" Marshall demanded.

Gretty trembled, swallowing a lump in his throat. "I think it was Harris, sir, but I'm not certain...."

Marshall retrieved a black-brimmed hat from his closet. "I'll deal with him myself." He adjusted his hat, and with his black longsword at his side, Marshall marched out to the deck.

He walked before the crewmen and removed his sword, raising the point toward the sky and ceremoniously lowering the tip, pointing it directly at the deck. Coated in a dark black finish, Marshall's sword struck fear into those who saw it in his hand.

"Harris." Marshall's voice was calm and firm.

Jesse Harris peeked out from behind one of the two rowboats on deck.

"Boss?" Mr. Harris asked in a shaky tone.

"Is there something you'd like to tell me, Jesse?" Marshall asked, not moving from his position.

"B-boss, I'm sorry about the map, this kid picked it up, Nicks was there ... and w-we lost sight of-" Harris began, stumbling over his words.

Near the central mast, a similarly nervous Mr. Nicalis covered his eyes with his red bandana.

Pouncing like a lion, Marshall grabbed Harris by the collar and pinned him against the mainmast in a firm choke hold. "Listen well, for I will only tell you this once. Everything that happens on this ship enters these two ears ... and not after we've sailed three days away from the scene! Is that understood?"

Harris opened his mouth to reply, but was tongue-tied, and nodded instead.

"Very well then. Consider yourself lucky, for there will be no permanent damage to you today. Just a simple reminder." Marshall released his hold on Harris.

Marshall started to turn away, but in a quick spin motion slashed two deep cuts into Harris' legs just below the knees, forcing the injured man to fall to the ground and cry out in pain.

Marshall wiped the blade clean on Harris's coat before returning it to the sheath. As he circled the crewman who was grasping his wounds in agony, Marshall changed his mind. "On second thought ... tie Mr. Harris to the stern after he is bound around the arms. Long enough so he can swim ... he will sail to South Cimmordia from there."

Marshall left the deck, leaving Harris curled up in agony, trying to cover his wounds with his clothes.

"Let Harris walk the wake of blood ... we embark at once."

Without as much as a word, the other men of the nine-man crew carried out Marshall's orders. Not one of them enjoyed what they were ordered to do, yet they would not fail to obey.

Harris quietly spoke the names of his children to himself as they lowered him into the waters behind the ship.

Nicalis did not participate, as he knew that he was responsible for Harris's fate. None of the crewmen seemed to object Nicalis's inaction.

Soon, the *Inferno* weighed anchor and began sailing for South Cimmordia. They dragged Mr. Harris behind with only a length of rope and a stream of blood into the shark-infested waters of the Sundrop Islands.

As had happened before, the crew understood that it was better to follow orders than question them. The *Inferno* was on its way toward the southeast.

When the *Inferno* arrived at South Cimmordia at dawn two days later, there was only a blood-stained length of rope trailing from the stern.

Legends and Lies

*A*board the *Valiant*, all was well. Into their third full week on the island, the crew had adopted a regimen of daily chores. One team would collect fresh fruit, while another team would perform fishing trips.

The first of many fishing days by the crew prompted Thomas to remember the signal conch that Acadia had provided. As the crew disembarked for the fishing grounds to the west, Thomas blew the signal three times as per their agreement. Not only were these fishing trips more successful than the very first one, but there were no mermaids injured during the process.

A chance discovery of a wheat patch on the western hills of Nemaris Island provided a harvest for grain ... but not one that would last long. Someone suggested that it was a patch of wheat left by the wizard, and nobody chose to dispute that claim.

Although stranded, the crew had been surviving well, and no man was ill or hungry. Thomas had continued to read Scyhathen's journal as time allowed.

September 24th, 1582. The winds have been starting to arrive, but our chances of breaking free remain questionable.

I write this next part with disbelief fast in my mind, as the truth is as hard to believe in writing as it is in reality. We have made friends with some of the mercreatures. One of the maidens, whom Smitty has informed me is named Cynthia, has given us some information about these islands. I'm not yet certain of what effect we have already made on her, but since Smitty began meeting with the maiden, I've been curious as to their interactions with one another. What surprised me most, however, was the other day when it was my turn to gather fruit for the men and I spotted her sitting upon a rock reading one of Mr. Smitty's books. No, he won't get attached to this woman, I be sure of that, but it is what he is teaching her that makes me curious. Perhaps I should learn more before I make assumptions.

Thomas stopped suddenly, and went back a few sentences to read a particular passage again.

"... since Smitty began meeting with the maiden, I've been curious as to their interactions with one another ..."

There it was in writing. Perhaps, just maybe, Mr. Smitty taught Cynthia reading and writing, among other learned skills, which she then taught to Acadia. Yes, it all made sense.

Furthermore, a captain has no right to question his crewmen behind their backs, especially ones as close as mine. Yes my crewmen are my brothers, and together we survive. Without them, I am nothing. I will write again once these assumptions of mine are proved—whether for truth or fantasy.

That was the end of the entry. But before he could get too much further, Jared Roberts and Roland Benson entered his cabin after a quick knock.

"Tommy, how you doing, lad?" Jared asked.

Thomas looked up from his reading. "Good, how are you sirs?"

"Jared tells me you're interested in fencing lessons," Benson said.

That got Thomas up from his cot. "Yes sir, I am."

"Roland is probably the second best swordsman aboard this boat, Tommy." Leaning against the door frame, Jared gave the boy a wink. "And the cap'n agrees that you're ready."

"Unless now is a bad time?" Benson asked.

"Not at all. Is there room on deck?" Thomas asked.

"Sure is." Jared tilted his head to indicate Thomas should follow. "Come on, you might need to use a sword someday."

They spent the next few hours training and fencing. Thomas was shown the basics. A canvas bag stuffed with palm leaves was used as a dummy for stabbing and chopping. With all the activity, soon stuffing was falling out across the deck.

"That's good Tommy, real good," Mr. Benson said as Thomas thrust and stabbed the dummy through the chest.

"But that's just a dummy." With a chuckle, Jared picked up some stuffing near the rail and tossed it overboard. "Good against the living, now that's a challenge."

"We'll practice fencing, won't we?" Thomas asked.

"In time, yes." Lowering the rapier he'd been using to demonstrate, Benson relaxed against the rail next to Jared. "Stick and move, feints, and the art of footwork will all come in our next lesson. But you remember, a gentleman's intent is never to kill. Nor is it in his best interest to flee."

"Yes sir."

"In my opinion, a buccaneer's intent is to disarm his opponents and defend what is his, not seek out that which is not." Benson wagged a finger at Thomas. "And doing so should not always involve swords."

Jared nodded. "Aye, it takes a bigger man to walk away, or find a better alternative than to slash another man to ribbons."

"So you suggest that I should learn to talk my way out of battles?" Thomas asked.

Roland smiled. "If we all could do that, we'd all be just like ol' Scyha-then. Desperate men live by the sword, Tommy. Sometimes, all you can do is try and defend yourself."

"We can't teach you everything about combat, Tommy, but it is important to know the difference between honor and aggression," Jared said.

Roland nodded. "Aye, and that'll be another lesson. That's enough for today." He began collecting the swords and training gear.

"Agreed." Jared sat down and began to play his fife.

From the crow's nest, Mr. Jennings glared down from his nap. "You're not still playing that, are ye?"

"Why not?" Jared gave him an unrepentant grin. "Maybe Miss Acadia will come and spend some time with us."

"Miss Acadia? Who is that?" Roland asked.

Jennings climbed down to deck level and took the gear from Benson. "I can see I won't be getting any sleep up here." He took the sword from Thomas. "I've got it." Jennings quickly headed inside.

"Thank ye … Tommy, who is Acadia?" Roland asked.

"I can bring her here if you want," Thomas offered.

"I'd like to see ye try," Jared said skeptically.

From out of his pocket, Thomas took out the small shell that Acadia had given him the night before.

"With a shell?" Jared asked.

"Watch!" Thomas blew on it as hard as he could in a long, smooth blow.

There was no sound, as expected, and no immediate response.

"Tommy?" Jared's look was a cross between curiosity and concern.

Roland cupped his ears. "I don't hear anything."

"Of course not. It only sounds underwater." Thomas pocketed the shell.

"Sure it does, Tommy." Roland started to go below deck, but just then, off the starboard side, Acadia surfaced.

"There she is now," Thomas said.

"Thomas? Did you need something?" she called.

Leaning over the rail, Thomas waved. "Hold on, Acadia. We'll be right down."

"We?" she asked.

Thomas reconsidered. "Okay, for now I'll be right down."

Jared stood to lean over the rail. "Good day, Miss Acadia!"

"Hello there," she replied.

"May I come with, too?" Jared asked.

"I don't believe we've met." Acadia's tone was playfully prim.

"Tell you what, Acadia. We'll meet ashore. Okay?" Thomas said.

"Yes, that would be more comfortable." She ducked underwater.

"You coming too, Mr. Benson?" Thomas asked. He turned to see that Benson had already gone inside.

"Don't worry about him...." With a wave, Jared dismissed their shipmate. "I's been looking forward to this."

"She's very friendly, Jared. I'm sure you'll get along just fine."

They took the rowboat to the beach on Nemaris, where Acadia joined them. She crawled just far enough ashore that the waves kept her tailfin moist.

Jared remained a gentleman, and didn't as much as stare at Acadia's tailfin once.

"Hello there," Acadia said as the two men pulled the rowboat out of the surf and joined her.

Thomas gave a little bow. "Let me introduce my good friend, Jared Roberts. Jared, this is Acadia."

"A pleasure to meet you after all this time." Jared accepted her hand and kissed it.

Blushing, she looked away. "That's very sweet of you."

"No, sweet of you actually. I understand now that you are the one who found my fife." Jared took it off of his belt.

"That was yours, then?" She gave a regal nod. "I'm glad you were able to get it back."

"Would you like to hear it?" Jared asked.

"He plays very well," Thomas said.

"That would be a treat, yes," Acadia said.

Jared took the fife and, holding it in the proper way to his side, put it to his lips and began playing a smooth, gentle tune. Acadia rocked back and forth with the rhythm as if she herself was part of the music.

When the song finished, she applauded. "That was wonderful, Jared. You play very well."

"Twas nothing, really. In fact, Acadia, you probably have more musical talent than I. It's just a way I express myself when words don't apply," Jared explained.

"You are modest, but I enjoyed it, for it was very good. Thomas, do you have any musical talent?" Acadia asked, turning to him.

"Me? No, not really. I have never been very good with such things." Although there had had been opportunities to learn music in Harper's Bay, it was something that Thomas had taken little interest in.

"But you are creative with other things, like with your rock carvings, yes?" Acadia asked.

"Right." Between reading the journal and learning to swordfight, Thomas had all but forgotten his carving project.

"I'm curious, Jared, Thomas. What caused your ship to get stuck like it is?" Acadia asked.

Jared sighed. "There was a terrible storm, actually. The crew and I were unable to control the ship, and the storm had its way with us. A miracle we were able to come to these islands without any damage, but now we're stuck in good and tight."

"We can't get the ship free, but we are not in much of a rush to right now," Thomas added.

"Everyone is okay, then." A small frown pulled at the corners of her mouth. "A shame that the ship is stuck, though."

"Do you know how far the hull is dug into the bottom?" Jared asked.

"There is sand below, as the beach continues for a very long distance in these shallow depths." She tilted her head in thought for a moment. "If you had a length of rope I might be able to measure how deep your boat is lodged into the sand."

"Should we do that?" Thomas asked.

Jared nodded. "Yes … the cap'n would like to know, I'm sure."

"Will you get some rope, then?" Acadia asked.

Jared gave his knee an enthusiastic slap. "Let's do it." He and Thomas returned to the rowboat, and Acadia swam after them.

Once they reached the *Valiant*, Acadia grasped the edge of the rowboat. "I'll wait here."

They connected the boat to the crane, but left it in the water. Jared climbed up to the deck and found a twenty-foot length of rope and brought it down to Thomas.

"Here, I'll hold it at to the surface as you swim down," Thomas said.

"Right." She took the other end of the rope and dove straight down. The rope was never tight, and a moment or two later she came back, holding onto it firmly.

"This is as far as your ship is above ground," Acadia said, holding the rope some thirteen feet from where Thomas held it.

"Hand it here," Jared said, taking the rope at the place where Acadia held it. He then tied a knot to mark the distance.

"I'll give this to the captain," Jared said, climbing up.

"I'll be right with you," Thomas said.

"Please, don't go yet. Could we go out together again?" Acadia asked Thomas, grasping his arm tightly.

Jared leaned over the rail and waved. "Go ahead Tommy… nice meeting ye, miss."

"You as well, Jared," Acadia replied.

Thomas held the rowboat steady as Acadia climbed inside the rowboat, then he released crane hooks and pushed away.

"Where shall we go?" Thomas asked.

"It does not matter. Where do you want to go?" Acadia asked.

That made him a bit confused. "I thought you wanted to go out again."

Acadia nodded. "I do. I'm just not certain where."

Thomas laughed. "We'll just go this way then." He headed west. They rowed in silence a few minutes, then Acadia spoke.

"Did you enjoy our time together yesterday, Thomas?"

"Yes, it was quite an experience," Thomas replied with a smile.

"Could I ask a personal question?"

Thomas slowed his rowing, and looked at her. "Of course."

"What does it feel like to walk?" she asked.

Thomas nearly dropped the oars. He immediately stopped rowing. "That's ... that's a trifle difficult to explain, really."

"Do you have to think about it?" she asked.

Thomas took a deep breath, and then gave his reply. "No, I do not. That's why it's hard to explain."

"Okay." Although she nodded, her expression suggested she didn't really understand.

"It's just something that happens, I suppose." Thomas thought for a moment. "When you swim, do you think about it?"

"Not unless I'm in a hurry."

"You just kick with your fin, right?"

She flicked her tail. "Something like that, yes."

"I just move my feet, and they touch the ground. Sometimes the ground is soft, other times hard." He laughed. "I guess I've never really thought about how to do it."

Her gaze traveled to the nearby beach. "Ever since I met you, I've wondered what it is like to both walk on land and swim in the sea."

"I can swim, yes, but not like you. The sea is your home, Acadia. The surface is mine."

"That is true." She turned back to him. "But, you can enter my home, and swim beneath the sea. I can enter your home, but flounder without the means of movement."

"How do you swim?"

"Simple strokes, like with your oars," she replied.

"Shall we swim together, since we can't share the land?" Thomas asked.

She smiled at that suggestion.

Thomas turned for the shore, as they were almost at the tip of Nemaris Island.

Acadia climbed out of the rowboat and splashed into the ocean as the boat drifted to the beach. Thomas pulled it ashore. He then removed his shirt and vest, leaving his trousers on. Next he removed his boots, socks, and everything in his pockets, leaving all articles in the bottom of the rowboat.

"Thomas, I feel lonesome out here," Acadia said playfully.

Thomas then jumped through the surf and swam out to join her. Although by no means an expert swimmer, by using standard swimming strokes he was beside her in moments.

"Do that again," Acadia said.

"Do what again?"

"Swim," she said.

He swam parallel to the beach a few strokes, taking breaths of air all the while.

"Watch me try." Acadia kicked her tail slowly while she moved her arms in the same fashion as she swam to meet him, leaving no trace of a wake behind.

Thomas laughed as she mimed his movements, albeit in her own style.

"Why do you use your arms so much?" Acadia asked, as she continued her undulating strokes in a circle around him.

"That's the way I was taught, actually."

She ducked under a moment. In an instant, he felt his toes being tickled, making him laugh profusely.

"Stop that!" he said through forced laughter.

Acadia resurfaced a moment later. "Why are you laughing? Are your feet sensitive?"

"Yes, they are very ticklish," he replied.

Acadia swam in another circle, and then made a soft kick so she'd float by Thomas with her tail straight out. "Am I ... ticklish?" she asked as she glided by.

He slowly reached his arm under her tail, and brushed his fingers along her tailfin as it passed. She giggled.

"I believe you are," he said, stopping.

Acadia came about and floated upright in the water next to him with a smile. "How about this? Tell me if you can do this." She dove under and swam quickly away from the beach. A moment later she shot out of the water and back in with sheer grace, just like a dolphin, surfacing again afterward.

"Not in a million years," Thomas replied with a smile.

She leaned back in the water bringing her tail close to her so she appeared to be in a kneeling position. She floated like that for awhile. "I'll bet you can't do this, then," she said confidently.

Thomas moved into the same position, and sunk like a rock. He recovered a moment later. Acadia again laughed at his predicament.

"Hey, that's not fair!" Thomas said, laughing at himself.

Acadia spun around and floated across the surface past him, kicking her tail every once in awhile to keep moving. "Tell me, Thomas, do your people ever swim for recreation?"

"They do, and I think some people do it to keep themselves fit, too," Thomas replied.

"What do you think would happen if you were stranded at sea, rather than here along the shore? Would you swim if you could?"

"Probably not, even if it was the captain's choice," Thomas said.

"Not if your captain was there. If it was just you and the ocean, would you?" Acadia asked, as she angled her tail to turn around.

Thomas also got into a floating position and gave his reply. "If that was my only option, I think so."

She then turned about and returned to an upright position. "Are you glad you found this place?"

Thomas flipped upright. "Of course! If we hadn't landed here, I would've never met you."

"Where would you have liked to have landed besides here?" Acadia asked.

"Anywhere else I would've met you," Thomas said.

Acadia smiled and gave him a kiss on the cheek. "You're the sweetest person I've ever met."

"I'm the luckiest person in the world to have met you," Thomas replied.

They were about to kiss again when a nearby rumble of thunder got their attention.

"Is that a storm?" Acadia asked.

Thomas looked to the northwest, where a large group of clouds were massing. Dark and foreboding, the clouds blocked the sunlight and were approaching swiftly.

"Aye, a storm's coming. I should get back to the ship." Thomas headed for shore.

"Take me with you," Acadia begged, taking hold of his arm.

Sputtering, he kicked back to the surface. "Acadia, you'll be safer underwater."

"I don't want to leave you just yet, please, take me with!" She sounded almost hysterical.

He recoiled. Had she ever seen a storm from the surface before?

"Thomas ... please!"

Thomas thought hard. She was asking to come with, but would the captain allow it? Most importantly, was it best for her? She would need water to live. Clearly, she didn't want to be alone during all this. That, and he had promised to protect her.

Knowing there wasn't much time, Thomas decided to bring her along. She had already made her choice, after all. His decision was helped by the large crack of thunder that sounded just then.

"There's no time to debate this, I suppose. Come on!" Thomas pushed the boat into the water so Acadia could climb inside. He put his shirt back on without doing up the buttons, the increasing winds causing it to flutter on his shoulders.

She shivered. "I've never seen a storm on the surface before."

"Thought not," Thomas replied as he quickly began rowing toward the *Valiant*.

"I spend most rainy days underwater."

Thomas nodded as he continued rowing.

"Oooh, that wind is cold," Acadia said as they approached the ship. She rubbed her wet skin warmly.

"Here." He removed his shirt and put it around her. As another gust of wind blew, she quickly held it closed.

"Thank you," she said. Thomas continued to row.

They arrived at the ship a moment later, and Thomas quickly connected the hooks from the crane to the boat and started to climb up the ship's ladder. Jennings was there to help.

"Tommy, the captain's been wondering about ye!" Jennings called.

"Mr. Jennings! Can you help us with the rowboat?"

"Us?" He leaned over the rail and gasped at the sight of Acadia in the rowboat. "Impossible ...!"

"Mr. Jennings!" Thomas begged.

Jennings looked around, knowing the ship was secured and the sails were down. "I don't know how the captain'll like this one," he muttered, raising the boat with Acadia in it while Thomas climbed the ship's ladder.

Together, they guided the boat onto the deck and then secured it just as clouds blanketed the sky overhead.

"We've got to get inside. This might be a wild one," Jennings said, stuttering. He was about to pick up Acadia, but hesitated. Seeing her tailfin up close, the sailor could only slowly back away.

"Thomas, I'm scared," Acadia said.

"I cannot lift you, I'm sorry," Thomas said. A blast of lightning flashed in the distance.

"Will you help me?" Acadia asked Jennings.

Jennings threw his hands in the air. "N-no ... I'm sorry, Tommy." He rushed inside to get someone else.

"What are we to do?" she asked.

Mr. Perry came out. "Tommy? Jennings just ran by ... is everything okay?"

"Perry, can you bring Acadia inside?" Thomas asked. Sheets of rain began to fall hard upon the deck.

"Hello," Acadia said.

"Miss," he said, bowing. He lifted her carefully out of the rowboat and held her firmly in his arms. Acadia's situation didn't bother Perry in the least, and even if it did, there was no time to show it as the deluge began.

Everyone on deck had gone inside, latching the oak door closed. Mr. Perry carried Acadia downstairs and into the mess hall, gently setting her down on a bench. Thomas quickly collected a bucket full of water from the water tank for Acadia to rest her tailfin in. She gave Thomas his shirt back, and he put it on despite its being damp.

Mr. Benson was reading a book at the table across from her. He didn't shift his focus from his book for a second.

Thomas placed the bucket of water under Acadia's fin before sitting next to her.

"Thank you, kind sir," Acadia said to Mr. Perry, who sat across from Thomas. The storm had begun to rage outside, even coming in the windows. Although a system of hooks and wooden boards covered them, the rain still penetrated through the sides.

"Acadia, this is Mr. Perry. Perry, this is Acadia," Thomas said. Perry bowed while Acadia followed suit, curtsying in her own way.

"Miss Acadia, I trust you are comfortable?" Perry asked.

Acadia nodded as she fixed her long hair. "Yes, thank you."

She moved her tail slowly around in the bucket. As she did so she looked at Mr. Benson, who was immersed in his book. "Hello," she said politely.

"Hello," he replied, his eyes never leaving the pages. "You must be Acadia, yes?"

Acadia nodded.

"Nice to meet you," Benson said. He had peeked over the book once, but continued to read.

Thomas leaned onto the table. "I'm sorry if we can't do more for your tail."

"I'll be okay for now, but I'm a bit cold," Acadia said.

Benson glanced at Thomas a moment, motioning to his coat that had been slumped over a chair in the corner. Thomas got it and put it around Acadia's shoulders.

"Thank you," she replied.

Jennings arrived in the mess hall with Mr. Ward and Captain Janes.

"Miss Acadia, what an unexpected surprise." Janes removed his hat and sat across from her.

"I hope it's okay I brought her aboard, sir. She didn't want to be alone during the storm," Thomas stated.

Jennings continued to be very nervous, keeping his gaze fixed toward the windows.

"Excuse me, am I making that man uncomfortable?" She motioned toward Jennings as he sat down at the table on the far side of the room, facing away.

"Please excuse Mr. Jennings. As you might guess, he's a little shy," Janes replied. Jennings took a quick glance before shying away again.

"Mr. Jennings, please do not be afraid. I mean you no harm." Acadia said to him.

Jennings stood up, but did not turn around. "I can't help it, not after the things I've said earlier."

She looked at Thomas in confusion. "I heard no such things."

Thomas whispered to her quietly. "He made a big deal earlier how … people like you … may not exist."

Acadia nodded. "What does your heart tell you, Mr. Jennings?"

"Harvey," Jennings replied nervously.

Acadia nodded. "Harvey, then. Do you believe what your eyes are telling you?"

Continuing to look away, Jennings slowly backed up closer to her table. Then, he nervously turned to look at her on the bench. His eyes passed over her several times as she sat motionless.

"I'm sorry, I can't believe this," Jennings replied, and he left quickly.

Ward watched him leave, but did not follow. "Don't worry about him, miss. He'll be all right."

Acadia nodded slowly.

Janes tapped his hat on the table. "How bad does the storm look, Tommy?"

"It spread far and fast, sir. Very menacing."

"I see...." The captain turned to their guest. "I do believe we shall need to set up something to accommodate you while you stay with us, then, Miss Acadia."

"I do hope I'm not intruding." A twitch of her tail caused the bench to move.

"Intruding? Nonsense." Janes flashed a charming smile. "This is the first time I've ever accommodated a person with your ... shall we say, unique needs."

"Of course." She still seemed unsure.

"On the contrary, Miss Acadia, it's quite an honor for us to have you aboard. We are prepared to do whatever it takes to make you comfortable," Ward said.

Acadia smiled. "Thank you."

"Mr. Perry, will you be able to escort our guest around if she desires?" Janes asked.

"Aye."

"There now." Janes stood and donned his hat. "Thomas, you two can remain here whilst Gritzol, Ward, and I devise a plan for this. Perry, I'll need your help for the moment, I believe ... Benson, you too."

"Aye," Perry said, as he left.

Without looking around, Mr. Benson marked his page and left his book on the table. "Hm? Oh, certainly,"

Pausing at the door, Janes turned to Acadia and smiled again. "Welcome aboard."

"Thank you, sir." She turned around on the bench, moving her bucket as well, so she could rest her arms on the table.

"Are you sure your coming aboard was a good idea?" Thomas asked her again.

"I'm sure," she replied.

A moment later, Ellis entered from the hall, taking a quick look at Acadia. "Boy, I tell ye … there's some strange sugar in that fruit ashore." He turned, and without a second glance went to his chambers, closing the door to the galley behind him.

"Thomas … who was that man?" Acadia asked.

Thomas shuddered. "Er … another crewman, Mr. Ellis."

"Oh … okay," she replied.

Outside, the storm had picked up. Those aboard, however, could only tell by the sound of the howling winds, as the boat itself had not budged at all.

"What would you like to do now?" Thomas asked.

"There isn't much we can do, is there?" she asked, aware of what she had gotten herself into.

"Tell you what. Would you like it if I told you a story?"

Her eyes lit up. "A story? About what?"

"About an adventuring bard." He was thinking of a story he heard from his Uncle Ian long ago.

"What are bards?"

"Bards are storytellers who travel from village to village, singing and passing on stories they learn from other places and about their journey," Thomas replied.

"Does that make you a bard now?" Acadia asked.

Thomas thought a moment, and then nodded slightly. "Yes, I suppose it does. But this story is about a different bard, a bard by the name of Sylik."

Acadia leaned on the table as she listened intently.

"Sylik always carried two things with him when he traveled: a lute and a small knife. He used the lute more than the blade, however, as he would only use the knife for self-defense or to make a meal out of an apple," Thomas began.

"I heard about apples from Cynthia." She grinned. "So how did he survive?"

"By storytelling. Rather than live by the knife, he lived off what those who heard his stories would provide. If he told a good enough tale to a farmer, he'd either end up with some vegetables or fresh fruit, depending on what the farmer offered him. He rarely took meat, however, as he did on what the farmer offered him. He rarely took meat, however, as he did not wish an animal's suffering to fulfill his needs. Somehow, he always got by," Thomas continued.

Tilting her head, she gave a thoughtful hum. "That sounds like quite a life."

"One day he came to a small village nestled in the mountains, where one could see the ocean on a clear day. Like most villages, this one consisted of some six or seven cottages, a church, a market and a tavern, nothing more. It was a sleepy village, as it was some distance from the sea and too small for a port, and the next nearest settlement was a week's journey by foot," Thomas explained.

"How far was it to the next town if someone swam?"

Thomas smiled. "It's inland, remember."

"You said it's close to the ocean." Acadia lifted her chin as though miffed.

Thomas chuckled. "About five days by swimming."

"Thank you."

"Anyhow, he went inside the tavern when he arrived, as it had gotten late and the men of the village headed there to meet with their neighbors and enjoy their company. Some of the men gave him an odd look as he entered," Thomas continued.

She seemed puzzled again. "Why did they give him an odd look?"

"Because he was a stranger—an outsider. Their little village did not get many visitors, partly because of its location and place in the world. Sylik approached the tavern owner and presented himself. He asked if he could do his storytelling act for the patrons. The tavern owner was a bit skeptical. He wasn't sure how a young man could entertain these older gentlemen, but the only lady present, the daughter of the owner, suggested he do his best." Thomas paused to take a breath.

"Was the daughter lovely?" Acadia asked.

He nodded. "As a matter of fact, she was. But since the town's younger men had left for other places with more excitement, there were none interested in a girl of her age. Sylik went to an open area at the end of the tables and took out his lute. He began playing a steady tune to draw in the men, who were usually were accustomed to drinking in quiet.

"One of the men spoke up. He asked the bard what he was trying to accomplish in a little village with a bunch of old men, and Sylik gave his response. 'Nothing, good sir. I travel from village to town, on a quest to entertain and learn about every town in this world of ours.' He continued to strum on the lute. A second man then spoke up, asking what would lead a man to such a life. Sylik again gave his response, saying, 'I come from a land where stories are forgotten. Heroes are never made, and journeys are seldom taken. By exchanging tales of grandeur and adventure, someday my hometown will share experiences similar to those of every hamlet on this great earth,'" Thomas continued.

"What did the men think of him?" Acadia asked.

"Well, most of them were somewhat impressed by his statement, and chose to listen. Only one man left, thinking this young man was either a criminal or ashamed of his past," Thomas said.

"He left?" Her eyes rounded. "Why?"

"Well, because his name was Ignorance. Since he was too ignorant to ask about the young man's true past and too arrogant to listen, he left. A second man asked another question of Sylik, asking him about his family. Sylik responded, stating that 'An orphan I have always been, never knowing my true allegiance nor my homeland.' The man also asked, since he had no family, if he hoped to find one, and the bard answered 'No, for I cannot choose my own destiny.' This man also left, thinking his time had been wasted on a homeless shell of a man," Thomas said.

"What was that man's name?" Acadia asked.

"Indifference. He didn't care what the bard said because the bard had no family to go home to. He believed his money and time would be better spent on his own family than a wandering fool. A third man asked of the bard's reasons for not being armed with anything besides the one knife that was sheathed on his belt. 'A weapon shows both fear and hatred in a man; I carry neither as I am neither afraid nor hateful. A tool I carry for my well being and defense, no more,' Sylik replied. This third man also left, and his name was Aggression. This man enjoyed hearing about other men's perils in combat and daily life. Unless the bard told tales of raw hatred between neighbors and opposing nations, the man would not be entertained, and left," Thomas explained.

"Were there any other men in the tavern?" Acadia asked.

"Only one, with the exception of the owner and his daughter. The bard continued to play, waiting for the fourth man to inquire about his intentions. After some time, Sylik chose to ask the man a question of his own. 'What pleases you, good sir? Have you a question of my travels?' The man shook his head."

"What happened then?" Acadia asked.

"The man gave his answer. 'I come for entertainment in any form, but your music soothes me. I toil in these lands all day to come to a home where nothing changes. Someday I will grow weak and die and leave nothing to my family except the work I left from the day before. I will never see the world as you have, but I shall enjoy it just the same,' the man explained."

"What was his name?" Acadia asked.

"Integrity. He knew what his life was going to be like the day he started it. He knew his life was going to be simple, and he wasn't ashamed of it. The bard put down his lute and approached the man. He took out a small bag that had a slight weight to it, and put it in the man's hand. 'What's this?' the man asked. The bard gave no reply, picked up his lute, and asked for a flask of water from the tavern owner. He left. The man opened up the bag, which was full of sand," Thomas explained.

"Why sand?" Acadia asked.

"The sand represented a place the bard had traveled to—a vast desert in a faraway land. Sylik knew that the man would never see such a land, and gave him a taste of the outside world, even if it was only simple dust."

"What about the owner's daughter? What did she do?" Acadia asked.

"She rushed outside to see if the bard would return and rest before going onward. The bard turned to look at her and shook his head. He said he wanted to continue to a place where he could share his stories. The daughter begged him to stay, but instead Sylik held her hand for a moment, kissed it on the back, and then put his finger to her lips. With a smile, he turned and left the village, never to return," Thomas said.

"That seems sad," Acadia said.

"There's more, though. The young woman knew that she had had an impact on the bard's visit, even though it was only for a few moments. She never forgot the man who journeyed from place to place and hoped that someday he would return with more stories," Thomas concluded.

Acadia smiled.

"The end." In the silence that followed, they could hear the wind and rain outside howling through the boards of the ship.

"That was a very good story. Is it your own?" Acadia asked, as she moved her tail in the bucket again.

"My mother told it to me a long time ago, and my uncle Ian told her before that. It certainly made an impact on me, telling me that there was always more to life than what you see and what was around you. That's why she gave me the glass orb and why I keep a bag of smooth rocks from the waterfall near my home in my cabin," Thomas replied.

Acadia nodded. "Thank you."

At that moment Perry entered. "Miss Acadia, the captain has prepared a washtub in the hold where you can be more comfortable 'til the storm passes."

"Oh, wonderful! May I see?" Acadia asked, removing her tail from the bucket to face him.

Perry nodded and picked her up gently. Thomas slid the bucket out of their way.

"Thomas, will you leave this here?" She removed Mr. Benson's coat.

"Certainly." He returned the coat to its former location on the chair.

The three of them went down to the lower deck and into the secondary cargo hold in the rear of the lowest deck, where a wooden washtub was set up and filled with water from the tank above. There was plenty of space, as the tub was some five feet at its longest and four feet at its widest. Also, at three feet deep, there would be enough room for her to be either submerged or sitting up and able to see out.

"Will this do?" Janes asked as Perry carefully helped her into the tub. She sank into it and gave herself a moisture bath before sitting up and giving her approval.

"Thank you, Captain Janes. This is wonderful."

"The storm shouldn't last longer than tomorrow, so I hope you will be comfortable here tonight. Mr. Ellis should be finished with the dinner meal soon, and we'll bring some for you then," Janes explained.

"May I remain here until that happens?"

Janes smiled. "Anything you wish."

"Miss Acadia, I will bring you some food when it is time. Do you have any preferences?" Perry asked.

"What is Mr. Ellis preparing?"

"Crab, I believe." Janes glanced at Perry who nodded. "Will that be okay?"

She clapped her hands. "Sounds wonderful. I do not need much, however."

Janes smiled again, relieved that she was not friends with their dinner. "If you need anything, let one of us know."

"I'll be down here, sir," Thomas said.

"Aye, you'll be next door, won't ye lad?" Janes said.

"Aye sir."

"Thank you," Acadia called as Janes and Perry went upstairs.

"Anything else you need, Acadia?" Thomas asked.

"No ... thank you, Thomas." She yawned.

"Did that story make you sleepy?"

She nodded.

"I'll be right next door if you need anything, okay?"

She slid under the water, but he could still hear her say, "Thank you, Thomas."

"Rest easy." He left as she fell asleep.

Above the Surface

$\mathcal{B}$ack in his room, Thomas suddenly felt it would be a good time to start carving the necklace he'd promised Acadia. Following his earlier sketch, he took his chisel, hammer, and knife and began carving. He would first carve a channel for the necklace itself to hang from. Then he would follow his design from there.

His work would need to continue well beyond that day, but it kept him busy while Ellis prepared the evening meal. Thomas arrived at the mess hall just as Perry was preparing Acadia's meal. They could still hear rain pounding into the deck above.

"Hello Mr. Perry," Thomas said, taking a bowl.

"Tommy," Perry replied. He selected some things for Acadia to eat, including shucked crab meat, pineapple chunks, a white sauce, and some bread.

They both loaded up in silence.

"Actually, Perry, I'll bring it. I'm going that way," Thomas said.

"Can you carry two of them?"

"I've got a tray. They'll both fit," Thomas replied.

"Aye then," Perry placed the bowl on Thomas's tray, then went back for his own meal.

Thomas descended the stairs carefully, as they were narrow and steep. He went into the cargo hold where a makeshift table had been made from scrap timbers and crates.

The smell of boiled crab filled the room.

Acadia surfaced. "Thomas? Why, what a surprise!"

"Where shall I set it?" He could use the table easily enough, but the same would be awkward for her.

"I can take it." She held out her hands for her meal.

"Careful, the bottom of the dish might be warm."

"What are these?" She picked up the knife and the fork from the bowl.

"A fork and a knife, used for cutting and getting it to your mouth," Thomas replied, setting his tray on the table.

Still examining the utensils in one hand, she sat so the dish would rest on her lap above the water line. "How do I use them?"

"Like this, see?" He took the fork and stabbed some crab then held it up so she could see.

"Hmm … oh, of course. Cynthia told me about these once." She skewered a piece of crab with graceful expertise. "I remember now."

Thomas was amazed. "You already know about eating utensils?"

"Well, Cynthia taught Marsha and I; she's an excellent teacher." Acadia took a few bites of pineapple.

"What else did she teach you, besides calligraphy and etiquette?" Thomas asked.

"Just a few other things." She gave a little shrug. "Language mostly, but that's all."

"I see," Thomas replied. He too went about his dinner, although he did so using better manners than he would normally use around the men.

Acadia gave her crab a thoughtful poke. "But tell me this, why do you cook the food before serving it?"

He thought a moment; it wasn't something he'd ever really considered. "Well, it tastes better warm, it brings out the smell and flavor, and there's less chance of one getting sick from eating it if the food is heated."

Acadia nodded. "Yes, it certainly tastes good. But, how did this practice start?"

"I don't know, but the idea caught on, apparently." He took another bite of crab.

"Yes, I believe it did … this is delicious."

The conversation paused while they ate.

"Do you know how old Cynthia is?" Again Thomas's curiosity got the better of his manners.

Acadia looked up, thinking for some time. "No, I do not."

"I suppose she doesn't want to give out her age."

"I don't think it's that. It's just that we never seem to age." She looked down at herself. "As long as I can remember, I've been about this size."

"How far back can you remember?"

Again she had to think about her answer. "Until when I was about ten or so, maybe."

"But, you don't know your true age?"

"I'm afraid I do not. You said you were fourteen years old, right?" She ate another bite of crab meat.

"Right. I was born on June 12th, 1609."

"Yes, of course. You call that your birth date, correct?" Acadia asked.

"Correct. I'm curious. Do you know yours, at all?" Thomas asked.

Laughing, she shook her head. "I suppose if I did I would have a better idea of my own age."

Thomas nodded.

"It is something I would like to find out, however. Maybe Cynthia would know."

"Maybe," Thomas agreed. The conversation lulled as they finished their meals.

"I must say, that was very tasty." She popped the last piece of bread in her mouth with the fork. "Please tell Mr. Ellis that he did an excellent job."

Thomas shuddered slightly.

"Is something wrong? Are you cold, perhaps?"

"It's just that … well, Ellis gives me the shivers," Thomas said.

"Is that so? You mean, you are afraid of him?"

Thomas nodded.

"Why is that?"

"You'd have to see him in action. Did you get enough?" Thomas asked, changing the subject.

She smiled. "Quite satisfied, thank you."

"Here, I'll take your bowl then." He added hers to his on the tray and stood to go.

"Thank you for sitting with me."

Thomas looked back before starting upstairs. "Shall I send Mr. Perry? Perhaps you'd like to meet the men in the mess hall?"

"Certainly, I would like to." She gave him a bright smile. "Please do."

He went up quickly, taking care on the staircase toward the mess hall. Before disposing of the dishes, he stopped to see Perry, who was meditating in the barracks.

"Mr. Perry?"

Perry slowly opened his eyes, but gave no response of distraction or discomfort.

Even so, Thomas felt like he'd intruded. "Did I interrupt something?"

Perry shook his head.

"Could you help Acadia come to the mess hall? She wants to meet the rest of the crew."

"Aye." Perry got up to retrieve her. Thomas bussed the dishes in the mess hall. Inside, Gritzol and Lewinston were discussing the islands. Benson kept to himself, reading the same book from earlier in the day.

"So I said we ought to find some other source of life on these rocks, but everyone knew that would never get over," Lewinston continued.

"You know the captain won't go for that one," Gritzol replied.

"I don't know. There must be something else here besides fruit and fish," Lewinston said.

"Didn't you hear Jennings muttering earlier? There is more than that on these islands," Gritzol said.

"What mutterings?" Lewinston asked.

"Tommy, you were there. I still don't understand why the washtub was set up in the middle of the day. What was all that talk earlier?" Gritzol asked Thomas.

"What talk?" Thomas had missed most of the conversation.

"Whatever it was that spooked Jennings so much," Lewinston said.

Benson sighed as he looked up from his reading. "Jennings has just got no respect for company."

"Company?" Gritzol asked.

"He was just surprised to see Acadia, that's all." Thomas put the dishes into a washing bin.

"Who's this Acadia?" Gritzol asked.

Just then Jared came in. "You're all making quite some noise in here, aren't ye?"

"Oh, so you're going to come along and clear this all up, then?" Lewinston asked.

"If I must. You're trying to figure out … what, exactly?" Jared asked.

"Who someone named Acadia is," Gritzol said.

Perry's footsteps echoed in the hall. A woman's voice could also be heard.

"If my ears don't fail me, it sounds like she's coming now," Jared said. Perry entered, carrying Acadia in his arms.

As if on cue, both Lewinston and Gritzol's jaws dropped. They quickly remembered their manners and endeavored to stop themselves from gawking.

"Good evening," Acadia said as Perry carefully helped her to a bench. Thomas sat across the table from her.

"Evening," Lewinston and Gritzol chorused, in their best monotone voices. Their faces did not shift from their previous gasp. Benson continued to read his book.

"Thomas, can you introduce me?" Acadia asked. Gritzol and Lewinston attempted to regain their composure.

"Certainly." Thomas gestured to each in turn. "Gentlemen, this is Acadia. Acadia, this is James Lewinston and Barry Gritzol."

"Nice to meet you," both men said.

Acadia laughed slightly. "Can either of you reply independent of the other?"

Again, at the same time, both men replied, but with contrasting answers consisting of "No" and "Yes."

"Don't worry about them, Acadia, they're fine," Jared said.

Eventually the crewmen were able to compose themselves around Acadia. The conversation soon included everyone aboard, save for Ellis and Jennings. Gritzol tended to the coals nestled inside the small furnace in the corner of the room, bringing with it a comforting warmth.

"Now that we're more comfortable, perhaps it would be best if you all said where you are from, and something unique about yourselves," Acadia asked as all six men joined her at the table.

"Who wants to start?" Jared asked.

"You start, Tommy," Mr. Lewinston said.

The boy shook his head. "She already knows about me."

"Roberts?" Benson asked.

Jared cleared his throat. "Very well. I'm the youngest hand on board besides Tommy, having been one of the earlier cabin boys back when I was a little younger than Tommy. I'm originally from Juniper Bay, a good distance west of here. I joined a cargo ship after my mother, rest her soul, passed away. My father then drunk himself silly. I needed to get away and find meself, and here I am."

"A shame about your mother," Acadia replied.

"Thank ye," Jared said quietly.

Thomas hadn't heard the part about Jared's father. "Your father isn't still a drunk, is he?"

"Not no more, thankfully ... but he still has trouble getting around with his peg leg though."

Gritzol stood up. "I'll go next. My name's Barry Gritzol, miss. A pleasure, by the way. My parents were quite well off, and I with them. But I was in a life of the ordinary and, wanting to see the world, bid farewell to me folks and found a ship. A decade or so later I left that ship and joined a navy, where I met Captain Janes, and have been serving with 'im ever since."

"Do you see your parents often?" Acadia asked.

"It's been awhile, but I've got a picture with me. I used to send letters, but I've not been getting responses lately," Gritzol replied.

"Acadia, do you know your parents?" Jared asked.

She shook her head. "I cannot remember them, no."

"Shall I go next?" Mr. Lewinston asked.

"Please," Acadia replied.

"Well, I actually had little choice about going to sea, as I was thrown into the life. I was taught most of my knowledge by pirate folks, and that's how I got this tattoo," Lewinston said, sliding his sleeve up for her to see. The tattoo was of a rather roughly scrawled skull and crossbones.

She reached out to touch it. "How ... lovely."

Lewinston sighed. "Aw, I guess so. Fortunately, I wasn't with those pirates long enough to get into the life too deep and was rescued by a fishing fleet. A number of years later, I'd sworn never to get into such a situation again. I met up with Cap'n Janes maybe some six years ago now, and I've been clean since."

Thomas had wondered about the tattoo, but it was the captain's part that seemed worthy of interest. "Where did you meet Captain Janes?"

"Somewhere north of 'ere, Jyrel Village, I believe," Lewinston replied.

"Are pirates as bad as I've heard?" Acadia asked.

"Aye." Lewinston gave her a grim smile. "If ye see one coming, get away from 'em as fast as ye can."

"Yes, I'll do that," Acadia said, with a slight yawn.

"Are you feeling okay, Miss Acadia?" Benson asked.

"I'm feeling a bit dry, actually." Her tail had been out of the water for nearly a half hour.

"Oh my goodness! I forgot the bucket." Thomas rushed to get it from the water tank in the back of the room. Filling it, he poured some water on Acadia's tail before placing the bucket on the floor so she could immerse her tail in it.

"Thank you, Thomas." She cooed, already appearing more awake.

"Shall I continue?" Benson asked.

"Aye, indulge us," Lewinston replied.

Acadia nodded. "Yes ... I've seen you twice today, but I do not know your name."

"Oh, forgive me. Roland Benson, madam," he replied.

"A pleasure, Roland."

"Thank you, it's easy to get lost in that book sometimes. I don't have as much sailing experience as the other men or even fancy stories to talk about. I'm an orphan, actually, and came into this business after having been trained in swordplay by Tallebeck's best trainers," Benson explained.

"Tallebeck ... isn't that a castle?" Acadia asked.

Benson nodded. "Aye, a nation to the west of here. I realized that joining a guard squad was out of the question for me ... as I had always found comfort in the breeze of the sailing life. And since I had grown up near the sea, I thought this to be my only option. I worked my way east and joined on with Captain Janes not long after he had got himself a ship. Yes, I knew that I needed some experience on the seas, but cap'n was good enough to teach me skills, provided I taught his other men fencing. I've been with him since, making it some twelve years since then," Benson explained.

"Yes, I too know what it's like to be orphaned," Acadia said.

"It's not a glamorous existence, but I've done well enough to hold my own, Miss Acadia," Benson replied.

"Mr. Perry, I haven't heard from you yet," Acadia said.

Perry looked up from his meditating state. "I've no past, Miss Acadia."

She blinked in surprise. "Are you certain? Everyone has a history."

"Well, he's partially right, Miss Acadia," Lewinston said.

"That's right. Apparently, Mr. Perry here came to us after a raid," Benson added.

"A raid?" Thomas asked.

"Aye," Perry replied.

Lewinston cleared his throat. "I think this is how it went. Perry was a prisoner on a renegade pirate ship who wanted our cargo. We believe it happened shortly after his own ship had been attacked. While the fighting went on, the pirate ship accidentally came too close to shore and struck some rocks. Our ship had been anchored, so we were safe. They began tossing out their treasures so nobody could pillage them later. Perry had been tied up with two others: one male, one female. The female went under, and never surfaced—presumed dead. The male was struck by a random piece of debris and was killed on the surface. A chance of fate left Perry alive and, as it turns out, he has been very important to our crew's success ever since then."

"Is that true?" Acadia asked, turning to Perry.

"Aye, I cannot remember where my home lies, or even me family. Only that my homeland is in Qui-Kinneas." Perry went back to his meditating.

"That's a distant nation far to the northwest," Gritzol said.

"Why do you close your eyes like that, Perry?"

Without opening his eyes, the big man answered. "It is a mediation that I have done since I can remember, miss. It is meant to cleanse the mind."

"I think that's everyone who's present," Jared replied.

"Who else is on the crew, then?" Acadia asked.

"Just Mr. Ellis, Mr. Jennings, Mr. Ward the mate and the captain," Gritzol said.

"Can you tell us about yourself?" Lewinston asked.

"I certainly can." Acadia shared some of what she had previously told Thomas, although they did not hear as much as he did.

Since the storm outside continued into the night, Perry later carried Acadia back to the washtub in the hold. Thomas had intended to do some more work on his carving, but gave it up and slept. He couldn't focus any longer that evening.

The rain did not let up until early morning, and by then there wasn't a cloud in the sky. The islands had returned to a state of paradise.

Fear on the Rocks

Morning arrived, and a groggy Thomas awoke to the sound of a sweet humming coming from the cargo hold next door. He had no idea what time it was, but there was no chance of getting back to sleep the way Acadia was singing.

He went inside the hold to see her combing her hair, sitting upright in the tub.

"Good morning," he said. She continued humming to herself.

"Hello there," she said between notes.

"You're in an awfully good mood, I see," Thomas replied.

"Why shouldn't I be?" Acadia replied. The melody stopped.

"You woke me up, that's all," Thomas replied.

Her comb paused mid-stroke. "Oh, my apologies."

"Not a problem, I just wish I knew what time it was … did you sleep well?" Thomas asked, looking away for a moment.

"Quite well. Is the sun up yet?" She glanced around her. "It makes it hard to know without windows."

"Let me go check. I'll be right back." Thomas rushed to the mess hall. Although the sun was up, most of the men were still asleep, but sounds of life came from the galley. He headed back and reported his findings.

"What did you find?" Acadia asked.

"It's dawn, but the men aren't up and about yet. I did hear Mr. Ellis at work, however."

"Okay, then. I'm sure they'll be along soon." Acadia continued to comb her hair.

"Should you need anything, I'll be next door. I'm sure we both have some things to do." He headed for his cabin.

"Thomas, is the storm over?"

Thomas turned before going into the hall. "Yes, it is."

"Oh, good." She was taken aback by Thomas's sleepy demeanor, but continued to fix her hair and decided to not let it ruin her day.

Thomas took the opportunity to read another entry in Scyhathen's book, as he wasn't quite awake enough to continue work on the necklace.

September 30th, 1582. A diabolical encounter occurred yesterday. We climbed atop the rocky plateau of Siren Island, and at first nothing seemed out of the ordinary. There was a large flat plain where some foundations were faintly traceable, but beyond that little else caught our attention. At least not until we searched further behind the peak of the isle, where a narrow entrance led to a cavern. Upon entering, we heard a deep voice, telling us not to go further unless we possessed magic. We were not about to argue with such a thing, certainly. Perplexed, we left to ask Miss Cynthia for advice.

At least, those were our plans. That was before we knew that there was another ship in the nearby waters. We hadn't seen other vessels, nor have we heard any reports from our scouts. What happened next to myself, Smitty, Banes, and Corvair was something I shall never forget. To be trapped so easily embarrasses me to this day, especially once we came face to face with our captor ....

Although the journal itself wasn't quite this detailed, Thomas could almost hear the encounter as if he were there.

A deep voice came rumbling through the thicket. "Halt there. Welcome, for you are now my prisoners."

"Who are you to imprison us? We are merely adventurers, no more," Scyhathen spoke in a calm tone.

"Correct you are, I have no right to imprison thee. Rather, I choose to." A menacing laugh echoed through the trees.

Scyhathen and his crew took a good look around to see where the demon was standing, but could not see anyone. Corvair gripped his sword tightly, while a nervous Smitty searched the trees. Banes also gripped his sword in preparation.

Above them a flurry of bats emerged from the darkness, their cries of terror soaring like a chilling breeze over the dark one's voice. "If you're trying to find me, you must look farther than up and down."

Scyhathen threw down his glove. "Enough! I demand to know who I am speaking to!" This game was far too childish to play any longer.

"My name, he asks." His chuckling intensified and grew gravely serious. "I no longer carry a name that such lowly knaves as yourselves could relate to. However, I have earned a nickname, if you will."

While he spoke, Mr. Smitty continued searching. He looked beyond the fallen trees for anything—a footprint, a hat. Again, his searches were in vain. It was clear that the evil captain was an expert at wishing not to be seen.

"Nothing, sir," Smitty reported.

Scyhathen turned to Banes and Corvair, who both shook their heads.

"Curses..." Scyhathen muttered.

"Quite right, dear captain. For curses may have created me ... breathed life into me ... and dubbed me ... Epoth."

A shudder passed through the men as a blast of lightning flashed overhead. Scyhathen remained steadfast.

"Very well then, Captain Epoth ... if I should call you that. Whatever do you want with us, then?" Able to negotiate his way through a typhoon, Scyhathen showed no signs of fear or unease.

"Magic and mystery are a divine combination, Captain. Methinks I shall bide my time rather than foolishly blurt out my secrets. If you can find your way out of this, so may your answers be found...." Epoth chuckled. The bats flew away and the wind grew quiet.

*It was then, I concluded, that we were not only being shadowed,
but attacked as well. Our assailant didn't wish to harm us physically, but rather mentally. Our cage was austere. We quickly discovered that his trap turned out to be no trap at all, only tricks
of the mind. Upon our return to the Nemaris, I plan to consult
Miss Cynthia in hope of identifying the first voice in the cavern...
She has been visiting with Mr. Mandalay in the cargo hold and
is surprisingly comfortable in the washtub ... despite her, shall I
say, situation. I grow weary now, so I shall write again, provided
Mr. Epoth refrains from his little games. Our own situation has
become much worse, and we are taking necessary steps to avoid a
second meeting with that captain.*

Reading onward, Thomas came to a short passage describing the sight-
ing of a second ship.

*September 30th, supplement. Mr. Larson reported to me, after a
quick tour of the islands, that there was a ship docked south of
Stewart Island. It appeared seaworthy, but in shambles. He admitted being fearful of going aboard as her deck had been damaged
severely, possibly by rot or weather damage. He continued to
describe several deep holes that extended to the bottom deck. How
such damage could occur mystified every single member of my
crew. Her sails were shredded ribbons, merely strands that could
scarcely hold a breeze. There were no inscriptions on the hull, nor
any colors displayed. How a vessel could've reached this locale
with naught a sail on her masts baffles every rule of seafaring that
I have ever known.*

*Larson was amazed that the craft continued to float, but it is our
expectation that it will sink one day. I shall keep an eye on it,
although I feel it will not survive any journey beyond these shores.
As with many of the features of these islands, its origin is a mystery. For now, I have ordered my men to avoid it at all costs, and
I shall do the same.*

*I have to report how troubling it all now has become ... for how
these islands that were such a paradise at our arrival, to suddenly
be a living nightmare.*

Thomas marked his page realizing by now the men would not only be awake but awaiting the morning meal.

As Thomas arrived in the mess hall, Acadia had been carried there and was talking with Mr. Benson.

Acadia gestured to Benson's ever-present compass. "What is that you carry, Roland?"

"This? It is a compass, something I bought in a distant port. Quite an interesting tool, if I do say so. It shows which direction north is." Benson removed it from his belt so she could see.

"May I hold it?" Acadia asked.

"Of course."

She took it and watched as the needle spun around a few times before stopping. Next she adjusted it so the needle covered the N. "If the N is north, then how do you find west?"

"N indicates north, yes, which the needle tells you. By finding north, you can find west, like this." Benson pointed to the W to the left of the N.

"So that is west, that is south, north there, and east behind me, correct?" Acadia asked.

"Yes, you have it exactly. Well done," Benson said, taking his compass back.

"What an interesting object," Acadia said.

Benson thought a moment. "Perhaps you would like one of your own?"

Acadia's eyes lit up. "May I?"

He removed a smaller compass from his vest pocket and handed it to her. It was attached to a short wrist strap, and Acadia slid it over her right hand.

"I've had this one for some time, but you seem a good fit for it."

She examined it with delight. "Thank you, I shall keep it in good condition."

"You're most welcome, my dear. I think you'll find a use for it sooner than ye think," Benson said.

Ellis came into the room. "Breakfast! Eat it 'fore I toss it to the scuttles!"

As everyone finished their breakfast, they began chatting quietly. Thomas found it hard to focus on the conversation, as he heard a faint voice outside, much different than the one he had imagined earlier.

"Do you hear that?" Thomas asked Acadia, who was sitting across from him.

She listened for a moment. "I don't hear anything."

The conversation continued until Thomas again heard a woman's voice.

"There it is again … it sounds like a woman." He stood to open a window.

"Is it Cynthia?" Acadia asked, looking toward Thomas.

He looked out the mess hall windows and saw a girl all right, but it wasn't Cynthia. She had light brown hair with a tiny hint of green, and a little bit more body under her bodice. It was difficult to tell by her expression, but by her actions she seemed to be worried.

"Excuse me? Are you Thomas?" the girl called.

"I am. Can I help you?"

"Is Acadia aboard? I've been looking for her!" she called back.

"Acadia, she's looking for you," Thomas said to Acadia.

"Who is it?" Acadia asked.

"What's your name?" Thomas called down.

"Marsha."

"Nice to meet you," Thomas called back.

"Marsha? Oh my goodness … Mr. Perry, can you help me to the deck?" Acadia asked as if she'd suddenly remembered a deadline.

"Of course, Miss Acadia." Perry hoisted her up.

Thomas opened the door for them and followed them upstairs. "What is it?"

"Something must've come up. I have to go home."

They went above deck, and Perry attempted to put Acadia into the rowboat.

"No, thank you," Acadia said. She climbed onto the ladder. Perry again helped her, and she quickly jumped down into the water.

"Thomas, I'm sorry. I'll find you later … when you're by yourself, please," Acadia said. Then, she dove under.

Marsha gave a little bow. "Thank you for watching after her." She also dove under, her reddish-pink tail splashing in the shallow water.

Thomas watched as ripples slowly dissipated across the surface. Perry stood by with a surprised expression.

"That was sudden," Thomas replied.

"Aye." With no other comment, Perry went below.

Captain Janes came out a moment later, adjusting his coat over what looked like bed clothes. "What was all that about?"

"Acadia left, sir," Thomas replied.

"She did? Well ... yes, of course. I do hope she enjoyed herself. Next time you meet, please tell her she's welcome here anytime, Tommy." Janes started back to his cabin.

"I will, sir." Thomas looked again to the waters. The ripples were gone, along with any trace of Marsha and Acadia's presence. Benson had mentioned practicing fencing without the dummy, so Thomas focused on that. He would soon forget about hasty departure of their guest.

The Burning Seas

Captain Marshall and the crew of the *Inferno* were once again docked at the port of South Cimmordia, having no success in the recovery of their lost treasure map.

Marshall paced inside of his cabin as the men returned from searching the town. Mr. Nyguard knocked at the door.

"Enter," Marshall replied.

"Boss, we've got some reports."

"Your findings?" Marshall asked.

"Indeed. Gretty found out that someone did in fact pick up the map at the drop," Nyguard began.

Marshall snarled. "Who was it?"

"A boy," Nyguard replied.

"A small kid ... I already know it was a small kid! Well? Tell me what you know!" Marshall ordered.

"Well, not exactly a small kid, sir, more of a teenager. Little older than the cabin boy's age, I believe," Nyguard added.

"Teenager, fine. Get on with your report!" Marshall growled.

"Yes, sir. We've got some reports that a vessel left in quite a rush shortly afterward."

"What kind of ship? You did catch the name, didn't you?"

"Had a white dove on a field of black and blue stripes on her flag, one man reported ... and a mermaid bust on the bow," Nyguard replied.

"White dove ... I have seen those colors before ... continue to gather info in the pubs, Leo. See if you can learn what their intentions might be. Leave me for now ... perhaps a single white dove will be our guide." Marshall turned away to think.

"Aye boss." Nyguard left to convey the orders. The captain contemplated their next move.

That evening after dinner, Thomas took the rowboat to the far side of Nemaris Island. He removed the signal shell Acadia had given him from his pocket. After pulling the boat ashore, he found a nice place to rest under some palm trees.

Facing away from the sunset, Thomas sat on the beach and blew through the shell and waited. Within a few minutes, Acadia arrived and joined him on the beach.

"Good evening," Thomas said.

"I apologize for having to leave so suddenly this morning. Marsha is my guardian, but sometimes she can be a bit over protective," Acadia replied.

"It's no trouble. I'm sure you were glad to get home."

She nodded. "Yes, I was, and … this may sound odd, but I enjoyed my stay with your crew. They are very interesting."

"Why does that sound odd?" Thomas asked.

"Well, it is odd of me to say it," Acadia answered.

"Perhaps it's because of your nature." He shrugged. "Traditionally, merfolk and humans have not had much contact."

Acadia nodded. "Yes, I have been told the same. You once mentioned myths. What are they?"

"Myths are a way to attempt to explain the unexplainable. Where should I start?"

She swished her tail, sending little waves away from shore. "Would the question of my existence be good?"

Thomas laughed. "Yes, that would. Some of the men were … afraid of you, because they often associate the appearance of mercreatures with misfortune and danger."

"You mean how Harvey acted, yes?" She smiled brightly. "Perhaps he will come around, once he gets to know me."

He couldn't help smiling in response to her positive attitude. "Yes … but let's not talk about Mr. Jennings. The truth is, sailors are away at sea for very long periods of time, sometimes for more than a year. They have little contact with their friends and family, which includes attention from girls, ladies, social events. They long for companionship in a way their shipmates simply cannot provide."

"A female companion?"

"Correct. The myth says that when a sailor sees a mermaid on the rocks, even if she was doing something as trivial as combing her hair or watching the waves roll by, he would have a few reactions." He ticked them off on one hand. "First, he'd probably deny his visions. Second he'd reassure himself that he didn't see what he thought he did. Should he continue longing for her affection, he would search the seas in hope of finding the maiden," Thomas explained.

Her eyes widened. "It would become an obsession of his, then?"

"Yes, exactly. The man would lose all interest in his shore affairs and be doomed to live his life at sea until the sea herself would welcome the sailor to her depths forever … that's how some of the stories go, I believe."

"Ah! So that explains his actions then."

Thomas nodded.

Tilting her head, she leaned toward him with a grin. "Answer me this, then. Why did you approach me?"

Thomas had to think hard for an answer to that question. Of course, he did not know she was a mermaid initially, but that was clearly not the answer Acadia was looking for.

Her eyebrows rose. "Can you answer?"

Thomas sighed, and shook his head. "No, I cannot."

"I'm glad you did," Acadia said with a smile.

Thomas reached over and held her hand.

Acadia returned Thomas's grasp. "I spoke with Cynthia today. She wishes to meet with Captain Janes tomorrow."

"Where should they meet?"

"South of the waterfall." She straightened with a thoughtful look. "Do you know who constructed that bridge? It's very well crafted."

While the compliment made Thomas proud, it wasn't as though he alone had done the work. "Mr. Roberts, Mr. Jennings, myself, and a few others. Thank you for the compliment."

"I'm certain I'll never use it, but it is very lovely to look upon," Acadia said.

"I don't know about that. You said Rhydar knew magic, didn't you?"

"He was a wizard, yes. He is no longer physically alive, though," Acadia replied.

"All I am saying is that you should not be so certain of your limitations. You see, I have learned never to make too many assumptions." He turned his gaze to the *Valiant*. "Especially since I joined this crew."

"For me to walk upon that bridge would be very far out of my reach, Thomas," Acadia said sadly.

Thomas nodded. "Perhaps, yes, but it's better to leave one's options open than close out all hope."

She perked up. "Yes, yes, maybe you're correct."

They sat together in silence for a few moments. The sun had come close to setting for the day, and Thomas knew that he should return to the ship while he still had sunlight.

"It's becoming rather late, Acadia...."

"Must you? Please, not yet." It was difficult to refuse her pretty pout.

"Why don't we ride together?"

Acadia smiled. "I would enjoy that."

They both climbed into the rowboat. With Acadia's guidance, they made their way back to the ship just as the moon came out. The sky had melted into a rich shade of purple as twilight set in.

"You should probably go home now," Thomas said.

"It is becoming more difficult to do so." She sighed. "But yes, you are correct. Cynthia asked me to tell you when your captain is ready by the waterfall, signal on the shell and we'll come as soon as we can."

"Certainly. I will see you tomorrow, then," Thomas said.

"Good eve, Thomas." Acadia leaned forward and kissed him.

"Good eve, Acadia," Thomas said, kissing her back. Under the starry sky, they shared a tender moment and then parted for the evening. Acadia splashed into the water. Thomas proceeded to raise the rowboat to the deck.

Not yet ready to sleep, Thomas spent an hour or two by the light of the lantern carving away at the stone pendant. It wouldn't be much longer before the little charm was complete.

Cimmordian Tea

$\mathcal{L}$ater that evening, Captain Marshall was conversing with Leo Nyguard as the men below finished sharing a bottle of rum before calling it a night.

"Can't those slobs keep it quiet when we're in port?" Marshall muttered as he looked over some charts.

"Aye, but they's almost done, boss," Nyguard replied.

Marshall sipped from his cup of tea. "For their sake, let's hope so. My memory's hazy, Leo. That ship's last known course was west to northwest, was it not?"

"Aye it was, from what our sources reported."

"And were the Nemaris Islands west to south west of here?"

"Aye, I reckon so. You don't think they's got the gall to go there, do ye?" Nyguard asked.

"No, even if they understood the writing on the map they wouldn't know where to find the islands," Marshall began.

"Sir, are you familiar with the colors of that ship? The white dove?"

Marshall pounded his fist against the already splintered table. "Dammit, Leo! I can't be called upon to remember every single ship I've attacked!"

Nyguard turned away. "Sorry, boss."

Marshall began to think. "There was one encounter that stands out, however ... hmm. Who's the captain of the *Valiant*?"

"*Valiant*, boss? I do not remember. Janes, perhaps?" Nyguard replied.

"*The* Christopher Janes? Of all people, he would have the gall for such a thing. And he would know how to read the map ... confound it!" Marshall cried. He stopped himself from pounding his fist on the table a second time. Due to the many times that Marshall himself had damaged the table, he recognized that another pound onto the splintered boards would surely cut his hand.

"Boss, should we replace that table? After all the times we've ... I've ... used a knife on it?" Nyguard asked nervously. Of course he knew it was his captain's doing, but he wasn't going to accuse Marshall of that.

"Stick to the subject!" Marshall growled.

Nyguard smiled nervously. "Right, boss! Er ... this Captain Janes ... he wouldn't know how to read that map, would he?" Nyguard asked nervously.

"He would," Marshall said coldly, dimming the lantern.

Nyguard nodded. "What are your orders for the crew, boss?"

Marshall stood up and paced slowly toward his bed. "All this business with the map must be terrible for my health. Perhaps I should rest, Leo. Take your leave, and inform the men that we sail at dawn."

"And if they ask our destination?" Nyguard asked.

"It is none of their business, Nyguard." Marshall removed his shirt.

"I would like to know, boss," Nyguard asked.

Marshall kneeled away from Nyguard to unbuckle his boots, but before straightening up gave his response.

"Nemaris Isles."

Nyguard nodded with a sigh and left.

Captain Marshall turned off his lanterns, one by one, and in the dim moonlight slipped under the covers and retired for the evening. At dawn's light, the *Inferno* was underway.

Demonic Dossier

When dawn broke over the Nemaris Islands, a mild rain shower was hiding just enough of the sun to make morning difficult to find. The smell of Mr. Ellis's muffins roused the crew, as the grain stock had been broken into at last.

Thomas soon met the other men in the mess hall. Captain Janes and Mr. Ward were discussing some methods to free the ship.

"I's just saying, captain, the sand must've been somewhat busted up by now. Can't we go down there with some long poles and try to free ourselves that way?" Ward asked.

"We have neither the manpower nor the equipment," Janes replied bluntly.

"Or what about the winds? Surely the sails have the power?" Ward suggested.

Janes shook his head. "Do you really think there's reason to leave in such haste? I've been waiting to explore that rocky island, myself. Just to prove some of them old sailors wrong about this place."

Thomas came by their table, getting Ward's attention. "Oh, morning there, Tommy. How are you today?"

"I'm well, sir. I don't intend to interrupt, but…" Thomas began.

With a hand, Janes indicated Thomas should sit. "You're a welcome distraction, Tommy."

"Well, Acadia and I talked again yesterday, and she asked me to let you know that Cynthia would like to meet with you."

"Miss Cynthia?" Recalling the name, Janes smiled. "Oh, yes, Miss Acadia mentioned she would arrange such a meeting later."

"Later today, in fact. I hope that is not too inconvenient?" Thomas asked.

The captain waved his concern away. "Nonsense. When did she wish to meet?"

"Midday."

"After our meal, then. Would you come as well?" Janes asked.

Cynthia had so many interesting things to say, Thomas had hoped he might accompany the captain and see her again. "Certainly, sir. I can do that."

"Excellent. We shall visit with her after the meal. Where did the lady wish to meet?" Janes asked.

"South of the bridge."

The captain nodded. "A fine place. I look forward to it, Thomas. I'm certain we'll have a valuable conversation."

"Aye," Ward said.

By now, the *Inferno* had passed Kalis Island and was well on its way to the Nemaris Islands. The time of their incursion into the tropical paradise was uncertain, but it was just a matter of when.

Following another of Mr. Ellis's meals, Captain Janes, Thomas, and Roberts rowed out to the beach and hiked inland through the forest. Crossing the bridge, they proceeded to the south side of the pool at the base of the waterfall.

"Tommy, is this where we were asked to meet?" Janes asked.

"Aye sir, right here. Shall I call for them?"

"Not quite yet...." He turned to Jared. "Roberts, you have the tea?"

"Yes sir, here it is." From a satchel, Jared pulled out a tin of tea, a teapot, a strainer and three mugs.

"Good." The captain indicated the stream. "Tommy, some water if you please."

Thomas took the pot and collected some water as Roberts used a tinderbox to get a small fire going. "Acadia claims that it is the purest water available."

The captain nodded, as he and Gritzol had already made several trips themselves for fresh water earlier that week.

Once a warm fire was burning and the tea water was warmed, Janes turned to Thomas. "Now then, Thomas. You may call your friends," Janes said, taking a seat on a nearby rock that, although hardly fit for a captain, was able to provide adequate support if not comfort.

Thomas raised the shell to his mouth, and blew a long, smooth breath.

The captain cupped an ear. "Perhaps you might try again, Tommy ... I didn't hear anything."

"It only sounds underwater, sir."

Jared huffed. "Seems to defeat the purpose of an instrument, says I."

"When do you expect them?" Janes asked.

As if on cue, Acadia swam up the creek and surfaced.

"Good afternoon, gentlemen." She was wearing a long, blue vest down to her waist, possibly a ceremonial gown for the occasion. However, it was too sheer to serve any purpose as clothing. She wore her silk bodice beneath. The ensemble was exotic, as the wet fabric clung to her body. Thomas fought the urge to blush.

Ever the gentleman, Captain Janes smiled at his guest and removed his hat. "Good afternoon, Miss Acadia. Is Miss Cynthia with you?"

"She will be here shortly. Did you bring the tea?" Acadia asked.

"It's here. Would you like some?"

Before Acadia could reply, Cynthia surfaced. She wore a vest similar to Acadia's, only hers was colored a subdued shade of violet.

"Please forgive my late arrival." Cynthia chose to sit on a flat rock just at the surface.

Thomas spoke in his best formal tones. "Cynthia, this is Captain Christopher Janes. Captain, I would like to introduce you to Cynthia." He also took a seat on a rock just by the water's edge. Acadia sat beside him on the shore.

"A pleasure to finally meet you," Janes said.

The mermaid inclined her head. "You as well. I understand you have many questions."

"I have been reading the journal of Captain Scyhathen, Miss Cynthia." The captain offered the ladies mugs of tea.

"May we talk on more casual terms, Captain? I do not wish for this to be too formal."

Janes nodded. "Of course. Shall I simply call you Cynthia, then?"

"I shall call you Christopher, as well?"

He smiled. "Please, just call me Chris."

"What shall we talk about, Chris?"

"In the journal, Scyhathen has written about a cave on Siren Island. He mentioned that he heard voices," Janes began.

"I am not entirely sure." She sipped her tea with an elegant poise that made it seem as though she'd drunk the beverage all her life. "But the voice must belong to the spirit of Rhydar. Although his body has left these islands, his spirit will forever live in this paradise."

"You have caught me at a disadvantage, Cynthia. I do not recall seeing the name Rhydar in my readings," Janes replied.

A delicate eyebrow quirked briefly as she paused. "I must apologize, Chris. I do not know what Scyhathen has written."

"Perhaps if we knew more about Rhydar, that would help," Thomas asked.

"Yes, of course!" Acadia replied.

Cynthia nodded. "A good idea, Thomas. Let me tell you about Rhydar, our generous host. He was a great storyteller ... and this is his story as it was told to me."

Rhydar was the one person who could create this land and invite its inhabitants to these shores. He was a wise and just wizard. He had been given the name Rhydar by his birth parents, whose names have been forgotten with the passage of history. There is little knowledge of his homeland, for he did not spend much of his life there. Rhydar was raised by a sailing crew, arriving shortly after his birth for reasons unknown to this day. It was believed that he was raised by a sailing man as a favor to his parents... but nobody is alive to verify that claim. Upon reaching the age of five, he began life as a cabin boy, similar to the DeLeuit boy. Magic came to him like tidal waves, as did teachings from his crew about things like reading and writing and arithmetic. Despite his young age, he learned at the pace of a scholar. He studied these subjects between his tasks for the crew. It was during this time he discovered his talents as a wizard, though he kept quiet about them. His life as a cabin boy was short lived, however, as a pirate ship soon attacked his shipmates.

These were among the most vile men to sail the seas in want of its treasures. Ruthless and with greed in their veins, these pirates showed no mercy.

As his crewmen were slashed through one by one, including his captain and the mate, Rhydar feared his young life would end. He quickly escaped to the ship's hold, hiding from the carnage that occurred above. Unfortunately, this was where the ship's only valuables were stored, and the greedy pirates soon found their way below.

One pirate kicked in the door to the hold. The light from the rogue's lantern flashed onto young Rhydar's face. He did not move an inch, frozen from fear.

The pirate called to his captain, unsure of what to do with the boy. They would either kill him and take the ship as their own, or keep him alive and enslave him. He was far too young to be trained to be a ruthless pirate, and for him that would be a fate worse than death.

The captain gave his order quickly. No prisoners.

Rhydar knew that his end would come unless he acted. As the pirate approached, he began chanting.

The pirate stopped, noticing Rhydar's mouth moving. Thinking that the boy was praying for mercy, he began laughing loudly at his victim's attempts to save his life.

But Rhydar was not praying. Continuing to chant, he placed the palm of his hand slowly on the wooden floor below, carefully touching all of his fingers to the floor as well. The boy then lifted his hand, and suddenly five of the six pirates shot upward. They flew through the upper decks, as if they were carried by a great updraft. They soared high into the air, eventually splashing into the water over a hundred feet away. The spell left gaping holes in both the decks of the ship and her sails. The remaining pirates fled for their lives, diving over the side and swimming in panic away from the child. They were not seen again.

Sensing that he was safe, Rhydar went through the ship to discover what remained on the silent decks above.

The musty crew quarters were thick with the breath of death. Severed limbs were strewn about the deck, surrounded by pools of blood. The pirate crew had been savage in their slaughter. The carnage was ornamented by an occasional stray limb. The bodies of the crew lay everywhere, their faces left in expressions of shock and surprise.

It was not entirely silent, as not all of the pirates had been disposed of. The pirate captain remained on board. Knocked aside by the flight of one of his own crewmen, he rose from the deck with the blood of his victims strewn across his face and skin.

The captain scowled at the boy. He had no idea how a mere child could've created such a wonder and reached for his black sword.

Rhydar quickly cast another spell, this one aimed directly at the evil captain. Sadly, the spell could not be completed. It was interrupted as the captain attempted to decapitate Rhydar. Although the sword never reached Rhydar's head, the spell reached the captain.

He flew back against the opposite wall, splintering the fortified hull of the ship. As the captain lay motionless, Rhydar fled from the scene.

The true purpose of the spell is unknown to this day, although it partially destroyed the captain. It is not known to what extent the spell affected him.

As the captain lay in a pool of his own blood, Rhydar climbed the deck. Using the rowboat that brought the six pirates aboard, he climbed aboard the pirate's galleon. He was fortunate to find it abandoned, with the sails at the ready.

Leaving his crippled ship behind, Rhydar cast a wind spell that brought him to these legendary islands.

The pirate ship brought him here, and it is here that it has remained. Her name is long forgotten. The men it carried are forever doomed to their deserved afterlife. The captain, however, was cursed beyond what the spell originally intended. All that remains known about him is that his ancestral name was Nepotherden.

"There has been much speculation among us as to whether Captain Nepotherden survived the spell that Rhydar cast. Rhydar made himself a home here, never wanting to leave the islands' enchanting atmosphere nor encountering any violent acts again. I was called to him years later, after he had already created many wonders. This waterfall we are now enjoying is one of them," Cynthia concluded.

"What happened to his ship?" Jared asked.

She sipped her tea. "I believe it later became his home on Siren Island. The day his mortal body died, it too vanished."

"I take it, then, that Rhydar lived the rest of his life on these islands?" Janes asked.

"To my understanding, yes."

Thomas found the prospect daunting. "That is a long time to be in one place with nothing to do but cast spells."

"He did more than that, Thomas," Acadia replied.

"Oh yes." Cynthia nodded. "Occasionally, he would use his magic to scan the sea for those who were like Captain Nepotherden, those men who would take what was not theirs. He would have them find their way to his islands, and then entertain himself with their efforts to escape. Some would occasionally escape him, but they would ever after steer clear of his islands. Those who didn't escape lost their ill-gotten treasures. Rhydar kept these items in a cave on Siren Island."

"The same cavern with the voice, perhaps?" Janes asked, remembering Scyhathen's journal entries.

"I do not know," Cynthia replied.

"Did he have a grudge against pirates in general?" Thomas asked

She nodded. "Perhaps because at the time of the attack, Rhydar's shipmates were the only companions he had ever known. I believe he would use his magic not only to keep himself occupied, but yes, also certainly to deter those who would gain wealth by immoral means."

"Yes ..." Janes sighed. "Greed is a depraved siren that man is prone to follow. Perhaps it is his greatest enemy."

"Excuse me, but this Rhydar ... he didn't take these treasures for his own?" Jared asked.

"Rhydar did it not to appease his own sense of wealth, but for punishment to those who chose such a life. I believe that the treasures became his incidentally. He had no interest or need for greater riches or power," Cynthia replied.

"I currently possess a map of these islands, and it leads, I assume, to that cave on Siren Island. Perhaps the treasure is larger than it is said to be?" Janes asked.

"If such is the case, Rhydar is guarding it not because he wants to own it, but so those who covet it cannot use it toward their own gain." Cynthia lifted a shoulder in a reserved shrug. "One day, he foretold, someone who is his relation will be allowed to enter his cavern and return each individual item to its rightful owner, so he or she may live as many days as he wishes in this paradise."

"But you said his ancestry is unknown," Thomas said.

She turned to Thomas. "Which is why Rhydar's spirit remains. If such a person exists, he or she will have to find his or her way here. Such a rare occurrence may not happen until we ourselves are gone from this world."

"Cynthia, you are very wise," Jared said.

Her gaze returned to the captain. "I have lived much of my life with Rhydar and remember it because I was there. These are merely events that occurred long ago."

Janes thought a moment, placing his hand across his chin. "What do you suppose would happen if this Nepotherden person were still alive?"

"Nobody could live that long ... right?" Thomas asked.

Acadia shook her head. "Wizards, like mermaids, share a longer lifespan than ordinary humans. But Nepotherden would have been cursed."

Cynthia nodded. "To believe Nepotherden alive, even remotely, is a possibility I shudder to even consider. Such a being left in that state would surely wish to take retribution for its misfortune. It would wander the earth in search of its creator."

"Rhydar," Janes said.

"Undoubtedly," Cynthia replied.

Thomas recalled the voice that day on the beach near his home, that it spoke of its creator. "You mentioned a Captain Epoth earlier. What does he have to do with all this?"

"Epoth is a nemesis of Scyhathen, not of Rhydar. If there is any connection, I do not know of it," Cynthia replied.

Thomas nodded his head slightly.

Turning her gaze westward, Cynthia finished her tea. "Chris, I feel our time together has been most beneficial, but sometimes stories are best served in small doses. I do hope that I have done my best to answer your questions."

"Indeed you have. I hope to learn more by continuing to read the entries in Scyhathen's journal. Perhaps there is a conclusion to this that is written between the pages, rather than what is at the surface," Janes replied.

A rare smile passed across Cynthia's lips. "Yes, I do hope you are correct."

"Will you meet with me later, Thomas?" Acadia asked.

"If you wish, certainly," Thomas replied.

It was then the third sister, Marsha, surfaced between Cynthia and Acadia. She wasn't as formal as her companions.

"So here you are! I have been wondering where everyone went," she exclaimed.

"Is everything well, Marsha?" Cynthia asked.

"I do not believe we've met, my dear," Janes said.

"My apologies, Captain. Marsha, this is Captain Christopher Janes. Chris, this is Marsha," Cynthia replied.

"I should also introduce my men, Jared Roberts and Thomas DeLeuit," Janes said.

"Yes, yes, I've heard about all of you. So nice to meet at last!" Marsha smiled.

"Now I have met all of you, if I am correct," Janes said.

"All of us that are currently here, yes." Marsha nodded.

"If I may, where do you fit in the group, Marsha?" Thomas asked.

"I was called here by Rhydar several years before Acadia arrived. However, I must admit, I am not often in the center of things." She gave a little pout.

"Sure you are, Marsha," Acadia replied.

"Like when?" Marsha asked.

Acadia thought a moment, before smiling playfully. "Okay, you're right. You're never in the middle of anything."

Cynthia sighed. "Please, let's stop. I thank you for our time together, Chris."

"You as well. Good eve," Janes said.

"Come along, Acadia," Marsha said. Cynthia returned her mug then ducked under and left.

Acadia handed her mug to Thomas. "Use the shell to call me later, please." She and Marsha also dove under and swam back to the bay.

Jared poured the remaining tea over the fire. "That Rhydar sure had a tragic upbringing. I might feel the same way about those darn pirates."

Putting on his hat, the captain stood. "Come on, boys. If we hurry, Ellis'll have supper prepared." He took his mug of tea along, leaving Jared to carry the rest.

"Come along, Tommy," Jared said, as Thomas had lagged behind a moment. It was all too mysterious for him. The conversation had left him with more questions than before.

The meal that evening came late. Thomas was able to spend time carving Acadia's charm before supper. After the meal concluded, Thomas took the signal shell with him and climbed into the rowboat. He left for the bay on the southern shore of Nemaris Island. He found a place to sit on the beach before calling Acadia.

She arrived a few moments later.

Acadia settled herself in the sand, as the surf gently splashed onto her tailfin. "Did you find our conversation interesting?"

Thomas nodded. "Quite interesting, yes. I never imagined Rhydar had such a tragic childhood."

"Although I remember very little of Rhydar, there is one thing I remember him telling me. He said that if I ever saw a ship with pirate's colors, to never let my guard down, nor succumb to their wishes. He also reminded me that sometimes it was better to flee than fight," Acadia explained.

"Yes, those are true words. Did he mention whether succumbing to their wishes meant letting your guard down?" Thomas asked.

"No, I do not believe so. I am certain he knew there is a fine line between such things," Acadia replied.

Thomas nodded again, watching the purple sky grow darker. He could see the remaining semicircle of the sun as it softly sank beneath the horizon.

"What lies beyond these islands, Thomas?"

"Mostly more ocean. Eventually there is a continent."

"Out there?" Acadia pointed northeast.

"Something like that," Thomas replied.

"I would like to go exploring sometime, to see what there is out there." Her cheerful tone turned slightly downcast. "But Cynthia and Marsha tell me it is far too dangerous."

"There is some truth to their warnings. Regarding the myths I spoke of, there are those who would enjoy putting a mermaid on exhibition."

She drew back slightly. "What do you mean by that?"

"Travel around the land on display and have people pay money to see." He shook his head, remembering his uncle's story of a snow bear he'd once seen displayed in a little cage for a copper a view. "A terrible practice and degrading to those subjected to it."

"Are you saying there are people ashore who will humiliate someone for profit?" Her eyes widened.

"Sadly, such acts have occurred. I have been fortunate enough not to witness it myself, although I have heard stories."

"Of mermaids?" Acadia asked, frightened.

"No, people with bad scars, or a disfigured face, that sort of thing," Thomas explained.

"I weep for those troubled souls." Acadia's look was so sad, it was easy to take her statement literally.

Wanting to steer the subject to calmer waters, Thomas forced a smile. "Worry not. Some are lucky and able to escape while they have some humanity left. Others become stronger from the experience and defeat their captors, leaving them to recover from their own curses."

Acadia smiled in return. "That is good to hear."

Thomas figured some probably had just the opposite occur, but he knew enough not to pursue that subject, since that would clearly upset Acadia.

"All those people on land...." She let a handful of sand sift through her fingers. "What do they do all day?"

"Most have a trade of some sort. Some men work the lands; others take from it. The elderly care for the young, and make goods for others to enjoy. My mother bakes bread and other baked goods for the market. She also rents a spare room for travelers seeking shelter," Thomas explained.

"She looks out for her neighbors," Acadia said.

"That's right," Thomas said.

"Why does she do it?" Acadia asked.

"Because it makes her feel like she is doing what she can to make a difference in this world," Thomas replied.

Acadia looked toward the stars a moment.

"Once my Uncle Ian told me a story, when I was very young. It was about an elderly woman who would always go to town and sweep any rubbish away from the center of the marketplace," Thomas began.

"What was this old woman like?" Acadia asked.

"She had reached an age where she could no longer tend to an oven, nor toil in a garden for vegetables. Her children had grown children of their own, and she had been widowed for some time," Thomas replied.

"But why did she sweep the marketplace?" Acadia asked.

"She did not do it for money, or for any one person. Sometimes careless people would drop their garbage, or a piece of food they could not finish, or even because they no longer wanted what they carried. These items, if let to collect, would make the market a place nobody would want to visit. She took it upon herself to keep the area presentable," Thomas explained.

"Because she wanted to feel like she was still useful?" Acadia asked.

Thomas nodded. "Exactly. It made her feel good to have a purpose. She continued to sweep the marketplace until she could no longer. In time, she returned to the earth that she toiled to keep beautiful all of her days."

"What a lovely storyteller your Uncle Ian must be. Do you see him often?" Acadia asked.

"No, my mother lives far from her brothers, and it is a long journey for visiting. He worked as a messenger for the nation of Xavier." He smiled thinking of the last time he'd seen his uncle. "When he came back from a trip, there were always stories to hear."

"I wish I knew more of my family, as you do." She drooped a little. "Sometimes I wonder about my real family ... who my siblings are, where they live, and what they are doing."

"I could not imagine what that would be like," Thomas said.

Straightening, she smiled again. "Perhaps someday I will ask Rhydar for help and learn about my own past."

"His spirit resides in that cave, then?" Thomas asked.

Nodding, she swished her tail absently in the waves. "That is what I believe, yes."

"Perhaps a day will come when you can ask such a question," Thomas said.

"I do hope you are correct." She yawned softly.

"You are tired, I see." Thomas didn't understand why he found her yawns so charming.

"As you say, it has been a long and interesting day."

"Was there anything else you wished to discuss?"

She shook her head and smiled. "I enjoy your stories, Thomas. They are comforting."

"It is enjoyable to share them with you, Acadia. For you see, if stories are not shared with anyone, they lose their meaning," Thomas replied.

"Shall I guide you to the ship?" Acadia asked.

"It is up to you. I can see well enough, if you are tired."

She yawned again. "Are you sure?"

"Yes, you go ahead. I shall see you tomorrow."

"As you wish, then. Good night, Thomas. Rest well tonight." She slowly inched her way back to the surf.

"You as well, Acadia. If you see Cynthia again, thank her again for her time today."

"I will." Entering the surf, she started to swim away but stopped to blow Thomas a kiss, which he caught. Then, Acadia dove under and returned to her grotto. The faint moonlight lit Thomas's way back to the *Valiant*.

He paused his rowing for a moment as he saw a glint of green light, as well as a soft splash from the nearby surf. Without another thought, he returned to the ship.

Young Love

*M*orning arrived quickly. Before Thomas could decide how best to spend his day, Benson and Jennings chose for him. They had arranged a fencing test and had used up most of the cargo area to do so.

"Lunge, withdraw, leap, guard, parry, feint, thrust, lunge, thrust, parry, feint, guard, stand ready, and present blade," Benson said, listing the commands as Thomas executed them. Jennings held a wooden shield, which was Thomas's target.

"How was that?" Thomas asked, lowering the point.

"You are getting pretty good, boy. Pretty good indeed," Benson replied.

"Are you ready for your test now, Tommy?" Mr. Jennings asked as Captain Janes stepped into the cargo room.

"Good morning, sir," Thomas said as the captain stood at the door, wearing his sword.

"Tommy," Janes replied.

"I asked if you are ready for your test?" Jennings asked again.

He became focused and raised his sword. "Uh, yes sir, I am ready." Jennings readied his rapier, and raised his hand.

"Prepare yourself," Jennings said, aiming his sword, although both swords were tipped with cork, so as to prevent any serious injury.

Thomas did his best to ward off the strikes that Jennings made, trying to sneak in his own strikes as well. It did not take long, however, for Thomas to lose the point to Jennings.

"Point to Jennings," Benson said, and the two resumed.

"Remember, anticipate, and act," Jennings suggested.

This time, however, Thomas earned a point shortly into the combat.

"Point to DeLeuit," Benson said. They again drew blades. Their fencing lasted a minute or two before Thomas earned a second point against Jennings.

"Point to DeLeuit. Match, Tommy," Benson said.

Jennings reached out and shook hands with Thomas. "Aye lad, you are getting much better indeed," Jennings replied, as he removed the cork and sheathed his sword.

"Thank you, gentlemen," Thomas said.

"Not so fast. Perhaps on your next test, you will take on the master swordsman aboard," Janes said.

"Well … that'd be quite a feat, sir," Thomas replied.

"Aye, he has some way to go, Cap'n," Benson replied.

"I'm certain you'll have him ready soon, gentlemen." Janes clapped his hands and gave an unsympathetic grin. "Mr. Ward needs ye for fishing duty, boys."

"Aye sir," the two men said, returning their weapons to the rack and going above deck.

"Do you need me for anything, sir?" Thomas asked.

"Just one thing, Tommy. See that old apple there?" Janes asked.

"Yes sir?" Thomas asked.

Janes removed his silver saber from its elaborate leather sheath. On the blade were elegant engravings in a sweeping curve. It was a spectacular blade, indeed.

"Toss that apple into the air, please." Janes readied his sword. Thomas tossed the apple upward with plenty of lift, and Janes slashed it into two clean pieces before it even reached the top of its arc. Each half smashed into the floor, and a sweet smell filled the room.

"How is that, eh?" Janes asked.

"Very impressive, sir … but aren't you worried about your blade becoming tarnished?" Thomas asked.

Janes smiled. "On the contrary, it is a blade of silver alloy and steel composite. One of the finest blades the blacksmiths of Mt. Faate have ever crafted. It was a gift from the young Princess of Cimmordia and is in no danger of growing dull, Tommy."

Thomas nodded. "It is a fantastic weapon, sir."

Janes wiped the rotten apple remnants from the blade. "Do not be too wary of our match, Tommy. I shall use a corked rapier, just like you."

"I am not certain if I should look forward to it or be wary, sir," Thomas replied.

"I think ye'll do fine, Tommy." Janes sheathed his sword and headed above deck. Thomas followed.

"What have you for today, Tommy?" Janes asked, as he looked across the sea.

"Not certain, sir. I do have plans to meet with Acadia, but not until later," Thomas replied.

"Of course." Cocking his head, he have the boy a kindly look. "If it is not improper of me to ask, do you possess feelings for her?"

Thomas did not respond immediately, rather, he joined Janes in his gaze across the sea. It took him a few moments to collect his thoughts into a response. "Actually, sir, I am not certain."

A second moment of silence passed between the men.

"Let me tell ye something, lad. When I was a young man not much older than you, a cabin boy myself, the ship I served once spent a week's time at a small town. There I met a young woman. We may both have been the same age. She was a lovely young lass, something like your friend there." The captain had a glimmer in his eye. "As it was a small town, most of the men she would've liked to keep an eye on either were too old or did farm work for money. Since I had been such a friend to her, she kept an eye on me, and we spent some time together," Janes began.

"What was her name?" Thomas asked.

"Gretta. We shared a picnic about halfway through our time together, and we connected. That entire week, we enjoyed each other's company … ahh, young love," Janes said, trailing off.

"What happened?" Thomas asked.

"Well, let me tell ye. The ship had to leave at the end of that week, and I promised Gretta that when I returned, we'd spend more time together, maybe even get married and spend our lives together. She gave me a rose petal to remember her by—which I still have, mind you—and that was the way it ended," Janes concluded.

"Did you ever make it back?" Thomas asked.

Janes nodded. "Yes, many years later. However, both of us had long since grown up, and she had already found a husband and started a family. She did name her oldest boy Christopher, after me. She remembered me well, and was glad to see me, although I could tell she was a little heartbroken that I had never returned for her."

"What a sad story."

"Aye, I suppose it is." The captain sighed. "Now some men will tell ye that this can't be, Tommy … but I'm not one of them."

"Sir? I don't understand," Thomas said.

"Because of Acadia being a mermaid and all … but a friend is a friend, don't you agree?" he asked.

"Yes, I do sir," Thomas replied.

"Good, that is a gentlemanly attitude to have. Now that story about Gretta may have cost me a friend, but I can see everything in Acadia that I saw in Gretta. And you … Tommy, I believe you can do anything. But the true moral of the story be this, lad. If there's something special taking place, and it has potential for something even more special, catch it and let it grow … and let life take its own course," Janes explained.

"I will, sir," Thomas replied.

Janes waved the boy off. "Now run along and spend your day wisely, Tommy."

"Thanks, sir," Thomas said. He returned below deck to work on Acadia's necklace.

Janes chuckled to himself softly. "Ahh yes … young love indeed."

While Thomas was spending his afternoon perfecting and polishing the nearly complete necklace, the *Inferno* continued its approach to the islands.

"What's our bearing, Gretty?" Marshall asked, standing behind him atop the navigation deck.

Gretty, who was manning the wheel, checked the compass on the stand and gave his reply. "Bearing west to southwest, Cap'n," he said.

"Full sail!" Marshall called.

"Aye Cap'n," the men muttered. They climbed the masts and adjusted the sails. The ship was already at full sail, but they knew that Marshall wanted the maximum speed possible. So, they went through the motions of adjusting the sails, even though they could adjust them no further.

The day passed rather uneventfully with the palm trees swayed in the light breeze coming off of the sea. It was far too nice of a day to remain secluded in his cabin, and Thomas went to the bow of the *Valiant*. He leaned against the rail by the mermaid bust and chipped and carved the last markings into the polished stone.

After finishing the last circle of the wave-motion pattern on the bottom half of the rock, Thomas took the rowboat and headed past the southern shore of Nemaris Island onto Stuart Island, where he could face the inner bay of the islands. There, leaning against a slightly bent palm tree, he continued to carve the top half of the rock. This would be the last carving to do before threading it into a necklace.

The tedious task of tapping the hammer onto the tiny rock continued long into the afternoon. Thomas was so focused that he never even noticed that he had company. Thomas held the stone up to look at it from a distance when Marsha spoke up.

"What are you working on?" she asked.

Thomas shook his head, distracted by her voice. "Oh my! Hello Marsha. You've startled me." He lowered his hand and the stone with it.

"It was not my intent to startle you. I just am relieved to know Acadia has a friend." She folded her arms around her tail as she relaxed next to him on the beach.

"Yes, a very special friend," Thomas replied.

"Did she ever tell you how Cynthia learned how to write and speak your language?" Marsha asked.

"No, she never spoke of it." He lightly tossed the rock in his palm. "From what I have read in Captain Scyhathen's journal, and from what Cynthia has told me, I believe the crew of the *Nemaris* taught her."

Marsha nodded. "You seem to learn quickly, Thomas. I was still young at that time, a child merely, so young that I never saw the men. I did, however, take lessons from Cynthia shortly after they departed."

"Departed?" That got his full attention. "So, they left these islands, and did not die here?"

"Cynthia remembers better than I." She had a far-off look for a moment. "But they did indeed leave with their vessel intact."

There was a part of the story no one had covered to Thomas's satisfaction. Perhaps Marsha knew more. "What was Onell's place in all of this? I am certain he was around back then, yes?"

"Yes, I am slightly younger than him. He spent most of his time watching for trouble around Rhydar's island, the one now called Siren Island," Marsha explained.

"I wonder what his feelings were after Rhydar's death," Thomas asked.

"I do not know. My guess would be that his feelings were no different from the rest of us, grief and despair." Her brow creased. "Males seem to never be able to share such feelings around others."

"Yes, human males act similarly to such situations. Perhaps he felt he failed Rhydar, even though it was caused only by old age," Thomas suggested.

"Old age, perhaps. It is difficult to judge on that basis alone, however," Marsha replied.

Thomas's eyes lit up. "What do you mean by that?"

"He never appeared old to our young eyes. I remember him walking the shore with a cane, but beyond that, no signs. No wrinkles, no crackling voice, not even a sore bone in his body." She shrugged. "Except for his gray hair and white beard, nothing."

"Physically fit, then," Thomas said.

"Yes, quite! Rhydar's death came as a complete shock to us. Cynthia spoke with him just before we last saw him enter his house. She has not shared their conversation with us." She casually made patterns in the sand with her fingers.

"Tell me, do you think Acadia will like this?" He handed Marsha the nearly completed pendant.

Marsha took a long look at the pendant, turning it over and over, following the carefully chiseled lines that Thomas had painstakingly carved.

"It is an amazing piece of art, Thomas. I did not know Acadia had an interest in such things," Marsha replied.

"We were talking once when she mentioned these stones, and asked what my hobbies were. I thought it would be good to make her a gift, since she gave me this shell to call her with." Thomas removed it from his pocket so that Marsha could see.

"I am quite confident that she'll appreciate such a well-crafted gift." With a smile, she returned the stone to Thomas's hand.

"I hope so. I've enjoyed our conversation together, Marsha. You seem to have a lot of knowledge," Thomas said.

"Thank you." She smiled again. "You see, I have never actually spoken to a human like yourself. You have some interesting thoughts on our situation as well. I am pleased Acadia has befriended you."

"I should finish this stone … I was hoping to give it to her later tonight. I even brought this thread for it." He took a durable black string from his belt pouch.

Marsha nodded her head. "I think I will go home for now, then. Unless you enjoy my company, as well?"

"Of course! But, if you feel you should go home, I won't keep you," Thomas said.

Marsha looked away. "I am certain you know that the three of us act like sisters together. I am always fearful of Acadia's safety, but now that I have met you…." She returned her gaze to Thomas. "I do not believe that a problem anymore."

He smiled. "Thank you, I'm pleased to hear that."

Marsha smiled back, and then slowly entered the water. As she reached the deeper part of the bay, she turned back. "Good day, Thomas."

"Good day," Thomas replied. He turned to work on the finishing touches on his necklace. A few more chiseled lines and the pendant would be complete.

A Dolphin's Lament

*B*ack aboard the *Valiant*, Captain Janes and the first mate were meeting with the rest of the crew.

"Good work, lads. We've got enough food for a few more days yet," Ward said.

"Wonderful … and we've plenty of grain, as well?" Janes asked.

Ward nodded. "Can't explain how, we harvested all the wheat we could the other day. Yet, the patch is still there, ready for harvest again."

"Interesting…" Janes began. "It was odd enough the first time, with this being spring and all."

"A question, Cap'n?" Jennings asked.

"Yes, Harvey?" Janes asked.

"Are there any plans to either free the boat or explore that fourth island? I feel that if we're going to be here any longer, we should see what there is to see," Jennings said.

"Aye, and we're getting low on supplies, like soap and rum," Gritzol added.

"And I can't stand cooking seafood no more. I can't get the smell out of me cabin," Ellis gruffed.

"Agreed, we are outlasting our welcome here. Simply put, this place can't support us as we'd like it to," Ward replied.

"So what're we going to do about it?" Jennings asked worriedly.

Janes held up his hands. "Calm down, calm down. Harvey, your point is well taken. Agreed, we should explore while we're here, but from what Miss Acadia and Miss Cynthia have indicated, if any exploration is to be attempted we must take proper precautions."

"And about freeing the hull?" Jennings asked.

"We've known since we got here that getting out won't be easy," Benson said.

"Aye, true. A shame, really. It has been twenty-three days since our arrival … and I should say, it is a challenge to remember what day it is." Ward gave a rare sigh. "It is far too easy to lose track of time while staying in a paradise that seldom changes."

"Twenty-three days … that is no small feat, gentlemen. I commend you all for performing admirably during these past few weeks," Janes said.

Ward concurred. "But, with the shifting tides, one would like to believe the hull has moved some."

"What about those two fishy girls? Can they help us, since they're here?" Lewinston asked.

"Here we go with the mythical talk again," Jennings said.

"Harvey, your suspicions notwithstanding, the information we have gathered from the two ladies has been quite valuable." He smiled. "Not to mention rather inspiring."

"Indeed. But asking them for our own gain wouldn't be proper. Rather, it would need to be our final resort," Ward added.

"Aye," Perry said, agreeing with his superiors.

"Hmph," Jennings muttered, sticking strongly to his own opinions.

"Well, perhaps we should explore the isle?" Jared sounded as though the thought of Siren Island had been on his mind a while. "After all, both girls couldn't give us straight answers, as I'm confident they themselves haven't gone there."

"Quite true," Benson replied.

"So we go ashore Siren Island then?" Gritzol asked.

"Tomorrow morning. Any volunteers?" Ward spoke up.

Ellis returned his attention to the galley. "Got too much to clean, Cap'n. Nobody else'll wrestle the rats."

Perry crossed his arms, nodding. "Captain, I will go."

Gritzol pulled Jennings aside. "Harvey and I are up for fruit duty."

Lewinston jumped to their side. "And I got fishing to do."

Benson did not commit either way. He instead reached for his book.

Jared grumbled. "There's nothing there that scares me. You fellas aren't afraid of demons still, are ye?"

"Bold words from a man who carries a fife instead of a sword say I," Lewinston muttered.

Janes stamped his foot. "Enough! The lure of demons is a valid note of concern, but leaving the ship unattended would be worse. Seriam, Perry,

Roland, Jared, and myself will go. The rest of you men hold the ship. Of course, we'll need Thomas as well. But I refuse to listen to any more talk of curses and demons!"

The men all responded with an attentive stance. "Aye sir!"

Janes then left the room, followed closely by Ward. "Perhaps there are demons on this ship, Seriam ... I'm not one to bark orders like a savage cutthroat."

"Rather on the ship than the isles, Chris. At least then we know what they look like," Ward replied.

It was nearing late evening. Thomas had enjoyed a late lunch, missing Ellis's meal and fixing a sandwich on his own from leftovers. Choosing to continue his work on the northern shore of Stuart Island, he was too far along with the moonstone pendant to stop. Finally, with a few carefully placed taps from the chisel, he marked his initials on the bottom of the pendant, "T.A.D."

He held the pendant up to his eye and inspected all his markings, pleased with his product. Then, after moistening some string in his mouth so it would pass through the hole easier, he slowly threaded the black string through the pendant, tying a knot on both sides to position the pendant at the middle. Taking a pair of small clasps he had found in his trunk, he tied the ends of the string to them, and snapped the pendant together, completing the circle that would eventually adorn Acadia's neck.

All that remained was to see how well he's guessed the length. Using the signal shell that hung around his own neck, Thomas called for Acadia. With one long breath, he called just as he had been instructed to. Quickly, he wrapped the pendant in a small handkerchief and placed it inside his vest to ensure the gift would be a surprise. Acadia arrived several moments later. She surfaced and gave Thomas a wave as she approached and joined him on the beach. There was a large smile on her face when she sat next to him.

"I can tell you are in a good mood," Thomas said.

"Have I told you that you brighten my day, Thomas?" Acadia asked.

The sentiment caused his cheeks to warm. "No, I do not believe so."

"Well, you do. And today is no different." She leaned against the large rock the two of them shared. "How are you? Is everything well on board?"

"Actually, I've spent most of my day here, watching the wildlife and waves pass me by," Thomas said.

She nodded, appreciating the view. "The scenery is very soothing, yes?"

"Very much so. But when you're here with me, nothing else compares." He rested his hand next to hers.

"I must know why you are so good to me," Acadia asked.

"If only I could tell you in words...." He felt too satisfied as he grinned about his accomplishment, so he looked away and laughed. "But since that is impossible, I shall do the next best thing. Will you join me in the rowboat?"

"Of course, but where are we going?"

"Worry not, is it near. It's a surprise." After helping Acadia into the rowboat, he pushed off from the beach and jumped in, taking the oars and rowing into the center of the bay. He positioned the boat along the north and south axis, so they could both look westward into the fading sunset.

"I am afraid I do not understand, Thomas. What is so special in the center of the bay?" Acadia asked. The rowboat rotated slowly in the gentle currents.

"Look there for a moment, into the sunset." As she did, Thomas reached into his vest pocket for the pendant.

"It is a lovely sunset, but I am curious as to what is so special about this sunset over any other one, Thomas." When she looked back at him for an explanation, she saw the pendant in the palm of his hand.

"Oh...." she began, gazing at the pendant's carved moon image. She tilted her head slightly to look at it from as many angles as she could before forcing herself to blink.

"I would much rather have presented this to you at the evening moon, but since we are here now I want you to have it." Thomas held it up by the string.

"You mean ... you did all this ... for me?"

"That is, if you would like to have it," Thomas said.

"It is so ... captivating ... please, may I?" She took the pendant into her hand and rubbed her thumb along the smooth face, around the moon itself, and along the wavy pattern on the bottom before lifting it up by the string. "Lovely, and the rock is very smooth."

"Here, let me help you." Thomas unlatched the string before reaching around her neck as Acadia held her hair aside.

Just before he could secure the clasp, Acadia heard a faint noise. She made an expression to match her sudden fear.

"What is it? Is something the matter?" Thomas lowered the pendant as she looked around.

"I imagined I heard something, something very serious. A voice of the sea crying out in terror...." She looked around anxiously as though seeking the source of the sound. "I cannot explain it, but it happened just now. I must speak with Cynthia." She climbed out of the boat and dove into the water.

"Wait! I want to help!" Thomas called, but she was gone. He held the pendant between his hands as the ripples vanished from the surface. Stricken, he pocketed the necklace and began rowing as quickly as he could toward the Cove. Even with the growing darkness, he felt there was no other alternative.

"Blasted marine life, getting caught up in the wake and breakin' our ships ... if they didn't get in our way we'd be much faster along," Nicks muttered as the *Inferno* passed a dolphin that had been harpooned through the torso.

"Nicks! What're you doing throwing them harpoons away?" Marshall bellowed.

"Dolphins getting in our way, boss! Them slimy creatures," he exclaimed.

"Aye then. As long as they're in the way," Marshall replied.

"Fallah! What's on yer sight?" Mr. Nyguard called.

"Not certain, skip, but I's see something in the way of the sunset," Fallah replied.

"Something in the way? Lemme see that there spyglass." Marshall snatched it and glanced toward the final rays of the sun. Along the water, there was something just distant enough to be an island. "That's an island, you fool!"

"Land ho! All hands, land ho!" Gretty called from the riggings. He had seen the island also, but waited until Marshall had seen it first to say so.

"Orders, Cap'n?" Nyguard asked.

Marshall glared confidently toward the islands. "We go within spy-glass range, and then anchor. Keep to the southeast corners, lest we spot any ships. A shame that I was unable to read the map before we arrived here...."

"What about Janes, sir?" Nyguard asked.

"If Janes is here, we shall find him in the morning whilst they be groggy!"

"Aye boss," Nyguard replied. The *Inferno* slowed before approaching the Nemaris Islands.

"As long as my name is Archibald L. Marshall, I will find you, Janes... your final freedoms begin now."

Thomas arrived at the Cove and called to Acadia.

"Acadia! Please, tell me what you are feeling! I don't understand this." But his only response was his own voice echoing endlessly upon the rocky cliffs.

He tied the rowboat to a shallow rock. Acting frantically, he removed his vest and dived into the deep water, searching for Acadia. With only a few remnants of sunset left, he held his breath tightly and again went deeper into the waters.

The water was clear, but Thomas was hampered by the many over-hangs and tall plants that blocked his way toward the bottom. It was an unfamiliar environment in the evening light, and he had difficulty finding his way.

He was forced to return to the surface for air. A deep breath later, he began his second dive, descending further into the waters. This time, he found himself navigating through a number of tall sea plants. Hoping to find Acadia swimming toward him, Thomas instead could only see more rocks and plants below, the bottom far beyond the light. Water pressure continued to tighten its grip upon his lungs and ears as he swam ever deeper, his determination unwavering. Where had she gone so quickly?

The bottom came into sight, far below. A thin overhang revealed a trio of openings on either side of the strait ... but they were too distant to ascertain their purpose, and his breath was gone. His lungs straining for air, Thomas was forced to the surface again. This time, his path was not as clear. Disoriented, he fought for an opening, again finding rocks bridged between each other. The maze of plants was impossible to navigate. Were those plants or reflections upon the surface? The light from above was fading fast.

Time was running out. Panicked, Thomas tried to follow the plants upward. In doing so, he only found another rock, hitting his head.

His eyesight fading, he saw a faint flash of blue scales in the clear water. Darkness embraced him quickly as he lost consciousness ....

"Thomas! Can you hear me?" Acadia's voice rang out in the darkness.

Thomas slowly opened his eyes. Salt water had clouded his vision, and everything was in a deep fog.

"Thomas! Please, speak to me!"

A sputter and a cough later, Thomas was finally able to clear the rest of the salt water out of his eyes. Opening his eyes fully, he looked up at Acadia, who was leaning over him across a flat rock in the Cove.

"Acadia ...." Thomas muttered.

"Why did you come for me? You would endanger your life for me, yet merely drown trying," Acadia replied. Thomas could hear her fear inside.

"I ... I wanted to help," he replied.

"Please, sit up, you should be well enough to do so," Acadia said with a smile. Thomas sat up. She guided him to turn and lean against a higher portion of rock.

"I apologize for leaving so suddenly. Unfortunately, I was unable to learn the true meaning of my vision, but it did involve a painful cry from a friendly neighbor." She shuddered. "Whatever caused it cannot be pleasant."

"A ... neighbor?" Thomas asked, still catching his breath.

"I heard a dolphin's cry ... one very near," Acadia said.

"A dolphin?" He had heard what she said, but was still disoriented.

Acadia looked toward the north. "I spoke with Cynthia, and she assured me that this may just be an isolated incident."

Relief began to steady Thomas's nerves. "I knew you wouldn't act so drastically unless you had a reason."

Acadia responded with a smile, although there was fear behind it. "Thank you for your concern. I could see the worry on her face, however. Cynthia's instructions were simple, to be cautious and alert of what might come."

"We should trust Cynthia in her decision. When I return, I will inform the captain," Thomas said.

"Yes, and we should not waste time … it will be dark soon. Come, I will guide you." With a hand from Thomas, she climbed into the rowboat.

Thomas would've liked to have given the pendant to her then, as the moon would've surely shined its light upon the Cove within the next hour. But knowing that a crisis could occur at any moment, he chose to leave it within his vest for the time being. He would wait until the moment arrived that she could wear it in safety, rather than fear.

In their weeks of isolation, Thomas had improved his rowing skills and made it back to the *Valiant* in short order. The tension eased as the sound of Jared's fife filled the evening. His music soared majestically into the evening sky.

"Is that Jared's fife I hear?" Acadia asked.

"It sure is. He does like playing it so," Thomas replied.

"I do not wish to interrupt him, but this is an important matter."

"Agreed." It impressed him that, even in a time of crisis she appreciated artistic beauty. He latched the rowboat onto the crane's hooks. "Do you wish to come aboard for the moment?"

"For the moment," she replied.

Thomas climbed to the deck and began operating the crane.

Seeing his shipmate's return, Jared slipped his fife in his belt and came over to help. "Hey Tommy! See anything special today? Ye missed supper."

"Jared, is the captain busy? Acadia and I need to talk to him."

Acadia came into view over the deck rail. "Good eve, Jared."

"Good evening, Miss Acadia." Jared doffed an imaginary hat.

"It's very important that we speak to him," Thomas said.

Jared hitched a thumb sternward. "Captain's in his quarters."

"I'll be right back." Thomas went to collect the captain.

Acadia reached out and touched Jared's hand as it steadied the boat. "I am not certain of this, Jared, but have I told you that I think your fife playing is exceptional?"

"You may have, but I always appreciate a compliment, milady." Jared managed to maintain a modest grin.

Thomas returned a moment later with Captain Janes and Mr. Ward.

The captain removed his hat. "Miss Acadia, I understand there's something you wish to tell me?"

Brows twisted with concern, Acadia sat up a little straighter as she conveyed her warning. "Christopher, earlier this evening I heard a cry of pain in the ocean. When I told Cynthia, she decided that I should tell you and your crew to be cautious and alert. She's concerned that something bad may happen."

"Something bad? Any idea what to watch out for?" Janes asked.

"I am not certain, Captain. I'm sorry," Acadia replied.

"Your information is more than helpful, my dear. In the event of some terrible thing happening, can we rely on your cooperation?" Janes asked.

Acadia nodded solemnly. "Of course, I will be with you Christopher. You may rely on us should it be necessary."

"I thank you in advance," Janes replied.

"Could it be more of them demons?" Ward asked.

Janes nodded begrudgingly. "Perhaps our demons are not on the ship… possibilities are nigh. If you'll excuse us, Miss Acadia, we must confer."

Janes started back to his cabin. Ward followed behind a moment later. They closed the door, and that was that.

"Guess that's it," Thomas replied.

Acadia was wearing her inquisitive expression. "What are demons?"

"Things that one should never trifle with," Thomas replied. He began lowering the boat so she could climb out.

"Thomas, if something does happen, please be safe."

"You as well. Good eve, Acadia … and thanks for what happened back there." Thomas wasn't sure he wanted the others to know about his frantic underwater search.

"You're welcome. Good eve, Thomas." Acadia kissed his cheek. With a smile, she slipped over the side into the welcoming surf. Thomas took the pendant from his pocket. After watching the moonlight catch on it for a moment, he returned it to his vest pocket and proceeded to stow away the boat and retire for the night.

Later that evening, Captain Janes and Mr. Ward discussed the next day's plan, but fatigue quickly set in. Soon both men agreed to make any decisions when the time arrived.

Before getting into bed, Janes scanned Scyhathen's journal for any clue that might aid their situation. Under the steady glow of an oil lamp, he discovered a noteworthy passage that related to the cave on Siren Island.

October 12th, 1582. This is indeed a dark day. The past week has been an eerie one, as we are under a cloud of fear and dread caused by the pirate Epoth. Once a day three of my best swordsmen patrol the beach ashore, and a constant eye is aloft in the crow's nest, but we are scanning for a being who appears to vanish with the tide. Among the crew, several of the men reported dreams of discovering treasure. All were quite certain they were delusions sent by Epoth to distract us from the real threats that are present here.

All is well aside, but the men are surely seeing with fear in their eyes. Personally, I still see the paradise that is these islands before us. Yet, I am beginning to share the same feelings as those of my men, that deeper and more terrible things can inhabit even the best of places. I have yet to speak with Mr. Mandalay on his latest encounter with Miss Cynthia, whom I have not heard reports of since Epoth's arrival.

Janes stopped a moment. Mandalay? He had heard that name before in previous messages, and also now recognized his distinct signature on the map that had been penned by the late navigator of the *Nemaris*. Paging backward through the journal, he came across an entry that caught his eye.

September 20th, 1582. An interesting event occurred earlier today. As Mr. Mandalay always carries a canvas among his things, much to Smitty's disapproval, he began a painting today that I'm certain has never been done before. I have seen his work, which is indeed of mark, although I consider it auxiliary to his duties as navigator and helmsman. I am certain that I do not mention it enough to him, so I will write it here with my other thoughts.

What makes this work more special than others is that it is the first actual portrait of a mythical creature of the sea, namely Miss Cynthia. I watched as she posed for him sitting upon a rock in the bay, looking off into the distance with a solemn expression. I am not certain if she had something on her mind or not, but I look forward to seeing the finished portrait.

"Hmmm ... Mandalay ... yes, he has done many artworks, but where else did I see his name before ...?" Janes returned to the previous entry.

October 12th, post addition. Mr. Banes and his party have made a discovery during their rounds ashore. A long red velvet scarf strewn with blood was found in the jungle, wrapped around a long pike that had been embedded in the dirt. From the incident in the cavern earlier, I wonder should it belong to Epoth himself, but such a conclusion is merely a speculation. Smitty calls it a sign of bloodshed to come. Although I respect his opinion, I am not ready to agree on the basis of such an obscure event. I have always worn clean coats, and a bloody scarf may be one way to symbolize terrible things to come. Perhaps those old tales of the sea truly are omens to fear. Nonetheless, If Mr. Epoth wishes to send me a message, may he do it honorably rather than by the way of a coward.

Janes read the last sentence again carefully, before removing his reading glasses and placing them on his nightstand. The book joined the glasses as he blew the lamp out and settled down to rest, unaware of what dangers would be lurking in the morning.

As dawn broke on the horizon, a second ship was spotted by her light off Siren Island. It was the flagship of the Sundrop Guild, the infamous galleon known as the *Inferno*. With her massive red sails and wide girth, she was far more intimidating than the *Valiant*. Without her sails furled and light out, the *Valiant* was not so noticeable, but as she was locked deep in the sands of the beach, she would be unable to avoid detection from an intensive search. Also, the crew would be unable to flee if confrontations were to arise.

"We've arrived at the Nemaris Islands, boss. What are your orders?" Mr. Nyguard asked.

"Any sign of other vessels?" Marshall ordered.

"None spotted, boss," Aramondo replied.

"Follow this shore south, but keep your distance from the rocks. And keep them sails trim ..." The captain gazed across the water with a hungry gleam in his eye. "They're here, I just know it. We'll sneak up on 'em quiet like. But remember, we could run out of ocean anytime."

"Aye boss." Gretty turned the rudder accordingly.

Morning aboard the *Valiant* remained pretty typical. Breakfast consisted of small biscuits made from the remnants of grain stowed below, which had become harder to keep due to the increasing number of insects infesting the cargo hold. Most other supplies aboard were unusable to them, including the ore, which would not be of use even if refined. Fortunately, the mysterious patch of wheat on shore continued producing grain for bread. Without grain supplies, they would eventually be hard pressed for proper nourishment.

Janes met with the crew and those who had agreed to investigate the cave ashore Siren Island. The volunteers consisted of Mr. Ward, Mr. Roberts, Mr. Benson, Mr. Perry, Captain Janes, and Thomas, who was drafted due to his knowledge of the history of the islands. The explorers were armed with their blades, including Mr. Perry's large Kah Lunaseif and Janes' silver sword. That left Gritzol, Jennings, Lewinston, and Ellis behind to hold the ship.

"There's one thing I don't quite see, Cap'n," Jennings spoke up.

The captain gave him a reassuring smile. "What's that, Harv?"

"Let's say your party goes to this cave and finds something. Or, we find nothing. Either way, we're still stranded here," Jennings said.

"I respect your opinion. Simply speaking, we'll have something to go home with. If there's nothing there, then there will just be more incentive to somehow dig the ship out of this rut," Janes replied.

"Sir, I'm beginning to think we'll get nowhere," Benson added.

"That may happen, too. I promise ye this much, lads. Should there be nothing there, we shall make preparations to free ourselves tonight. Mr. Ellis, how is the grain supply?" Janes asked.

"Picked a cadre of bugs out of the bag this morn', Cap'n," Ellis replied.

"How much grain would you say is left?" Ward asked.

"Dozen and a half pounds," he muttered, "but that won't go far with them insects pick'n at it."

"Maybe that patch of mature wheat ashore will be replenished again ... I'd like to know if that was Rhydar's ...." Janes began, trailing off.

"The jerky and the dried fruit?" Ward asked.

"Dried fruit's long gone. Jerky's doing okay, but like everything else it won't last forever," Ellis gruffed. "Shall I plan on preserving some of the filets?"

"Agreed, we may find ourselves suddenly without supplies. We shouldn't waste time. Mr. Gritzol." The captain turned and patted the man on the shoulder. "Since you'll be the senior crewman aboard, I leave you in command. Should you find anything to dig with, try to determine how long it might take to dig just enough sand to free up the keel."

"I'm no engineer, but I'll see what I can do, Cap'n," Gritzol replied.

"We'll do our best, Cap'n," Lewinston added.

"Aye," Jennings said.

"I trust you'll do what ye can. Come on lads, to the rowboat." Janes headed for a crane.

The crewmembers who were left gathered on the deck.

"Something tells me there's a better way," Jennings muttered.

"Yeah, like freeing the ship," Lewinston said.

"Well, there's a good southern wind today, but for all we know the sand may have shut us in for good," Gritzol said.

"There's another rowboat here. Why don't we take that to the mainland?" Ellis suggested.

"Never! That's suicide," Jennings cried.

"Agreed. Besides, the captain's orders were clear, aye? Let's see how much sand we'd have to move to do any good," Gritzol said.

"I's not liking this plan," Jennings said.

"What would you like?" Gritzol waved his arms as thought summoning the wind. "Some sort of magical power source to propel us to the mainland? Or maybe some renegade pirate force to kill us all, make our misery disappear? Come on, let's see what we can do."

The men moved down to the mess hall and began to strategize a possible way to free themselves from the tight hold of the beach.

As the morning grew on, the *Inferno* passed by the southern end of the channel leading to the Cove.

"Keep going around along that next island, Gretty. Can't fit through there—far too narrow," Mr. Nyguard said.

"Aye boss," Gretty replied. They sailed on along the south shore of Nemaris Island.

"Wait; go south along that smaller one next. It's small, but big enough to hide a ship behind," Marshall ordered.

"Aye boss," Gretty repeated, altering course. Now they followed the soft shores of Stuart Island to the south.

At about that same time, Janes and the rest of his crew arrived on the eastern shore of Siren Island. They found a spot where they could anchor and climb to the plateau.

"Tommy, where is your lady friend today?" Ward asked.

"Not certain, sir. Shall I call Acadia?" Thomas asked.

Janes waved the idea away. "No, Tommy, don't bother her now. We'll ask questions later."

Jared tied the boat to a suitable rock, and Perry dropped an iron anchor into the waters. The water at this landing was much shallower than the water around the rest of the island.

One by one, they climbed onto the shore and up the rocky walk to the grassy plateau above, taking along their swords and a lantern.

"Now then, where was that cave?" Janes asked.

Ward pointed. "According to the map, toward the west shore, if I recall."

"Aye," Benson said.

"Let us be off, then." Janes directed Perry to lead the way.

They journeyed through a strip of jungle until they came to a clearing. There, a few wooden foundations could be seen protruding from the ground. They were mysteriously free of rot and preserved exceptionally well.

The captain paused to remove his hat and mop his brow. "What do you make of this, Tommy?"

"This must've been Rhydar's home," Thomas replied.

Ward checked the dimensions. "Almost looks like the size of a small ship, like it was upside down or something."

"Too small for that," Benson added.

"Maybe an older one," Jared suggested.

"Either way, it's not there anymore," Thomas said.

Janes nodded. "Tis true. I recall hearing Miss Cynthia mention that it vanished when Rhydar passed ... aye?"

Ward nodded. "I believe so, that sounds correct."

"Aye then. There's nothing more to see here, then. Let's move on." Janes donned his hat, and they continued through the jungle.

It was now mid-morning, and the *Inferno* had come around the far corner of Stuart Island, approaching the final bend around Nemaris Island.

"Anything yet?" Marshall asked.

"Not yet, sir, not yet," Aramando reported.

"Hmmm ... where is she?" Marshall muttered to himself. Gretty continued to steer along the shore.

Greed and Betrayal

Janes and his party continued their way through the jungle. The path to the cave was very clearly marked, perhaps even made by Rhydar himself. Coming around a bend, they heard a soft rustling in a nearby thicket of trees.

"Hold! What's there?" Janes drew his sword. The other men did the same. So did Thomas.

The commotion grew louder, and from out of the brush walked a tiger. She appeared very tame, standing at attention as if expecting the men.

"Keep still … no sudden movements," Janes ordered.

The tiger took a few steps toward them. She came to within a few feet of Thomas and then sat down on the grass. She licked her chops, apparently waiting for a treat.

Thomas slowly put his sword away.

"Tommy … what are you doing?" hissed Benson.

"Do we have anything to give it?" Janes asked.

Ward glanced a Jared. "Did you bring that jerky?"

Jared nodded nervously.

"Well, go on." Janes made a little tossing motion.

Jared shook his head, all but frozen with fear. The tiger did not growl, but instead remained patiently seated as she continued to lick her chops.

"Looks pretty hungry," Benson observed.

"It almost seems to know us," Jared said.

"Curious, this is," Perry added.

"She respects us, like a master," Thomas said.

Everyone looked at Thomas.

"A master?" Janes asked.

"You? A master? That's ridiculous," Benson said.

The tiger growled at him.

"Okay, okay. I yield." Benson held up a pacifying hand.

The tiger slowly returned its gaze to Thomas.

Thomas looked at the tiger. "I'm sorry, I have nothing for you."

The tiger blinked a few times, licked its chops, shook its head, and then casually turned around and went into the bushes from whence it came.

"Quite mysterious this is," Perry observed.

Jared nearly collapsed from his relief, but quickly regained composure and patted Thomas on the shoulder. "Well done."

"How'd ye do that, lad?" Ward asked.

Thomas shook his head. "I have no idea, sir."

Benson sighed. "Phew ... that was a close one."

"Aye, it was. Well ... come along; let's keep moving." Janes sheathed his sword, and they continued onward.

Traveling to the edge of the jungle, they came to an opening. The path ended atop a high overlook. From there, they could see the rocks along the eastern edge of Nemaris Island and the entire Cove below.

"Seems we've gone as far as we can," Janes said.

"There was another path to the north," Benson said.

"Aye then. We go north," Ward said, turning around and taking the lead as the others followed. Thomas looked from the cliffside to the cove below.

"Looks awful high from here ...." Thomas thought to himself.

"Tommy! We're not wanting to get separated," Jared called. Thomas quickly rushed to catch up.

As the *Inferno* sailed around the western cape of Nemaris Island, Nyguard spotted the *Valiant*. The ship was situated in her resting place some thirty yards offshore.

"Cap'n," Nyguard motioned for the captain to look.

"Ahh! There she is! There she is ... an apple waiting to be plucked from the branch. But...." Marshall held up a hand, using the width of his palm for a hasty measurement. "Nyguard, is she resting awful close to shore?"

Nyguard nodded as a wicked grin creased his face. "Seems so."

"Watch carefully, Leo. This is where the fun begins." Marshall strode over to his helmsman. "Gretty, take us about a hundred yards astern, right along the drop off. We don't need to be getting too close. It looks awful shallow where she's beached."

"Aye." Gretty adjusted course.

Taking the northbound trail, Janes and his crew left the jungle for rockier terrain. As the crew progressed further, the trail narrowed into a rocky valley. They soon discovered a cave opening at the end.

"There it is! Have you the lantern, Benson?" Janes asked.

Benson unhooked it from a clip on the back of his belt. "Aye sir."

"Light it. We're going in." The captain's enthusiasm was almost palpable.

"I's got a bad feeling from that place, Cap'n," Perry said as Benson ignited the lantern with a tinderbox.

"I share your feeling, Perry." Ward shook his head. "Nothing keeping us out but our fears."

"I'm starting to agree with 'em, Cap'n," Jared muttered.

"Roberts, buck up, aye?" Ward ordered.

Janes rubbed his hands together with a grin. "Aye. Come on then, lads. Let's head inside."

"You lead, Benson. You have the lantern," Ward said.

Benson took a deep breath. "All right, 'ere goes." He cautiously started into the cave. As the shadows increased and the light of the lantern flickered quietly, they explored the cavern's antechamber.

A thick, cool musk hung in the air. Stalactites flanked the ceiling's smooth arches as if it were a cathedral. A faint dripping echoed in the distant darkness where the cavern sloped deeper into the earth.

All things considered, the cavern appeared to be rather ordinary.

"Huh..." Jared's posture began to lose its tension. "Why, it almost feels comfortable in here."

"Perhaps too comfortable. Like it could be a trap methinks," Benson said.

Ward turned to Janes. "Wasn't there a loud voice in that journal, Captain?"

"Aye, there was." The captain nodded. "And I haven't heard one yet."

"That's proof enough for me. Let's go back," Benson said.

Janes turned sharply. "Roland, you're the bravest man I have on my crew. Don't be making a fibber out of me now, hm?"

Benson cleared his throat and nodded slowly. "Aye Cap'n. I can do this."

"Good then. Let's keep going. If we hear a voice, we can turn back then," Janes said.

"Aye," Ward agreed.

They wandered further into the darkness of the cavern. A faint whine echoed from the depths below.

"Did you hear that?" Jared asked.

"Seems perfectly normal to me," Ward reported.

Janes listened for a moment then nodded. "Aye, just the wind."

They turned a corner that blocked the light from outside, and the true darkness of the tunnel became apparent.

Suddenly, an ominous shudder rumbled through the cave. The wind was so strong, that the flame of the lantern flickered violently.

"What's that?" Benson asked.

"This does not bode well!" Perry cried in what was by far the highest level any of them had heard his voice reach.

"Peace, everyone!" Janes ordered, holding them back. The ominous shudder rose to a voice that echoed in the cavern.

"Go back to your ship, sailors. For it is there that your strength and efforts are needed. Your time has not yet come," the voice thundered.

Benson jolted. "I shan't argue with that!" He made a mad dash for the cave entrance, passing the lantern to Jared as he rushed by.

Thomas stopped a moment. The amplified voice was strangely familiar to him. He was unable to determine how or why as he was dragged outside by the others.

"My, that was a close one," Janes gasped as he knelt outside the entrance.

"What did it mean, the ship is where our strength should be?" Jared asked.

"I've found it good not to argue with thundering disembodied voices, thank you," Benson replied.

"Same here, we should return to the ship," Ward said.

Janes raised a hand. "Hold a moment. Thomas, you had a strange look on your face when the voice spoke. What are you thinking?"

Thomas blinked and shook his head a few times. "Very strange, sir. Almost as if I have heard that voice before."

Jared's eyes rounded. "You know that voice, Tommy?"

"I do not know. It does not seem to me that I should."

Ward gave a whistle that even the captain was forced to pay attention to. "Come on. Our time may be up."

"Right, right." Standing, Janes dusted off his knees and straightened his hat. "Let's go now. We can discuss all this after we return to the ship."

The group made haste to the *Valiant*. In their absence, an unexpected scene was beginning to unfold.

"Ahoy there!" Captain Marshall called.

Gritzol and Jennings came atop deck, and looked out to sea where the *Inferno* was anchored just beyond the shallows surrounding Nemaris Island.

"Just what we need...." Gritzol muttered quietly.

"I say, ahoy, and good morning to you!" Marshall called again. "Whom do I have the pleasure of speaking with?"

"Hold on ... that's the *Inferno*, isn't it?" Jennings whispered to Gritzol, his gaze remaining focused upon Marshall.

"Aye ... I'd recognize those sails a league away," Gritzol whispered back.

"You sure?" Jennings asked.

Gritzol gave Jennings a stern look, keeping his voice hushed. "Aye I'm sure. You were there too, ye scalawag! I know Marshall better than the King of Cimmordia ... we're not taking any chances with him ... not after last time."

"We're in for it now," Jennings whispered quietly.

"Ahoy! I would caution thee, good sir, to keep your ship in deeper waters, for your own protection, as the sands are very shallow here," Gritzol called.

"Aye, but it is I who cautions you! I also offer my apologies, as your situation has indeed become much worse. Is your captain about?" Marshall called.

"Any ideas?" Gritzol whispered.

"Napping," Jennings replied quietly.

"He is napping, good sir." Gritzol called back. "Shall I send for him?"

Marshall turned away, growling quietly. "Napping...? Hogwash!" Turning back to the *Valiant*, he spoke in the same prim tone as he had before. "If it wouldn't trouble you, send for your captain right away. I do not wish to cause any ... unpleasantness."

"Please excuse us a moment," Gritzol replied, and went with Jennings just below deck, where Ellis and Lewinston were waiting.

Lewinston was in a state that was a cross between furious and frantic. "I thought I saw the *Inferno* outside! What's Marshall want? And how did he find us?"

"Shh ... keep your voice down. I don't know, but he didn't come for tea." Gritzol grimaced. "Revenge, probably."

"How big is his crew these days, anyhow?" Ellis asked.

"He recruits his men by fear, rather than loyalty. And he's always too much of a braggart to carry a force with him. I'd say not more than twelve," Gritzol replied.

"Aye." Scowling, Jennings nervously ran a hand through his short hair. "But that's more than we can handle without Perry or Benson."

"Perhaps we draw them a few at a time. At least he's playing the civil card as always. Hmm...." Gritzol's eyes lit with inspiration. "Ellis, how well can you act?"

"Act? I'm no prancy actor," Ellis gruffed.

"You look old enough to be a captain." Gritzol gestured to help convey his idea. "We give ye a big brimmed-hat and a blue coat, like the cap'ns, and go out and talk to Marshall. Talk about limiting bloodshed and have a few of his men come over for discussions. We get them down here, ambush them, and capture the commander for ransom. Can you handle that?"

Ellis shrugged. "No assurances, but I'll give 'er a shot."

"All I ask, Captain," Gritzol replied with a smile.

"I've got an old hat," Lewinston said, going for the barracks.

"And I'll borrow one of the captain's old overcoats," Jennings said.

"Good, that'll work well. Meantime, I'll set up Marshall." Gritzol returned to the deck.

"I's not liking this plan too much," Ellis muttered as he heard Marshall's voice.

"I have little time to converse, good sir, is your captain on his way?" Marshall called.

"Aye he is, good sir, he will be but a moment," Gritzol called.

Little did Gritzol know that a rowboat was slowly approaching from behind Siren Island.

Once the bigger ship came into view, Janes let out a rare groan. "The *Inferno* … just what we need. Keep us behind Opole Island, Perry."

Perry nodded, rowing quietly.

"What are you thinking?" asked Ward.

A sly smile crossed the captain's lips. "You'll see."

Benson, Jared, and Thomas each remained silent.

Marshall grumbled as he called to the *Valiant* again. "What is your predicament, good sir?"

"It concerns the shallow water, actually. Nothing a little effort and a high tide can't remedy, mind you," Gritzol replied. Mr. Ellis signaled that he was ready.

"Ahh! Here he is now. Captain." Gritzol stepped back, letting "Captain" Ellis come forward.

"So! If it isn't my old friend … Christopher Janes, correct?" Marshall asked.

"Uh…" Ellis began quietly, before speaking more confidently. "On the contrary, Janes is dead. Allow me to introduce myself. Captain Horatio Ellis."

"Dead, is he? Yes … such a weakling, best for him I suppose … Captain Ellis, then. It appears that I have a quarrel with your crew, good captain. I suspect you have my property on your ship. Since I cannot divulge its purpose, I may be forced to capture your ship. I do hope you wish to cooperate," Marshall called.

"You must forgive me. I am at a disadvantage, sir. I do not recognize your colors," Ellis called back.

Gritzol rolled his eyes. "Come on Ellis, Marshall hates it when he's not recognized … don't buy into flattery," he muttered to himself.

"I get it, Barry. Relax," Ellis replied through gritted teeth.

Marshall spoke over them. "Captain Luther Marshall, of the galleon *Inferno*. I say again, Captain Ellis, an item of mine may have made it aboard your vessel. We are both gentlemen, Captain, and if you cooperate I shall leave you and your crew in your predicament. Should you allow it, I will be sending a few of my men over to search for it at once."

"That sounds fair. However, I give you my full assurance that I have no knowledge of possessing any unusual property, sir," Ellis replied, then hissed to Gritzol, "What do we have of his, anyways?"

"No clue," Gritzol replied.

"I look forward to meeting your men, Captain," Ellis called back.

"Simply wonderful! I shall send them on their way." Marshall turned to his men. "Nyguard, take Morrey and Irving with you in the rowboat. Janes must be alive ... draw him out. He must be hiding something yet."

"Aye," Nyguard said.

"Aye boss," Morrey and Irving chimed.

The three men climbed into the rowboat. As they began rowing over, Mr. Gritzol went by the doorway to ready the others.

"Swords ready?" he asked without turning towards the door.

"All ready," Lewinston replied.

"Three of them. Do you have my sword too?" Gritzol asked.

"It's here." Jennings rattled it in its sheath.

Gritzol's flexed his hand in anticipation. "And Ellis has his under the coat. Leave mine on the wall. Jennings, behind; Lewinston, from the front. In the mess hall. Let's try to knock them out ... and don't screw it up. We'll only get one shot at this."

"Aye," Jennings and Lewinston chimed.

Gritzol walked out and stood beside Ellis as the men tied their boat to the port side and climbed on deck.

"Welcome aboard, gentlemen. Right this way, please." Ellis gave them an officious nod. He and Gritzol followed behind their "guests."

"Hey, don't I know you from somewhere?" Nyguard asked Gritzol as the group went down the stairs.

"No, sir. Please, this way." Gritzol gestured toward the mess hall. As they entered, the crew went into action.

Quickly, Jennings held his sword abreast of the first man, Irving. Lewinston held his sword against the neck of the second man, Morrey. Gritzol retrieved his own sword from the hall and held it against Nyguard. Ellis did the same.

"All right, which one of ye is the commander?" Gritzol asked.

"Him," Morrey said, pointing to Nyguard.

"You fool!" Nyguard tried to kick him.

"Good then." Lewinston left his sword trained on Morrey as Ellis took everyone's weapons.

"Marshall will have your heads for this," Irving threatened.

"Shut it." Lewinston gagged both men. Morrey resisted and earned himself a punch to the face from Gritzol.

"Now wait a minute, he's an innocent," Nyguard began.

Gritzol gave him a look sharp enough to cut wood. "Innocent what? Murderer? Under Marshall's command too, I'm sure. Tie 'em up."

Ellis took some rope from the kitchen and tied up Nyguard and the other men. Jennings went about closing the portholes in the mess hall-except for one on the bow end of the room. He then lit the lanterns. Morrey and Irving were tossed unceremoniously into the refuse bin, leaving Nyguard detained for questioning.

"Do I seem familiar now?" Gritzol removed Nyguard's sword from his sheath and threw it onto the floor in the corner.

"Barry Gritzol... I should've known." Nyguard spat on the floor, causing Ellis to grumble.

"If your captain hadn't called the retreat, you might not've lived to see this day, Mr. Nyguard," Gritzol replied with a fierce grin.

"Your threats mean nothing to me, you blaggard," Nyguard scoffed.

"Let's not resort to names." He gave the man a hard pat on the back. "We're old buddies, right?"

"Curse you," Nyguard snapped.

Ellis made a sound of disappointment. "Straighten yourself up, man. You're a captive now."

Nyguard rounded on him, nearly losing his balance. "You're not captain at all, are you? Who are you, really?"

Ellis took off the hat and the coat. "Just a simple cook."

"A cook?!" Nyguard moaned.

"A wonder why Marshall was foolish enough to send you rather than more of his hired hands." Gritzol shrugged. "But the game is in our court now. What is it that your captain wants?"

Nyguard stiffened. "Nothing. I'll speak only to Captain Janes."

"Ellis." Gritzol turned to the cook. "Have you got any of that leftover chum? I'm curious as to how potent it is."

"Aye, me too," Ellis said with a devilish smile.

"He seems hungry to me," Jennings muttered to Lewinston.

Nyguard sang like a canary. "Okay! Okay! A map! Marshall's looking for a treasure map of these isles! A silly map!"

Gritzol frowned. "We have no such map."

"Marshall knows that you do. Your cabin boy, along with a man carrying a fife, picked it up!" Nyguard explained.

"Jared ... and Tommy?" Lewinston asked.

"So let's assume we have this map." Gritzol gave the man a good poke in the ribs. "What good is it to us, being stranded here, eh, Nyguard?"

Taking on a pitying expression, Nyguard sighed. "Marshall'll kill you for it."

"All for a piece of paper?" It seemed unfathomable to Gritzol.

"Yeah, laugh it up, you'll get yours!" Nyguard cried.

"When the cap'n gets back, we'll know if there's any treasure at all," Lewinston replied.

"Janes lives!" The news seemed to cheer Nyguard. "I knew it!"

"Aye, he lives." Jennings gave the man a look that could curdle milk. "And when he returns he'll decide what to do with the likes of ye."

"But first, do me this favor." Taking his captive by the arm, Gritzol turned him to the uncovered window. "Call to your captain and tell him it may take some time to search."

"And if I refuse?" Nyguard replied.

Gritzol shrugged. "As much as it would honor me to kill you in combat, I'd have to kill you where you stand."

Nyguard nodded, and Lewinston and Jennings dragged him to the open window.

"Captain!" Nyguard called.

"What is it, Leo?" Marshall called back.

"It may take some time to search effectively, sir!"

"More men, then?" Marshall called back.

"Well ... sir ...." Nyguard began.

Gritzol pressed his sword hard against Nyguard's back.

"Not necessary sir, but give us some time!" he called with a slight quiver to his voice.

Suspecting something, a sly smile crossed Marshall's face. "Aye then. Come back when you've finished." He then ducked into his cabin.

Pulling Nyguard away, Gritzol lowered his sword and blocked the window as well.

Nyguard jerked his arm out of Gritzol's grasp and glowered at him. "So, what's your plan now? Or are you just making this up as you go?"

"There's a small storage room right here." Gritzol made a mockingly gracious gesture as though seating a lord in their best chair. "You just sit tight and keep your crewmates entertained for awhile, and we'll get back to ye when we come up with something."

Jennings opened the door to the small refuse tank containing the slop from the kitchen. The smell was appalling. Aside from the buzzing of numerous fruit flies and struggling noises from Morrey and Irving, it was very quiet inside.

"Ish, what died in there?" Nyguard gagged, turning away.

"You, if it comes to that." Gritzol shrugged again. "Nothing personal."

Ellis pushed him in. Lewinston closed the door, sealing it with a wooden crossbeam.

"Jim, keep an eye on Marshall and an especially close eye on their boats. Harv, don't let those boys in the refuse bin out even to piss," Gritzol ordered.

"Got it," Jennings and Lewinston replied.

"What about their boat?" Ellis asked.

Gritzol crossed his arms in thought. "We'll leave it alone for now … I just hope the captain returns safely."

A few moments later Janes and the others approached the ship from the starboard side so Marshall and his crew couldn't see them. It was just a chance of fate that they got back as easily as they did without being seen.

Lewinston took over keeping watch as everyone met in the mess hall.

Gritzol greeted his captain with a hearty handshake. "Captain, it's good to see you."

"So … Marshall found us after all." Despite their predicament, Janes seemed perfectly calm. "What's the situation?"

"He sent over three of his men, one being the mate. A man of your acquaintance," Gritzol began.

The captain sputtered. "Nyguard? That fool is still at Marshall's side?"

"He should know better than to serve a man like Marshall," Ward added.

Raising an eyebrow, Janes gazed at the men who'd handled the *Valiant*'s invasion. "Where are they now?"

Gritzol's tried to hide his grin and failed. "In the refuse bin, locked safely away."

"How did you do it?" Ward asked.

"We tricked Marshall into sending over a few men, to search for...." With a frown Lewinston shrugged. "Whatever it is they want ... some piece of paper or something."

"The map," Ward stated.

"Not the same map that," Thomas began.

Janes nodded. "Aye, Tommy. That same map."

"What map is this?" Jennings asked.

"A map revealing the treasure of Rhydar," Janes explained.

"So that's what's in that cave!" Benson exclaimed.

"Aye ... the riches of men who traversed the seas and of those who earned it dishonorably," Perry added.

"Must be pretty valuable stuff down there if Rhydar's spirit guards it." Jared seemed more enthusiastic about their trip to Siren Island.

"Beyond the dreams of most men," Gritzol said.

"I don't know..." Ward huffed. "That Marshall can dream up a lot."

"So why don't we go down there and get it first?" Ellis asked.

"Marshall'll never allow that. Hmmm...." After a moment's contemplation, Janes made for the door. "Ward, Tommy, with me. The rest of you, make sure to sharpen your swords. Gritzol, untie their rowboat and let it drift. Make sure you're not seen. Maybe Marshall will think they went ashore or something ... once that's done, we continue our routine business like nothing is wrong." He started for his cabin.

"I'm on it. I'm an expert at avoiding wandering eyes, sir," Gritzol said.

Janes nodded. "Good."

"What about the prisoners, Cap'n?" Mr. Jennings asked.

"Double bar the door, and seal it up tight. There's no doorknob on the inside, but we don't want them escaping."

Jennings nodded, as Lewinston went over to the refuse bin. "We'll take care of it, Cap'n."

"Good ... and be ready for anything," added Ward. Then, he and Thomas followed Captain Janes.

"Aye sir," the men called after them.

Thomas and Ward followed Janes into his cabin. He closed the door and kept the curtains drawn, focusing his full attention on Thomas. "Okay, I want to know what happened on the island, Thomas."

"Sir?" Thomas asked.

"The tiger, the foundations, the cave. What happened?" Janes asked again, taking a seat at the table.

"Honestly, sir, I cannot explain any of it."

"Captain, maybe the journal can explain more of this," Ward suggested.

Janes sighed. "My apologies, Tommy. All this mystical poppycock ... and now with Marshall back into the picture ... I can see why even Scyhathen grew impatient."

"Shall we look further into the book, sir?" Thomas asked.

Janes nodded. Thomas opened it to where Janes had left his bookmark and read the next passage aloud. The entry was only a few sentences long.

November 2nd, 1582. There have been no recent encounters with Captain Epoth. He has yet to make a second appearance, and we are beginning to wonder at his true intentions. Both Smitty and I are not convinced that Epoth exists fully in this world. My crew is starting to feel the effects as well, particularly Kid. He seems to be experiencing some odd dreams, he reports. They are rather unique.

That was the end of the passage.

"Now I wonder what he means by that?" Ward asked.

"I share your wonder, Seriam. Hmm...." Drumming his fingers in the table, Janes turned back to his cabin boy. "Tommy, you haven't had any bad dreams recently, have you?"

"Not anything unusual," Thomas replied.

"Read the next passage," Janes asked.

Thomas turned the page. "That's odd ... sir, the next passage is dated November 32nd."

"The 32nd?" Moving behind Thomas, he looked over the boy's shoulder. "How is that possible?"

Janes waved for him to continue. "Read it, please."

November 32nd, 1582. I am somewhat curious as to the condition of Mr. Banes after he gave me the date for today, but nonetheless

I will trust his reports. Due to the unusual weather conditions we had yesterday—or was it the day before—there have been some odd occurrences, and I can believe anything. This was apparent when I saw Mr. Larson and Mr. Corvair casually building a snowman on the beach. It actually snowed in the tropics, and not just a few flakes, but rather a full-blown snow storm. I've never seen anything like it, especially when Kid informed me that he had a dream where it snowed all night. If this is an act of Epoth, and he has somehow influenced my crew, I shall make an example of his treachery. Such attacks against us will surely end his life, whatever trace of it remains.

"Snow in the tropics?" Shocked, Ward moved away from Thomas. "Just over yonder, ashore?"

Janes gave a dismissive wave. "Nonsense! It could never happen."

"I can assure you I have not had any dreams with snow in them, at least, not recently," Thomas responded.

"No, I wouldn't think so," Janes said.

"Who is this Kid person?" Ward rubbed his chin. "Was that the cabin boy's name?"

Janes gestured to Thomas to give him the book. "It would seem so. I recall seeing an entry where Scyhathen covered his crew in more detail. It was toward the back, so I'll keep the page first." He replaced the bookmark before paging through the journal. When he found the correct passage, he read it aloud.

… I feel I should take the time to recognize my crew in these pages. For without them, we could not have survived the trials put before us upon these islands. First, there is Mr. Gerald Banes, my faithful timekeeper and expert navigator. His tireless efforts have not only kept us mindful of the passage of time, but also our location, and the details of these four islands we now call home.

Second, Mr. Oswald Smitty, my loyal friend and mate. There is not a man alive who knows more about winds and how to ride them anywhere on the sea. Some days, I wonder if I am truly who I am, were Smitty not there to help clear up any situation we might be in.

Then there is Mr. Rhudell Corvair, a man whose skillful use of ropes and pulleys have kept the sails in prestige condition since the Nemaris came under my command.

Mr. Allen Larson is a man who can feel a storm a league away. Both of these men are skilled beyond their years.

Next, the artistic Nelson Mandalay, who has such a skillful taste for art that his works should be placed adjacent to the famed works of Liffellno or Casteletta the Great. Mandalay is also a skilled navigator and tactician, and with him and Banes at the helm, we are never lost. Nelson is an excellent cartographer. He has drawn many maps and other items of reference, including a small sketch of these islands that he drew today. I requested that he copy it for my records towards the end of this journal.

Mr. Barnaby Jones, a cook of excellent taste, is quite creative and has done wonders with the meager materials he has been forced to work with since our arrival here. As I am sure I have indicated many times, without him this journal would be left blank; I would be too weak and hungry to write.

And last, but not least, the young cabin boy, who the men usually call Kid. He has been with us these past few weeks and has taken to the seas like a fish. I was a good friend to his father, Lowell DeLeuit. After his mother died of an unknown disease the boy was sent to me for training. Rest her soul, she was too lovely for such a tribulation. As for young ....

Thomas gasped. "DeLeuit? Young DeLeuit? Is that possible?"

"Surely it must be an unrelated coincidence," Ward said.

"Does it mention his real name?" Thomas urged.

Janes turned the page, and a new entry was there instead.

"That's actually the end of the entry," Janes said softly.

"Perhaps a page is missing," Ward suggested. Some ruffled strips of paper were sticking out of the binding of the book.

Thomas groaned and lowered his head.

"Tell me, Thomas, what do you know about your father?" Janes asked.

Straightening, Thomas met his captain's gaze. "Very little, except that he started as a cabin boy when he was very young, not more than four or five years old."

"Seriam." The captain turned to his first mate. "Do you suppose this DeLeuit could have been named Gregory?"

Ward shrugged. "Based on the evidence, I would say that the chances are rather good."

"A pity we cannot discuss these findings with your mother at this time, Tommy." Janes sighed.

"What are we to do about Marshall?" Apparently more concerned with the practicalities of their situation, Ward moved to peek through a curtain at the *Inferno*. "It cannot be the same as last time. We lost too many good men ... Nyson ... Vicks...."

"Aye, good men indeed...." After a thoughtful moment, Janes turned back to his cabin boy. "Tommy, perhaps you should refine your fencing techniques before it becomes too dangerous. Seriam and I have some things to discuss."

"Sir, about my mother. I'm not sure if she knew exactly...." Thomas began.

"I'm afraid the matter will have to wait until there is more time for it. Go train some, make sure you do so in the hold," Janes said softly.

"Yes, sir."

Thomas made his exit, and Ward took the seat Thomas occupied. "What are your thoughts, Chris?"

Janes sighed deeply. "I share Captain Scyhathen's woes, Seriam. This is a paradise ... but not while Marshall is around."

All the while, Marshall was becoming impatient at the lack of progress from his men.

"That ship is smaller than ours ... what could be keeping Nyguard?" Marshall growled to Gretty.

"Perhaps Janes pulled a maneuver on us, boss?" Gretty speculated.

"A maneuver indeed! Only Christopher Janes would be so crafty ... but Janes is dead?! Does that seem right to you?" Marshall thought aloud.

"Boss, I'm sorry that I do not know Captain Janes as well as you do, but from what I have heard from Nyguard, he was a good swordsman," Gretty said slowly.

"A *good* swordsman, say you? What would that make *me*, then, Gretty?" Marshall asked, standing up.

"A *spectacular* swordsman, boss?" Gretty answered with a large smile.

Marshall nodded his head. "Aye indeed. I think I've played their game long enough. Perhaps we should pay … Captain Ellis … a visit."

"Aye boss. Who shall I send for?" Gretty asked.

"Bring me Nicks and Benks, and maybe Fallah too…" A satisfied sneer stretched across Marshall's lips. "If Janes is pulling a maneuver, I want to be prepared for it."

"Aye boss, I'll get them for you," Gretty said.

"Be quick and quiet about it. There will be no tomfoolery this time." Marshall sneered coldly, making Gretty shiver.

"Aye boss!" Gretty said with a slight jump to his voice.

Marshall grumbled to himself silently, then turned to his wardrobe and selected a coat to wear for the upcoming meeting.

In the mess hall, Jennings was complaining. "This is a bore … I was hoping for a bit more action."

Lewinston added a mumble of agreement, keeping his eye on the *Inferno* through the one open window.

"Could be worse ye know," Ellis replied.

"How so? We's stuck on a lovely island, but can't adventure it. We's holding prisoners that we can't do nothing with. We's just sitting here, waiting for the captain to make a move. It's quite a bore, mind you!" Jennings rambled.

Pausing as he wiped the buffet table, Ellis looked at his shipmate like he was an idiot. "Marshall could've sent all his men at once. Would ye rather be dead?"

Lewinston shrugged. "At least then we'd get some exercise."

Jennings scoffed toward Ellis. "Since when do you give a bother? Usually ye just sit in yer cabin and do … whatever it is ye do."

"Maybe I've been getting tired of waiting myself." Ellis straightened with a gleeful gleam in his eye. "We could raid Marshall's boat. After all, 'Captain Ellis' does have a ring to it."

"The day I call you captain…" Jennings began.

Thomas walked into the mess hall, getting Jennings's attention. Without a word, Thomas took a seat and rested his head on the table.

Happy for the distraction, Lewinston turned from his post at the window. "Tommy ... what happened upstairs?" Each man quickly agreed it was best not to bicker with Thomas present.

"Yeah Tommy, what lies with you?" Jennings asked.

"Just something we read in Captain Scyhathen's journal," Thomas mumbled.

"What are they talking about now?" Jennings asked.

"They asked me to leave, but I wasn't really paying attention," Thomas said quietly.

"Important matters, Tommy. Best to keep your mind on other things," Lewinston said, returning to the window.

Straightening, Thomas burst, unable to contain the news any longer. "They believe my father came here with Captain Scyhathen."

Jennings looked away a moment. "Gripes, I ain't no good at these things ... Scyhathen, huh? What'd ye read, anyhow?"

"An entry that mentions a cabin boy with my last name," Thomas replied.

"A cabin boy? From the *Nemaris*?" Jennings asked, looking up.

Thomas nodded. "Aye, but no first name."

"Huh..." Jennings's expression softened slightly. "What was your father like, Tommy?"

Ellis went into the galley and closed the door, removing himself from the conversation.

"We've never met," Thomas replied.

"Seems you and I are kinda alike, then." Jennings sat down across from Thomas.

That got Thomas to focus on something other than his fidgeting fingers. "Alike? How so?"

Jennings took a deep sigh and then blinked a few times. "I don't usually talk about this ... me own father threw me out one day. Said to me, 'Boy, go get a life, and don't come back until you do!'"

Thomas's eyes grew wide. "You were thrown out from your home?" He couldn't imagine how horrible it would be.

"Aye, my own father threw me out on the road." Jennings shrugged. "I was only seven years old."

"Seven...?" It took effort for Thomas not to gape at his shipmate. "And you were on your own? Any family?"

Jennings shook his head. "I have little family left. Distant relatives, mostly, but after my mother died my father went crazy. Blamed me for the diseases Momma suffered. One day, I'd like to look him in the eye and show him what a strong man and tough worker he threw away...." Vengeance grew within his voice.

It was bad enough only having one parent, but Thomas thought losing both that way was beyond awful. "I'm sorry about your mother."

"A damn saint, she was. A saint." Jennings started to calm down.

"If I may ask, how did you survive?" Thomas asked.

Jennings stood up and paced around the table. "The first week was probably the worst. With only the shirt on my back, the pants around my legs, and the boots on my feet, I walked north as far as I could. I reached a small town and collapsed inside a poor man's inn. He had little business, and could only afford to keep his daughter and himself fed. So he threw me back out on the road! Not even a coin for my troubles. He only gave me a drink of water and a loaf of stale bread—barely a slice of life itself."

"That guy didn't know what he threw out, either," Thomas said.

"Aye, he didn't. With only poor folks like the innkeeper in that town, I continued east, to a port town." He paused to glance out the window. "It was there I met a man who worked in a shipping warehouse. He took me in and gave me food and work. After a year or two and as my strength increased, he secured a position for me on a merchant ship." Jennings shrugged again. "With no connections elsewhere and a desire to leave my past behind, I took it. What had I to lose? And so my life as a sailor began."

"When was the last time you saw your father?" Thomas quickly did the math. "Twenty years?"

"Something like that, I don't remember anymore. I could care less, really ... I may never forgive my father, though. Not a day came when he 'preciated the things I did for him, just to keep my stomach full." He sat down at the table again.

"Did you ever get back to see him?" Thomas asked.

Jennings shook his head. "Once I found the courage to confront him, he had been dead for nearly two years by then. Just as well, I reckon."

A thought occurred to Thomas that he'd never really considered. "Guess I started pretty old for a cabin boy, then?"

"Times are changing, boy. How old are ye now, fourteen?" Jennings asked.

"Right."

He gave Thomas a friendly cuff. "You're getting stronger. Keep at it, and someday you'll be as strong as ol' Perry."

"Yeah," Thomas said, getting up.

"Guess if Marshall and his crew come over, I'll be waiting for them," Jennings said.

"You will?" Thomas asked.

"I don't fear 'im. Should Marshall be foolhardy enough, I'll be glad to end him. Even if he dies honorably," Jennings said.

"And I've your back, Harv. No matter what," Lewinston said, turning from the window.

Jennings nodded. "You and me both, brother." He looked back at Thomas. "Got your sword still? If you do, best you practice with it whilst ye can."

"Aye, I'll do that," Thomas said, going out into the hall and down to the cargo hold.

"Boy's had it too easy. He's gotta toughen up lest it tear 'im apart," Jennings said, fixing his gaze on the refuse door.

Thomas found it hard to focus on his fencing. Putting the sword away, he picked up Acadia's shell and looked at it a long time. In the time he had spent with her, they had shared many great moments. As he thought more about it, he began to take it to heart. From what Jennings told him, he tried to imagine what life could've been like if his father were around. Thomas could've learned about the seas early on, even heard amazing stories about the exotic places his father had traveled to in his sailing career. Thomas also wondered what would happen if he could stay with Acadia always above ground, below water, always together no matter what. The longer he thought about it, the more he began to wish it were possible.

Overwhelmed, he drifted into a midday nap and his thoughts shifted from his woes to friendlier waters. Instead of swimming around the Nemaris Islands, however, Thomas and Acadia were swimming together near the waters of Harper's Bay. They were both carefree and happy. He didn't have to think about Epoth, or Rhydar, or his daily toils, or the predicament of the ship. It was just him and Acadia ... and that was a beautiful feeling.

In his dream they had played all day together, and a new day was dawning. Thomas drew the signal shell to his lips and blew once, long and smooth, to summon Acadia to his side.

Perhaps he was dreaming, or perhaps he really did blow into the shell. It rested gently at his side as he laid in his cot, a smile on his face.

Under the waves, the sounds of the shell passed through the waters, to the grotto of Acadia some distance away. Hearing his signal, she swam toward the *Valiant* as she had agreed with Thomas to come when called. Perhaps it was about the gift? Or another story about the ways of people ashore? Little did she know that Marshall was about to take his second rowboat on a conquest mission.

Lewinston watched as the crew of the *Inferno* lowered their rowboat to the waters below.

"Harv ... they're on the move."

Jennings nodded, not leaving his post at the refuse bin. "Ellis ... go get the captain."

Ellis opened the door to the galley. "Someone say something out here?"

"They're on the move," Lewinston said.

Ellis wiped his hands clean. "I'm on it."

"Okay boys, keep your oars low. We are not here to attract attention," Marshall ordered. The men took care to row quietly.

"What have you planned, boss?" Gretty asked.

"There's nobody on deck, then? A foolish act, Captain Ellis. One should know better than to leave his ship unguarded ...."

"Boss?" Gretty asked.

"Silence!" Marshall snapped. Then in a more sedate tone he explained, "I'm planning."

"Isn't it obvious, boss? They's afraid," Benks said.

"Aye, they's lily-livered ninnies," Nicks added.

Marshall looked up. "Did I not order silence?" he asked in a subtle voice.

"Yeah, we think you did," Fallah replied as Benks and Nicks agreed confidently.

"Then be quiet," Marshall growled, making all three men cower.

A few silent moments passed as they continued their approach toward the *Valiant*. Gretty slowed his rowing. "They can probably see us by now."

"Aye … we climb aboard, and call them out. Got that belaying pin with you?" Marshall asked Nicks.

Before they left, he had untied one of the wooden club-like pins that the riggings were often tied to. "Aye boss, it's here." Nicks retrieved it from the bottom of the boat and hefted it in his hands.

"Good … keep it handy in case you lose your weapon like last time." He gestured toward the side of the ship. "Ready that rope, and tie the rowboat alongside her. Ever since Mr. Harris' departure we've been short an anchor."

"Aye boss, I got it covered." Remembering the harsh treatment Harris had received in the past, Gretty wasn't about to be tied to the ship, bound and thrown overboard.

Marshall nodded as they slowly approached the *Valiant*. Just astern of the ship, not far from Marshall's rowboat, Acadia surfaced. She had seen the rowboat from below, thinking that it was Janes returning from shore or that Thomas had called her for another boat ride during the sunset. But instead of seeing Thomas in the rowboat, a grim face glared back.

"Oh?!" she cried, seeing Marshall.

"My my my … and just where did you come from, missy?" Marshall grabbed her shoulder.

She winced. "Wh-what do you want?" Acadia asked. Her voice quivered from the sharp pains caused by his tight grip.

"Maybe she knows some of these sailors, boss?" Gretty asked.

"Nobody just comes up from the ocean, boss," Benks said.

"No way could she have held her breath forever! She came out of nowhere, she did," Nicks said.

Acadia looked around for a way out, wishing she hadn't surfaced so quickly.

Marshall gave her an insincere smile. "It would seem to me that you are in a predicament, milady. I think if you join us aboard the *Inferno* all your troubles will come to an end." He tightened his grip on Acadia.

"No, I do not want to go with you," Acadia said, trying to break away.

Marshall pulled her closer. "My dear, I am afraid you have little choice."

Gretty took her by the left arm and Marshall took her by the right. Lifting her by the shoulders, there was little she could do until her tail came free of the water. Marshall's men backed off in shock at what they saw.

"Great Caesar's ghost!" Benks cried.

"By Davy Jones's beard!" Fallah exclaimed.

Acadia took the opportunity to defend herself best as she could, swinging her tailfin at Nicks. The blow knocked him back against the side of the *Valiant*, easily knocking him out. The belaying pin in his hand flew away, splashing into the waters beyond.

Even this final act of desperation did not save Acadia, as Gretty and Marshall already had her pinned in the rowboat. With Benks and Fallah holding her down, she squirmed to fight free as best she could. Unfortunately, the men were much stronger than she. Her strength quickly waned, as her efforts shook off whatever water drops had remained on her shimmering, blue scales. She slowly slumped into Gretty's arms.

"So . . . like most fish, water is both your strength and weakness," Marshall observed.

Acadia couldn't reply, and only moaned as Gretty laid her between the benches of the rowboat.

"Perhaps Ellis can wait, Gretty. If there is a connection between this fishy maiden and Janes, we'll find it. Let's return with our new bartering chip," Marshall declared. Fallah and Benks began rowing back toward the *Inferno*.

Nicks regained consciousness after they were clear of the *Valiant*. Acadia's blow had earned him a bloody nose and a large lump where his skull had met the side of the ship. He remained disoriented during the trip back to the *Inferno*.

Acadia, however, struggled just to breathe as she rode in silence.

A Fish for a Fool

anes watched from his cabin window, as Marshall and his men rowed away with Acadia lying across the bottom of their rowboat.

"Goodness me. Now matters are much worse." Janes sighed sadly.

"What do you mean by that?" Ward glanced up from some charts.

"Seriam, look there." Janes pointed to a narrow gap in his curtains. "Tommy's not going to like this."

Ward came over to see Acadia passed out in the rowboat, her blue scales glimmering in the sunset as Fallah continued to row away. "Miss Acadia! Come on, we've got to do something!" He turned to see Janes slowly walk to his chair to sit and outrage turned quickly to frustration. "Why are you sitting down? Chris, is there nothing we can do?"

Janes shook his head. "Not without risking Miss Acadia's well-being. If we act now, her life may be at risk. So, we will have to strategize first."

Hands clenched in fists, Ward drew close to tower over Janes. "Captain, I rarely question your actions, but I cannot just sit idle and allow this to take place. Please do not force me to go alone."

"A straight fight?" Janes shook his head again. "Even if we could all reach the *Inferno*'s deck in safety, I will not risk an open melee with Marshall's men. If we are to help her, it will be done ashore, but I do not know where yet." He gave his mate a quelling look. "Seriam, there is much at stake here ... and bloodshed will only be my last resort ... especially for Miss Acadia's sake."

Ward sulkily paced, stopping and slapping his palm against the wall in frustration. "Okay, okay ... what do you have in mind?" He took a deep breath, trying to control himself.

"Right now, nothing."

Ward looked at him wide-eyed. "Nothing?"

A cool smile echoed the tactical gleam in the captain's eyes. "Nothing. Refraining from acting is a strategy in itself, Seriam. Marshall assumes that we are oblivious to what has transpired just now." He spread his hands as though he'd just revealed a battle plan on the table. "Therefore, if we play along with him in the coming hours, we will have more to work with. Careful planning, in respect to his plans, will give us opportunity to find his weakness."

Ward accepted his captain's plans. "You suggest a risky proposition. But, if we are successful there will be less bloodshed on both sides."

Holding a finger aloft, Janes emphasized a critical facet of his scheme. "And, a far better chance to rescue Miss Acadia when Marshall doesn't see it coming."

There was a knock at the door.

"Aye, come," Janes said.

It was Ellis. "Marshall's on the move."

"Horatio, we saw. Close the door, please." Janes waved him closer.

Ellis closed the door and came inside. "So Lewinston and Jennings aren't just yanking my gizzards? Thought for sure it'd be another one of their games."

"I assure you it is not. Marshall planned to come aboard, but as an unlucky turn of fate Miss Acadia chose to surface just then," Janes said.

"They went back to the *Inferno* with...." Ellis frowned. "With this Acadia person?"

Ward nodded. "And now they've a captive of their own."

"Beg your pardon, Captain, but who is Miss Acadia again?" Ellis asked.

"The mermaid," Ward said.

Ellis gave a confused look, oblivious of all that had transpired.

"She was on board for a day or so, remember?" Ward asked again.

Ellis shook his head, unsure of whatever he had been drinking. "There must be something strange in these waters ...."

"Aye, now you've got it," Ward said.

Janes stood to look out the gap in the curtains again. "The matter here is that Marshall has a prisoner now. If I am following this correctly, he believes you are the captain?"

"Aye, that he does, but I fail to see..." Ellis began.

Turning back to his men, Janes wore a congenial smile that belied the wicked gleam in his eyes. "Perhaps you should invite Marshall to tea this afternoon. All we need to come up with is some sort of enticing tale. Say Nyguard and his men are searching ashore for his map, distract him, that sort of thing." He waved the details away. "In the meantime, we ambush his ship and rescue Acadia."

"You want me to distract Marshall?" Ellis held up his hands in protest. "Now wait just a damn moment. I can't keep him alone for...."

"Alone?" Janes shook his head. "Nonsense. Gritzol and Lewinston will be with you. That should leave Ward, Perry, Tommy, and myself to raid the *Inferno*. Jennings, Roberts, and Benson will hold the ship in case he has a counterstrike planned." Pausing, he tapped his chin for a moment before pointing at his cook. "You should invite him to tea around mid-afternoon, the proper time."

Ellis's face was grim. "Let me understand this, Captain. Your idea of a rescue attempt is ... a tea party?"

Janes dismissed the suggestion. "My plan is a distraction. And you often grumble about never having anyone to enjoy your tea with."

Ellis sighed deeply. "I suppose I should see if we have any crumpets in the galley ... but I ain't bringing no flowers along." Tea was one of his intrests he often kept private. Grumbling, he turned to leave.

"I thank you, Horatio," Janes called after him.

"Have Gritzol go on deck and catch someone on the deck of the *Inferno* before you go," Ward added.

Ellis muttered some more before closing the door behind him.

"Are the odds in our favor with this plan, Chris?" Ward turned his attention back to the captain. "Last time we took on Marshall, he had at least twelve men."

"With Nyguard, he sent two other men, who are bound and gagged in the refuse bin."

Ward nodded. "That rids us of three men, but that could still leave nine more."

"Aye ... but I know Marshall too well." He chuckled grimly. "He would never leave his ship alone, and would never leave his ship unprotected." Wagging a finger, Janes gave a nod of acknowledgement. "As you mentioned, this is a risky proposition. But for Miss Acadia, I feel taking that risk is our only option."

"Shall I inform the crew?"

Janes nodded. "If we fail ... then I can only shudder at what Marshall might do."

Mr. Ward headed for the door.

In a cabin lit only by gas lanterns, Acadia regained consciousness.

"Feeling any better, my dear?" Marshall asked.

She took a moment to look around. It was a captain's cabin, all right. Acadia was amazed to see that it was much more elaborately decorated than any of the rooms she had seen aboard the *Valiant*. It had a rich purple carpeting with a gold border. The walls were clad in wooden panels, decorated with artwork and prized weapons. Trophies, Acadia decided. There were five windows—two on either wall with a larger one along the stern. This person apparently liked it dark, she thought, because even though the stern of the ship faced away from the afternoon sun, the thick curtains were closed.

She could not feel her charm on her wrist. Perhaps it was taken, she decided. For now, there were more pressing matters.

"Am I aboard your ship?" Acadia lifted her chin so she could look down her nose at him.

"Very sharp for a young lady." Marshall gave her a falsely gracious smile. "What else do you know?"

Trying to move her arms, Acadia found that they were free. However, her tail was tied with two thick ropes around the chair she sat upon. The chair itself was situated inside a shallow wooden tub. Her ropes were knotted along the bottom edges of the tub, well out of reach. The tub itself was filled with only an inch or so of water, which she assumed collected there when the captain—or whomever—tried to revive her.

She ignored his question. "What do you want with me?"

"It is not for you to ask questions, my dear." His tone was patronizing. "On the contrary, it is you who will divulge information today. Perhaps you can tell me who you know on the good ship *Valiant*."

Acadia looked around for a quick exit, but the windows were all closed. The door could be an option, but she couldn't tell if it was locked. Even if she could untie herself, she could not in any way move quickly enough to escape.

"It would seem you are uncomfortable, yes? My apologies for the bonds." With a mocking bow, Marshall took a seat on a trunk he kept at the end of the bed. "After what happened to Nicks, who I am certain earned his head injury, I decided a precautionary measure was necessary. We can do without any more violence."

She gave a regal shrug. "Why should it matter who I know on the *Valiant*? What is it to you, for you already have me."

"Everything matters, my dear." There was an almost fervent gleam in his eyes as he leaned closer. "Everything from the time of day to the condition of the seas … which, I suspect you have some knowledge of. The pattern of the waves on the sands, and even what the monkeys are dining on nightly. But, there are some things that matter more than others, such as who your friends are." Leaning back, he grew calmer. "Certainly you must have a reason for surfacing in the location you chose."

Acadia decided silence was favorable to betraying her friends, especially Thomas.

"You may choose not to respond if you wish. That will not upset me. But know this, my fishy friend…" Marshall pointed at her with such vehemence the lace on his cuffs shook. "In your current situation there is little you can do to help them. When you cooperate, I treat you well. Should you resist, I will not treat you well. You cannot live without water, and I am sure you cannot live without nourishment." Marshall's gaze drifted away from her and toward his artwork as though the outcome didn't matter to him. "The choice is yours."

Acadia considered her options carefully, quickly realizing how much power Marshall had over her. "What would you like to talk about?"

Marshall turned back to her with a smile. "Let us keep it simple, my dear. Perhaps I should introduce myself." Feigning shock, he put a hand to his chest. "How rude of me to wait so long into the conversation. Captain Marshall, at your service. And what may your name be, my dear?"

"You're nothing but a fiendish pirate!"

Marshall laughed, a demonic but playful laugh that gave Acadia a cold chill. "Yes indeed. I see my reputation has preceded me! But I know nothing about you, my dear. Surely you have a name?"

Acadia closed her eyes, and blinked a few times as a small tear escaped. "Acadia."

"Miss Acadia … a very lovely name for such a lovely creature." Marshall clapped his hands at their progress. "Now, enough with pleasantries, Acadia … you are familiar with the *Valiant*, yes?"

"Yes," she replied softly.

"But of course you are ... perhaps you'd like to discuss the name of the commander?" Marshall asked.

Acadia looked away. "I ... don't know," she whispered quickly.

"Forgive me, but the sounds of the ocean outside tend to drown out even the loveliest of the ocean's creatures, don't you agree?" Marshall stood and walked toward a nearby window.

Acadia remained silent.

"Did I hear the sound of a fish being scaled?" Marshall said, trailing his voice a little, making Acadia shiver in fright.

"Okay! Okay ... I'll talk," Acadia said softly.

Marshall turned to Acadia and smiled, even though it was the most devilish smile Acadia had ever seen. As he leaned close, she felt his breath on her face and cringed away, but could not escape from his poisonous gaze.

"Who is in command of the *Valiant*?" Marshall demanded.

"Christopher Janes," Acadia said under her breath, looking away.

Marshall came up to her and lifted her chin. Inches from her nose, he asked again. "Speak loud enough to be heard, or you will never see the ocean again."

"Captain Christopher Janes."

Marshall stood up quickly. "So ... not dead as we were led to believe. A crafty one, he is ... Gretty!"

Gretty opened the door and came in. "Yeah boss?"

"What's the condition of the cargo hold?" Marshall asked.

"Dry and dusty, boss," Gretty replied.

"Tidy it up for Miss Acadia here." With a hospitable wave he indicated their captive. "She'll be staying with us awhile."

"Aye boss," Gretty said, going to work.

"I told you what you wanted. What more value am I to you?" Acadia asked.

Marshall turned to her. "Quite simple, really. You're worth more than any treasure on the seven seas."

It took effort not to ball her hands into fists of frustration. "There is nothing I can do for you, and nobody around to showcase me to. Someone will come to my aid before you can leave these islands, and you will never get the treasure you seek."

She could smell something sour on Marshall's breath as he tied her arms to the back of the chair with some more rope.

"My dear, your thoughts are your own business. Your rescuers shall come, and they shall be killed. We are free to leave these shores; your friends are not." Finishing his task, he moved in front of her. "I will find what I've come for, and there is little you can do about it. After all, I shan't be the one to tell you what you are … and that you cannot simply walk away." There was a knock at the door. "Come!"

"All set boss," Gretty said.

He waved at her dismissively. "Take her away. Make sure it's nice and dark inside."

The men picked up Acadia, chair and all, and hauled her into the hall and downstairs. As she was taken away, Acadia heard devilish laughter, the kind that only a man as evil as Marshall could produce. Indeed, the laugh was familiar somehow, as if she had heard it before.

After getting the men to remove the tub from his cabin, Marshall took a breath of fresh air on the deck. "My word … for a mermaid, that girl sure smells like fish."

Through the narrow halls of the ship, both men worked feverishly to transport her through the lower decks. While being lowered down a narrow staircase, she caught a glimpse of fear in Gretty's eyes, even though she expected hatred and aggression. Surely all pirates were as vile as Marshall; Thomas had said not to trust any of them, yet these men were just as shaken as she was.

"You fear your captain … why?" Acadia asked.

Neither man responded. They averted their gaze, instead focusing on the task at hand.

"Am I correct? Even after leaving his presence, you continue to tremble."

Again, they did not return comment. Acadia was suddenly flustered; perhaps these pirates were not the same as their captain.

In the cargo hold, the two men plopped her onto a shallow wooden tub similar to the one used before and poured a bucket of water within. They removed the chair, but left the thick bonds in place.

Although Acadia had the strength to fight back, she did not pursue the opportunity. She had to confirm her suspicions.

"The boss ordered that you get only one gallon, miss, we're sorry." Gretty seemed sincere if unrepentant.

"Sorry?" She gave them a pitying look. "I feel sorry for you, taking orders from such an evil man."

Benks nodded his head. "Aye ... to think I fell for his trap that day ..." he trailed off, leaving the room in a rush.

"You should be so lucky to even have water. Most of his prisoners never receive such treatment," Gretty said, turning tersely toward the door.

"Such words could only come from a prisoner, as well," Acadia said.

Gretty stopped in his tracks.

"It is true, then? Why do you continue to serve him?"

Gretty shook his head, refusing to face her.

Acadia put as much warmth and persuasion into her voice as possible. "Do the right thing, Mr. Gretty."

"Ross," he replied.

"Ross, then. Of all people, you know my being here is wrong."

"I cannot, I am sorry." Gretty shook his head again.

It didn't make any sense to her. "Dear me, what has Marshall done to you?"

Gretty quickly left the room, leaving Acadia to wonder. If indeed these men were prisoners on their own ship, perhaps her rescue would come all the easier.

From the *Valiant*, Gritzol called. "Ahoy captain!"

Marshall spun around, apparently surprised. He suddenly realized that Nyguard hadn't yet returned.

"Ah, some news at last! Good day again, good sir. Have my men completed their search?" Marshall called.

"Afraid not, sir! They decided to search on shore ... but perhaps we could discuss the matter over tea? My captain wishes to cooperate as fully as possible, you understand?" Gritzol called.

Marshall grumbled quietly. "You're such a fool, Nyguard." He composed himself and addressed Gritzol once more. "Very well, sir, you put me into a peculiar position. Tell your captain that I accept. Shall I bring the tea?"

Gritzol bowed. "You need not concern yourself, leave it to us, sir! We shall meet you shortly, near the waterfall."

Marshall nodded, watching the man on the *Valiant* leave the deck. Then, he pounded his foot on the deck three times. "Gretty! Aramondo! On deck, now!"

Both men quickly arrived and stood at attention.

"Aye boss?" both chimed.

"Turns out the good Captain Ellis wants a meeting this afternoon for tea. I think it should be good to find out the truth behind his generosity," Marshall said.

"You want some guards, boss?" Aramondo asked.

Marshall nodded. "I would have preferred you said escort, but that is your chief purpose. Just in case he has something planned."

"What about the girl?" Gretty asked.

"Benks and Fallah will be outside the door, plus Geynall and the cabin boy," Marshall replied.

"The cook? He's not good with a sword, boss," Aramondo said.

"He can use a knife just fine. He's a cook, isn't he?" Marshall asked.

Gretty nodded.

"Are there any other orders? Boss?" Aramondo asked, quivering slightly.

"None for the moment."

Aramondo made for the ladder below.

"Gretty?"

"Yeah boss?" Gretty asked.

"Did you give the girl, as you called her, some water?" he asked in a bit of a hush.

"No boss, I haven't given her anything." Gretty was willing to chance a white lie if it meant better treatment for Acadia.

"Do so." With a nod he turned for his cabin. "Do not let her dehydrate, although you may let her starve."

"Aye boss."

Ward hurried down to the lowest deck to find Thomas alone in the cargo hold, practicing his fencing once more.

"Tommy," Ward said, leaning on a barrel that had once contained grain.

Thomas lowered his training rapier. "Hello, sir."

"I see you've been practicing hard, that be good to see."

"Aye sir, Mr. Benson wants me to keep my training consistent."

Crossing his arms across his chest, he gave the boy a meaningful look. "What if I told you that training may come into use someday?"

"I suppose it might one day, sir." Thomas shrugged.

"What if I told you that day was today, Tommy?" Ward asked again.

Thomas responded with a confused look. "I do not understand, sir."

"Did you happen to see Miss Acadia today?"

Thomas shook his head. "No sir, not today. We were ashore."

Ward raised his hand. "I know … Thomas, the captain saw Acadia, but not face to face."

"Sir?" Thomas asked.

Ward took a deep breath. "He saw her from his cabin window."

"His window?"

"As she was taken into Marshall's rowboat," Ward concluded, softly.

With a gasp, Thomas sat upon the nearest box. "That is … horrible."

"Aye, but I know this much." Ward straightened and placed a comforting hand on Thomas's shoulder. "Acadia is waiting for you."

Thomas felt a surge of adrenaline begin to build. "I'll waste him."

"Whoa, easy!" Holding up his hands, Ward shook his head. "We're not going after Marshall."

"No! Let me, please!" Thomas was on his feet, grasping at Ward's shirt as though to shake the man.

"You're no match for him. If you're slashed through by Marshall, you won't be doing yourself or us any favors." With little effort, Ward disengaged the boy from his shirt, and pushed him back toward the box where he sat. "Acadia is waiting for you, but she must be helped first. Myself, Perry, and the captain are planning on going over to the *Inferno* later today. I was hoping you would come with."

Thomas nodded. "If Acadia is waiting for me, there is no choice, sir."

"That is the decision of a man." Ward gave him a slap on the shoulder that rattled his teeth. "We shall meet in the mess hall after lunch. Ellis will prepare for tea with Marshall ashore."

"Mr. Ellis? Is he going ashore?"

Ward nodded. "Of course. He's the captain, as much as Marshall knows."

"Mr. Ellis, the captain?" Thomas suddenly felt sick to his stomach.

"It does not matter now. Continue to practice your fencing, it may do you credit sooner than you think."

Thomas stood and took a guard position. "I will sir, you can count on me."

"Good, because Acadia already is." With a nod, Ward left.

After thrusting with his training blade a few times, Thomas switched to a scimitar he found mounted on the wall. Since he knew of nobody who was using it, he took what little time was left to practice with it as best he could.

As Gretty returned to the *Inferno*'s cargo hold, he stopped at the mess hall and picked up a few small biscuits. When he arrived in the hold, he opened the door and found that Acadia was sleeping quietly, even though she was still securely tied up.

Taking the nearby bucket of water, he poured it over her scales. She woke as the water refreshed her, and he untied her arms and hands.

"Mmmm ... Ross?" Acadia asked, opening her eyes.

"Here, eat these." He handed her the biscuits.

"Bread? This is not on order from your captain, is it?" Acadia asked, taking them.

Gretty turned away. "No, he has no knowledge."

Acadia took a small bite of the biscuit and held it aside, turning her gaze toward Gretty. "Why do you look away? Is it my appearance?"

Gretty shook his head. "I do not mean to offend, miss, but when I look upon your face, I am reminded of Adriana, my eldest daughter."

"Ross, why do you let Marshall do this to you?"

"What would a son think if his father was cut down in cold blood by a coward?" Gretty replied, taking a seat on a barrel.

"So you have a large family?" Acadia asked with concern.

"Aye, I did once. Six years ago ... by now my oldest should be a man."

"I sympathize, Mr. Gretty. How many others?" Acadia asked.

"My oldest was fifteen. I also have two girls, ten and eight ... my youngest was still unborn when...." Gretty paused.

It seemed to Acadia that many sailors had sad personal stories. "I will listen, if you wish."

Gretty gave a deep sigh. He used a handkerchief to wipe a tear before continuing. "I was along the port, with my oldest boy, taking our harvest to market. I was a wheat farmer, that's all ... just living from my father's fields, and … leaving Garrett, my son, to run the farm when he was almost ready.…"

"Garrett … your eldest son."

Gretty nodded. "Aye miss."

"And Marshall came, and kidnapped you?"

"While Garrett delivered the grain to the mill, I went to get some ale, but never made it back to tell him the secrets of our trade. And … I may… never get to.…" Gretty hid his face, too ashamed to show his tears.

"Ross, will you not stand up for your own honor? It pains me to see you submit to Marshall so easily." Acadia had seldom seen tears, least of all for the living, and they tugged at her heart.

After a moment, Gretty stood. "Prisoners have no honor." He headed towards the door.

"Thank you for the bread," Acadia said.

"Please, forget you received it." He closed the door behind him.

Acadia continued to eat the biscuits. She felt sorry for Gretty, and began to wonder if the other men under Marshall's command shared his plight. With such new and complex situations to consider, she was almost able to set aside her own troubles.

"Okay, now let me understand this one last time," Ellis began, as he leaned against the rail. He was decked out in one of Janes's old dress coats while the captain wore a simple coat over a plain shirt and breeches.

Janes let out an exasperated sigh. "Horatio, I have told you the plan four times now. Must I continue to explain?"

"I'm just thinking this be a bad idea," Ellis muttered.

"'I *believe* this is a *terrible* idea.' Horatio, you must sound more civilized," Ward said, adjusting the cook's collar.

"Marshall and you are simply meeting casually, like two old friends. Is that so difficult to grasp?" Janes asked.

"All right, all right, so let's say—assume, that this scheme, er…" Putting on his captain's hat, Ellis straightened a bit and pompously held a lapel of his coat. "Let us assume this plan of yours, works. How shall we know it has succeeded?"

Janes gave an approving nod. "A good question. When we return from the *Inferno*, Mr. Roberts will start playing his fife loudly. So when you go ashore, make sure you stay in the open or you will not be able to hear it."

With a final tug at a cuff, Ellis was ready, and the group exited to the deck. "Fine then ... since there be no getting out of...." Ellis paused and cleared his throat. "Let us get this party underway."

Gritzol and Lewinston joined them on deck.

"Good tidings, gentlemen," Janes said with a bow.

"On your order, Captain," Lewinston said with pride.

"Aw, hush up Jim," Ellis muttered as he climbed into the rowboat. Once the rowboat was manned and lowered, the captain and Ward went into the cabin as the three men started toward shore.

Meanwhile, Marshall was also loading his rowboat.

"Boss, do you know those two men o'er yonder?" Gretty asked, seeing Janes and Ward leave the deck.

"Who?" Marshall said, taking a quick glance. He only saw Ward for a quick moment, as Janes had already left his view.

"Did you see them, boss?" Gretty asked.

"You are trying to worry me, Gretty." Marshall's voice steadily became more menacing.

"N-no, boss, I's serious," Gretty replied quickly.

Marshall gruffed slightly. There were no other men aboard the *Valiant* he could see. "No matter, for we have an appointment to keep." He climbed into his rowboat, fully unaware of the cunning plan Janes had put into work.

While he waited for the moment to storm the *Inferno*, Janes continued reading Scyhathen's book by the light of a lantern. Coming to an unusual passage, he made sure to read it very carefully.

December 9th, 1582. We continue to exist here, even now as the waters have gone cold. The peculiar events that have plagued myself and my crew have not ceased. The occurrence of these incidents seems to have increased since we explored Siren Island.

Kid has been involved in the most interesting of these encounters. One such episode occurred when the boy, myself, and Smitty went ashore to gather fresh fruit. Several monkeys had gathered in the trees and seemed almost in awe of the boy. When Kid began climbing the trees, the monkeys, rather than fleeing in fear, handed bananas to him by the bushel, making our task effortless.

A few days ago the boy and Mr. Mandalay were making some sketches ashore, and a mother tiger came to watch. Rather than defend her territory, the tigress stood at attention until Kid shared his lunch. Although he had already eaten most of it, the remnants of his bread roll seemed to be enough. Yet tigers are carnivorous, and there is little enough meat on these islands. Bizarre was the word Mr. Mandalay used to describe the scene. Such events are becoming commonplace. As exceptional as they may be, I dread each new day, for the next dawn may bring the return of Captain Epoth.

Janes began to think. What of Thomas and the tiger today? Was there some connection? And if so … who was this Kid DeLeuit that Scyhathen kept writing about? Somehow he'd find the answers to his questions, but first Miss Acadia must be returned to the sea. He retrieved his silver sword from the wall, along with a whetstone, and readied himself for the coming raid.

Ellis and the others arrived ashore much sooner than Marshall's clan. They soon were able to establish a place where they could see both ships. It was far enough ashore that the pleasant sounds of falling water could be heard.

"This spot looks good, Ellis," Gritzol said.

"Aye … and there's even a stump to use as a tea table," Ellis replied.

"You think Marshall will come to this unarmed?" Lewinston asked.

Gritzol huffed. "Of course not. He'd never do that."

"Aye, I fully expect him to be armed." Ellis tapped the side of his nose. "That's why we brought ours, ye know. Should the subject come up, we will simply say that they were for defense from … I don't know … from the wildlife."

Having spent weeks trying to catch some meat, Lewinston chuckled. "Good call, Captain."

"A response like that'll keep him on level terms." Gritzol glanced at the *Inferno* as he set out the teapot and cups for the "captains" and mugs for the men.

"If only long enough to give the captain and Mr. Ward enough time," Ellis said.

"Aye," Gritzol said.

"Start a fire, then." Ellis gave them an officious wave. "This special brew of tea that I blended myself is best plenty hot."

"No problem." Lewinston used a tinderbox and soon had a good fire started.

As Marshall's rowboat past the *Valiant*, Janes watched it carefully.

"It seems that Marshall took the bait, Chris," Ward said.

"Ahh, Marshall. Still predictable, I see, trying to keep a prim edge even now." Janes turned from the window back to his blade. "We shall give them some time, Seriam. One needs plenty of time to confer, you know." With a fluid motion, he sheathed his sword with a lethal snap.

"Just give the word, and the men will be ready." Ward turned to head below again.

"Soon, Seriam." Picking up his tea, Janes sipped it while watching through the gap in his curtains. "Our time shall be worth the wait."

Aboard the *Inferno*, Benks entered the hold with a small bucket of water and a few slices of bread, buttered and topped with jelly.

"Oh my, what is all this?" Acadia's eyes lit up with surprise.

"The cook was wondering how hungry you were, so I took the opportunity to serve, miss," Benks said.

"I believe I am at a loss, mister…?" Acadia began.

"Jed Benks." The man gave a little bow. "I have much experience in service."

"Service to Captain Marshall, perhaps?" Acadia asked, as Benks added water to her washtub.

"Since he removed me from the service of my master, yes," Benks replied softly.

"I see Mr. Gretty's situation is not unique on this craft, then?" She sadly shook her head.

"We are all prisoners, but by serving him we get better treatment than those who do not." Dragging an empty crate over, he placed the tray adjacent to the washtub.

"Am I correct to assume that I am one of the fortunate ones?" Acadia asked.

Benks nodded. "Those who resist with swords are defeated, and those without usually walk the plank."

"Excuse me, the plank?" She blinked at him in confusion. "I am not familiar with that. Can you explain?"

"Why, it is nothing more than a long piece of timber attached to the deck, madam." He glanced at her tail and smiled politely. "But I can see how it should not concern you."

"I do not understand. Is it because I cannot walk it, Mr. Benks?" Acadia asked, still confused.

"Because it is my belief you are an adept swimmer," Benks replied.

Acadia smiled graciously. "Yes, that is true. Do you know how to keep yourself afloat, Mr. Benks?"

He gave her another polite smile. "Not as well as you, I would suppose."

"If Captain Marshall ever has you walk his plank, simply stretch your arms all the way out, and keep your legs straight." She stretched her arms out to demonstrate. "If you are not too heavy, you should be fine until you reach the shore with the tide."

Benks started to leave. "Usually they'll tie you up so that you cannot use your arms, but I shall remember." With a bow he closed the door behind him.

"What a foolish method of torture," Acadia fumed as she nibbled on a piece of bread.

As Captain Marshall approached Captain Ellis's camp, the tea just finished steeping. Ellis strained the amber liquid into one of the two fancy teacups resting on the cloth they'd used to cover the stump. There were even crumpets on a silver platter.

"There it goes then." Holding his cup daintily, Ellis tried a sip.

"I say, may I join you?" Captain Marshall stepped from behind a tree.

Ellis stood up as Gritzol and Lewinston closed in behind him. "Greetings, Captain Marshall. I had high hopes you would join us." Ellis spoke in as lofty a tone as possible.

"Please, do not stand at attention. We are simply gentlemen enjoying tea and a crumpet or two." Marshall took a crumpet from the platter. The two men behind him grumbled. They had come hoping for action, not tea.

Ellis sat down, with Gritzol and Lewinston standing uncomfortably behind him. "Please, help yourself to this exquisite tea of my own concoction—with raspberry and mint." Ellis strained some tea into Marshall's cup.

"Smells delectable." Accepting the cup and saucer from Ellis, Marshall took a sip.

Mr. Gretty watched carefully as Marshall took a larger drink. "Is it okay, boss?"

"Quite okay, Gretty." Marshall waved a hand at the men behind him. "Captain, my esteemed associates, Mr. Gretty, and Mr. Aramondo." With a gesture from their captain, they eagerly sat down.

Ellis nodded haughtily. "Mr. Gritzol and Mr. Lewinston. It was too nice of a day to sit inside the cabin, you understand, so they opted to come with."

Gritzol and Lewinston quickly sat down as well.

"Of course, too true, these men had the same idea, didn't ye boys?" As Marshall looked at them in turn, each made a solid grin and nod, returning to a more sullen look afterward.

"What shall we talk about, Captain? I trust you have a well-rounded crew, yes?" Ellis began as Marshall sampled the tea.

"They are adequate, perhaps dispensable at times, but a good crew." Marshall lifted his cup in salute. "Tell me, how did you create this tea of yours? Rarely does one find mint and raspberry in the same brew." The men behind him exchanged disgusted looks.

"A hobby of mine, as the journeys we make sometimes involve the ports of the tea trade, Captain." Ellis made a modest little shrug and strained some into the mugs for the crewmen. "One only needs a taste they like with an aroma that appeals...."

As they chatted quietly, Gritzol and Lewinston were amazed at how civil Ellis could be. Perhaps it was all for Captain Janes, but nonetheless Ellis and Marshall found themselves speaking on many things, from trade winds to the cultures of distant nations ... no topic was forbidden. Despite the convivial air, it seemed just about every other word that came out of Marshall's mouth was an insult toward his crew, which did nothing to dissuade Gretty and Aramondo's animosity toward their captain.

While Ellis and the others kept Marshall occupied, Captain Janes, Mr. Ward, Mr. Perry, and Thomas took to the rowboat and embarked for the *Inferno*, which lay quiet and still. Securing the rowboat to the hull, they climbed up the side of the *Inferno* and removed their swords. As expected, the deck was empty.

"Come quickly." Janes headed to the one door that was visible. "The cabin must be this way."

They were a bit surprised to find a small landing with ladder leading down. Janes closed the door quickly, hearing footsteps.

"Is this all we do, just go in headfirst?" Ward picked up a nearby belaying pin just in case.

"If anyone has any other ideas, now is the time to speak out." The captain waited a moment, but heard no replies. "Well then. Come on." He opened the door again.

Inside, the cabin boy was preparing to swab the deck. He grabbed his knife as quickly as possible, pointing it at them with a shaky hand. "Who are you?! And just where do you think you are going?"

"Get out of the way, boy," Ward said.

"Boss told me nobody gets through! And that means you, it does!"

"Keith! What're you mumbling fer?" a voice from below called.

Janes pointed his blade toward the boy's throat. "You're only talking to yourself." It was not a request.

"Off it," the cabin boy said, knocking the blade down. Within seconds, four blades were on the boy's neck.

"What's your name, boy?" Janes asked.

"What's it to ye, ye codfish?" the boy spat back.

Ward raised an eyebrow at the unusual epithet. "Kid's got quite a lip."

"Boy, you better be swabbin' the deck like boss told ye to," the voice called again.

"You don't want to be here, do ye, boy?" Janes's voice was as smooth and sweet as fresh cream.

"What do you care?"

"If you know what's good fer ye ..." Ward began.

"O'Nuss! You hearing me?" the voice called a third time.

"I ain't talkin'!" the boy cried.

"Enough of this." With a quick, efficient move, Ward disarmed the boy and gave him a shove toward his bucket and mop. With the entry clear,

Janes and Ward started down, but the boy wasn't going to give up that easy. He tried to attack Perry from behind.

Perry turned and stared down at the boy, his massive sword at the ready. "You, fight me?" His accent was thicker than usual.

"Um … ah … ahhh!!!!" The boy bolted onto the deck.

"Stupid kid.…" the voice from below muttered as footsteps echoed in the hall.

"Here he comes," Janes said. Ward waited around the corner by the staircase at the end of the short hall. The cook came out with his knife ready.

"I'll cut you good for this—ugh!"

Ward threw the belaying pin at the man's forehead, knocking him to the ground. The large man breathed deeply, but did not stir.

"Looks like the cook," Thomas said.

"Aye … chances are his cooking isn't as good as Ellis's," Ward said.

"Shall I pull him aside, Captain?" Perry asked.

"We do not have much time. Come on now." Janes started deeper into the ship.

They came by the barracks and continued farther into the nearly deserted ship, reaching the cargo level to find Fallah and Benks guarding the door. Both men drew their weapons as Janes's rescue party approached.

"Hold it, who are you?" Benks asked.

"We've come for the girl." Janes gestured with his sword to indicate the room beyond them where he knew she must be. "You can either let us through or be defeated, the choice is yours."

Benks stepped back, lowering his sword. "Take her."

"Please, return her to the sea, sirs," Fallah added, letting them pass.

"Are you sure?" Ward asked, bewildered.

"You don't put up much resistance, do you?" Thomas asked.

"Tommy," Janes said sternly.

"There is no reason to, boy," Benks said.

"And why is that?" Janes asked, also confused.

"Cap'n, they're prisoners too," Perry replied.

Benks's eyes lit up. "You are Captain Janes, then?"

Janes nodded.

"Will you take us with you?" Benks asked eagerly.

"Sailor, I came here for a mermaid, not to recruit pirates." Janes stepped around both men and entered the hold.

"Please, Marshall will kill us if you take her," Fallah began.

"Then you had better come up with a good excuse, sailor." With a shrug, Ward entered the cargo room.

"Excuse me," Thomas said, as he and Perry went by.

"Guard the door, eh?" Benks said aside to Fallah.

"Hmm..." Fallah began.

"Christopher ... Thomas! And Perry ... at last!" Acadia cried as Janes and Thomas came in and undid her remaining bonds. Once she was free, she hugged Thomas tightly.

"Miss Acadia, are you well?" Janes asked, kneeling next to her as she hugged him.

"I am quite well, thank you," Acadia said.

"I will carry you now, Miss Acadia," Perry said.

She held her arms out to the big man. "Thank you, Perry, Thomas! Thank you all."

"Acadia, why did you surface so close to Marshall's boat?" Thomas asked as Perry took her into his arms.

"I heard a sound from the shell, so I came." She gave a dainty shrug. "It looked like any other rowboat to me."

"You mean ... my shell?" Thomas began, holding it in his pocket.

"Tommy, it must've been an accident," Ward said.

"I ... um..." Suddenly overwhelmed with guilt, Thomas wracked his brain to try to figure out how it might have happened.

"Do not blame yourself, Thomas. As you say, an accident." She looked up to the man carrying her. "Perry, may we go now?"

"Aye, let's be off then." Janes started toward the door; however he found it blocked by Benks and Fallah.

"Captain, I cannot allow you to leave. I'm under orders, sir," Benks began.

"Sailor, we can do this the easy way or the hard way. According to my math, it would appear that there are two more of us." He nodded to their liberated young lady. "Three if you include Miss Acadia here."

Benks and Fallah looked at each other with disgust. "All right, take her," Benks said.

Janes nodded in gratitude. "You have made the right decision, sailor. I shall try to remember your cooperation today." He and the others began upstairs.

"Wait, there's one more thing," Fallah replied. He removed Acadia's shell charm from his pocket and held it out for her. "I took it when she was unconcious.... I just took it, although it was not mine to take."

Janes had recognized the charm from before. Without a word, he placed it onto Acadia's wrist and headed up the stairs.

"Thank you," she replied softly as Perry carried her away. The rest of the crew followed.

Watching the rescue party leave, Fallah shook his head morosely. "Marshall'll have our heads, ye know."

"Maybe. But with most of the men already missing, he doesn't have many of us left." Benks headed toward the barracks.

"Aye, I s'pose you're right," Fallah replied, following behind.

The day began to fade into a blazing orange sunset, Ellis and Marshall were still chatting. Ellis was growing impatient for the signal from Mr. Roberts, as the conversation was growing stale.

"And that was the last time he ignored my orders, Captain," Marshall replied.

"Hmm ... I can see maintaining discipline, Captain, but that is a bit harsh, yes?" Ellis asked, in reference to the late Mr. Harris.

"Oh, tis not that harsh; Jesse was always a bit of a bother. He and his ability to fail at everything ... but enough about him. Is there anything else we shall talk about? My missing property, perhaps?" Marshall asked.

Gritzol had a thought that Marshall's statement about Harris was somewhat exaggerated, but he chose to continue sipping his tea rather than create an argument.

"I have noticed the grand condition that your ship is in. Is it fast?" Ellis asked.

Marshall made a confused look. "Fast? Yes, but, did you not ask me that question earlier?"

Gretty spoke up. "He did, boss."

"What of the trade routes, Captain?" Lewinston muttered to Ellis.

"I'm sorry, I must've drifted off. This tea, it is too good to ignore," Ellis said.

"Yes ... perhaps I've had too much," Marshall said, finishing his cup.

"Are you leaving so soon? We haven't discussed what item it is you were looking for, or where your crew might be?" Ellis sputtered.

"They'll show up … although that doesn't explain…." Marshall began. Suddenly, he saw in the distance an empty rowboat riding the waves along the lagoon.

"I beg your pardon?" Ellis asked quietly.

"Nothing, captain. I enjoyed your tea … if you'll excuse me." Tapping his hat in lieu of a bow, Marshall took off for the beach. Gretty and Aramondo followed close behind.

"Wait! Please take some with you!" Ellis called.

"Forget it, Ellis. Come on!" Lewinston chased after their "guests."

"The captain's not going to like this," Gritzol muttered, following after his crewmate.

Ellis turned around and saw the rowboat hit the beach. It was the *Inferno*'s second rowboat that had been allowed to drift along the shores.

"Captain's not going to like this at all." Ellis let out a vexed huff and hastily poured the remaining tea onto the coals. Taking his sword in hand, he ran to catch up with the other men.

It was at that moment Janes and his crew finished the arduous task of getting a mermaid up a ladder and reached the deck of the *Inferno*. Although there was no sign of the cook, the cabin boy blocked their exit.

"Still fighting, are we?" Janes asked.

"You aren't getting away from me this time!" He held his knife steadily.

"Out of the way, boy," Ward ordered.

"I'll take him, sir." Thomas drew his scimitar.

"A sword? I'm not taking you on with that!?" the cabin boy cried.

"Fine then. Mr. Ward, may I borrow your sword?" Thomas asked.

"A fair fight, good form." Ward instructed, handing his to Thomas then tossing the scimitar to the *Inferno*'s cabin boy, O'Nuss.

"Ugh!" he cried, dropping it.

Janes held up a hand. "Let him pick it up."

Thomas did so, and soon O'Nuss was ready. However, by the way the other boy held the weapon, it was pretty obvious that his skill with it was limited.

"Ready," Thomas said, quite comfortable with the saber. O'Nuss held the scimitar awkwardly, a noticeable shake in his boots.

"Be careful, Thomas!" Acadia said.

"Have at it!" Thomas said, making the first slash. O'Nuss defended it, and soon both young men were fencing ferociously. A low slash from O'Nuss and Thomas feinted, jumping over O'Nuss's blade and cutting his opponent's arm on the return slash.

"Augh!" O'Nuss cried.

Thomas paused. "Do you yield?"

"Not yet!" O'Nuss yelled back. He lunged at Thomas, who dodged and parried back. With a few more hits, Thomas's superior technique became clear. The scimitar flew to the side of the ship and landed next to the port rail, leaving Thomas's point hovering in front of the boy's chest.

"How about now?" Thomas asked.

"I yield; I yield!" O'Nuss said.

Thomas didn't remove his point right away.

"He's yielded, Thomas." Janes's observation had a hint of command in it.

Thomas nodded then lowered the weapon and reached out with his left hand to help the boy up. Instead, O'Nuss drew his knife and swiped at Thomas's wrist, slashing the middle of his lower arm.

"Ugh!" Thomas cried, tripping backward in surprise.

"Thomas!" Acadia shrieked.

"Enough of this." Ward picked up the scimitar and thrust it at the boy.

"Whoa!" O'Nuss backed up against the railing.

"Tommy, you okay?" Ward asked.

Janes wrapped his handkerchief around Thomas's wound to slow the bleeding.

"He'll be fine." Janes adjusted the tourniquet, ensuring that it was tight.

"Go below and don't come up unless you want more pain," Ward said, keeping the scimitar fixed on the boy.

"Just you wait until next time!" O'Nuss blurted, scurrying below deck.

"Thomas, you fought bravely," Acadia said. Perry put her down next to him.

"It's ... nothing." But his reply was unconvincing, as it came through gritted teeth.

She held him around the waist, her tail moving back and forth along the deck. "Thank you for defending me."

"So ... you sent a decoy to me after all!"

They turned to see Marshall's head above the starboard railing.

"Lower your arms, boys ... we have run out of time," Janes said quietly. Thomas and the others sheathed their weapons just before Captain Marshall climbed onto the deck. If there was to be more fighting, they agreed, it would have to be done ashore. There, Acadia wouldn't be hurt so easily.

"If it isn't the honorable Captain Janes, from beyond the grave." Marshall struck a dramatic pose as though confronting a ghost. Gretty and Aramondo climbed up behind their captain.

"Beyond the grave, Marshall? You should talk," Janes countered blandly.

"I am uncertain how you planned this, but I commend your efforts. Tell me, where is my property?" Marshall asked.

"Gretty, check on Benks and Fallah," Aramondo said.

"Aye," Gretty said. He rushed below, and the crew of the *Valiant* didn't stop him.

"You have us, what more do you want?" Acadia asked.

"Yes, my dear. I do have you ... all of you. I hope you enjoyed a little fresh air for the moment ... Aramondo, take their weapons," Marshall ordered.

Janes yielded his sword to Aramondo without a word. Ward and Thomas did as well, but when Aramondo reached for Perry's, Perry took him by the collar and lifted him off the deck. Janes quietly shook his head, and Perry let go.

"Ugh." Aramondo had to catch his breath. Then, he took the massive blade and put it with the rest of the weapons just inside the cabin door.

"Ah, Mr. Perry, always the strength behind Janes's blade...." Marshall sauntered up and patted him on the cheek. Perry flinched, but did not resist further.

Gretty returned from below with Benks and Fallah, although the cabin boy did not show. "The cook's shaken and coming around. I couldn't find the boy ... but these two are okay."

"And you two allowed them to retrieve the girl?" Marshall demanded.

"They spared us, boss," Benks said.

"So be your mistake, Janes," Marshall replied, turning away.

"You want some silly map?" Janes seemed disinterested in the whole affair. "I do not have it here."

"Then where is it?" Marshall asked, sneering into Janes' face.

Janes didn't flinch for a second. "I am the only one who can lead you to it, and if you kill any of us, you'll never find it."

Marshall took a step back. "Very well. We'll play your little game."

"Have I your word, Marshall?" Janes raised an inquisitive eyebrow.

"The word of the king may as well be mine, Janes. You of all people know that," Marshall replied.

Janes nodded. "We shall see."

"I ask you again, where be the map?" Marshall asked, a little calmer this time.

"Ashore. On Siren Island, within a deep cavern." Janes bluffed; the map was still safely locked away in his safe.

"Is that so? You would have us meet ashore, when the map is so nearby? Where is the logic in that!? No, that is too convenient, I do not believe it," Marshall countered.

"The choice is yours to make." With a shrug, Janes turned his attention to his fingernails. "I noticed how empty your cargo hold is. Waning supplies will make your wait unpleasant."

Marshall drew closer and poked the other captain in the chest with a finger. "It is you who can wait as long as you wish." He turned back to his crew. "Gretty, take the cabin boy and bond him."

Gretty tied Thomas's hands, along with his legs. Thomas thought about struggling, but chose not to. He knew he was a competent swimmer.

"What do you want with the boy?" Janes asked.

"Please, no!" Acadia begged.

Marshall paced in a circle, ignoring Acadia's pleas. "Oh, he's worth nothing to me. But I can see he might be to you, my dear," Marshall said, turning to her in mid-sentence.

Thomas shook his head. "Acadia, no. Don't endanger yourself."

Anticipating his captain's intentions, Aramondo set up a long wooden plank over the edge of the ship.

"How heroic! And how brave!" Marshall went so far as to withdraw a hankie and mockingly dab his eyes. "But all for naught, once you walk the plank, young man!"

Acadia gasped. "You cannot do this!" Even though she knew Thomas could swim, she didn't want to see him try while he was tied up.

"Oh my, but I can do this! Be reasonable, my dear! What can you do to me? You certainly can't rescue your boyfriend from above the waves!" With a gesture from Marshall, Gretty pushed Thomas into position.

Janes continued to weigh his choices. He didn't want to lead Marshall into the cave, especially without his sword, but his options in the cavern would be somewhat of an advantage—as long as Thomas lived.

Acadia closed her eyes, her fear overwhelming.

Cynthia and Marsha were in the Cove at the time and sensed Acadia's fear right away.

"What is it?" Marsha asked.

"Acadia has trouble … come, there's no time to explain." Cynthia jumped into the water and swam ahead.

"Acadia? Oh! Wait for me!" Marsha followed close behind.

"Marshall, perhaps we can deal after all. I will show you to the cavern myself, but only if you take my men with," Janes replied.

"I think that can be arranged." Marshall nodded. "More mules for moving the treasure, says I. But only if I get your mermaid, too. She is not out of the fire yet."

"I will not last on the shore," Acadia replied. Fear rang clearly through her voice.

"Bring enough water for her, and she is yours," Janes said.

Acadia couldn't believe her ears. "Christopher…."

Perry, who was still kneeling next to her, whispered in her ear. "Worry not, you will be safe with me."

"And she is mine from then on?" Marshall asked.

Janes remained steadfast. "From then on…."

"Put the boy into position!" Marshall cried. Gretty poked his sword into Thomas's back.

"Ugh!" Thomas said, as he walked slowly onto the plank so he wouldn't trip.

"You were saying something, or should the boy walk?" Marshall threatened.

"From then on … she's yours," Janes said softly.

"Ah ha then! Gretty, get the rowboat ready," Marshall replied.

"Aye boss!" Gretty called, pounding his foot too close to the teetering plank. It sent shockwaves onto the board. Thomas lost his balance, and fell in with a large splash.

"No!" Acadia cried.

Gretty winced, hiding his anguish from Marshall.

"Tommy!" Ward called.

"Oooh, bad, Mr. Gretty, bad. Tsk tsk … too shameful." Marshall shrugged. "Get the sails ready, and take that mermaid back to the tub." Turning, he left for his cabin.

Gretty glanced over the side, then tied up Janes's hands. Fallah, Nicks, and Benks tied the hands of the rest of Janes' men. They tied Acadia's too, but did not go to the trouble of restraining her tail this time.

"Thomas, please be all right," Acadia said to herself.

Kidnapping for a Kidnapping

*U*nderwater, Thomas struggled to free himself from his bonds. He was able to loosen his legs before his hands. His air didn't last long enough, however, as he was unable to get a full breath when he pitched into the water.

As his feet touched bottom, his air gave out. But just before he blacked out, Marsha swam forth and took hold around his torso. Rather than bring him directly to the surface, she and Cynthia swiftly brought him to the far side of the *Valiant*, avoiding Marshall's view.

"Thomas, cough it out." Cynthia thumped his back as Marsha held him above the water.

Thomas spit up seawater. He sputtered and coughed and shook his head, very surprised to discover that he was still alive. "Cynthia … Marsha … am I glad to see you … where am I?"

"Acadia called for us, and we arrived just in time. Are you okay?" Cynthia asked.

"I am now, thanks to you." Thomas couldn't help grinning like a fool.

Cynthia smiled, patting him again on the back. Marsha removed the rest of the bonds from his legs and hands.

Despite the trauma of nearly drowning, one question remained clear in his mind. "She never opened her mouth. How did she contact you?"

"Not by words." Cynthia rested a hand over her heart. "She sent us a message conveying her emotional fear for your safety."

Thomas shook his head, unsure. "What?"

"Acadia sent an emotional message to both Marsha and myself, Thomas. Mermaids can sense emotions, such as fear or concern, from one another. It also works with other marine life, as with the dolphin the other day," Cynthia explained.

"Acadia's fear at that time was so strong, the message could be felt as far away as the mainland, if need be," Marsha added.

Thomas nodded.

"We were unsure what to look for. Then we saw the other ship. I noticed the plank overhead, and you entered the water," Marsha explained.

"Can you tell her that I'm okay?" Thomas asked.

Cynthia closed her eyes a moment. "She knows of your safety."

"What do you think I should do next? The captain and the others are Marshall's prisoners now," Thomas said.

"But not all of your crew, I hope?" Cynthia asked.

"No, there are some men ashore as well as on our ship," Thomas said.

"I suggest you strategize a plan with your remaining crew." Her gaze turned away, as though she could see through the *Valiant* to the ship carrying her sister. "As for Acadia, I have faith in your captain. I do not believe he will allow her to come to any harm."

Thomas swam to the ladder on the hull. "Thank you for saving my life."

Cynthia held up a hand. "Wait, Thomas, do not climb just yet. Marsha, check the other side for rowboats."

Marsha nodded, diving under and swimming to the other side of the *Valiant*.

"What is it?" Thomas asked.

"Should more of Marshall's men come aboard your ship, you do not want to be re-captured. In fact, when you do go aboard, take care to hide your remaining crewmembers, lest they be captured too," Cynthia warned.

Thomas nodded. "I will."

Marsha re-surfaced. "All clear … in fact, the other ship is leaving."

"Go quickly, Thomas, and remember…" Cynthia touched his hand. "Only you can save Acadia and your captain."

"I will, thank you again." With a nod, Thomas headed up the ladder.

Cynthia and Marsha dove underwater. Marsha suddenly realized that Cynthia had a strange thought in her mind. "Cynthia, what are you thinking about?"

Cynthia came to a stop, remaining underwater. "I do not know, but there is something in Thomas I have sensed before. … something very familiar."

"Familiar? I have not sensed anything," Marsha replied.

"Perhaps Acadia has sensed it without knowing." Cynthia glanced up at the *Valiant* looming above them. "I cannot explain it, but something very familiar is there."

"The last time you spoke like this was when Scyhathen's ship was still here," Marsha said.

"I don't recall. It may have been nothing. But, there are more pressing matters at this time, and there is work to do." A flick of her tail sent Cynthia speeding away.

Marsha nodded and followed as they swam toward the Cove.

Back aboard the *Inferno*, Marshall kept Acadia and the others in the cargo hold as they traveled toward Siren Island. On deck, Nicks, Benks, and Gretty were discussing the situation. Marshall supervised nearby.

"How is your head feeling, Nicalis?" Gretty asked.

"I'm doing okay now, Ross," Nicks replied.

"You'll live, Nicks, you'll live," Marshall muttered.

Nicks rubbed his head, still sore from the impact caused by Acadia's tailfin a short while ago. "That mermaid is dangerous, boss, how can you trust her untied?"

"Once we go ashore, we'll keep her wet enough to live, but not a drop more. If that Perry fellow carries her, he won't be able to attack us, and she won't have enough strength to hit us," Marshall explained.

"Good strategy, boss!" Benks said.

"Enough of your praise." Marshall left for his chambers.

"I'm just saying," Benks began.

"Shut up before you lose your knees, Jed," Nicks cautioned.

Benks sighed. "Aye."

Aboard the *Valiant*, Thomas went below deck. He found Ellis and the others in the mess hall.

"Tommy, where's the captain?" Gritzol asked.

"They've been captured, all of them!" Thomas explained.

Roberts jumped up. "Everyone?"

"The captain?" Gritzol asked.

Lewinston smacked his forehead angrily. "I never should've left my watch … we could've done something!"

"Aye, but now everyone's captured ... Acadia too." Thomas took a seat on the bench.

Benson rushed over to him. "Tommy, Tommy, this is no time for sitting down!"

"I'm just lucky to be alive, I suppose," Thomas replied.

"That explains why the *Inferno* left so quickly ...." Gritzol began.

"Where are they going?" Roberts asked.

"Siren Island, to the cavern." Thomas raised his hands in frustration. "Everyone's going."

"That doesn't leave us many options ... unless ..." With a thoughtful grin, Gritzol's gaze turned to the refuse bin. "We get some help."

"Harv, whatever happened to that Nyguard fellow?" Lewinston asked.

"Let me find out." Jennings went to check bin.

Inside, Nyguard was still alive, but in very bad condition. Aside from his dry mouth and gurgling stomach, his face had a green tint to it. His odor, on the other hand, was considerably less than pleasant. Irving and Morrey were also alive, but indisposed, as they had both passed out from the fumes.

"Feeling okay, Nyguard?" Jennings asked.

"W ... w ... water, please?" Nyguard begged.

"Ellis, get him some water and a bite of food," Gritzol said.

"Aye." Ellis went into the galley.

"Come out of there, and get some air," Jennings pulled him into the mess hall and resealed the door behind.

"Smells nice in there, doesn't it?" Lewinston asked.

"You ...." Nyguard began with a scowl.

Gritzol pinched his nose and waved. "Ick—wash that man!"

Benson filled a nearby bucket from the tank and doused Nyguard with it. Loose particles of rotted food was now strewn across the floor. With a nearby broom, Jennings brushed aside the mess for the time being.

"Cold...." Nyguard sputtered a moment. "Thank you, I think. What do you want with me?"

"How badly do you want to go back to Marshall's command?" Gritzol asked.

"He'll kill all of you for this outrage!" Nyguard replied.

Holding up a finger, Gritzol pointed out a significant detail. "Right now, he doesn't know you're alive."

"He chose to take the rest of our crew, and another prisoner, to Siren Island instead of coming back here to find you." Thomas thought it was important to mention that part.

Ellis returned with a biscuit and handed it to Nyguard. Nyguard took it, choking at Thomas's statement. "Siren Island? What does he want there?"

Lewinston let out an isn't-it-obvious snort. "That item you were looking for."

"A map, perhaps?" Thomas asked.

"How do you know that?" Nyguard asked.

Gritzol's look hardened. "We know more than you think. Like how every man on that crew—except you and Marshall—are kept there by fear, not by choice."

"They are all prisoners," Jared said.

"Yeah…" Nyguard began.

"Excuse me?" Gritzol asked.

"All of them, even me," Nyguard said louder.

Pulling up a chair, Ellis waved a gracious hand as he sat, as though he were still playing captain. "Enlighten us."

"I … I can't, it happened too long ago," Nyguard began.

"What happened too long ago?" Jennings asked.

"Dammit, I've become a friend to Marshall after all this time; I can't just ignore those years!" Nyguard cried, frantically trying to change the subject.

That didn't sit well with Thomas. "Even though you know that he keeps his men by blackmail and threats of murder?"

Nyguard waved him off. "What do you care? You're just a little cabin boy!"

Thomas raised his hand to his chest. "I …! I … unngh!" He'd forgotten about his wound; it hurt all the more knowing he'd earned it fighting in Acadia's defense.

"This cabin boy has just fought for a friend of his, for honor!" Jared said, before whispering to Thomas, "Right, Tommy?"

"Acadia," Thomas replied with a slight nod.

"Who the bloody heck is that?" Nyguard asked.

"A mermaid," Gritzol replied.

Nyguard rolled his eyes and laughed. "You're all in cahoots on this ship, aren't you?"

"Look at this boy. He bleeds for her. And for us," Jennings replied.

There was no denying the boy was wounded. If he'd been wounded defending the ship, the sounds of fighting would have reached the bin, but it had been quiet. There was no reason for any of them to go to the *Inferno*, least of all the cabin boy, unless they'd intended to rescue someone. "Hmm … well, if you're speaking the truth, she must be pretty special, then." Nyguard's tone was almost compassionate.

"So, you do know what it's like to have a close relationship with someone, after all." Thomas couldn't keep the hope from his voice.

"Enough about me past." Nyguard turned back to Gritzol. "What is this plan of yours?"

All business, Gritzol's hand settled on the hilt of the sword at his waist. "Here's the deal. You help us get our friends back. And maybe, if Marshall is unable to continue his role as captain of your ship, we might just consider bringing you with us."

"Leave?" Uninterested in a possible Marshall-inspired death, Nyguard shook his head. "I'm not leaving Marshall's side for anything."

"Throw him back in there." With a frown, Gritzol turned away.

Jennings and Jared grabbed Nyguard's shoulders.

"Wait!" With his hands raised in a placating manner, Nyguard tried to shrug out of the men's grips. "Wait … all right, I said I'll never leave his side, and I won't. But, I will help you free your friends."

"How can we trust you?" Jennings asked.

The pirate put a hand over his heart. "I give you my word. I swear on it with my life."

Turning back, Gritzol jabbed a finger at their captive. "All right, then. I shall hold you to that." His gaze shifted to Thomas. "Now, you say they were going to Siren Island, Tommy?"

"Yes," Thomas replied.

Benson checked the window. "They've got to be well out of sight by now."

"We've given them a head start … they're probably ashore by now." Gritzol turned for the door. "Get some swords; we're going by rowboat. Come on."

"You're really going ashore?" Ellis asked.

Gritzol looked back at Ellis. "You'd like to hold the fort, right?"

Ellis nodded.

"Take care of yourself, and double bar that refuse bin. We should be back by morning," Gritzol said.

"Aye," Ellis muttered.

Shortly, the rest of the crew was armed to the teeth and rowing quietly toward Siren Island as the sun was waning in the west.

By the time the *Inferno* arrived on the western shore of Siren Island, there was only enough light to see the rocky cliffs.

"There, that looks like a good place to climb the cliff," Marshall said.

"But boss, all the rocks, are you sure we can get that close?" Gretty asked.

"Hmm...fer once I might agree with ye, Gretty." He pointed eastward. "Take us some hundred yards out. There may yet be rocks underwater."

"Aye boss."

He glanced at the two rowboats on deck, having claimed the rowboat used by the *Valiant*'s crew earlier. "We will go in two groups, Fallah myself and the captain first. Then you will bring the rowboat back and collect the rest ... I will not risk your losing another rowboat. If you do..." Marshall warned.

Gretty's eyes drifted toward his knees. "No, boss! Of course! You won't lose another rowboat, I swear!"

"See that you don't!" The captain paced across the deck with a look of disdain toward the rocky island.

Below, the mood among Janes's crew was subdued and somber.

"Tommy ... so young," Ward began.

"Aye, I do not look forward to returning to Harper's Bay with such bad news," Janes replied.

"Thomas..." Perry muttered, lost in his meditations.

Acadia looked around. "Why do you feel sad? Thomas may yet live."

"Acadia, dear, very few men survive walking the plank," Janes replied sadly.

"Miss Acadia, you do feel for his life, yes?" Ward asked.

"I can assure you I would, if I was certain he was dead," Acadia said.

"How do you mean?" Janes asked.

"Thomas can swim; I know that. Perhaps he was bound, too. Should I find him washed ashore beyond breath, only then would I grieve." She gave them a reassuring smile. "But he is alive and well as we speak."

Even in the dim light, Ward could see the conviction in her eyes. "Why are you so certain?"

"Simple." She smiled again. "Cynthia and Marsha have helped him, and he is safe and sound."

Janes shook his head. "Impossible, I watched him fall. How would they know to be there?"

"I told them," Acadia replied.

"What?" Ward asked in disbelief.

"Not directly," Acadia explained. "But my sisters were able to sense my fear for Thomas, and in a similar way they later told me of their relief for his safety."

"A miracle ...!" Perry exclaimed. Ward breathed a sigh of relief.

Janes nodded, accepting the truth. "Marshall must not know. I trust Tommy found the others and is coming to our aid, then."

"We must forget about Tommy's whereabouts for now." Ward's stern gaze swept them all. "Nobody speaks of him until we are free from Marshall's ears, aye?"

"Agreed," Janes replied.

"Aye," Perry and Acadia chorused.

There was a brief moment of silence. Acadia chose to break it.

"Christopher, why do men like Marshall exist? What drives him to take things and hurt people?"

Janes sighed. "There is a side of men that craves possessions and wealth, and greed is its name. A terrible side, one that should never be seen."

"Aye. And Marshall practically wrote the book on it," added Ward.

"Greed is a fickle mistress, and oftentimes, it wants more than it can swallow." Janes tried to shift into a more comfortable position, but his bonds prevented him. "But every time she gets hungry, reason and justice need to keep her in check."

"Marshall will get what he deserves, Miss Acadia," Perry said.

Acadia nodded. "But in the meantime, we are prisoners here."

"We shall play along with Marshall's plan for as long as we must. Should a chance for escape present itself, we will not take it," Janes explained.

Ward gave him a cross look. "We should not try to escape?"

"Marshall knows I am a man of my word." Janes shrugged. "Also, I know how he thinks. He will use any excuse to treat us as poorly as possible. If I've learned anything, it's that better behavior yields better treatment. No struggling, no fighting back, not even talking back. If we are told to be quiet, we'll be quiet. Understood?"

"What if he refuses to give me water?" Acadia asked.

Captain Janes reached out to hold her hands tightly. "I am prepared to risk my life for you, Acadia. Should he refuse to give you water, I will find a way to convince him that we are not taking you unconscious."

"I as well, Miss Acadia," Perry replied.

"Perry, I cannot thank you enough. All of you," Acadia replied.

"It is our duty, miss," Ward said. The ship lurched as activity echoed through the boards above.

"Keep your voices down. The ship is slowing," Janes said.

Acadia took several handfuls of water and doused her tail with it as much as she could before Nicks opened the door to the hold with his sword ready. Aramondo was with him as well.

"All of you, on your feet," Nicks ordered. Janes, Ward, and Perry all stood up.

"What about me?" Acadia asked.

"You, the brawny fellow, pick her up," Nicks ordered.

Without a complaint, Perry reached out his bound hand to her. With some effort, she settled herself into his arms and reached around Perry's neck with both hands for support.

"Upstairs," Nicks ordered. Aramondo led the way.

They quietly filed up the stairs, following Aramondo to the waiting rowboat as ordered. Once their hands were unbound to allow them to climb, Janes and Ward climbed into the rowboat below. They did so at swordpoint, but neither officer made any effort to fight back.

Before Acadia was put in, Gretty ordered Perry to place her on the deck.

"Put her down here," Gretty said.

Perry did so, carefully resting Acadia down in front of him.

"Aramondo, hobble them," Gretty said.

Aramondo took a thick rope and wrapped it around the base of Acadia's tailfin, near her fins. He then took the other end of the rope and tied it tightly around Perry's ankle.

"If you jump out, you'll break his ankle," Aramondo said.

Acadia nodded, not making a sound.

Aramondo then turned to Perry. "If you try to run with her, you also will break your ankle. I trust you will comply."

Perry nodded.

"In the boat," Gretty ordered. Acadia had to hang onto Perry's back as he climbed down the edge of the ship. Then Gretty joined them and rowed ashore, joining Marshall and the rest of the men waiting for them.

"Have your canteen, Benks?" Marshall asked.

"Here, boss." Benks held it up.

"Fill it," Marshall ordered.

There was no fresh water to spare, and since Benks figured Acadia lived in saltwater, he filled it from the shore.

"Will that be enough for her? It is a long walk," Janes asked.

"I have no idea." With a dismissive twirl of his hand, Marshall smiled. "We shall have to trust your directions, Captain."

Janes fought to contain his anger at Marshall's obvious contempt for Acadia's health.

Gretty looked around the small shore. "Which way do we go, boss?"

"Aye yes ... what say you, Janes?" Marshall asked.

"Toward the jungle." Janes pointed. "There is a path already cleared."

"This one ... here?" Marshall said, pointing toward the north.

"Not that one. There," Janes said, motioning toward the west.

"Ahh. This one, then." Marshall gestured for Gretty to lead.

"What a fine evening for hiking. A good thing we brought the lantern after all, wouldn't you agree, Mr. Gretty?" Marshall asked, in a cheerful tone.

"Quite so, boss."

Ward sneered at Marshall's mockery of the situation.

"If I get off course be sure to tell me, Janes. After all, it is I who have all the time in this world, not you," Marshall said, still jovial.

"I shall," Janes muttered quietly.

"Janes!" Marshall slowed to come alongside his fellow captain and give him a friendly pat on the back. "Aren't you enjoying this walk? Your lady friend is, yes? To see the land above the sea at last?"

"I'm sorry, I find it difficult to sightsee right now," Acadia replied.

"Hm." After a momentarily thoughtful look, Marshall smiled and shrugged again. "So it be your loss then." He turned back to Janes. "You never told me how lovely this island was, Janes! Such lovely country ... maybe better suited for our headquarters than our old place!" Marshall exclaimed as his men laughed, even though Gretty's response appeared to be forced.

"A left here," Janes said, as they approached a fork in the trails. Marshall began going the wrong way.

"Oh yes, it's so easy to get lost in the dark, isn't it?" Marshall said. He turned to follow the correct path as they started their way through the jungle.

Beneath the Mist of Sirens

Aboard the *Valiant*'s remaining rowboat, Gritzol and Lewinston each manned an oar. Benson and Jennings counted their supplies as they traveled through Rhydar's Maw. All managed to fit into one rowboat, although it was a tight fit. Both crews had a missing rowboat, although the crew of the *Inferno* had kept the one used for Acadia's first rescue attempt. For now, this single boat would have to suffice.

"Okay, let us count one more time. Seven of us, seven blades, at least six of them, and four prisoners. Is that correct?" Jennings asked.

"That's the drill. Keep your voice down; they may hear," Benson ordered.

"Do you think Ellis will be okay aboard?" Lewinston glanced back at the *Valiant*. "What if they double back?"

Nyguard shook his head. "Marshall will be focused on the map, but don't expect him to leave his ship guarded."

"Marshall, leave his ship unguarded? You're taking us for fools," Gritzol said.

Nyguard steadied himself. "He has too many prisoners to contain. He'll bring all hands."

"And if it is guarded?" Roberts asked.

"Then you shall encounter some resistance." Nyguard shrugged. "Depending on who it is."

"Like who? Who would side with Marshall?" Gritzol asked.

"I do not know," Nyguard said bluntly.

"Who?" Benson said, thrusting his hilt upon Nyguard.

"A-anyone, perhaps?" Nyguard replied quickly.

"Anyone, you say? I should hate to execute your crewman if it comes to that," Benson began.

"I do not know, honest!" Nyguard held up his hands. "Do you want my help or not?"

"It's your word, so keep it," cautioned Gritzol.

"Shh ... we're too close now," Thomas said. They approached the *Inferno* from the port side.

"All right, plan to dock." Gritzol's gaze scanned them all. "We'll be looking for our crew's weapons, and we'll need to carry them with."

"Carry them on your backs or over your shoulders," Benson said.

"Right," Jennings nodded.

One by one, they boarded the quiet ship and climbed onto the deck. There was no sign of anyone, not even the cabin boy.

"Are you feeling okay, Acadia?" Janes asked.

A lantern was their only guide in the dark jungle, as they continued hiking beneath the twinkling stars overhead. Yet, even in the dim light he could see that she was a bit limp.

Acadia did not respond right away. Perry had held her tighter, as she had slumped within his arms.

"Acadia?" Janes stopped.

Marshall stopped as well. "I see no cave here, Janes. What keeps us?"

Janes walked over to Acadia. "Acadia?" She was breathing comfortably and slowly opened her eyes.

"She was only sleeping, Cap'n," Perry replied.

"Where are we?" she asked softly.

"Inside the jungle. Is everything okay?" Janes asked.

"I feel dry and a little tired," Acadia said.

"Give her some water," Janes said to Marshall.

Marshall spun around and rolled his eyes. "Very well. Benks." Benks poured some of the sea water from the canteen onto her tail, getting Perry's vest wet also.

"We're not there yet, are we? Ahh, the path goes this way," Marshall said. He continued on as Gretty followed with the lantern.

"Please, try to stay awake, Acadia. I do not want to lose you," Janes said. Ward patted her shoulder softly before continuing.

Acadia nodded quietly.

Gritzol tossed a blade to Jennings. "One for you, one for you." He handed Ward's sword to Roberts. "And you take the captain's, Roland." Gritzol passed the captain's silver blade to Benson.

"What about Mr. Perry's, sir?" Thomas asked, retrieving his scimitar.

"His blade is pretty big, I'll take that one. Come on, we've no time to waste." With the Kah Lunaseif on his back, Gritzol climbed out of the *Inferno*'s hold and down the side to rejoin the crew in the rowboat. They approached the island along the cliff, tying their rowboat on the other side of the natural dock before going ashore and heading toward the cavern.

Marshall was growing tired of walking through the jungle in the dark. "So Janes, do we have any chance of reaching this cavern before morning?"

Janes looked toward the west. They had reached the cliffs overlooking the cove. A brief walk to the north would take them to the cavern.

"We are almost there," Janes replied.

"I think you have been leading us astray," Marshall said.

"It's just to the north, Marshall. Let me show you," Janes said.

"You lie!" Marshall delivered a swift jab to Janes's face, hitting him square in the cheek just below the eye. Even though Janes was a tough man, it was enough to knock him to the ground.

If it meant showing weakness, Janes would do it to keep his favor with Marshall.

"Oh!" Acadia cried. Ward and Perry watched silently, holding their tongues.

"Are you finished with your lies?" Marshall growled. Janes sat up. A trickle of blood flowed from his left nostril.

"The cave is to the north. There are only cliffs to the west of here," Janes replied in a low tone. Although his face had been bruised, his determination wasn't.

"Well then. I trust your lies will end here and now." Marshall and his men started along the north trail.

Ward extended his hand to Captain Janes, who refused. "I'm all right," Janes replied, picking himself up.

"Why would Marshall do such a thing?" Acadia asked.

"It's all an act, Acadia," Ward said.

Janes nodded. "Quite right, I'm fine." He used a handkerchief to clean up some of the blood, before dropping it to the ground.

"Are you in need of more encouragement?" Marshall called from ahead.

Benks and Aramondo held the hilts of their swords at the ready. "Boss said to keep moving."

"We're coming," Ward said. He started along the north trail. The others followed closely behind.

"Tommy, are you sure this is the way? We seem to be off course," Gritzol said as Thomas led with the lantern.

"Quite sure, sir." The boy looked back with an apologetic expression. "Although it would be easier in the daylight."

"Do any of you have a plan for when we catch them?" Nyguard asked.

"Well, it shall take some cunning, perhaps luck, and skill. But I assure you, it will work out in the end," Lewinston replied.

Nyguard scoffed, his voice doubtful. "You haven't a clue, do you?"

"It's never stopped him before," Jennings said.

Benson raised his lantern, seeing a bloody handkerchief in the grass.

"Look at this! Surely this must belong to the captain," Benson said.

"My apologies for losing trust in your judgment, Tommy." Gritzol gave him a pat on the back. They continued along the path to the north.

In the dim moonlight, Marshall followed close behind Gretty. They walked on a narrow mountain trail between high towers of rock. Overhead the moon was in plain view. Aside from moss and vegetation along the narrow edges of the rock, there was little else of scenic value.

"Shouldn't the cave be here, Janes?" Marshall complained.

"There it is, just around the corner," Janes replied in a shallow tone.

"Gretty, shine that light around the corner," Marshall ordered.

"Yeah boss." Cautiously, Gretty rounded the corner.

"Anything?" Marshall asked.

Gretty's light faded into darkness. He replied with an omnious echo to his voice. "Nothing, boss."

"What be that?" Benks asked.

"An echo … there be our cave!" Marshall said.

"As I told you," Janes replied.

"What now, boss?" Gretty asked.

"Go in, of course. See if it's safe, Gretty," Marshall said.

A strong breeze passed over the rocky valley, and it made a sound that echoed deep throughout the cavern in a menacing hum. It was enough to make the men quiver. His knees knocking, Gretty hesitated.

"Go on then, keep your wits about you! Go on," Marshall ordered.

Gretty nodded. He started forward slowly while Marshall and his other men looked on. Nicks followed, managing to find a gopher hole before his path. His legs fell out from under his feet.

"Ugh!" Nicks said, as he crashed to the ground, hitting his bruised head on the rocky terrain beneath.

Aramondo and the others each drew a sword on a member of Janes's crew, just as Gretty returned with the lantern

"No more games," Marshall said to Ward.

Ward held up his bound hands. "I did nothing."

Marshall looked down at Nicks. A trickle of blood seeped from his bald head. "The man always was somewhat clumsy." He shrugged. "So it be his folly."

Benks and Fallah tried to wake Nicks up.

"The cave looks clear, boss," Gretty said.

"This time you go first, Janes. I want to know if something'll kill me before it happens," Marshall ordered.

"That is fine with me." Janes went just ahead of Gretty toward the cave.

As the others continued in formation, Nicks sat up and felt himself bleeding. He tore a large piece of fabric from his tunic and wrapped his head. He hobbled as he ran after the others, his balance lacking. "I'm not dead! Wait for me!" Nicks called. He did his best to catch up as they entered the cave.

Although this was the same cave they had ventured inside earlier, it no longer had a welcome feeling. It seemed as if spirits themselves were awake with evil intentions. A soft rumble echoed quietly, creating a definite ambiance of threat.

"This is an abysmal place." Benks's voice echoed far into the cavern depths.

"Aye," Fallah added.

"I sense uneasy spirits within," Perry spoke up. Acadia nodded, not fond of entering the cave herself.

"Silence, you. Forward, Janes," Marshall ordered.

Janes continued down, followed closely by Gretty with the lantern.

"Boss, I'm not liking this place," Aramondo said.

"Can we wait outside?" Nicks asked.

"You cowards!" Marshall turned on them with a furious gaze. "There'll be no waiting outside! Forward!" Marshall cried. His echo shook throughout the cavern.

Janes tread carefully down the cavern, stopping at the point where the strange voice had echoed earlier. There was no voice this time.

"Why do you hesitate?" Glancing around, Marshall noticed nothing different. "Pffft! Fine then, if you have no courage…." He took the lead and headed into a large chamber. The cavern split into two passages. "Well Janes, which way shall we go?"

"It was…" Janes did his best to appear sincerely uncertain. "It was to the right, yes, that's correct."

"Funny thing, you couldn't have been here that long ago, and yet you forget so easily? Your lack of confidence worries me …" Marshall turned to Acadia and Perry. "Do you know the way, mermaid?"

Marshall's men exchanged confused looks. How could their captain think someone without legs could have reached the cave?

Acadia tried not to be startled by the question. "I've never been in here."

"Fine then. Left," Marshall ordered.

"Right," Janes muttered in agreement.

"Right?" Marshall paused. "Left or right?"

"I agreed with you, to the left," Janes said.

"Did you say right?" Marshall asked again.

"He said to the right, boss." Fallah pointed that direction.

"So? Perhaps left is a trap, then?" Marshall asked.

Janes shrugged. "I would have no reason to trap it."

"Your efforts will never break me." After a deep breath, Marshall seemed to calm himself. "Very well. We go right, if you're so smart."

Acadia removed the tiny compass from her wrist, allowing it to fall to the ground. Perry noticed it, and with a wink walked deeper into the cave.

✷ ✸ ✷

Gritzol and the others soon arrived at the cave.

"How do you know they'll go all the way in?" Nyguard asked.

"We don't," Gritzol replied. Roberts adjusted the light of the lantern.

"If they come back, should one of us wait here?" Thomas asked.

Benson shook his head. "No, we don't split up. That'll weaken our numbers if they should return while we are in a different part of the tunnel."

"Aye," Jennings replied.

"Guess we go where they did," Gritzol replied.

"Aye," Roberts said, adjusting the flame of the lantern.

When they reached the split caverns, Gritzol began going left.

"Wait, are you sure that's where you want to go?" Jennings asked.

"I don't see why not. Roland, what do you think?" Gritzol asked.

"It seems the cave has been continuously turning to the left. It may be a shorter passage," Benson replied.

"And if Marshall took this passage, then what?" Nyguard asked.

"Yeah, it might be a trap, you know," Jennings said.

"Fine then, we decide as a group. All for right?" Gritzol asked.

Three hands reached for the cavern ceiling.

"Now, for left?" Gritzol asked.

Three hands as well. Jennings didn't raise his hand for either.

"Harv?" Gritzol asked.

"I's not sure if we should go either anymore...." After an impatient glare from Gritzol, Jennings shrugged. "Fine, I say left, if you's thinking it be shorter."

Gritzol then spotted a glint of light near the ground. "Hold on ... what's that there?"

He walked over to the right path, where a shiny compass with a wrist strap lay in the dirt.

Jared held his lantern closer. "Roland, isn't that yours?"

Benson nodded, pocketing the compass. "Acadia … she left us a clue. They're taking the outside path."

"Then we'll take the left path, and hopefully find them sooner," Nyguard said.

"A deal is a deal only so long as you keep your word, Nyguard. Let's move on." Gritzol led onward with the lantern.

Back aboard the *Valiant*, Ellis was quietly walking the deck. His browsing would eventually lead him to the captain's quarters.

"Hmm … Captain Janes won't mind if I stop in here for a moment. After all, I was the captain myself for a day," Ellis muttered quietly. He carefully opened the door and stepped inside.

Finding the cabin dimly lit by the reflection of the moon from outside, he lit a lantern. Looking around, he discovered the book upon the table. It was the journal of Captain Scyhathen.

"What have we here? Scyhathen … is this the one that Janes has been reading about?" Ellis took a seat, opening the journal to a bookmarked page.

> *January 12th, 1583. It seems our supplies are becoming exhausted, as are I and the rest of the crew. Kid and I are on a quest for any remaining sources of food. In this pursuit, we have journeyed back into the cavern of Siren Island. Sadly, there was little of anything inside. We did not journey any deeper. Outside, at least, our situation has begun to improve. Winter has begun to arrive with increasing storm activity. Although the weather is a harsh realization of nature, the strength of the wind is welcome in activating the sails after so long. We are hopeful that the Nemaris shall again become free of the sands beneath her hull. As the winds grow stronger every day, we are testing the potential of our sails. With luck, we shall free ourselves using our sails.*

"Hmm … so they were caught in these sands as well … using the sails would be an option, one I cannot perform by myself, however. Course, that wind has been picking up. I wonder…." Ellis muttered as he read the next passage.

January 13th, 1583. Through the efforts of Mr. Smitty and Mr. Corvair, we have discovered that if the winds keep steady our sails should be able to provide the power needed to free ourselves from the sand. Of course, that will require a change in the direction of the wind and riding it long enough to send us far from shore. With Mr. Banes's navigational assistance, our chances should be very good of returning to a more comfortable locale, say Cimmordia Castle or Teraske. Frankly, we shall be happy to reach any locale. The men and myself are in great need of fresh food and company. To be rid of Mr. Epoth as well would be most welcome ... and our next visit to these islands shall only be in my dreams.

I have sailed the seas for much of my life, and my time to spend upon them is limited. Never have I enjoyed the comfort of a family life, and never shall that security be achieved, I fear. To those I have enjoyed company with these past decades, I thank them. Of my current crew, I can say this. These have been the best years of my life, and for that I am thankful. If bringing these men home is to be my final hurrah on this earth, then with that my life shall not have ended in vain.

I find myself reflecting on the legends of Davy Jones daily. His old self, fishing on a quiet beach, waiting for old men like me to arrive. I still wish to see the distant shores of the Phrynn continent, but sometimes one has to let a dream die. Perhaps my duel with Mr. Jones is too evident, but such is the imagination of a salty old sailor.

Should my fate lie with one of Mr. Smitty's mercreature friends, I would not protest. In fact, I welcome the day an old mariner like myself should enjoy a good conversation with a person as wise as Cynthia. But, I digress. My honor shall lie with Mr. Jones, as he has allowed me to stay afloat for more than 40 years. I shall welcome the day I shake his hand.

With that thought in mind, Ellis yawned quietly, drowsily slumping onto Janes's bed behind him. Although the reading did not bore him, it was late at night. Rather, it was incredibly early in the morning. And a morning that even the eventual dawn wouldn't bring peace to.

Walking without rest, Marshall's group had continued their way into the cavern, beyond the junction of the two routes, following the cavern downhill.

"This cavern is indeed long, Janes. Does it ever end?" Marshall asked.

"I tell you honest, I have not seen the end. But I assure you that the map is near," Janes replied.

Marshall made a sour face. "Your lack of confidence overwhelms me, Janes."

"My crew hid it very well and then gave me a full report. You would do the same with your crew, yes?" Janes asked.

Marshall grumbled something, before speaking in his usual prim tone again. "Very well then, we continue on. But there will be a reward at the bottom, if it be something other than the map that leads to the riches of Rhydar, it will be my victory over your head." He ran his finger along Janes's neck.

From behind, Gritzol stopped Roberts. "Shh ... I see another light ahead."

"Have we caught up to them already?" Roberts whispered back.

"Hood the lantern for a moment," Benson said. Roberts covered it with a leather hood, halving the light in the cave.

"What now, sir?" Thomas whispered to Gritzol.

"Quiet, at all costs. This cavern has good resonance, but only for those who wish to be found," Gritzol replied.

"Aye," Nyguard said.

"Come, but tread lightly," Gritzol ordered.

Toward the back of the group, Acadia asked Perry what he knew about human conflict. Perhaps it was an inappropriate time to speak of such things, but there was little else to keep her awake.

"Perry, why do men fight among themselves?" Acadia whispered to him.

"They want what others possess, Acadia. Greed fuels man's aggression," Perry replied.

"But Christopher does not possess anything Marshall wants. I see no reason that would drive him to violence," Acadia asked again.

He shook his head. "Your understanding is too perfect, Acadia. Beyond lies only speculation with unanswered questions."

"It seems there is more to this circle of greed than lies on the surface," Acadia agreed.

Perry nodded as they approached a large cavern. Along the ceiling, stalactites sparkled from the light of the lantern. Beyond, the light traveled some distance before fading into a further passage. Before them, a stream of water split the chamber in two, its sound created a soothing rhythm. A long rope bridge crossed the gentle current. The ropes were well preserved, as if the bridge had only been constructed a day or so ago.

"Wow ... look at the size of this place!" Gretty exclaimed, his voice echoing immensely.

"Is that water below?" Acadia asked.

"Aye, but we're not going swimming," Marshall said, inspecting the bridge.

"I wonder where the water goes to?" Benks asked.

"Keep up yer yapping and you'll find out. You, cross the bridge and see if it's safe," Marshall said, pushing Ward forward.

"All right, looks okay." Ward took a deep breath and stepped onto the bridge. It didn't even sag.

"One at a time, come on ..." Marshall waved them on, glaring at Acadia as Perry walked by. "And don't even think about trying out the water, missy."

"Captain Marshall, you are not a kind person." Acadia replied calmly.

"Thank you, my dear; I shall do my best to live up to your standards." Marshall gallantly lifted his hat to her as she passed.

"Peace, miss," Perry said. He carried her across the bridge.

Marshall crossed last. They continued into the next part of the cavern.

As the *Valiant*'s crew followed just behind, Benson inspected the rope bridge Marshall had crossed only moments earlier.

Gritzol spied several footprints in the dirt. "They've certainly come through here ... but what do you make of this bridge?"

"It seems solid, we can cross," Benson reported.

"Of course it is. Marshall's smart enough that he wouldn't cut off his only escape route," Nyguard replied.

"How does he know that? There may yet be another exit underwater." Jennings pointed to where the stream's current carried the water out of the cave. "Perhaps at the end of the stream?"

"We have no way of knowing how long that is. And furthermore, we'd be in the dark the entire distance, be it ten yards or ten hundred," Gritzol added.

"Marshall wouldn't know it either," Lewinston replied.

"I am not prepared to be disloyal," Nyguard said in Marshall's defense. A plan was formulating in his mind.

"You gave your word, you best be," Benson said.

"Can we cross the bridge? We have no time," Thomas said.

"Aye, agreed." Roberts crossed with the lantern. "Come then."

"You're right, Tommy. Off we go," Gritzol said, pushing Nyguard onto the bridge.

Acadia seemed to be nodding off as they approached a narrow passage.

"Captain," Perry spoke up.

"Yes?"

"Miss Acadia is leaving us," Perry said.

Marshall looked back, grumbling. "Enough with the idle chat. What's wrong now, Janes?"

Janes leaned close to Acadia, who was neither breathing nor sleeping. Instead, she was slumped against Perry, her scales sticking to him because of his sweat. He snapped his fingers next to her ears several times. She was unresponsive.

"She needs water, now," Janes said.

"So what else is new ... go ahead, Benks," Marshall was clearly annoyed with their lack of progress toward the end of the cavern. Benks took the flask out, and proceeded to pour whatever was left in it. However, only a few drops trickled onto Acadia. Sadly, this was not nearly enough water to bring her around.

"That's all of it, boss," Benks said.

Gretty sighed, very apologetic. "What a shame."

"Gretty? My, you sound almost compassionate!" Marshall sneered.

"I don't feel right letting the miss waste away, boss," Gretty replied.

"Then take the flask back to that stream there. Leave the lantern," Marshall ordered.

Gretty's eyes rounded. "How am I to see, boss?"

"You've been through there." Marshall waved at him dismissively. "You know the way."

Taking the empty flask from Benks, Gretty sighed. "Aye," he muttered. Leaving the lantern with Nicks, he trudged back toward the stream. Fallah and the others decided to sit down and rest, allowing Perry to sit down a moment as well—although he continued to hold Acadia in his arms.

"Well Janes, you are getting what you wanted. When shall I receive mine?" Marshall demanded.

"It cannot be much further. We have gone quite far," Janes said.

"There's something I've been wondering, Janes … you say the map is in here, yet you seem to have never been here before. How do you explain that?" Marshall asked.

"I trust my men with that information, Marshall." He gave Marshall a bland smile. "You trust your men, don't you?"

Marshall scoffed. "I hope you're enjoying this little game of yours … and for your sake, I hope it ends quickly."

"Aye, there be little island left before we go below sea level," Ward said.

"So says you." Shaking his head, Marshall smiled grimly. "Your predictions had better be true, lest one of you taste steel."

As Gretty trudged back toward the underground stream, Gritzol and his troupe were in the passage coming his way.

"Miserable excuse of a captain, sending his most trusted replacement-for-a-second-in-command in the dark … if he didn't know where my family lived I'd slice his throat in his sleep and sprinkle his blood across that cursed ship…." Gretty grumbled to himself as he carefully felt his way through the cave.

Thomas stopped suddenly when he heard Gretty's ramblings. "Do you hear that?"

"Hold…." With a lift of Gritzol's hand they all halted. "Aye, it sounds like a rambling sailor."

"Clear to the side," Benson ordered. "Jared, hood that lantern."

Roberts covered the lantern, bringing darkness to the cavern. Only a small amount of light seeped against the stone wall. All the men ducked to the side, except for Nyguard, who was yanked to the wall by Jennings.

Gretty approached the group. "Where be that light source?"

"Gretty?" Nyguard asked.

Gritzol and the others drew their blades as Jared unveiled the light. "There be too many of us for you to take on, sailor."

"Leo?" Gretty didn't seem to care that he was surrounded by the *Valiant*'s crew. "You're alive?"

"Aye I'm alive. Where's Marshall?"

Everyone sheathed their swords for the moment.

"Up ahead in the cave, in a narrow passage." Gretty hitched a thumb in the direction he'd come. "We ran out of water for the miss, so he sent me back."

"Is Acadia okay?" Thomas asked.

"She be drying out...." Apparently just taking notice of Thomas, Gretty blinked in surprise. "Say, how did you survive that fall?"

"Never mind that! We have no time." Lewinston snatched the lantern and went back toward the stream. The others followed the light.

"We must hurry! She is not breathing," Gretty added.

"Wait a minute. How can we get to her with Marshall nearby?" Roberts asked.

Suddenly it became silent in the cavern. Nyguard looked to Gretty. "Gretty, Marshall expects you to return. You go first, and we'll be close behind you."

"With the swords drawn?" Benson asked.

"That's right," Gritzol said, taking the lantern from Lewinston.

"Ahh ... been waiting to get some action on this accursed island." Jennings slowly drew his weapon.

"Right with ye, Harv." Lewinston unsheathed his own blade.

"Mr. Gretty, leave the water with me," Thomas said.

"Tommy?" Gritzol began.

"If Marshall's busy yelling at him, I can sneak by and toss the water onto Acadia," Thomas said.

"Hmm ... perhaps we can capture Marshall then." Gretty handed the flask over.

Nyguard remained silent.

"That plan sounds pretty dangerous, Tommy," Robert replied.

"This entire ordeal has been risky." Thomas hastily filled the container then stood with a resolute look in his eyes. "I would choose to throw away everything for her, including my life. I am also the quickest one here. Marshall thinks I'm dead."

"A distraction would give us the jump on him," Roberts said.

Gritzol nodded. "All right, Thomas. You've convinced us. Looks like you're becoming a man really quick."

"We all knew you'd make it there someday, Tommy," Roberts added.

They heard a voice in the distance.

"We should hurry. Marshall should be getting impatient by now," Nyguard said. The group proceeded.

Nyguard's Word

The midnight waves broke softly. A few seagulls coasted along the surf as the starlit sky left a soft glow along the horizon. Moonlight seeped into the Cove, where Cynthia surfaced and sat upon a rock. She had a pained expression on her face, as she sensed evil unseen since before Epoth came to these islands. Although she knew not of Acadia's whereabouts, there was enough evidence in her mind of an approaching evil. She'd thought it would be best to remain unseen beneath the waves until a clear message was received, but from where this message would arrive she did not know.

"Where in creation is Gretty?!" Marshall fumed.

"Probably tripped and broke his skull," Aramondo said.

"It can happen." Nicks gingerly touched his battered head.

Benks offered his crewmate a sympathetic smile. "You of all people know best."

"Aye," Fallah added.

"Quiet, all of you!" Marshall snapped. "He'll return soon if he knows what's best for him."

Just then, Gretty came into the lantern light. "Boss, you've got to...." Gretty stumbled. Everyone, including Mr. Perry, stood up at once.

"Gretty, for goodness sake what kept you?" With a sweep of his hand, Marshall indicated the cave ahead of them. "There's a map somewhere in this cavern, and you take your time like a schoolboy during the summer!"

"Boss, there's something in the cave back there ... I can't explain it!" Gretty said, trying to cover for Thomas.

"Gretty, Gretty, Gretty. Are you afraid of the darkness? And did you lose the flask?" Marshall began, as Aramondo and the rest of his men chuckled slightly.

"But boss, I's serious!" Gretty sounded like he was about to rant. Marshall covered his eyes and shook his head in disbelief as Gretty continued to ramble.

Which was just the chance Thomas was looking for. As Roberts uncovered the lantern, doubling the light in the tiny passage, Thomas shot past Gretty and toward Acadia and Perry. When he tossed half of the water onto Acadia's tail, she woke on the spot.

"Wha? Huh?" she cried, opening up her eyes suddenly.

"Tommy!" Janes and Ward exclaimed as Thomas backed toward Gretty. Gritzol arrived to face Aramondo, and Roberts stood against Nicks.

"So ... you survived that little fall did ye?" Marshall stood and drew his sword. "Your luck ends now!" Thomas grabbed the nearest sword, taking Janes's silver sword from Gritzol's back.

"Whoa!" Thomas said. He tried desperately to hold a blade that was too heavy for him to handle. Benson rushed in and blocked Marshall, allowing Thomas to recover.

"We'll take him, boss!" Aramondo said, drawing his sword. Ward tripped Aramondo, dropping him onto Nicks. Aramondo's sword cut Nicks's leg, spurting blood onto the dirt below as the battered seaman cried out in pain.

Marshall laughed wildly. "Using a blade far too heavy, boy? I love it!" He advanced toward Thomas as Gretty drew his sword.

"Here!" Thomas said, tossing the blade toward Janes. It stuck in the ground. Thomas switched weapons.

"Hah!" Marshall said, swiping at Thomas. Thomas managed to dodge, but in doing so fell backward. Marshall raised his sword to strike, and Janes reached his foot out and kicked Marshall, causing the man to stumble. The others arrived.

"Acadia, watch your fin." Janes pulled his blade out of the ground and cut the rope between her and Perry.

"Thank you, captain ... Perry, all of you ... be careful!" Acadia cried.

"Aye miss, I have you." Perry hefted her over a shoulder. Even with one hand holding Acadia and one free hand, Perry still managed to ward off any who came too close. Aramondo was the first, but Perry was quick to dodge and used the Kah Lunaseif as a shield.

"We've got you, Marshall!" Gritzol engaged Marshall. Benson took Benks as Jennings and Lewinston took on Aramondo. Combat in the narrow cave was touchy, but Aramondo was no match for the two swords-men. Lewinston delivered a close slash, and the spry Aramondo narrowly avoided what may have been a fatal attack.

Roberts guarded Acadia as Perry choked Fallah, who was nearly turn-ing blue before dropping his sword. Nicks was already subdued from blood loss, passed out away from the battle in the dirt.

Nyguard remained behind the group as Ward took his sword and went after Gretty, who surrendered instantly before even crossing swords.

"I yield." Gretty held his hands up in defense.

"Fine," Ward said, then joined Gritzol and Janes in taking on Marshall. Marshall was defending himself as best he could, yet gave no appearance of defeat.

Swords clashed in the dim light. "You can't win, Janes! Even if you fight me off now, I can return with a full complement of armed pirates! I have the Sundrop Guild behind me!"

Gritzol punched Marshall, sending his black blade toward Acadia. Roberts blocked the blade with his own, knocking it to the ground.

"We best move!" he cried, picking her up. Unfortunately, there was no escaping the battle as Janes and Gritzol pushed Marshall toward them.

"Jared! I have an idea!" Acadia whispered to him.

Marshall lunged with his knife, but the battle was already lost. A swat from Acadia's tail knocked Marshall down as three swords pointed in his direction. "Okay, gentlemen, it seems you have me."

Perry took the remaining rope that had been around Acadia and tied up Aramondo and Benks with it. Soon Aramondo and Fallah had sur-rendered, Nicks and Fallah were unconscious, Gretty had switched sides, and Marshall stood alone.

Gritzol claimed Marshall's blade and passed it to Lewinston. "We've been behind you since you entered this cave. It wasn't that difficult to find you, Archibald."

Marshall sneered. "My name is Luther."

"I know your name … Archie!" Gritzol taunted.

"My name is Archibald Luther Marshall!" Marshall bellowed.

Acadia laughed. "Archibald," she said between laughs.

"I yield, does that make you happy?" Marshall waved his hands wildly, like a child throwing a tantrum. "I say I yield! No more will you taunt me!"

"You are fortunate to be a captive of a lenient man, Marshall." Janes sheathed his sword and attached it to his belt. "I give you one chance to return to your galley and flee to your home port. There is nothing here you will take, and nothing here I will take."

"You still have the map." The other captain pointed an accusing finger at Janes. "You'll return and take the treasure as your own!"

"I plan to burn it upon returning to my vessel. It is of no use to me, for those whom I serve with make me feel richer than I would with a few dusty jewels," Janes replied.

"You would let me go? Even after I attacked you, kidnapped your crew, and nearly killed your lovely friend?" A smile crept onto Marshall's face.

Janes rethought his plans a bit. "Marshall, you really are a fool. You rest upon your oars through life as greed fuels your sails. When offered compassion, you spit back in its face. Perhaps what you deserve is a few years of pain and turmoil. I'm sure the constable in Cimmordia Castle could find a place for you."

Nyguard thought about what was happening. Knowing that Janes and the others were free from Marshall, he picked up a discarded sword from the ground and slowly crept unnoticed behind Lewinston.

"Prison?" Marshall laughed. "There are no laws on the sea, Janes! And I know the constable in Cimmordia! He'd have no choice but to free me!"

Janes shrugged. "There are others who will know what to do with you, and I shall find them."

Nyguard had heard enough. Taking his sword, he drove it into Mr. Lewinston's back, creating an exit wound through his chest. A gasp came from Lewinston's lips. Nyguard pulled the blade out, and Lewinston collapsed.

"Mother…" Lewinston whispered before breath left him.

"That's for leaving me in the refuse bin, you filthy miscreant," Nyguard spat.

Jennings thundered and drew his sword, attacking Nyguard much like a relentless wind. "You gave your word!" Jennings cried. He slashed angrily. Both men locked their blades in intense combat. Perry took his sword from Gritzol and prepared to catch Jennings' back if he fell, too.

Marshall found an opportunity to flee as the others gawked at Lewinston's body. He picked up his black blade from the ground, snatched the lantern from Gretty with a swift jab, and took off toward the surface.

"Nyguard! Come!" Marshall called. Nyguard parried Jennings's constant strikes as he made his way after Marshall.

"Harv, let him go!" Janes said, as Ward went to Lewinston's side.

"Never!" Jennings cried. Nyguard punched him with the basket of his sword, knocking Jennings back.

"It doesn't end here!" Nyguard snarled before following after Marshall. Jennings was about to give chase, but Roberts and Gritzol held him back.

"I'll kill 'em! Let go!" Jennings struggled but couldn't break free.

"Harv, he's gone. Think of your friend," Gritzol said quietly. Jennings fell to his knees and broke into tears.

"James…" Janes began.

"Captain, he's already dead," Benson said.

"Hold your breath, Roland, he knows," Ward said.

"James, I'm so sorry." Tears seeped from Acadia's eyes.

"Perry, can you take him into the river chamber?" Acadia asked.

Perry looked at Acadia curiously. "Please, the current will bring him to sea from there," she said. With a nod, Perry put her into the arms of Gritzol. Then, he took Lewinston's body with both hands and started for the large chamber.

"What about us?" Gretty asked.

Jennings jumped to his feet and directed his blade toward each in turn. "You're going where Lewinston didn't."

Janes shook his head. "Lower your weapon, Harvey." Jennings reluctantly obeyed. He remained ready, still intent on seeking revenge for his friend.

Gretty kneeled, joining Aramondo and Benks, and held out his hands to let them be bound with what rope remained.

"Please, spare us, Captain." Benks shook his head. "We owe no allegiance to Marshall or Nyguard."

"Aye, we were kidnapped like the fish girl," Aramondo said.

"Mermaid," Thomas said coldly.

"Sorry, miss," Aramondo said, trying to sound more like a gentleman.

Acadia blinked a few times, but didn't say anything.

"What about those two?" Ward asked, referring to Nicks and Fallah.

"We're all prisoners," Benks said.

"Wake up." Benson kicked Nicks and Fallah lightly. They woke up, and upon finding out what happened, joined their fellow men in the kneeling position.

Janes rose to his feet and stood before them. "I know of your plight. Stand."

"We have attacked you, Captain, and we should not have," Gretty said.

"I ordered you to stand!" Janes repeated. The five men quickly stood up, although Nicks had to lean on Benks.

"Who is your captain?" Janes asked. He paced in front of them.

"We do not know your full name, sir," Nicks said. He continued to struggle on his bad leg.

Janes stopped and turned to them. "I am Captain Christopher Meriwether Janes, captain of the *Valiant*. I do not run a ship full of pirates, seeking fortunes of gold and jewels. We are buccaneers, and I command an honorable crew. If you accept, say so now."

All the men saluted. "Aye!"

Gretty stepped forward. "Captain Janes, sir, we shall serve you, but I think I speak for all of us when we say we wish to see our families."

"When the time comes, Mr. Gretty, I will not force you to stay. I only have room for one crewman to take the spot of the late Mr. Lewinston. I look forward to having you aboard, but first we must clear to the surface ourselves and care for the fallen." Janes had his new men freed from their bonds then led them all back to the water.

"We should have Ellis here for this, or at least do it proper at sea," Jennings said quietly.

"Situation as it is, this will have to do. Thomas, fill the flask before we begin," Janes whispered to him.

"Aye," Thomas replied, reaching down and filling the flask to capacity.

Janes gestured to the stream. "Mr. Perry, you may place our honored dead into the sea." Perry carefully lowered the body into the water, where it sank and vanished from view. As some blood had spilled onto Perry, he spread it across his chest, with a ceremonial gesture. Janes and the other men took a knee.

"I hope he doesn't float into the Cove," Acadia said quietly, wiping a tear.

"Shh ... it'll probably be all right, miss." Gritzol held her tightly.

"Mr. Ward, sir ... will you perform the eulogy?" Jennings asked, his tears beginning to return.

Ward nodded, and stood over the water as the others listened from behind.

"Make it quick, Marshall's getting away," Benks said.

"Show some respect, sailor," Benson hissed.

Mr. Ward took a deep breath. "And so ends the life of our beloved Mr. James Richard Lewinston. A greater sailor we have not yet met. Let Captain Jones favor you, lest your sailing days be at an end. May your homecoming to the endless shores of the afterlife be a pleasant one ... and rest assured that your life was not in vain nor will it be forgotten."

"Well put. We'll have a moment of silence later." Janes stood up. He then started for the cavern's entrance.

"I'll bleed for ye, mate," Jennings said, rushing behind Janes.

"Poor James," Acadia said. Gritzol carried her away.

"He's better off now. Acadia, he doesn't have to face Marshall's wrath," Gritzol said. He did his best to catch up with the rest.

Perry stopped and took Acadia from him, lightening his burden.

"Thanks Perry."

Leaving Lewinston behind, they took the shortest route back to the entrance.

Marshall, rushing along with the lantern dangling beside him, stopped momentarily to see who, if anyone, was still following him.

"Boss, what is it?" Nyguard asked, as he caught up.

"Where are the others?" Marshall asked.

Nyguard shook his head. "They haven't followed. I would guess they chose to side with Janes."

"So be their folly, then." With a disdainful sniff, Marshall turned back toward shore. "There is an old anecdote for these situations; he who sides with the losing side loses along with it."

Nyguard rolled his eyes. "Poetic, sir, very poetic."

"Forget about them. We can always find another crew, Leo. But now, we need to get that map of Janes's before he can get back to his ship."

"Aye boss, it's in his cabin, for certain," Nyguard said.

"Pick your feet up; we've no time!" They hurried as quickly as the poor light would allow.

Janes's crew journeyed with haste toward the surface. Any treasure kept by Rhydar would come second to the life of Ellis and the fate of the *Valiant*.

"Have we lost anyone?" Janes called as they reached the upper level of the cave.

"No, everyone's here," Ward called from the other end.

"Almost everyone ... I'll get that Nyguard," Jenning's pace hastened.

"Acadia, you well?" Perry asked.

She patted his arm. "Just keep running, Perry. I'll be okay"

"We're almost there, lads!" Benson called from the middle of the pack.

Echo of the Winds

*I*t was still nightfall when they finally reached the cavern entrance. Finding their way to the southwestern end of the island, they discovered that Marshall had anticipated their chase. A group of brush and branches appeared to cover part of the path leading east.

"Hold here, look at these trees." Benson pointed to an uneven patch of foliage. "They weren't down before."

"A trap, maybe? Nyguard's got a talent for those things," Gritzol said.

"This does not look good." Janes had stopped to consider their path. "He seems to have left this passage open, perhaps to trigger something."

"Aye, we should take care to go around it," Thomas said.

Ward thought a moment. "Maybe we can stall Marshall in the same manner."

"What are you talking about, Seriam?" Janes asked.

Ward went up to Acadia and Perry. "Acadia, I am in need of your services."

"Certainly, what can I do?" Acadia asked.

"How fast can you swim?"

"I can swim faster than Cynthia, but not as fast as Marsha," Acadia said.

"But fast, yes?" Ward asked again.

"Of course," Acadia replied.

Thomas came up to them. "What are you planning, sir? Acadia is a very proficient swimmer. I've seen her first hand."

"Can you swim around to our rowboat on the other side of the island? For you, it must be easier to go around the island than through the jungle," Ward asked.

Acadia thought a moment. "It is, but I do not understand...."

"Yes, I think I see it now." Janes nodded and turned to his newest crewmen. "Gretty, your rowboat was over yonder too, wasn't it?"

"Aye it was," Gretty replied.

"And ours was right next to it," Gritzol said.

"Yes ... exactly. Perry, come over here," Janes started toward the Cove. After a short hike, they looked down, some thirty or forty meters, to the waterway.

"Yes, of course. Tommy, you showed me this earlier. That's the channel below," Janes said.

"You want me to bring your rowboat here?" Her tail twitched as though anticipating the fall. "It is a long drop, Christopher."

"We can worry about climbing down later," Janes said.

"Acadia, we need you to swim around to the moor, and untie both crafts. But bring ours around here, so we can get a head start to the *Valiant*," Ward said. He then added instructions while he whispered into her ear.

Acadia nodded enthusiastically. "Yes, of course! Perry, thank you for carrying me."

"You are quite welcome, Miss Acadia." He placed her on the ground near the edge.

"I'll be back shortly." With a flick of her tail, Acadia dove far from the cliff and into the deep water. She then swam toward the eastern side of the island as fast as she could.

"Sir, will all of us fit into your rowboat?" Benks asked.

Janes shook his head. "With the amount of men we have currently, we'll have to make two trips. Mr. Ward, Mr. Benson, and Mr. Perry will go first. Two of your crew should go with also. The rest will wait here until Acadia brings the rowboat back so the rest of us can catch up with the others."

"I volunteer," Benks said.

"I as well. Marshall will get what is coming to him, sir," Fallah said.

"Good, I'll expect nothing but your full efforts, gentlemen." His gaze was confident but critical as he scanned his new recruits. "I am taking a calculated risk, but from what I can guess of your past years aboard the *Inferno* there shouldn't be cause for concern."

"You have our word, Captain," Aramondo said.

Swimming with full strokes, Acadia soon reached the southeastern tip of the island. Checking the shore to see if all was clear, she began working on the knot holding the rowboat to the south, which belonged to the *Inferno*. Once it was free, she pushed it adrift as hard as she could. Then, releasing the other rowboat from the shore, she took it's rope with both hands and pulled it back to the Cove. She had to stay close to the surface, but was easily able to pull it along at a steady rate.

She wondered why Marshall may have only used one boat to ferry them in two trips earlier, but did not let the question dwell in her mind.

Marshall and Nyguard arrived at the landing site some ten minutes later, only to find one rowboat slowly moving adrift toward the *Inferno*, about a hundred yards away.

"Where did those fools learn to tie knots?" Marshall bellowed.

"That knot was solid when we passed through earlier," Nyguard said.

Marshall waved after it. "Well, go on and collect it! You can swim, can't ye?"

"Aye sir, leave it to me." Removing his coat, Nyguard dove into the water. He wasn't the most elegant swimmer, and the rowboat seemed to drift further and further as he advanced.

"Avast there! Can't you catch a simple boat?" Marshall cried.

"It keeps floating away, boss!" Nyguard called back.

Neither Nyguard nor Marshall realized that Marsha had taken the rope of the rowboat and was leading it in circles around Nyguard.

"Come back here you!" Nyguard cried. Marsha laughed beneath the waves.

Acadia returned to the Cove with the rowboat behind her.

"Captain, the lass's back," Nicks said.

"Ahoy, Acadia! Were you successful?" Ward called.

"Marsha is keeping them occupied, yes! Be careful on the rocks, the water isn't deep everywhere," Acadia called back.

"Benson, you're the best climber. Go first and then talk us down," Ward ordered.

"Aye," Benson said, slinging his sword over his back. Carefully crawling over the edge, he was unable to find a foothold.

"There are no footholds, sir," Benson said as Perry pulled him up.

"You said it's deep, right?" Janes asked Acadia.

"Very much so, but there's nothing below you," Acadia said.

"Better go before I change my mind…!" With a yell, Benson fell straight into the water below. He surfaced a moment later, and with Acadia's help, climbed into the rowboat.

"Just keep your legs straight and don't think about it, sir!" Benson called to Ward.

"I'm too old for this." Ward muttered as he jumped. Benson helped him aboard the rowboat. Fallah and Benks followed, with Perry making a big splash in the end.

Acadia shook the water off her hair from Perry's tidal wave.

"My apologies, Acadia," Perry said as she guided him to the rowboat.

"On the contrary, Perry, a little water in the face can be quite refreshing," Acadia said. Benson and Benks pulled Perry aboard.

"Acadia, can you go with them and bring the rowboat back here when they're aboard the *Valiant*?" Janes asked.

"I promise to return swiftly," Acadia said. Benson and Perry helped her into the boat while Benks and Fallah each took an oar and began rowing toward the ship.

Benson reached into his pocket once Acadia had settled aboard. "Your compass, miss."

Acadia put the compass around her right wrist once more, offering Benson a kiss on the cheek. "Thank you for returning this."

Janes watched them leave as he leaned against a tree. "God speed."

"I have but one question, Captain," Jared asked.

"Aye, Roberts?"

"Once we get to the ship, we're still stuck in the sand," Jared said.

"Aye, we are." Gritzol let out a frustrated huff. "I'll be honest with you, I do not know how we are to free ourselves from that predicament."

Janes nodded. "I had thought it a tall order."

"Have you raised the sails?" Nicks asked.

"Hasn't been enough wind to bother," Jennings muttered.

"Was kinda windy earlier. Maybe the wind'll change?" Gretty said.

"I don't know; it's pretty calm now," Gritzol replied.

"I fear we cannot rely on the wind alone." Unused to stubble, Janes scratched his chin. "Perhaps in our absence, Mr. Ellis has come up with some ideas."

"I'm not sure I trust Ellis's ideas," Thomas said.

"Aye," Jennings said.

Janes chuckled. "I would be willing to listen to any ideas that might liberate the *Valiant* from the sand."

"Aye, sir," Thomas said.

Gretty held up a hand to get their attention. "Who is this Mr. Ellis, anyways? I thought he was the captain to start with?"

"Ship's cook," Jennings said.

"What? A simple cook?" Gretty cried in disbelief.

Janes smiled. "Not only just a cook, but quite a versatile man."

"And a fine actor as well," Roberts said.

"Although you wouldn't know it upon first impressions," Thomas said, remembering his previous encounters with Ellis.

"I'd hate to be Marshall if I knew about that!" Nicks laughed.

"Marshall is just a troubled individual. Personally, I feel sorry for the man," Janes said quietly.

"Sir? After all he has done to you?" Fallah asked.

Janes shrugged. "It's not good form. His actions are despicable, yes, but all in good judgment for a man with his condition."

"I's not understanding, boss," Aramondo said.

"It's quite simple, really." Rubbing his thumb over his fingers, Janes made the universal gesture for money. "Greed."

Roberts shook his head in confusion. "Greed, yes, but how can that be in good judgment?"

"And the death of your crewman? All because of ... greed?" Gretty asked.

"Lewinston was taken by Nyguard's interpretation of greed, but I won't discuss that now. You see, greed is quite simply wanting what Marshall cannot have," Janes began.

"Could you explain it further, sir? I think we have the time," Gritzol said.

"Certainly." Nodding he turned fully away from the cliff. "As I said before, his actions are based on greed. It can be man's greatest ally or his worst nightmare. You see, greed is like a circle, and its history will often repeat, if not in one man's life then in another's. For it is greed that comes to a man who has hit bottom, reasoning that the only way for him to get what was once his is to resort to covetous behavior. Greed fuels this passion. From greed, comes wealth, from wealth comes power, and from power comes fear. Fear of losing his power, wealth … everything. This fear flows into the souls of his fellow men, from which greed is again produced. Greed fuels want, and want creates bloodshed. Then, the cycle repeats … until another man falls into its vortex," Janes explained.

"You imply that Marshall was once rich," Gretty said.

"I know he was. It was long ago, when Marshall was the commander of Cimmordia's royal armada." The captain turned his gaze back to sea. "He had money and women, lived an aristocrat's lifestyle, but had no real power. Indeed, he held authority over the royal merchant marine and navy; but in secret he was a ruthless pirate, sailing from his hideout in the Sundrop Islands and raiding merchant ships from other nations: Derrisburg, Grand Point, Tallebeck … Dieteria, even the powerful and mighty nations of the North. When the king of Cimmordia began to grow older, he decided it was time for a prime minister to oversee the nation's needs, although the king was reluctant to give up his duties. Of all of his aids, Marshall and a wise diplomat named Rebecca were his two choices. The king had always thought of Marshall as a man of action, rather than peace. Knowing that Marshall had more capability as a naval captain than as a diplomat, the position was given to Rebecca," Janes explained.

"Which was when Marshall lost most of his wealth?" Thomas asked.

"Not quite." Janes turned back to them. "When Cimmordia Castle moved its central port to South Cimmordia, there came a movement to streamline the royal navy. Since most naval forces were in the control of regional admirals, Marshall's post was no longer necessary."

"Which was why he lost everything," Roberts said.

Janes nodded. "Marshall resorted to raiding ships and cargo on the seas where the laws of Cimmordia Castle did not apply. Since he was still recognized by the people of Cimmordia, he adopted a split personality. On shore he acted dignified and proper, leaving his true and ruthless nature on the seas."

"All because of greed," Aramondo said.

Janes nodded.

"You sound like you know Marshall better than yourself, boss," Gretty said.

"I may not have spent as much time in Cimmordia as he has, but I know people." He scratched his chin again. "Rebecca, for example, was once the representative to Dieteria, and my brother still meets with her on a regular basis."

"But, if Marshall inherited all this greed, who had it before him?" Nicks asked.

"The old Ranthath Cult, maybe?" Gretty asked.

"Probably, but that's a subject reserved for the philosophers now." Janes straightened as he spotted Acadia returning from the *Valiant* with the rowboat.

"Christopher? Are you ready?" Acadia called.

"We are!" He turned to Jennings. "You go first."

"Why me?"

"You're the nimble one." Janes waved at the edge. "Go on."

Jennings took a deep breath. "I can do this."

"Come on, Harvey!" Acadia called.

"Okay, the girl's down there … okay … okay," Jennings muttered.

"Harvey, we have no time for this," Janes replied.

"Haa … naaa!" Jennings cried as he fell toward the water, sinking deep below the surface before Acadia helped him up and into the rowboat.

"Well done; you were wonderful!" Acadia said.

"Remind me when we get to the ship," Jennings muttered.

The rest of the men, one by one, splashed into the waters and boarded the rowboat. Then, as soon as Acadia was in, they embarked for the *Valiant*, hoping to arrive before the *Inferno* and Captain Marshall recaptured them all.

As it turned out, Marsha had kept Nyguard busy for some time. Eventually letting go of the rope for her own safety, Marsha left and fled to the Cove, allowing Nyguard to finally catch the rowboat.

"There are some strange occurrences on these islands, boss," Nyguard said as he rowed the boat back to pick up Marshall.

"Someone is playing games with us, Leo." Marshall looked over his shoulder. "They must be close behind us."

"But there's one thing I don't understand, boss. The other rowboat was moored right here," Nyguard said.

Marshall thought a moment. "I don't know how she did it, but I know she did it!"

"Who, the girl?"

"Aye the girl! We must hurry!" Marshall climbed inside the rowboat, and they headed for the *Inferno*.

Janes's group cleared the sheltered cliffs of the cove, and quickly discovered that the winds were quite strong, as if a storm were headed their way from the south. They had picked up suddenly, and seemed almost unnatural.

Acadia shivered. "My, what a cold wind this is."

"Here, we'll sit together." Thomas moved next to her.

"Take this." Janes put his coat around her shoulders.

"Thank you, you're both such gentlemen," Acadia said with a smile.

"We should be to the left, here," Janes said to Gretty, who was rowing alongside Nicks.

There, where it always had been, sat the *Valiant*. It looked like Benson and Benks had already gotten the sails rigged, as the canvas had been unfurled and readied.

"This is your best idea yet, Ellis! If this wind keeps up, we should be free of the sand in no time!" Ward called as the rowboat approached.

"Ahoy, Captain!" Benks called down.

Benson manned the crane. "I'll pull you up!"

"Good work, gentlemen! I see you had the same idea as myself," Janes said.

Ward leaned over the rail, shaking his head. "Actually, sir, Mr. Ellis came up with this one."

"Horatio? Well, that's astounding! I am very impressed!" Janes said. Roberts secured the crane's hooks to the rowboat.

"Acadia, you should probably go now," Thomas said, taking her hand.

Acadia gave him a confused look. "But I'm coming with you, Thomas."

"How can you? This is your home, and ... well, you need to be in the water. It is where ... you belong." In his heart, he would rather she came with too. "Captain, I need a moment," Thomas said to Janes.

"Only a moment, Tommy. I'll need this boat secured." Janes directed the other men to climb up the hull.

"You ... don't want my company?" Acadia asked.

"Acadia, of course I do." He took her hands in his. "I've always enjoyed your company. And I swear to you, I will never forget you and our stay here. The thing is, it would be best if I returned to my home ... and you returned to yours."

"My home is where you are," Acadia said.

Thomas smiled, his gaze turning toward the islands. "These islands are a wonder, Acadia. You are a wonder, yourself. Should you come away with me, these lands will be losing a part of that magic. If I could take you with us, I would in a heartbeat; but life on the seas, or even life ashore, will not be a pleasant experience for you. As in the cave, going day to day, waiting for a bucket of water ... I don't want to see you like that." Thomas looked into her eyes intently.

Acadia could only look back as tears seeped from her eyes.

Thomas cleared his throat and reached into his vest pocket for the pendant. "Here, I meant to give this to you earlier, but it was not the time. So, I shall give it to you now, so you can keep a part of me here, with you." He placed it into her hand.

Acadia looked at it in the first rays of the sunrise. "I remember you showing me this earlier."

"It's a carving of the full moon. I hope that when you wear this on a clear night, with the moon shining, you can be with me," Thomas said.

Lifting her hair, he secured the charm around Acadia's neck. She adjusted it to the center where it hung comfortably.

"You are indeed a beauty; it becomes you."

Acadia dried her eyes. "Perhaps you are right, Thomas. It does sound rather daunting, when you put it that way, going from bucket to bucket each day."

"Tommy! We need you up here!" Benson called as the winds picked up.

Thomas looked at Acadia closely, knowing that he would always remember her, just as she sat now, until the next time he could see her.

"One day, Acadia, we will meet again." Thomas removed the captain's coat from her shoulders.

"Yes, perhaps so ... our time together will not be forgotten, Thomas."
She climbed out of the rowboat and into the water. "I assure you that I
shall never forget you, and I hope you do not forget me."

Thomas took her hand and kissed it just as Gretty began lifting the
rowboat from the water.

"Captain, *Inferno* ahoy!" Benks called. Acadia sadly watched as
Thomas was lifted away from her. Behind her, the *Inferno*'s red sails came
sailing around the far side of Opole Island.

"You'll know we are safe by two tones on the shell. Go, Acadia!"
Thomas said.

"Be careful!"

The rowboat was brought onto the deck, separating her from Thomas's
view. He stood up for one last glimpse, but by then she was already beneath
the waters. Now that he was on deck, Thomas could feel the powerful
winds.

"Thomas, the boss wants us to secure this. How we do it?" Gretty
asked.

"Uh, this way," Thomas said, forgetting himself for a moment. He
jumped out and secured the rowboat to the deck. Gretty watched carefully,
and did the same to his side. Just then, the sails caught the wind.

"Ah ha! You're a genius, Ellis! It shouldn't take long now!" Janes
said.

"Jennings! Keep an eye on that mainsail! If it starts to bend too far,
untie it before it gets torn apart!" Ward called.

"Aye sir!" Jennings called back. He made sure that his knot was secured
along the top of the mainsail.

"Hold on tight!" Benson called back from his side of the rigging.

"Mr. Benks, distance of the *Inferno*?" Janes asked from the bridge.

"A thousand yards boss," Benks replied, as the *Inferno* came around
the northern coast of Opole Island.

"Come on, you worthless excuse for a wind! My grandmother played
the pipes louder than you!" Ward cried out.

A strong gust of wind met the mainsail with great force, extending the
ropes to their breaking point. As a main rope began to stretch thin, Benks
spotted it.

"Benson! Your rope is coming loose!" Benks cried.

Quickly, Benson snatched the other side of the damaged rope, able to hold on tightly before it failed. It took all of his strength to hold on.

"Urggh! She's gonna split!" Benson cried.

A sudden lurch then shook up the men. It was the ship!

"Hold tight, Benson! She's coming loose!" Janes held onto a stabilizer. Ward, Gretty, and Thomas did the same. Nicks ran to assist Benson.

"I'll help!" Nicks said, even though his leg had yet to be properly tended.

"Nicks, your leg!" Gretty called.

"It'll be fine!" Nicks said, climbing up the mainmast. As the *Valiant* slowly came free of the sand, the *Inferno* approached.

"Okay Nyguard. While they're stranded, we charge aboard and take Janes by force!" Marshall called.

"It'll be a pleasure, boss!" Nyguard called back.

By then Nicks had climbed next to Benson, and using the last amount of his strength, Nicks swung down and collected the loose rope, allowing Benson to maintain his own hold on the mainsail.

That was the precious moment they needed, as the ship came free of the sand and sailed into the deeper waters off the coastline, away from the beach and into the open water. As the sun began to rise behind them, Benson tied a sheepshank knot in the damaged rope, securing both ends to each other so it would hold even in the strong wind. This way, they could splice the rope during calmer weather.

Nicks, fatigued, dropped to the deck below.

"Mr. Gretty! Spin us around and head toward the mainland!" Janes called.

"Aye boss!" Gretty cried out. The men cheered at their freedom.

Marshall watched them gain speed in disgust. "No! It cannot be!" The much faster *Valiant* sailed beyond his view.

"And with our crew, too! How shall we find them now?" Nyguard asked.

Marshall hit Nyguard with his hat. "You fool! Don't give up so easily! We know they're heading northwest. It's only a matter of time until they hit land."

"What do you suggest?" Nyguard asked.

"Plot our course, and be quick about it!" Turning back to the sea before him, he shook his fist. "No, Janes, you will not escape me this time … not while you still carry my map!"

"Sir … if I work the sails we can chase…."

"You heard my orders, Leo! Get at it!"

Knowing that his captain was letting the *Valiant* escape, Nyguard went below deck and found their bearing quickly, to please Marshall. He worked swiftly, fearing that Marshall might decide he didn't need an uncooperative first mate.

"Brandon, you okay?" Benks asked Nicks, who had obviously aggravated the injury to his leg further from the fall.

"This has sure been a bad couple of days." Nicks was seeing nothing except stars.

"Could someone give me a hand, here?" Benks called. "Looks like he needs some rest."

Jennings came to help him up. "That leg don't look good," Jennings said. He and Benks carried Nicks on their shoulders to the crew quarters.

"Aye," Nicks muttered. "You were friends with him … yes?"

Jennings pushed open the cabin door as Nicks collapsed. "Aye he was … and I'll thank you not to bring it up."

"We don't mean to." Benks wrapped a handkerchief around Nicks' leg. "Just know that Nyguard's loyalty was driven by fear. If I had the chance, I would've done Nyguard in myself."

Jennings stammered as he helped Nicks to his feet again. "You want help or not? You'll be losing your leg if we don't treat it now."

Nicks nodded. "Sorry about your friend. I truly am."

Jennings gave a nod. With Benk's assistance, they helped Nicks below.

Thomas looked back toward the islands from the stern, even though the sun had risen enough to impair his vision. Roberts joined him.

"What be your thoughts, Tommy?" Jared asked.

"If I could play your fife you'd know," Thomas replied softly.

Jared put his hand on Thomas's back. "She's already missing you, and I can see you miss her. Acadia'll never forget you; I assure ye of that."

"That doesn't make her any closer to me," Thomas said.

"I know it doesn't, Tommy. It's not going to get much easier from here out," Jared replied.

Thomas took a deep sigh as the winds grew steadier.

"Cheer up, lad." Jared patted his back. "There'll be a time when you can throw away your cares and return to those islands. And when that time comes, she'll be waiting for you."

Thomas nodded. "I hope you're right."

"That's for you to decide. If you want it bad enough, it'll happen again. Just make certain she knows you're safe." Jared took out his fife and playing the same note two times and went below.

Thomas looked up, and remembered what he had said to Acadia before she left. He had forgotten to signal on the shell! Taking it from around his neck, he blew as hard as he could into the shell twice. Although it failed to make a sound, doing so made Thomas feel much better than before. Taking the shell with him, he too went below deck.

With the islands behind him, his thoughts returned to the journal and the crew of the *Nemaris*. Wondering what had become of Captain Scyhathen, he retrieved the book from the captain and opened it to the bookmarked page.

Discovering that someone had read ahead, he turned back a page, reading the passage describing the chance escape that Ellis had read earlier.

"Well ... looks like the good captain had the same idea that we had ... that sounds too good to be a coincidence...." Thomas muttered to himself.

Ignoring the similarities, Thomas turned the page and read onward.

January 15th, 1583. Due to the quick thinking of Mr. Smitty and Mr. Corvair, and not forgetting the grace of nature for providing the winds, their planning to free our ship from the sands has proven most successful. Although not all of the men are quite ready to leave these shores, I feel it is in our best interest to do so. After all, even if I choose to end my days here, it is not my decision to choose the fate of my men, especially in a place inhabited by the demon who calls himself Epoth. Perhaps when I return to the common lands I will label these islands as a place to avoid in the future. On the other hand, a land of such wonder is hard to stay away from. Maybe I shall have to return in a personal craft, but not until I can properly promote Mr. Smitty to captain the Nemaris. I think he is ready and would be a fine captain of the crew. Not only that, he seems to be making more decisions than I lately. I am confident he could sail to Phrynn without incident. I shall have to discuss it with him.

We found the islands hospitable. By all rights and appearances we had no reason to want departure. Yet the sands held my ship firm, and soon the islands would appear much more than iron bars and shackles. Our prison was a paradise, indeed, and while we sail free I am conflicted. I must fight the urge to remain ashore.

Although we are leaving in haste, our time to leave has come. Our supplies are razor thin, and if not for the fruit and vegetables found on shore the islands we would all have perished from starvation by now. Our hope lies in South Cimmordia, a two-day sail east. A welcome sight it will be.

Perhaps someday I will retire on these lovely islands. I would be there still, even if I would find it difficult to live there with that Epoth. ... What has created that apparition I shall never know. Living in a state half alive, half dead; it is more than I can possibly imagine. To be stuck in such an existence must be a horrible curse, and I pity him. I sometimes wonder what his face may have looked like, having never shared the honor to cross swords.

All things considered, though I do have plans to return ... I do not know when. Yes, I shall consider the Nemaris Islands forbidden. It is best that a man would preserve the islands with their wonders and mysteries, especially those who would give into man's most covetous natures. For those seeking pleasure and fantasy, it is a paradise. But to those who wish to partake of the sorcerer Rhydar's treasure, which I learned of from Miss Cynthia, may they take caution of the demon Epoth and know of his wrath. A demon of terrible evil and dread... a demon that I'm certain was awakened by my arrival.

Thomas turned to the next entry, but it, along with all the following pages, were blank. Apparently, this was the end of the journal. Thomas observed that a number of pages had been removed from the book. Counting the number of ruffles, some five or ten pages had been torn out, including a page or two from earlier entries. It seemed as if someone wanted to keep certain things secret.

His mind began to race. Certainly Scyhathen had stopped writing at that point, but shouldn't the blank pages have been about Scyhathen's tour of the southern continent? Why had it ended where it did? Why did the *Nemaris*'s experiences so closely match those of the *Valiant*? Why had the islands faded from the minds of sailors if there was a journal about them? How had the journal arrived in Thomas's attic?

The mystery would haunt Thomas's dreams.

Calm Seas in Crystal Bay

Back on Nemaris Island, Acadia was crestfallen by Thomas's sudden departure. Much of her time in the water was spent moping about, and eventually she found her way to the waterfall. She arrived at the bridge that Thomas and the others had; it seemed like it had happened a long time ago. She climbed out of the water and sat upon the bridge, her tailfin dangling toward the creek below.

With this the only evidence of the *Valiant*'s visit to the islands, aside from the pendant that Thomas had given her, it was here Acadia chose to be alone with her thoughts. Holding the pendant tightly in her clasped hands, she hid her head and sobbed, since nothing else would help her move on. But it was not easy to let go. There had been far too much excitement during their stay, the most she'd ever had in her life.

"Thomas, I miss you," she said between tears.

She sat there for the remainder of the day, leaving only to refresh her dry scales before returning again to her spot on the bridge. As sunset approached, Marsha came to the surface of the creek, amazed to find Acadia there all alone.

"Acadia! There you are! I was starting to worry." Marsha joined her on the bridge.

Acadia sniffled. "I haven't gone ... anywhere."

Marsha nodded her head. "You know what? Your response to those humans coming here ... Cynthia did the same thing when that other ship was marooned."

Acadia perked up, astonished. "What? What ship? When?"

"A very long time ago." A wave from Marsha indicated the distant past.

For some reason, this made Acadia feel calmer. "Marsha ... I have always trusted your words. Please, I do not remember."

"You were very small, Acadia. Just as you are now, Cynthia was heartbroken about the departure of her Nelson." Sighing, Marsha absently twirled a lock of her hair between her fingers. "Such a creative man, he made a wonderful impression on her. The cabin boy, too, much like your Thomas. His arrival to these islands was predestined, I believe, especially with the then recent passing of Rhydar."

Acadia interrupted her. "Wait, I remember Thomas speaking of a connection between Captain Scyhathen's cabin boy and his father."

"A connection?"

Acadia thought a moment, and then gave her reply. "Actually, he never addressed it directly, but Captain Janes also hinted around it during our walk through the cavern."

Marsha drew back. "Of course…I remember something very odd about Rhydar's last days. Maybe…." She paused thoughtfully then dropped into the water. "Cynthia will know for certain. Come on!" Marsha sped toward the sea with Acadia following close behind.

After a few day's sail, the *Valiant* arrived at the island town of Crystal Bay, a small port northwest of the Nemaris Islands. Located atop a small island nestled between Cyeel Point and the southeast corner of Tabia, Crystal Bay was sheltered from most evils of the world. In accordance with Mr. Ward's calendar, they had been marooned for little more than a month … and the men were eager to restock the supplies.

As they came around Cyeel Point and the rocky harbor came into view, a breath of relief passed through the men.

Located a considerable distance from Tallebeck's capitol city of Feirmarin and outside of the main circle route taken by many of the South Centra Sea's merchant ships, Crystal Island was isolated from most other regions. To the west, the coast of the Tabia continent was riddled with rocky cliffs and waterfalls from the mountains above. Quite picturesque, it also was an excellent haven for fishermen and merchants alike. Most of the townsfolk enjoyed their isolation, content that travelers would rather take the long way around Tabia to avoid the Nemaris Islands. For Captain Janes, it resulted in unusual conversation after their arrival.

"You say you have been marooned on the Nemaris Islands for an entire month?" The docksman's brows rose skeptically. "Sir, I find that very unlikely."

In an attempt to remain polite, Janes fought to keep the incredulity from his voice. He was unused to not being taken for his word. "What's so unlikely? The lands are actually quite comfortable, sir. You and I both know of the rumors, and the demons, yes. But of all the tattle, I can assure you most of it is false."

"Sir, if I have been told true," the docksman replied, "one cannot survive on those islands for more than a day. Even the stores aboard your ship would be corrupted from the very air nearby. Or, have I been misinformed?" He looked Janes up and down then noticed Nicks, still feeble from his leg wound. "No, I think malnutrition has left your thoughts in disarray, Captain. A strong storm, perhaps? Or even a touch of scurvy?" The docksman gave him a friendly pat on the shoulder. "But whatever brought you here, I think I have the cure. Would your men like some fresh pineapple? We grow the sweetest variety that can be found along the Centra, ye know."

Janes smiled pleasantly, changing his tone. "Perhaps you are correct. Our maps are incomplete, and I may be deluded. Forget I mentioned it. In fact, pineapples sound mighty good right now." It wasn't his intent to argue with common belief.

"For you, captain, I shall waive the price. We sailors have to look out for one another," the docksman said. He took some pineapples from a crate and handed them to Janes.

Janes smiled. "I thank you for your generosity today. You may know that my men will greatly appreciate this gift."

"As you had mentioned, you may forget it. Just doing what you'd do for me," the docksman said.

The captain delivered the pineapples to the men in the mess hall. They were chatting quietly about their entire ordeal.

"Gentlemen, a generous gift from a local." Janes put the pineapples on the table.

"Those look mighty ripe," Ellis said.

"If you would cut them up, that would be most welcome," Janes said.

"Aye," he said, taking a few into the galley.

"I didn't mean to break into the conversation. Did I interrupt?"

"No boss, we were just speaking of those islands," Gretty said.

"They were quite a scene," Benks added.

"Gentlemen, you have missed out on a grand adventure ... why, it all started in South Cimmordia," Janes began.

"Oh, they already know about most of it, Cap'n," Gritzol said.

"All of it?" He seemed anxious to recount the story in his own words.

"Aye, we've filled them in already," Ward said.

Janes nodded sadly. "Oh. Well, no need for repetition then." He sat down at the table as Ellis entered with a fresh cut pineapple.

"We were curious about our next destination, sir," Benson asked.

"Only a few places to go. We've got some ore to unload, and a few bags of cotton, but afterward I plan to head back toward Dieteria Castle and Harper's Bay," Janes replied.

"And after that?" Benks asked.

Janes bit into a piece of pineapple. "That is up to Mr. Gretty. I understand you men have some folks to talk to."

"Aye, we are looking forward to seeing them again, boss," Aramondo said.

"I would like to make a pass by Vesper, if it's not too inconvenient," Gretty said.

"That would require a pass by the Sundrop Islands ... I'd rather not pass by Marshall's hideout so soon. Does anyone wish to go by Derrisburg or Grand Point?" Ward asked.

"Uh, captain? I have a young- er, I have a wife waiting for me in Derrisburg," Nicks spoke up.

"And I need to visit my brother's home on Valiavista Island," Aramondo said.

Janes nodded. "Perhaps we can work Vesper in after departing Harper's Bay, Mr. Gretty."

Gretty and those who had served with him on the *Inferno* nodded.

"Captain, what if we run into Marshall again? I don't think he'll be too friendly next time," Jennings asked.

Licking his fingers clean, Janes shrugged. "It will be a chance we have to take. Should we keep to the shores, we should be okay. If a confrontation is unavoidable, we outnumber Marshall five to one. He will not be a burden to us again."

Jennings looked across the table towards the bench where Lewinston usually sat. "Okay, captain, should it come to that."

"I know what you're thinking, Harv." The captain's expression grew solemn. "James was killed dishonorably. But when, and if, Marshall is foolish enough to chase us, he will get what is coming to him. For now, we should focus on getting this ship back in shape. Mr. Ward, you'll need some volunteers to help carry supplies back from the marketplace."

Ward finished his pineapple and stood. "Aye. Gretty, Roberts, Perry, and Benks, you're with me."

"Aye," the four men replied.

"As for the rest of you, we should inspect the sails and clean up that refuse bin. Jennings, you'll have to drain any water left in the tank and clean out any mold that may have grown inside," Janes said.

"Aww, I hate doing that," Jennings said.

"Beats getting sick," Ellis muttered.

"Aye," some of the men muttered.

Gritzol got up. "I can help."

"Thanks, I'll need it," Jennings replied.

Janes gave an approving nod. Camaraderie among the new and old members of his crew had been good. "I think if we all work hard, we can be sailing toward Teraske in two days. I realize we all want to relax from our journey on the islands, but we've relaxed enough for now. A little work won't hurt any. We should be at Teraske by the end of the week."

"Sounds good, boss," Fallah said.

"What about my leg, boss? I can't work none on it," Nicks said.

"We'll see that you get someone to look at it, Nicks. Perhaps a splint and some rest willl do you good," Janes replied.

"Aye," Nicks replied.

"Any questions?" Janes asked.

"No sir," and "No boss," rumbled through the room.

"Okay then. We've got some work to do," Janes said, heading into the hall.

"Captain, what about those two left in the rubbish bin?" Gritzol asked, turning back for a moment. The rest of the crew went about their orders.

"It's been what, two days? You gave them water, didn't you?" Janes asked.

Ellis nodded. "Only to shut 'em up. Last I checked they were breathin'."

"Open the door," Janes ordered. They went over to the refuse bin and removed the wooden barricade. The air was foul inside, and both Irving and Morrey were laying amongst the garbage on their backs. The thick smell seeped into the mess hall as a voice moaned quietly.

"Anyone alive in here?" Gritzol asked.

Morrey moved first, while Irving was slow to rouse. "Here, sir ... but Theo is gone." Morrey muttered in a dry tone.

Janes shook his head. "Barry, get those men out of here, both of them," Janes replied. They each took a shoulder on Morrey, and then pulled him into the fresh air of the mess hall. Gritzol went back for Irving, who was moments from succumbing to the harsh environment.

"Where ... where am I?" Morrey asked.

"Crystal Bay. And free from Marshall, if you want to know," Janes replied.

"Free? Marshall ... gone?" Morrey asked.

"For now. You may sail with us or go about your own way ... but if you choose to leave, I encourage you to not cross either mine, nor Marshall's path again, aye?" Janes asked.

Morrey nodded. "I get it, and I will take my chances on my own. I have no quarrel with you, or your men, Captain ... I had to follow orders. Just promise me that Marshall gets what he deserves."

"I will make no such promise, crewman," Janes replied.

"Farion Morrey, sir."

"Marshall has done enough for today and will be judged accordingly, but not by me." He helped Morrey onto the deck and gave him a few coins. "For now Mr. Morrey, I suggest you head ashore and get yourself cleaned up and try to rebuild your life."

"There's an inn just to the right of the docks. You might head there first," Gritzol replied.

Morrey looked at him and nodded. "Good day to you both ... and thank you for sparing me," he replied, heading down the gangplank and into town.

"What about him?" Gritzol asked, motioning to Irving.

"Theo? You there?" Gretty asked. He slapped Irving's cheeks, rousing him alert.

Irving opened his eyes, but just barely. His voice was weak. "Is that Gretty?"

"Theo, Marshall lost. We escaped him and are finally free of his command," Gretty said.

Irving continued looking around the room, dazed from his experience.

"Gretty ... Marshall ... will ... never give up ... so easily," Irving muttered before closing his eyes.

Janes called over Fallah and Benks. "See that he gets to the nearest tavern, and see that he gets the help he needs. Should he return to Marshall's side, that will be his choice and not ours."

Fallah and Benks picked up Irving by the shoulders and carried him atop deck. As he left the room, it was not clear if he was walking on his own feet or not.

For the remainder of the season, Theodore Irving would recover from his ordeal in the Diamond Head Hostel, Crystal Bay's local tavern. Irving would never sail again. He had been Marshall's closest ally.

As the *Inferno* sailed north, Marshall began plotting destinations that Janes might have taken.

"Derrisberg?" Marshall asked Nyguard, who was manning the wheel.

"More north than west," Nyguard replied.

"Teraske?" Marshall asked.

"We could check there first; it's where I'd go if I were Janes," Nyguard said. "If only that foolish cook Geynall hadn't used that map of ours to start a cooking fire with earlier ... too bad he can't be replaced until we find a city," Marshall muttered.

"Replaced, boss?" Nyguard asked. He wondered if Marshall hadn't killed off the only other crewman aboard, leaving him to do all the work.

"You know, *replaced*, Leo," Marshall sneered.

That confirmed that question, Nyguard decided. "Oh. And the cabin boy, boss?"

"He must be hiding someplace ... I'll deal with him soon enough."

Nyguard nodded. "Well ... what are your orders?"

"We try Teraske. Search the countryside. If not there, Derrisberg, Grand Point ... then perhaps to Sundrop for another map," Marshall grumbled, before going toward his cabin.

"I trust we'll find them boss," Nyguard said.

Marshall trailed off into non sensible jammer, mouthing foul language and other ramblings. He slammed his door behind him.

Two busy days in Crystal Bay passed. The ship was filled with supplies in the form of food, dried fruits, whale oil for lanterns, and a rowboat to replace the one that had been taken by the *Inferno*. These things done, the *Valiant* was again ready to sail the seas for her next destination.

"Ready for departure at your order, captain," Ward said. Janes stood beside Jennings at the wheel.

"Aye, there be a good southern breeze today! Our only destination for now be the port of Teraske." Janes chuckled dryly. "I'm sure Mr. Morgan is waiting impatiently for his shipment of ore."

"And Mr. Grimbeck his lumber ..." added Ward, "That is, what's left of it."

Janes nodded.

"Is the word given, Captain?" Gritzol asked.

"Perry, weigh anchor. Benson, Gritzol, Gretty, draw the mainsail. Jennings, you man the wheel." Janes clapped the man on the shoulder. "Man it like Jim Lewinston would've done."

"Aye sir!"

"The rest of ye, draw the rest of the sails." Janes pointed to the nearby peninsula. "Take her around Cyeel Point, veer north and follow the coastline to Teraske."

"Aye sir!" the men cried, glad to be doing their jobs at sea again.

Meanwhile, the *Inferno* was having difficulty in their search for the port of Teraske and the *Valiant*.

"Honestly, Nyguard, haven't you found the coastline *yet*? One would assume it would be an easy task!" Marshall cried.

Nyguard grumbled slightly, clearing his throat. "Sir, would it help if I called out to the shoreline and asked it to come closer?"

Marshall glared at Nyguard. "Do I look like a fool, Leo?"

"No, boss. But I do know that we're not far from the Sundrop Islands. According to our compass, we've been going north to northeast since we lost sight of the *Valiant*," Nyguard replied.

"North? They went west!" Marshall cried.

"I was trimming the sails, boss. The rudder must've drifted, and it takes more than one man to run a ship."

Marshall growled. "Just get us back to headquarters ... I don't care how." He then slammed the door to his cabin.

Nyguard muttered to himself. "Sometimes I think that man would drown in an inch of water if not for me." He adjusted the wheel and steered toward the Sundrop Islands.

As the *Valiant* sailed north, Thomas returned to the simple pleasure of swabbing the deck. It was a chore he had come to relish, and the deck was in dire need of it. Aside from that, with the journal being already read through and with no more rocks to carve, there was little else to do. Benson had his swordplay, Jared his fife, but Thomas? A mop and a bucket.

As he dragged the mop across the deck, he thought only of Acadia, back at the islands. He also wondered about the cabin boy of the *Nemaris*. No, there was no getting those thoughts out of his mind. So much so, in fact, that the mop seemed to be taking on a blond color, almost like Acadia's hair.

"I can't do this anymore." Thomas dropped the mop and went to speak with Captain Janes in his cabin.

"Tommy, where ye going?" Jennings asked.

"You're not leaving that, are ye?" Benks asked.

Jared held them back. "Let him go. I think he's got something big on his mind."

Thomas opened the door and went in to see Ward and Janes talking.

"And that barmaid was quite a picture, wasn't she? Voice and the face of an angel—Tommy, hello!" Ward said, seeing Thomas.

"I apologize for intruding, but who were you talking about?" Thomas asked.

Janes smiled. "Just someone we talked with at a tavern in Crystal Village. Something on your mind, lad?"

Thomas nodded. He sat down where Janes motioned for him to. "I find it difficult to do my work, sir. I cannot focus. My father, Acadia, the islands, Captain Marshall—I cannot sort it out."

Janes stroked his chin and nodded. "You are not the only one to feel this, Thomas. Remember when your mother agreed for you to come with us? What did she hope for you to discover?"

Thomas had to think a moment. It had been a long time since he'd spoken with his mother, and even longer since he had looked into the glass orb she'd given him.

"Learn the ways of a sailor, explore a little, and learn how my father lived," Thomas replied.

"Yes, and have you discovered those things?" Janes asked.

He looked up. "Aye sir, I have."

"That, and more, yes?" Pouring himself a cup of tea, he offered some to Thomas and Ward, who both refused. After a sip, he smiled. "You, myself, Seriam, the rest of these men. We've all encountered something that nobody else has ever seen and been able to tell stories about. Your friend Acadia, and her kin. That story alone will live with you until the day you leave this world for the next, Thomas! Oh sure, the men will tell it. I will probably tell it, and I'm sure you'll tell it to others someday. Those others may contest it to the end, but you'll know it to be true. That will be enough for you to share this tale, the next tale, and the next!"

"You see, Tommy? You returned from the forbidden islands … you've met a fantasy come to life. No matter what anyone says, you did that, and that's saying something," added Ward.

Thomas's thoughts seemed a little less jumbled. He felt a lot lighter, as if the burden of those thoughts had been tucked away until he could sort them out one at a time.

"Aye sir, I see it all now." Thomas stood to go.

"One more thing." Janes held up a hand to stop him. "I said I'd pay ye for your work, as I do the rest of my men."

"Pay?" Thomas sat back down.

"Of course. I did tell you I'd pay you for your services on this boat. Let's see … it's been a month, and I haven't paid you much of anything…" He turned to his first mate. "It was two microns a day, Seriam?"

Ward nodded. "Sounds right, Chris. A Dictare per week."

"I do not remember if we had a discussion, sir," Thomas said.

"No, I believe I worked it out with your mother. Either way, for four weeks of work, I believe you are due …." Janes began.

Thomas shook his head. "Sir, I kindly refuse. I do not believe you can pay me for my services, with the experiences I have earned aboard this ship. Whatever the amount, I cannot accept it."

"At least send it to your mother, Tommy … you're certainly entitled to it," Mr. Ward said.

Thomas thought a moment and then nodded in agreement.

Janes nodded. "As you wish, Thomas. When we return to Harper's Bay, I will settle with Marianne. But should you need money for any reason, you are due to it."

"Thank you, sir. May I return to my work now?" Thomas asked.

"Anytime you wish to talk, Thomas, feel free. I only ask that you knock before entering?"

Thomas nodded. "Of course, sir, I apologize again." Thomas backed out and closed the door behind him.

Ward chuckled. "Just as I expected. The men are the same way; I think they have too much fun here, Chris."

"I can't seem to give away any of my money, Seriam." Janes took a sip of his tea. "If it wasn't for my savings guild at Dieteria Castle I cannot imagine what I would do with the leftover funds."

"Chris, you surprise me. I had imagined that you and I put everything into this ship," Ward said.

"Seriam, I share all secrets with you. Aside from what the men get paid and what I keep in this safe, there is very little leftover. When passing by the castle, whatever excess Dictares I have go into the guild there. A percentage is given to the children of the castle in times of need, which is okay by me. I only keep what I use, and of that there is plenty," Janes explained.

Ward nodded. "Of course. Money is plentiful, and the men do get paid well. Forgive me for implying otherwise."

"Of course. As always, your honor with me is the highest."

Under the deepest reaches of Nemaris Island, Acadia left Cynthia's grotto. She headed for her own in haste.

"Impossible! Thomas must know about this!" Acadia entered her chambers and gathered a few things into a small knapsack of broad seaweed leaves.

Marsha caught up with her, blocking the entrance. "Where are you headed off to? What is this all about?"

"I must find Thomas … at any cost, he will need to hear what I've found out. He must know … I am sure of it!"

Marsha blocked Acadia's path. "You cannot just swim into the deep ocean! What would Onell say? And besides, it is far…."

Swirling to face her sister, Acadia raised her hands in exasperation. "Far too dangerous, and you will be eaten alive by giant squid and mermaid-eating sharks, because in the safety of these islands such creatures do not swim here … I know the risks, Marsha. Either I go alone or you can come with me." She synched her knapsack shut.

Marsha was about to refuse Acadia departure, but she knew it would not work. "Okay, but I do not agree with this course of action at all." She quickly made her own sack and hurried to catch up to Acadia, who had begun swimming northwest.

"Are you coming?" Acadia called back to Marsha.

"Yes! Acadia, please do not swim so fast! Wait for me!"

Twilight Reunion

$\mathcal{I}$t took a day, but the *Inferno* eventually found its bearing toward the Sundrop Islands. Late at night, Nyguard used a sextant and the ship's compass to get them on track.

"Some days, you truly impress me, Leo. I never have fully understood these navigational tools," Marshall said.

"Thanks, boss," Nyguard said.

"I'll take over the wheel in a few hours," Marshall said, heading for his cabin.

"Aye."

The *Inferno* continued to sail, following the heading carefully, a day's sail to the Sundrop Islands.

As the two mermaids continued their journey, somewhere between the Nemaris Islands and the port of Teraske, Marsha became convinced that Acadia was nearing the point of insanity.

"Are you certain of where we are going?" Marsha asked.

"Not actually, no." Acadia slowed down to take stock of their surroundings.

"We must be lost then." Marsha crossed her arms and mournfully glanced back the way they had come.

Acadia reached into her knapsack. "Have a little faith. See what I have here?" With the compass that Mr. Benson had given her, she held it level in her palm and spun in place as the needle discovered magnetic north.

"What do you call that contraption?" Marsha asked.

"Roland gave it to me. He called it a compass, to find north," Acadia said. She confirmed that they had been going northwest, as planned.

"Well? How does it work?" Marsha asked curiously.

"Easy! We have been going northwest the entire way, the direction Thomas went. They cannot be very far from here!" Acadia said, putting the compass away. She continued swimming northwest with Marsha following close behind.

✳ ✱ ✳

The *Valiant* had arrived at the humble port town of Teraske, working quickly to deliver the cargo that they had held during their stay at Nemaris Island. The lumber was delivered at last, despite a long delay.

"I tell you, Seriam, some folks have no patience," Janes said as they walked the gangplank back onto the deck.

"Well, Mr. Grimbeck's shipment was a month behind schedule," Ward said.

"Yes, and only one month. He claims that the Dieterian calendar is slower than his ... but the man needs to realize who's calendar is the standard." The captain crossed the gangplank.

"Hopefully next time he'll be a bit more accommodating," Ward replied.

"Aye, but there was no need for him to mention the six hours, three minutes, and twenty seconds. That man is tighter to his schedule than the sun is." Janes sighed. "But, I suppose we should be glad to get some money out of it."

"At least Mr. Morgan was happy to get his ore," Ward replied. Janes nodded.

"Captain on deck," Gritzol said, upon the captain and first mate's arrival.

"Conditions in the hold, Barry?" Janes asked.

"Looking good, sir. All hands accounted for, with the exception of Mr. Fallah. He has gone ashore with no word of return," Gritzol replied.

"No word? Has he left us, then?" Janes asked.

"I believe so, boss, he has a home in the mountains," Gretty replied.

"Well, we wish the best to him then. Make a note of it, Mr. Ward?" Janes asked.

"Aye," Ward replied.

"Sir? Are we heading to Derrisburg next, sir?" Nicks asked, who had his leg in a splint but was making himself useful peeling potatoes.

The captain nodded. "It's our next port, Mr. Nicalis."

"Shall we set sail, Captain?" Benson asked.

"I see no reason to remain any longer, do you?" Janes asked his mate. Ward shook his head.

"Let us be off then, while the winds are still strong." Janes walked the stairs up to the navigation deck.

"Sir? Shall I take my post, sir?" Roberts asked.

"Not today, Jared. Help with the anchor, I'll man the wheel once we get going. Seems to me I'm a tad removed from practice," Janes explained.

"Aye sir." With a grin, Roberts left to help Perry weigh anchor.

They sailed north along the coast, taking little time to savor the rocky shores.

Sailing well into the evening, the *Valiant* stopped between Teraske and Derrisburg shortly before sunset.

"Weigh anchor, Mr. Perry. We won't get much further tonight," Janes ordered.

"Aye."

The other men lowered the sails.

"We shall try for an early start tomorrow, just before sunrise. I suggest every man get his sleep," Janes said.

"Aye boss," Gretty and the other men echoed.

As the rest of the men headed below deck into the barracks, Jared took the opportunity to take out his fife and begin playing to himself.

Jennings stopped on his way to the door. "Roberts ... are you playing that thing again?"

"I am."

Jennings looked at him for what seemed to be an eternity. "Play something James would've liked."

"Sure thing, Harv." Jared played a soft melody that Acadia had taught him shortly after they met.

Thomas was swabbing the deck, his last chore of the night, but the music made him pause. "That's very nice, Jared."

"You don't mind hearing this, do ye?" Jared gave him an understanding smile. "I know what she meant to you."

"Actually, I find it very soothing," Thomas replied.

"Thanks, Tommy." Jared was about to play then lowered his fife. "Say, I've been meaning to ask ye. When we get back to Harper's Bay, are you planning on coming back out with us?"

"I'd like to...." Dunking the mop in the bucket, Thomas shrugged. "I haven't really thought about it yet."

"Well, whatever you decide, I must say it's been great working with you."

"You as well, Jared ... I miss my mother's baking, Jared, but I think I can manage."

Jared nodded, sighing. "And that's all a sailor can do, Tommy."

Thomas noticed Jared's expression. "Jared, when did you last see your mother?"

"Me mum? Well...." Jared turned his gaze away.

"I'm sorry, I should not have asked," Thomas began.

"No, it's okay Tommy." He raised a hand to stop any further apology. "I know what it means to ye, not knowing where your father has been all that time. It's no good not talking about me mum, since she's gone and all. Course, you already know I was raised in Juniper Bay, aye?"

Thomas nodded.

"Yessir, raised by Miles and Mildred Roberts ... me mum was the talk of the town, best oyster cook in the bay. And pappy, well, he only had one leg, but that didn't stop him from taking a walk around the island every day. He and mum would always walk together." Jared smiled at the memory.

"What happened to her?" Thomas asked.

Jared sighed, looking toward the ocean. "It was to be their fifteenth wedding anniversary. Pap took mum on a sunset cruise through the bay ... and Juniper Bay's among the rockiest and worst harbors in the land, Tommy. Sure, pap knew his way around it ... he'd even navigated it in a fog once ... but he didn't count on that trader ship from Tallebeck."

"There was a collision?"

Jared nodded. "They managed to pull me pappy from the waters, but they couldn't find mum. Since then ... pap hasn't gone in the harbor since. But a year after the incident, he gave me this fife." Jared held it up, playing several notes.

"And ... then you left for the seas?"

Jared nodded. "The summer after that. I haven't been back in a long time ... but Pappy's still there, even though he doesn't walk as much as he used to."

Thomas nodded. "Thank you for telling me ... perhaps it is time I returned home to see my mother again."

"There's a lot going on in your life right now, Tommy. Why not rest on it? No point in deciding this moment."

"Good night." Thomas put the mop away and headed below.

Jared leaned back upon the stern and continued to play a melody on the fife.

As the mermaids continued to swim north, Acadia heard a faint noise. "Wait, there it is again! Can you hear that?"

"Sounds like a bird singing." Marsha tilted her head, listening carefully.

"No, it's not a bird ... but it is very familiar. I'm going to get closer." Acadia swam toward the surface where a ship floated in the water.

"Acadia! Don't surface!" Marsha floated by the anchor chain.

"Why not? It's dark out, nobody will see us."

"Now hold on! I am not entertaining your adventures anymore!" Marsha stopped as Acadia hovered above her.

"There's nothing to worry about."

"That's what you said before nearly getting eaten by that shark yesterday," Marsha muttered.

Undaunted, Acadia continued upward. As she came to the surface, she looked around. There were rocky cliffs to the west, and a moonlight starry sky above. Turning to her right, she saw the ship that was there, one that had a mermaid sculpture on the bow. It also had a familiar looking flag, with a dove on it.

"Oh my gosh!" Acadia had hoped to be quieter, but her excitement gave her away.

On deck, Jared heard the commotion and stopped his song on the fife. "What was that?"

"Jared! I'm coming up!" Acadia approached the hull and climbed up the ladder along the side. She had to fight her way up using only her arms, occasionally using her flukes for leverage. Despite having no legs she was able to make it.

"Who is that?" Jared asked again, looking around. An exhausted Acadia crawled over the railing and flopped onto the deck of the ship.

Jared turned and saw her sitting along the side. "Acadia? So it was you who called my name." He left the navigation deck and kneeled by her side.

"It must be a miracle that I found you," Acadia gasped, catching her breath.

"Why did you come here? Especially so far from the islands?"

"I had to! I missed you all too much," Acadia said.

Jared smiled. "Yes, we miss you too, but we could always return to the islands. You didn't come all this way alone, did you?"

"No, Marsha is waiting beneath the surface." She glanced past the railing then back to Jared. "I may have come here against her wishes, but I need to tell Thomas something very important."

"I see ... does it concern the captain also? Perhaps that would be best?"

Acadia nodded. "I hope I will not be a hindrance to you."

"No trouble, madam, I can carry you." Jared picked her up and took her to Captain Janes' quarters.

Janes stirred in his bed. He woke up and stared as Jared entered his cabin.

"Wha? Jared, what is this all about?" he asked as the light from the hall entered the room.

"Captain, we have some company." With some effort, Jared placed Acadia onto a chair at the table.

"Acadia? My, what a pleasant surprise!" Janes got up, put on a robe, and sat across from her. Jared lit two of the cabin's lanterns and stood near the door.

"Christopher, I apologize if I am intruding," Acadia said.

He waved the thought away. "Nonsense, you're a sight for sore eyes. But tell me, why would you endanger yourself by coming so far?"

"Be assured I did not come alone." Her look grew solemn. "But I have a message for Thomas, one of great importance."

"Shall I get him, sir?" With a nod from Janes, Jared left.

"It involves the *Nemaris* cabin boy, Gregory DeLeuit," Acadia said.

Janes nodded slowly. "Cabin boy, Gregory DeLeuit ... just as we assumed."

Acadia nodded. "Cynthia told me everything. Although I have no evidence, all the answers can be found at the end of the Siren Island cavern."

"From what I have learned about you and Miss Cynthia, I can trust your instincts. As for Thomas, he may wish to have more solid proof."

Thomas arrived panting, as though he'd run there. "Acadia!" He rushed over and embraced her. Seeing her face again after their time apart felt like seeing the dawn after a cloudless, stormy night.

"Thomas, I thought I would never lay eyes on you again." She held him tightly.

"You're so far from the islands ... was it only a message that brought you here?"

"A very important message, Thomas, even at this late hour," Janes said.

Thomas's expression changed from concern for Acadia's safety to curiousity.

"Thomas, you remember telling me about your father, yes?" Acadia asked.

Thomas nodded. "Yes, that day on Opole Island."

"Remember how you wanted to know the truth about him?"

"Of course, anything to know the whole story." Thomas sat next to her.

"I was unable to bring the entire story." Touching his hand, Acadia smiled. "But you may be happy to know that the cabin boy of the *Nemaris* was named Gregory DeLeuit."

Somehow, he had known the truth since reading the incomplete entry in Scyhathen's journal, but having his suspicions confirmed was a bit overwhelming. "So the journal did tell of Father's role...." Thomas leaned to the table for support.

Acadia nodded. "Cynthia mentioned that Captain Scyhathen had regarded the boy as a very special being. She had always felt a certain something in him, something she has also sensed in you."

"Does she know of any other visits my father made to the islands?" Thomas asked.

"She knows of one visit...." Acadia's expression turned slightly downcast. "But she chose not to discuss it with me openly, hoping to tell you when the time was right."

He shrugged, disappointed that many of his questions remained unanswered. "I suppose she has her reasons. Everything makes perfect sense now, the connection between Scyhathen and my father, and what happened to us the islands themselves."

"Not everything." Janes held a finger aloft to emphasize his point. "What about that demon, Epoth?"

"If Epoth still exists, Cynthia said, only one of Rhydar's kin could complete the spell to remove his spirit from this world," Acadia replied.

Thomas looked away a moment. "As amazing as this all is, it still leaves a question unanswered."

"What question is that?" Acadia asked.

"If your father is still alive," Janes said, speaking for Thomas.

Thomas nodded in agreement.

"There still is a way." She grasped his hands in hers. "If you returned to the islands, perhaps the proof you need could be found by reaching the limits of that cavern. With Marshall out of the way, there would be nothing to stop you."

"Except for the rest of our voyage." Thomas turned to his captain. "Sir, I would rather help Marshall's men find their families before mine. I began this quest myself, and they were brought into it against their will."

"A noble view, Thomas." Janes shrugged. "Even so, the rest of the crew may not wish to return to those islands so suddenly."

"You have taught me much, sir. I would be willing to sail there myself if it meant finding the answers I seek. Knowing the truth about my father is worth the effort."

Janes nodded. "We shall discuss it in the morning. It is very late. Acadia, if you should need accommodations, it can be arranged."

"I would welcome it." She gave him a grateful smile. "But Marsha may not be as willing. I should go back so she doesn't worry ... she was afraid this might be a different ship."

Janes nodded again. "Of course, but let us know if you need anything."

"I will," Acadia replied. "Thank you."

Thomas stood and reached for her. "I can take you to the deck."

"Good eve," Janes said as Thomas carried Acadia outside then closed his door and returned to sleep.

With less effort than he expected, Thomas placed Acadia near the railing and sat down before he spoke.

"You've gotten stronger since we first met, Thomas." Using her arms to lift herself, Acadia settled into a comfortable position. "Do you remember the time you first held me? We both fell to the beach like rocks on the tide."

Thomas nodded, but his thoughts were elsewhere. "Acadia ... all I ever wanted to know was why my father wasn't home. I owe you so much already. And now, you came all this way to help me again. I cannot imagine how to thank you for this knowledge."

"You are my friend, Thomas. Seeing you again is enough."

Thomas's eyes drifted to the moonlight sky. "Acadia.... you didn't come just to tell me about my father, did you?"

Her smile gave it away. "You know me too well, Thomas."

His thoughts swirled. He had always suspected that there was something happening between them, but now that it was out in the open, Thomas wasn't ready to admit to himself that he felt feelings for Acadia as well. More pressing questions remained.

"I've talked it over with the captain. I will return to the islands, and I suspect the captain wants to return as well. Marshall will chase us all across the Centra Sea for the treasure, no matter what."

"And when he catches you..." Acadia began. A tear seeped from her mournful face.

"Marshall will do anything for that treasure." He remembered how Rhydar often defended his islands. "Rhydar would do anything to protect his home.... so maybe I can understand his reasons if I see the treasure for myself."

"Your father would be proud of you, Thomas, for showing such bravery, but also for protecting me from Captain Marshall." She held her pendant tightly. The white carved surface of the pendant glowed in the dim light, just like the moon above.

"It looks wonderful on you, Acadia."

She smiled. "Thank you. It's a long way back home ... but I know we will meet again."

"My only wish is for your safety, Acadia. Go join Marsha and abide to her wishes. I will arrive at the islands as soon as I can, whatever happens tomorrow."

"You will never leave my mind, Thomas," Acadia said.

Thomas helped her over the railing and to the ladder along the hull. "Farewell." He kissed her hand.

"Until then." Wiping a tear from her eye, she dove from the ship and back into the waters.

He watched her leave quietly. There was a deeper respect for her now, as Acadia had risked so much to come this far. All that mattered now was the safety of the islands.... even the thought of finding his father alive seemed secondary.

Thomas took a deep breath, looked up to the moon, and walked in silence back to his cabin.

Marsha was nearly in panic when Acadia finally returned. "Well? What was that all about? I was worried when you went aboard."

"It was them. I gave Thomas his message," Acadia replied quietly. "You no longer need to humor me; I know how worried you've been since we left home."

"And why should I be otherwise?" Marsha's tail swayed in agitation. "What would Cynthia say if I returned home alone? Then what?"

"I know what she would say, Marsha. We can go home now."

Marsha saw how depressed she was. "If Thomas cares enough to learn about his father, then he will return to our islands as soon as he is able. At that time, you'll be together again. And you always have Cynthia and me, okay?" She gave her sister a hug.

Acadia nodded. "Yes, I will be less reckless from now on." She found a bed of sea sponges to snuggle up with for the night.

"Just until we get home. You can be as silly as you want after that, okay?" Marsha said with a smile.

"Okay, goodnight."

"Sweet dreams, child." Marsha snuggled up next to her. They kept each other close for the rest of the night.

Before the crew got underway the next morning, Janes met with the men in the mess hall. "Gentlemen, I have a question for you. Tommy, I'm sure everyone knows Acadia visited us last night, aye?"

"Aye sir," Thomas and Jared both replied.

"So you want us to go back to those accursed islands?" Ellis asked.

"Despite that dastard Marshall?" Benks asked. Nicks and Aramondo shook their heads in disagreement with the plans.

"Count me out," Jennings said, thinking about the loss of his friend.

Holding up his hands, Ward quieted the hubbub. "Okay, one at a time. From what Miss Acadia and Miss Cynthia have told us, there may be more to this whole ordeal yet."

"More about the cabin boy of the *Nemaris*?" Gritzol asked.

"Indeed." Janes paced as he spoke. "We believe that the answers to our questions lay at the bottom of that cave on Siren Island. And the only way to find them is to return."

"Which is quite a risk, considering how Marshall feels about the treasure there," Ward added.

"We're going for his father, not the treasure. Is that it?" Jared asked.

The captain nodded. "Aye, exactly."

"Seems a noble quest," Benson said.

"What about us? With Marshall out for blood ... I'd rather not be involved," Nicks began.

"I understand some of you wish to go home." Janes turned to his new men's leader. "Mr. Gretty, I shall leave you and your men with more than enough funds to travel to any location you wish, should you ask of it."

Gretty looked around to his crewmates. "I think I speak for the four of us, boss, when I say that is most gracious of you. But first, I shall have to deliver news to the other families."

Janes nodded. "Yes, I should take responsibility for the deaths of some of the other men Marshall had serving for him ...."

Gretty shook his head. "No, you were not at fault, Captain. Captain Marshall had a grudge against the cook, Geynall, and he would often intentionally cook Marshall's least favorite foods in retaliation. Perhaps his day would've came soon. Harris, whom you did not meet, was killed by sharks en route to South Cimmordia. He left behind six children and his wife, and was Marshall's first target in almost every instance." Gretty took a breath. "Irving, on the other hand, was probably Marshall's biggest supporter, and was third in command after Mr. Nyguard. Had he not survived the refuse bin, I would feel no remorse for his death."

"Morrey and Irving were also his best swordsmen," added Aramondo. "And Morrey resisted the most when Marshall captured him. It's nice to see him free, I guess."

"Harris was killed when you took the map," Benks said.

Gretty nodded sadly.

"Aye, but he was marked for dead before that event," Nicks replied.

"My only wish is to send word to Harris's family of the situation. But the issue here, Captain, is that we hope to return to our former lives." Gretty turned to the others. "Boys?"

"I still have dreams of working Blyster Bay's best fishing fields," Aramondo said.

"There's plenty of time to be spent with my wife, if she remembers me." Nicks sighed, absently scratching where the splint rubbed against his shin.

"I'm looking forward to finding myself a small inn and setting up shop," Benks replied.

"Yes, yes, that is all understandable." With a smile, Janes nodded. "It can be arranged, too. That leaves the issue of the return to Nemaris Islands."

"I don't want anything to do with that place," Jennings said outright.

Gritzol huffed. "You never agree."

Sitting between them, Benson clapped a hand on each man's shoulder. "Come now, gentlemen. I can see going back if it means helping Tommy. After all, he's been great on this voyage."

"I appreciate the training I've received from you, sir," Thomas said.

The captain turned to Jared. "Roberts?"

"I want to go back. There's a lot at stake." Jared shrugged. "And personally, I liked it there."

"For Tommy and Miss Acadia, I go too," Perry replied.

"Count me in," Gritzol said.

"Ellis, what are your thoughts?" Ward asked.

"The shellfish was all good, but I's impartial. I'll go where the boat does." With a dismissive wave, Ellis headed back into the galley.

"Harv, you seem to be the only one against it," Ward said.

Jennings shook his head slightly. "For Tommy's father ... fine, I guess I'll go."

Janes rubbed his hands together in satisfaction. "So it's settled, then. Gretty, we'll leave you and your men at Derrisburg with fifty Dieterian Dictares to divide evenly. Is that satisfactory?"

"I's not sure, that doesn't leave much for each man, and...." Gretty began.

Tapping the table lightly, Janes leaned forward a bit for emphasis. "All right, one hundred then. Consider it my gift to you all."

Each of the men's eyes lit up. "That's ... very generous of you, Captain," Aramondo said.

"I know that Marshall took a great deal from you gentlemen, and this should help you to return to your homes. Perhaps it will provide a fresh start." The captain stood to go.

"If there aren't any more questions, I think we can set sail for Derrisburg then," Ward said.

Gretty, Aramondo, Nicks, and Benks all nodded. "We are indebted to you, Captain Janes."

"Should we meet on the open seas again, gentlemen, you all owe me no more than a cup of tea. For now, we have work to do." Janes led the way to the deck.

Soon, the *Valiant* was sailing at full sail toward Derrisburg.

A Change of Colors

*I*t had been tough days for Marshall. Since the cook had been done in by Marshall's rage, there was nobody to cook sustaining meals. All the crew had deserted him, leaving none to sail the massive *Inferno*. If not for his usefulness, Marshall surely would've murdered Nyguard simply out of anger.

Finally, with all of Nyguard's efforts, the two found their way back to headquarters at the Sundrop Islands. There, Marshall was able to restock his ship and collect a crew consisting of a group of loyal followers of the Sundrop Guild, his own pirate clan. They were a crew of ruthless savages. Marshall personally trained the twenty-five men recruited for raids on ships and islands across the Centra Sea.

As the *Inferno* sat in the harbor between the two islands, it was outfitted with a pair of sizable longboats for transporting the larger compliment for attack. Each man also carried his own weapon, varying from sturdy cutlasses to deadly rapiers. Because he was a man of respect in Cimmordia, only when he was working for himself did Marshall bring his battle squad to sea.

Once the *Inferno* was manned and ready, they prepared to set sail.

"All men accounted for, boss. What course shall we take?" Nyguard asked.

"First we sail to Teraske. Then Derrisberg. And Grand Point after that … Janes will have no escape route this time." Marshall struck a determined stance from behind the ship's wheel.

"Aye sir," Nyguard said.

"Victory, lads! Victory!" Marshall cried. His new crew raised their voices in a rumbling war cry.

"Nobody crosses Archibald Marshall and gets away with his life," Marshall muttered to himself.

The *Valiant* arrived at Derrisburg early the next day. Leaving with twenty-five Dieterian Dictares apiece, Gretty and his men parted ways from Janes' crew. It was a bittersweet scene at the town docks.

"Captain, I thank you for your compassion to us." With tears in his eyes, Gretty shook Janes's hand.

"Just promise me you'll find your family safe, Mr. Gretty." The captain gave him a pat on the arm. "I'm just doing what I can."

Gretty shook hands with the captain, and then went off with Aramondo, Benks, and Nicks, who walked with the aid of a cane.

"Anything else for us to tend to?" Ward asked as he came to Janes.

Giving the men a final wave, Janes turned back to the *Valiant*. "Just that scalawag Marshall. Start us east, then turn south midday. If I know Marshall well enough, he'll start at the closest point to our last location and go north, from Teraske I believe. If we keep to mid-sail for a day and are far enough offshore, we should be able to avoid confrontation."

"And placing someone into Mr. Lewinston's post?" Ward asked.

Janes took a deep breath, pausing. "I suppose there is plenty of time to worry about that task. The other men can dual task for awhile until Tommy's escapade is behind us." With a nod, he kept walking.

"Christopher, you know I always trust your judgment." Ward was using the tone of voice reserved for the rare times he disagreed with his captain. "But what if this story of Thomas's father is all for naught? What will the men think? And young Tommy ... I'm sure his mother is beginning to miss him by now."

Janes looked at him, again stopping before climbing up the gangplank. "Your argument proves noteworthy, Seriam. I did give her my word, after all, that he'd be back to see her in one month's time. Maybe our departure can wait for Tommy to write his mother a letter, should he still wish to entertain this quest."

"I think it would be proper, and yet still fulfill your promise." Glancing away, Ward added, "I myself wrote a note for my mother every other time I was in port."

"Aye then, I'll go find him." Chuckling, Janes returned the ship.

Janes found Thomas in his cabin and explained to him what should be done.

Thomas looked sheepish. "Goodness … with all this activity I have nearly forgotten about Mother."

"So you understand what you are proposing to do, then?" Janes asked.

Thomas stood up from his cot and went to the sack hanging along the wall. Reaching inside and removing the glass orb that his mother had given him, he held it toward the light from his lantern and peered through it.

He could almost hear the sound of Diamond Falls in the distance, the smell of a freshly baked loaf of bread, and the crashing of the waves all at once. A few butterflies even seemed to fly by. Bobby Lewis and a younger girl were fighting over the fate of a beetle in the town square, and the skies were crystal clear.

"I understand fully, sir." Thomas put the orb back in the sack.

Gesturing for Thomas to follow, Janes made his way through the hold. "There is some paper in my chambers. Once your letter is mailed at the town hall we will want to catch the winds, so there's little time to waste."

Using a quill pen and some paper, Thomas hurriedly scribed a letter to his mother. He made several mistakes, but managed to write an adequate letter.

Dear Mother,

I am writing to tell you I am well. We ran into a storm west of Cimmordia Castle a few months ago and have spent most of my journey marooned just offshore the Nemaris Islands. We ~~met a few locals~~ had an interesting adventure, finding ways to live and see the islands in their splendor. One ~~person I met~~ day was interesting because I found a clue saying the cabin boy of Captain Scyhathen was actually Father, and that he had long been attached to these islands. So, after we freed our craft from the sands that had marooned us, we sailed north and refreshed the ship's stores. We now return south to learn the rest of the answers. I must know what happened to Father, and I am certain you wish to know as well. So I write this letter in good health with a prayer to return home again soon. Tell Bobby that there were no death traps on these islands and that ~~I~~ may have met the ~~girl~~ woman in that painting.

~~Forever~~ With love from your son,
Thomas A. DeLeuit

P.S. The captain and the crew say hello.

"Tommy, you should take more care in writing," Mr. Ward said, noticing the crossed out areas.

"I did my best, sir." Thomas blew on the ink so it wouldn't smear.

"What painting are you talking about? Your mother may be a bit curious," Janes commented, reading over Thomas's shoulder.

"A friend and I found a painting in Elder Harrion's things," explained Thomas. "Back then I did not know who it was, but I am now certain that it was a painting of Cynthia."

"Miss Cynthia? Then...." Janes tapped his chin. "I see. Yes, I have seen that portrait in Elder Lewis's things ... I wonder how the artwork of Mr. Mandalay reached Harper's Bay if the *Nemaris* never returned to port?"

"Likewise ... sometimes I wonder how that journal made it," Ward added.

Janes nodded in agreement.

"Were you sure it was by Mandalay, Thomas?" Ward asked.

Thomas nodded. "I am certain of it. In fact, Scyhathen mentioned it in the journal ... I cannot forget that image, sir. And when I met Cynthia, it all became clear to me."

"Very interesting ... perhaps it will be explained upon our return." After folding it, Janes used some wax to seal the letter with his signet ring then handed it back to Thomas. "Run this to the town center for shipment to Harper's Bay, and be quick about it."

"Aye sir." Thomas took the letter and left.

Janes began to steep a pot of tea. "Do you suppose DeLeuit may have survived the adventure back to port?"

"Surely he must've, to meet Tommy's mother and make a family with her." Ward moved to a window to watch Thomas run down the docks. "But a painting? Salt water is murder for fine art. It must've been salvaged somehow."

"I am not certain of anything anymore. All I ever heard about the *Nemaris* was that there was no wreckage ever found, by anyone." Setting out his favorite teacup and saucer, Janes snorted in vexation. "Even more mysterious than the islands she sailed from."

"This be getting too deep for me, Chris. I's not sure we shall ever learn the truth."

As soon as Thomas returned from town, the *Valiant* hoisted anchor and followed Janes's plan to sail east before south. If the plan succeeded, they would mask their direction from Marshall. Fortunately for them, the *Inferno* had already sailed west to Teraske when Janes turned south.

"You three, search the docks, you six, search the town outskirts, and you nine, search the town and taverns!" Marshall ordered. In a flurry of activity, the men left to comb the entire area.

"Are you sure that's necessary, sir? We would've seen the *Valiant* before reaching the docks if she were here," Nyguard said.

"I want a full sweep, Leo! For all you know the bloody ship may have been taken ashore board by board just to avoid being spotted by us!" Marshall cried.

Nyguard strove to hide his obvious cynicism about Marshall's delusions. "Umm ... yes, sir."

"Where are you, Janes? Your time will come, I assure you," Marshall intoned in a low growl.

His men began their fruitless search.

It would take another three days for the *Valiant* to reach the Nemaris Islands. With little activity on the ship, Thomas chose to sleep it off rather than remain very active. All he could think about was the relationship he and Acadia had shared during his stay. He longed to be by her side again. Although he wouldn't admit it to anyone else, this return trip was as much due to his desire to remain with her as his need to know the full truth about his father. If there was nothing in the cavern, he would have no reason to sail anymore. He could return to Harper's Bay, and memories of the sailing life and of Acadia would be enough. But, if there was something ... then maybe his father's legacy would show him a new path in life. Either way, Thomas could only sleep and imagine what might be.

As for the *Inferno*, their search of Teraske proved futile, leading them north to Derrisberg. Not even one member of Marshall's crew could find a single man who had gone with Gretty; for all of Marshall's previous crew had left town quickly. The only lead was from a quiet young man who watched the waves every day.

Marshall decided to investigate personally and tromped to where the boy sat by the docks. "You boy, how long you been here?"

The boy had a cane by his side and replied in a raspy voice. "All day, sir."

"Clear your throat, boy. Speak up now," Marshall said.

"I's sorry, sir." The boy ducked his head apologetically. "I had a terrible cough several weeks ago, and me mother says I'll be like this forever. I said I be here all day."

"Fine then. Have you seen any ships with a dove on her crest?"

The boy nodded. "Aye, I served on it once. The *Valiant*, she was."

"And you saw it but today?" Marshall demanded.

"Yesterday, sir, for only a short time." The boy stopped to coughed deeply. "I couldn't move fast enough to greet the captain, sir."

"Aye ... and where did the *Valiant* sail to, boy?" Marshall asked.

"I saw her sail east. Her crew was in quite a hurry," the boy replied.

"That all?" Marshall asked.

"All I know, sir," the boy replied, his voice growing thicker.

"I see ... rest your voice, boy."

Marshall left to collect his crew.

"Where to, boss? Grand Point?" Nyguard asked.

"No, never. To the south—the Nemaris Islands once more!" Marshall said.

"We're going where?" one of the men shouted out.

"Can't get me to go there!" a second said.

With the grace of a lion, Marshall pounced on the man and drew his sword. "You'll visit Davy Jones's locker if you speak again! That's our destination!" Marshall growled.

The man gulped nervously.

"Full sail! To work! One, two, one, two! To work you worthless dogs!" Marshall cried, shouting out orders before they could take their next breath. The men were already rather uneasy due to their captain's obsessive behavior, and the prospect of going to the Nemaris Islands did nothing to calm their fears. Indeed, working with Marshall was never an easy experience. With men running all over the deck, the crew went to work in hot pursuit of the *Valiant*.

As the ship sailed away, a second flag ascended, replacing the *Inferno's* standard colors of black and red. With a red skull and crossbones on a black field fluttering in the wind, the *Inferno* bore its true colors. Similar to the ship's main sails, the flag had been singed along the edges, giving it a ruffled and scarred appearance. The *Inferno* was primed for battle and sailing south in anger, bound for blood.

It took the *Valiant* three days of nonstop sailing to reach the Nemaris Islands. Rather than risk being stuck in the shallow sands a second time, they weighed anchor in the bay along the northeastern shore of Opole Island. After spending a few hours of preparation, they locked down the ship.

"Padlock your things, men. Seal everything you're not taking with you, and leave no valuables behind," Janes ordered once the anchor was secured.

"Why all the baggage, Cap'n?" Jennings asked.

"We're taking an awful chance coming back here, Jennings. Remember last time Marshall got angry, Gritzol?" Janes shook his head. "We were lucky to get away with our arms intact."

"Aye, he brought an army of scabs. We held 'em off though, Cap'n," Gritzol replied.

"Probably'll raid us if we all go," Ellis muttered.

"We're counting on him doing just that. Bring your dinner kit, Horatio. No doubt we be in for a long stay," Ward said.

"Aye," Ellis muttered.

Thomas packed quickly. He brought clothes to last three days, and stowed the rest between the cot and the mattress. Of the possessions in the trunk, he packed the journal, his glass orb, and anything that appeared valuable. Although he had forgotten it was there, he also brought a jeweled bracelet that had been inside the trunk originally. Adorned with gems, the bracelet seemed too valuable to leave behind.

Everyone carried what they could in backpacks and sacks. They took the two rowboats and journeyed to Siren Island. Before they began inland, Janes pulled Thomas aside. "Tommy, I need your services."

"Aye sir?"

"Can you still summon our friends?" he asked.

Thomas removed the signal shell from his pocket. "Shall I, sir?"

"Please do."

Thomas blew into his shell whistle once. Moments later, Acadia breached the surface, practically jumping ashore with her speed. "Thomas! You've returned!"

Janes removed his hat, setting it on some nearby gear. "Miss Acadia, please listen carefully."

"Christopher? My ... you've all came back!" Acadia began, happily.

"Acadia, I'm happy to see you as well, but this is not a social visit."

The mermaid looked crestfallen. "Captain Marshall?"

Janes nodded slowly. "He is most surely pursuing us as we speak. Are you, or Miss Cynthia, absolutely certain of what is inside the cave?"

Acadia shook her head. "I am sorry, Christopher, I am not. As for Cynthia ... I have not seen her since you first left. The sky has been cloudy lately ... things are strange here, Christopher. I can say this, though ... Cynthia assured me that the cavern is the place to go."

Janes nodded. "Then, I shall trust her judgment, as I have before. I must ask you to be very careful these next few hours, though. When Marshall arrives, he will probably bring with him twenty or thirty men...." He checked to see that Mr. Ward had already gathered the crew ashore and out of ear's range. "We may not return from this adventure, because once we enter the cave, there will be no escape."

"Oh my," Acadia said quietly.

Janes held a finger over her lips. "I need you to take our rowboats to the cove for us again."

"Yes, I can do that."

"And one other thing." Janes passed her a hand-cranked drill. "In the outside chance we do not survive, I want you to take this drill and sink the *Valiant*."

"Christopher?" Acadia asked, unsure of his reasons.

"I hope to be able to explain this to you later ... but I suspect Marshall will claim her as his own if we do not return." He held her hands so they wrapped firmly around the drill. "So please."

Acadia gazed at the drill, nodding. "I ... I am prepared to do so if necessary."

"In the meantime, please be mindful of your safety and stay in the depths of the Cove, where Marshall cannot find you."

"Only if you are as careful, Christopher."

Janes put his hands on her shoulders. "You have been a good friend to us. I cannot promise to see you again, but it is in our hopes so long as it is in yours."

"Good tidings, Captain." She leaned forward and gave him a kiss on the cheek.

He smiled modestly, although his expression remained morose. "Now, go."

Thomas nervously watched her swim to deeper waters. She turned, blew a kiss toward him, and dove under, pulling a rowboat along the surface behind her.

"Sir?" Thomas asked.

Returning his hat to his head, Janes took Thomas back to the group. "She has her mission, Tommy, and we have ours."

Thomas nodded. "Aye sir."

Janes called to the rest of the men. "No looking back now, lads. Come, we've no time to waste." They followed the trail to the caverns.

Raiders of Rhydar

Their return to Siren Island came in the late evening. The islands seemed much different and darker than before. While only the cavern had felt less friendly in the darkness of their previous visit, now the jungle shared an equally shadowy presence. Even the brush seemed to have grown thicker, appearing to lash out toward any passersby. The wind ruffled the grassy blades, brushing together in an unearthly choir.

"Perry, see if you can clear a path here," Ward said as he used his sword to swat at few stray branches. Perry went to work with the massive Kah Lunaseif, swinging at the brush and clearing the path ahead effortlessly.

Ellis picked up a broken branch and tossed it aside. "Thought you boys came through here a week ago."

"I don't recall there being so much brush," Benson said.

"Aye, this is not at all like last time...." Gritzol looked around them, shaking his head. "And there's a strange feeling in the air now too."

"Very eerie," Jennings said.

"Aye," Roberts added.

Janes paused to remove his hat and mop his brow. "Something doesn't want us to go this way."

Thomas shrugged. "If a secret this big didn't want to be found, it would remain a secret."

Janes and the others nodded. "You present an excellent argument, Tommy. The path went this way." They continued to carve a trail through the jungle.

As the moonlit night grew cloudy, a second vessel loomed on the horizon. It was the *Inferno*, making its approach to the *Valiant*.

"There ... she waits like a gold nugget in the river...." Marshall lowered his spyglass with a satisfied sneer. "Take us starboard; get your swords lads!" As he raised his sword in the air, a distant blast of lightning lit the sky. "Uwoo ... bah, no storm will keep me from my prize. Leo, get the men lined up!"

"Aye boss." There was a slight smirk on Nyguard's face. He was ready to get his revenge too, especially after having to stew in the refuse bin for so long. Now, the rest of the *Valiant's* crew ... and Janes ... would get what they had coming to them.

They approached the *Valiant* and anchored at her side. The men placed a solid wooden plank across both railings and made ready to climb aboard the sleepy vessel.

Marshall laughed to himself. "Nobody on deck to greet us ... such foolishness, Janes!"

Marshall faced the men, standing to one side of the plank with his sword ready. He spoke with a vengeance, but in a way that was calm and collected more than aggressive.

"Kill anything that breathes."

With loud shouts, the men rushed across the plank and onto the *Valiant's* silent decks.

In trios, groups of men spread throughout the ship. The first group started in the mess hall, finding the refuse bin clean and empty. A second team searched the confines of the galley, discovering all that remained were a few utensils and stray items that Ellis had not been able to take with him—nary a morsel remained in sight. The barracks across the hall yielded similar results. Anything that wasn't locked tightly consisted of bulky furniture and solid oak lockers that were secured fast to the walls. The third team was unsuccessful at finding anything of value. The locks themselves were of high quality, providing a good defense against even a master thief.

A fourth team searched the cargo deck, finding the hold devoid of anything worth the slightest farthing, with the exception of extra stores and supplies for long voyages. What they found was worthless to a man seeking fortunes.

A final team searched Thomas's humble cabin, finding inside only a cot and an empty trunk, vacant even of clothing. A bag of rocks hung from the wall, and nothing else. The book of Scyhathen was safe ashore with Thomas.

Each team reported back to Marshall, offering similar findings.

"The ship be abandoned, boss. Nobody 'ere and nothing to gain," a spokesman of the crew replied.

"Nothing? Not even an old training knife?" Marshall asked, shocked.

"There's still Janes' cabin, boss," Nyguard said.

"Aye. Come on." Marshall stalked to the cabin door.

"Guard here," Nyguard said to the crew. He followed behind.

Finding the door unlocked, Marshall opened it and lit a lantern on the central table. The walls were bare, revealing only royal blue wallpaper. The trunk placed at the end of Janes's bed was empty, save for a few dust mites at the bottom. His wardrobes were so empty one could see each individual knot in the cedar. The bed was covered in ordinary sheets and appeared to have been left untouched in years. Even the safe was open a crack.

"Janes hasn't collected much for a man of his years," Nyguard said.

"Nonsense ... it's all here," Marshall said, throwing the covers off of the bed and onto the floor nearby. Underneath there was nothing except a mattress made of down, again appearing very ordinary.

"Nothing," Nyguard said.

"Janes is a crafty one, but he missed an obvious answer," Marshall said cordially. He took his sword and stabbed the center of the mattress. A cloud of feathers exploded from the mattress, flying into Marshall's face. He could only cough and gasp in disgust.

"Ugh ... feathers, feathers, feathers!" Marshall fumed, spitting and hacking wildly.

"It's a mattress," Nyguard muttered flatly.

"Enough with your smug attitude, Leo! Where else would you check, huh?" Marshall roared, inches from Nyguard's face.

Nyguard backed off a moment. "An open safe, perhaps?"

Marshall looked toward the small black safe in the corner. "Leo, Leo, Leo ... there were many opportunities to point that out, hmm?" He went up to the safe. Looking inside, he opened it to find a handful of Dictares, along with a hand-written note.

"Well, some money after all...." Marshall said, picking up the Dieterian coins and pocketing them. He then sat on the chair by the table and opened the note. In the lantern light, he discovered his name had been written on the outside, along with a seal marked by Janes' signet ring.

"It's addressed to me? I don't understand." Marshall unfolded the note and read it aloud.

Marshall—My compliments on finding my ship. I'm sure it took you endless hours to do so. Now I offer you a more difficult challenge. If you can find me and my crew, I might be impressed. You may keep that spare change if you wish, but if you want the rest you'll have to find me.
Captain C. M. Janes

P.S. I should mention, I have your treasure map in my front pocket, in case you are curious.

Marshall took the note and glared at it in rage, tearing it to ribbons.

"Janes! Your head will be mine!" He spat into the lantern and knocked the table over, storming out of the cabin afterward. It was fortunate the lantern was extinguished before crashing into the floor.

"Orders, sir?" Nyguard asked.

"Back to our ship. Find Janes."

Marshall stomped across to the *Inferno* and toward his quarters.

"And the *Valiant*, sir?" Nyguard asked.

"Let it rot." He slammed the door to his cabin.

"All right men. Let's go." Nyguard directed the men back to the *Inferno*. They weighed anchor and headed south toward Siren Island.

Meanwhile, Janes and the rest of his men had already descended into the cavern. They made their way toward the bottom. Thankfully, no loud booming voices were heard to impede their progress.

"Do you suppose Marshall found the ship, Chris?" Ward asked as he walked beside Janes.

The captain nodded. "Just like he was supposed to."

"Cap'n, what about your stuff? Your collection?" Gritzol asked.

"It's all safe."

"Forgive me, Cap'n, but your bag isn't big enough to be carrying everything," Benson said.

"Correct, Roland." Janes raised a finger with a smirk in his voice. "Most of it is safely stowed in the water tank where nobody would suspect it."

"No foolin'?" Jennings chuckled. "That's why ye ordered it dry."

"Never thought you'd be smuggling stuff there," Ward said.

"Marshall may want my head, but those are artifacts, not treasure. I wonder if he found the note or not." Muttering to himself, Janes crossed the subterranean creek.

✳ ✳ ✳

As the *Inferno* came around the northern coast of Siren Island, Nyguard watched carefully for any rowboats in the short bursts of light created by the increasing lightning strikes.

Marshall joined him on deck. "They took both their boats, so finding them shouldn't be too difficult."

"Boss, you don't suppose they went back to that cavern, do you?"

The prospect made Marshall grin. "Janes would be foolish enough to do that, wouldn't he?"

They approached the eastern edge of the island, but there were no rowboats.

"Not seeing anything, boss," Nyguard observed.

Marshall sneered, running a finger along his chin. "Another missing element. I see your pattern, Janes. Make it look like nothing is here. Nothing is happening. You go back to the island and take whatever riches you can … No! It will not end the way you wish, Captain. Leo!" Marshall yelled in Nyguard's ear.

"S-sir?" He shook his head as his ears popped.

"Ready the longboats. We're going where they went. He's already shown us the cavern once; we'll follow their footprints. If nothing else, we'll get some treasure for ourselves."

"Aye boss." Nyguard left to gather up the men.

✳ ✳ ✳

At the very bottom of the cavern, Janes and the crew came to a wooden door. Beyond it, they could only imagine the fabled treasure trove of Rhydar the Wizard remained, silently awaiting eternity. There was an oversized doorknob, but it appeared to have no obvious lock.

Whistling, Janes sized up the massive door. "This must be where Rhydar kept his collection."

"Do you think it's trapped or anything?" Roberts asked.

"Benson, check it out," Ward said. The other men backed off.

Benson took out his knife and stuck it in between the jamb and the door, sliding it as best he could along the crack on all four edges. Then, he did the same between the jamb and the rocky wall. As the hinges were probably on the inside, there was nothing to be gained. "Cannot get in too far, but she seems fine to me."

"Rhydar wouldn't trap it. His voice at the entrance would probably be enough," Thomas suggested.

"Perry, go ahead." Janes gestured to the door. Perry approached and gripped the handle, but pulling on the door did nothing, not even with Mr. Perry's strength.

"Hmm?" Gritzol scratched his chin. "Maybe you have to push it?"

"But of course!" Jennings replied sarcastically.

"Well, the hinges bend inward," Roberts said.

"Aye, try it anyways," Ward said.

Perry pushed on it, and the results were the same. The door refused to budge.

Janes crossed his arms with a frown. "This doesn't seem to be working too well."

"Can't go around it, either—that rock's too solid," Benson said.

"Must be some sort of puzzle or something," Thomas said.

Jared looked carefully around the door. While nothing seemed to stand out, the doorknob itself seemed a bit odd in appearance, as if something was intended to hang around it.

"Roland, what do you make of this?" Jared showed him the thickness of the doorknob.

"That does seem a bit large for a handle, now doesn't it?" Benson replied.

A thought came to Thomas. He looked inside his pack, almost hearing something call out to him. Digging through his possessions, he found the silver jeweled bracelet that had been kept inside his trunk.

Ward noticed the jewelry at once. "Tommy, what do you have there?"

"Oh my ... sapphire, diamond, emerald, ruby ... wherever did you find this?" Gritzol asked.

"My father had it in his trunk, which I acquired with some other things. I ... just now thought of it." Thomas was unsure of his own thoughts.

"Tommy, might I try something with that?" Benson asked.

Thomas nodded, handing it to Benson. He took the bracelet and unclasped it at the bottom. Placing it around the doorknob, he secured the clasp. The jewels glowed with a bright hue before returning to their lifeless state.

"Did you see that?" Roberts said as the other men watched in awe.

"Try it now, Perry." Janes nodded as Perry grasped the handle again. It opened effortlessly, as if it were a much lighter door.

"Well, that was easy," Jennings said.

Ward patted Thomas on the back. "That was the key."

They filed into the next chamber.

Everyone's eyes lit with excitement as they entered the massive cave. Piled high along each wall rested artifacts and treasures of immense value, ranging from priceless vases and pottery to jewel-encrusted goblets and housewares, some made with more diamonds and precious gems than metal. The collection included shelves of glassware in exotic colors and priceless paintings hung between them. Rugs sewn from gold and silver thread draped the floors, each one incorporating various gems and rare metals. Gold, silver, and platinum were stacked high in one corner, in bars that varied from one to twenty pounds. A rack on one wall held dozens of gold chains, some longer than six feet with upwards of two hundred links. Opposite the artifacts, there were two large bins, each some six feet long by three feet wide and five feet deep. The first of these was half-filled with coinage of all sizes and denominations. The second bin contained jewels and precious stones, of all colors and sizes, some as small as peas while others as large as eggs. On a group of shelves between the two bins, paper money was sorted by both denomination and country of origin. On another group of shelves, just beyond the bin of gemstones, some ten dozen gold bars sat, accompanied by three dozen more of silver. Other items in the archive consisted of mysterious weapons, elegant swords crafted from unfamiliar metals, wooden staves, long metal rods, books of all sizes, and miscellaneous magical items that would surly require a wizard of Rhydar's skill to use. With just the money cached in this archive, a man could live in luxury for five lifetimes. The artifacts and valuables would make a fine addition to any collection, some of which would be right at home in the mightiest castle or King's vault.

Although their first instinct was to stuff their pockets to the brink, Janes wouldn't allow it.

"Here's to my retirement!" Jennings said, digging his hand into the coin bin.

"Jennings, no! These coins do not belong to us, nor anyone here." Janes yanked Jennings's hand out of the bin.

"That Rhydar fellow doesn't need them," Jennings retorted.

Janes slapped Jennings across the face. Hard. "Get a hold of yourself! Rhydar didn't own them either."

Jennings held his cheek.

Ward patted his crewman's back. "They belong to those who had them taken away unjustly."

"To those from whom they were stolen by immoral means," Thomas added, eyeing the weapons longingly.

"Aye, they not be ours to take," Perry said.

Jennings meekly looked around. "Can't I at least hold them a moment?"

Janes shook his head, a stern expression on his face.

"Aww...."

"Quite a collection...." Roberts pointed to one of the most unusual items in the cavern. "Sir, look at this! A crystal and gold washbin ... this surely must've belonged to a wealthy king or queen who used it before state dinners, perhaps?"

Benson gestured to the item that had caught his attention. "And here ... a gem-studded longblade, Cap'n. All for show I'm sure, but lovely."

"Lovely, yes." Janes sighed, looking over the shelves of glass and crystal. "I shall admit, we can admire these works, but they're not ours to touch."

"Sir, back here. What do you make of this?" Gritzol pointed out a large, rectangular outline on a back wall to the left of to the gold bars.

Janes approached and took a closer look. "This is peculiar, isn't it now?"

"Looks like a door almost." Benson walked over to see for himself.

Gritzol inspected the rock with his hand. He found it was plenty solid.

"Seems solid all right, but there's something that don't feel right," Ward observed.

"Can't be anything, I suppose." Janes shrugged. "Guess that's all."

"Let's at least take account of what's here." Spreading his hands, Ward indicated each area in turn. "Touch nothing, but get a good idea. Benson, Perry, watch the door."

"Aye," they replied. Both men went back toward the entrance.

"Sir ... there's no handle on this side," Benson said.

Janes nodded nervously. "And with that dastard Marshall coming anytime ... keep your swords ready."

"Aye sir," Perry said.

Thomas took a good look at the magical weapons that had been stored here. One item that seemed to be in reach was a tall staff, crafted from a young beech tree. Although it appeared ordinary, somehow he knew it contained very powerful magic.

"What do you suppose that does, eh, Tommy?" Jared asked.

"Must be pretty powerful," Thomas replied.

Jared nodded. "Aye, from what I've heard about wizards, they're always carrying something like that. Some sorta staff or wand, and that it is their most versatile tool next to their spellbook."

"That one is really bizarre." There was another staff Thomas noticed that was deep blue. Crafted of a wood similar to oak, the blue color seemed to be a stain of some sort.

"Not familiar with that kind of tree," Jared said.

"Aye." Thomas leaned back toward the outlined wall. Instead of it supporting him, he fell through it as if nothing were there.

"Augh!" he cried as he hit softer ground on the other side. His upper body was on the other side of the wall, and his lower still in the treasure chamber. The experience made his head spin.

"Tommy, I've got you!" Jared pulled him back.

Somehow, Thomas appeared undamaged. "I'm okay," he reported as he sat up.

"What happened?" Janes asked as he rushed over.

Jared offered the boy a hand up. "Tommy found a way through the wall."

Janes slowly moved his hand toward the opening. He again felt a solid wall.

"I cannot sense anything unusual ... Thomas?" Janes asked.

Thomas reached his hand toward the opening; it passed through easily, unlike the others before.

A gasp of wonder came from the crew as they watched Thomas's hand disappear into the wall.

"Well, Tommy, I guess that path lies before you, not us," Janes said quietly.

"Sir...." The prospect of continuing alone was somewhat daunting.

"Go on, Tommy. We'll hold things here," Mr. Ward said.

Taking a deep breath, Thomas nodded. "Aye, sir." Hesitantly he walked through the solid wall. After going completely through it, he quickly looked behind him to see if it appeared to be a solid wall from that side, and it did. The room was lit, but he could not identify the source of light.

"I wonder what he sees back there..." Ward said.

"Sir, can you hear me?" Thomas asked.

Gritzol huffed. "Probably more treasure or something."

No, they could not hear him. However, he could hear them. At least, if they were in danger he could come back through the wall and assist. But for the moment, Thomas was alone.

Beyond Time

*W*ith the treasure behind him, Thomas walked into the chamber that lay beyond.

The room behind the false wall was much different than the one containing the treasure trove. Here, the walls were smooth with ornate lines in a dark bluish gray. The ground was much softer, with a feel more like a mossy forest floor than stone. Oddly, the room was sparsely lit ... the light seemed to flow like water from the various designs and up from the floor below.

No additional treasure was stored here. It was simply a large chamber with many ornate designs on the walls. Thomas didn't understand the designs, but they resembled the faces of large clocks.

Another hall continued in darkness on the opposite side of the room, but it was almost as if a veil of light separated him and the rear alcove.

Thomas cautiously walked forward a few paces. Then, he heard a strangely familiar voice that spoke in echoes.

"Thomas ...." it began.

Thomas stopped walking.

The voice spoke again. "Thomas ... you have come at last." It was definitely a man's voice, though Thomas could see no one.

Suddenly, all the light in the cavern went dark. Unable to see further, Thomas stopped walking. Instead of choosing to feel his way through the darkness, he responded to the voice. "I have heard your voice before."

"Of course you have. Once, a day long ago in mists. At Diamond Falls," the voice replied.

Thomas thought back. When he had visions at the falls, the conditions were always marvelous. The mists that came up from the falls created an atmosphere that brought feelings of wonder every time he went there. Except for that one time, right before he left his home....

"Yes, I know of the shadow you encountered, Thomas. But I am not that dark voice you heard those weeks ago. Rather, I was the voice you cherished on those shores. All those years … working the docks, tending to your mother's wishes … you were learning to care for yourself and respect the ways of others."

Knowing it was not the menacing voice was reassuring, but it didn't help Thomas figure out whose voice it was. "If you know all about me and were there all this time, why did you not talk more often?"

"There was no need to. My presence would only have complicated things. Your life was yours to choose; that path was yours alone. I'm just happy your path led you here," the voice explained.

"Then tell me this much. If you know me so well, may I see you? I wish to see your face," Thomas asked.

The light inside the cavern returned to its previous level. The hall across from him became clearer and brighter, opening a new path. "Please, join me," the voice invited.

Thomas followed the hall around a series of corners to where the light stopped before entering another chamber. Again, as before, he could not see a thing.

"A finer man I have yet to meet, Thomas. You have grown up so well."

Silently, someone had stopped behind him. The lights returned to a normal level again, and Thomas discovered there were clock patterns in this room as well. Yet another veil of shadows blocked the opposite side of the room. "Are you here?"

"Turn around," a man's voice said, no longer sounding echoed or distant.

Thomas was awestruck, but calm. It was as if he were in the presence of his parent's love.

He desperately wanted to turn around, but couldn't. No, it was not because he had no control over his legs, nor was it because of the effects of a magical spell. He couldn't because of his fear of what he might see. Everything in his being told him to turn around, but he couldn't bring himself to do so.

"Please, I want to look upon you as much as you do me." The voice was much closer than before.

It seemed like an eternity, but Thomas eventually brought himself to turn around and face the man who resembled himself.

The man was tall, standing six feet in height, and of a similar stature to that of Thomas. He was well built, developed from the daily chores of a sailing man. He had the same color hair as that of Thomas, but with some gray at the edges. He wore his hair tied back in a ponytail that extended to his shoulders. His attire matched that of a typical sailor, but these clothes were discolored and aged, having been worn many times. His face was quite familiar, much like Thomas's own but accented by stubble on his chin. It was as if he was gazing into a mirror, a mirror that added thirty years to the resulting image.

Thomas had never seen this man before, yet knew exactly who he was.

"Father...?" Thomas asked slowly.

"Son."

In the higher levels of the cavern, Captain Marshall and his clan had passed over the stream and were quickly approaching the treasure trove at the bottom. It would only be a matter of time until their arrival.

Gregory DeLeuit and Thomas DeLeuit shook hands. Thomas could not hold back any longer and hugged his father tightly. A special bond between a father and son had been restored, after so many years apart.

"Why did you leave mother?" Thomas asked once he had control of his voice.

"I had to. Not for myself, not for her, but for these islands. You have read through the captain's journal, right?"

Thomas nodded, "Aye- I mean, yes, I have."

Gregory laughed in a rich voice. "I see you've learned at least one thing on the seas, son. What did you find when you reached the end the end of the journal?"

"A few missing pages, and many unanswered questions."

"I can understand you wish to learn the truth." With a nod, he spread his hands to indicate everything around them, both inside and outside the cavern. "You see, when I first came to these islands with Captain Scyha- then, I didn't know much about myself. My mother, your Grandmother Eleanor, had died in a mysterious accident when I was two years old. My father, your Grandfather Lowell, was a feeble man, several years older than mother. Knowing that he couldn't care for me as he wished, he made an offer to Captain Scyhathen, who took me under his wing and trained me as a buccaneer."

"Grandfather threw you out?" Thomas asked.

"No, not at all. Yes, I did leave my home, but it was for the best." He smiled sadly. "My father had a crippling disease and was not long for this world, dying some months later. I sailed with Captain Scyhathen for several years, ones that I remember fondly. The captain taught me much, and everything was well until we took a new course south from Grand Point," Gregory explained.

"In 1582, when you discovered these islands," Thomas said.

His father nodded. "Yes. It was during that voyage that my time with Captain Scyhathen came to an end."

"What can you tell me about the captain?" Thomas asked.

"I wonder if you don't know a great deal already. Cynthia has told you much, hasn't she?" he asked.

"Much about his past, yes."

"Scyhathen was exciting to watch. You would've loved him, Thomas...."

Thomas listened to his father's words, much like he was hearing a bedtime story.

"Scyhathen had been sailing the seas aboard the *Nemaris* for nearly twenty years. I only served with him a short time, but in those few years he became a father figure to me." Gregory paused to scratch his chin. "He was gallant in command, an elegant gentleman who always knew the proper course to take. He was uncannily adept at it—be it making a strategic move against a rebel galleon... or choosing which wind to follow. His choice of action invariably saved our lives, and rarely did we end up in battle. I will always remember the sword on his belt—a remarkable blade for a remarkable man."

Thomas remembered all the times his crewmen had mentioned Scyhathen's blade, and he visualized it as his father continued.

"An elegant weapon, it was. A durable long sword, crafted from the fires of Mt. Faate and forged with a heart of mythril. Kept razor-sharp, it could cut through anything with ease." His face brightened at the sword's description. "Gold had been used to decorate the edge, creating a gilded appearance. He carried it at all times, although I never saw it leave his belt in anger. Instead, it was only removed from the sheath for its weekly encounter with the whetstone and polish, keeping its edge and hilt in pristine condition. He called it the Spirit of the Sea."

Gregory leaned against a nearby wall. "But although the sword came with him everywhere, Scyhathen always found another option than fighting. There was always a way out, and it was never to flee. There was always another option."

Again, Thomas was reminded of his crews admiration for Scyhathen's legendary negotiation skills.

"No matter how many times we found ourselves in trouble, Scyhathen always got us through. The only time he would fail was here, on these islands," Gregory explained.

Thomas could only imagine such a magnificent blade. "How did he become such a good swordsman if his sword never left the sheath?"

"Although this was his primary longsword, he would practice with a plain blade similar in weight and length. Believe me, his skill was unmatched by any other."

Thomas nodded. "From what I've read about him, he was a prime example of honor in a captain."

"Yes, indeed. He was the best of the best. However, once we came to the islands, I saw a weakness in him that had never been seen before," Gregory began. "Every day, an undermining fear grew among my crewmates. A feeling that something had been kept here against its will, hoping to destroy the one who had created it. It fed on our emotions, our hatreds, our deepest worries, and began to grow in strength. These were spirits who had been summoned back to their creator in hope of uncreating themselves. Soon we would be attacked by a constant menace who brought caution and dread to the winds of the islands. As our imprisonment continued, that day would come and our fears would reveal that person at last...."

"Captain Epoth," Cynthia's voice echoed out of the darkness. The light in the chamber extended to a vestibule in the very back, where the lifeless body of Captain Scyhathen lay entombed.

"Yes, Thomas...it was Epoth you heard that day. And now, with hope, you will be safe from his terrors in this sanctuary," Gregory explained.

Thomas wanted to cry out at the sight of the gallant captain, but surprise held him back. The captain's body had been perfectly preserved, appearing fleshy and warm as in life, the longsword still at his side. For all appearances, he may have simply been asleep.

Cynthia was there, sitting on a second bench to the left of the captain.

"Captain Scyhathen?" Thomas asked.

"It is only his body, Thomas. This chamber is ageless, and all kept within will not experience the effects of time. How you see him here is how I saw him upon his return to these islands, shortly after the *Nemaris* departed from our shores," Cynthia replied.

"Cynthia … how did you get here?" Thomas asked.

She pointed to a dark corner of water just behind the bench she sat upon. "There is an underwater path leading to the ocean under the island. I do not come here as often as I once did, but today is a special occasion." Cynthia replied.

"Thomas, what are you feeling right now?" Gregory sat next to Cynthia.

Thomas held up his shell, wondering if it would be of any use. He wanted to tell Acadia of these findings.

"Acadia does not know of this chamber, but she knows of your joy," Cynthia replied.

Thomas remembered how Acadia, Marsha, and Cynthia could all share their emotions with one another.

"Cynthia, how does Rhydar fit into all of this?" He sat down on a third bench across from Cynthia, adjacent to the one Scyhathen rested upon. He did not dare sit directly next to the corpse.

Gregory nodded, resting his hand on Cynthia's lap as she took his hand. "I had hoped you would ask. Cynthia, will you explain?"

"Thomas, do you remember the vision Acadia and I shared so long ago?" Cynthia asked.

"Yes, I do."

"It was a vision from Rhydar himself. It was sent from his consciousness back in the year 1575, before Gregory's arrival to these shores." With a graceful wave, she indicated the room and beyond. "These islands have a lot of magical power, Thomas … and have so ever since he created them. Each tree, rock and shrub were placed with purpose, and his animal pets were provided with homes of their own. During that time Rhydar foresaw his mortal death, and had made plans to pass his living entity into another lifeform, perhaps an unborn human boy," Cynthia explained.

"Into my mother, Eleanor DeLeuit. I was born later that year. Although it was my father Lowell who conceived me, it was Rhydar who entered my mother's womb, Thomas." Gregory shook his head. "I don't expect you to fully understand."

"Gregory grew up as you did, unaware of the spirit living inside of him," Cynthia added.

"Father, how did you learn about him?" Thomas asked.

"Rhydar has always lived with me, but not as a voice, or even as a conscience. Rather, I was like his son, instead of Lowell's," Gregory replied.

"And Gregory became educated and familiar with his magical skills after arriving here, following the shipwreck of the *Nemaris*." Cynthia reached under the bench, and pulled out a wooden case. She handed it to Thomas, who opened it.

Inside, there were twelve pages, each of which had been torn out of Scyhathen's journal. They contained the last entries from its pages, and unlike the rest of the journal, they had not aged or yellowed in any way.

"This explains it all," Gregory said.

Thomas looked over the entries. "Why are they in different handwriting?"

Cynthia perked up. "The captain was still alive at the time, and I offered to write for him, since he was unable."

Thomas looked over the passages, reading them to himself.

January 20th, 1583. I should mention forthwith, my gratitude to Miss Cynthia for taking these final words down. My apologies to my honorable crew, who in a horrible storm, died in lightning and fire. The mainmast of my little craft suffered a direct blast of lightning, perhaps from Epoth himself. The rain doused the fire, and mercifully, some of the ship has survived. I hope that Kid will be able to salvage what he can. I must recognize Kid today, for it was Kid who managed to keep the rest of the ship intact, save for the bow and her keel. A miraculous feat he displayed ... and I shall not attempt to explain his actions this day. Although I am certain I will never discover the true source of his power, he has told me of a wizard named Rhydar, who was the caretaker of these lands.

Cynthia has told me what happened, and that it saved my body from the deep. I will not ask her to repeat it all, as I do not understand it myself. Gregory, Kid's actual name, is, in all respects, Rhydar's son. He has inherited the skills Rhydar himself had in life, before his alleged death in the year 1575, well before our arrival. I grow weary now; I hope to discuss these events again tomorrow.

January 21st, 1583. Fate has allowed me to speak again. Cynthia continues to write. Thanks to you, Cynthia. Gregory has visited my smashed ship and salvaged what he could, including both my beloved journal and the last artwork Mr. Mandalay was able to create before the tragic end. To fully acknowledge his death, along with the remaining compliment of crew, is a pain I cannot endure, even with the comfort of my present company. A captain is traditionally obligated to die with his ship, regardless of circumstances. I now have failed to die honorably with my crewmates. In doing so I am able to convey this information for history, but at what cost I may never know. Along with the portrait, a few personal possessions have been recovered, including the trusty Spirit of the Sea, which I have always worn. While I have never found a reason to wield her in anger, my last wish would be to clash swords with Epoth for what he has done to my crewmen. A more unforgivable act I cannot imagine... Weary I have become. I beg your pardon, gentlemen.

January 22nd, 1583. Forgive me, Cynthia, for asking you to do these writings daily. Mr. Banes is no longer available to keep records, and Mr. Smitty can only listen to my ramblings in spirit. Oswald, my oldest friend, we always agreed we'd either die together, or one after another. You won, Smitty. But I feel your prize would rather be shared with those who served alongside you rather than a cold, dying man who once was your friend. Whenever my death comes, I hope for your forgiveness, which has been proven unwavering time after time. Cynthia tells me the weather is clear today. The birds are singing in the sky. A gentle breeze shakes the coconuts on palm trees free from the safety of the trunk. And sometimes I think of my dream to settle down, on a small homestead at the beach, with a wife at my side and my son and daughter playing in the surf. If my favor lies with Davy Jones, then in a few days that dream may finally play out like an opera. That is enough for today.

January 23rd, 1583. Kid tells me that there is little else he can salvage from my vessel. So be it then, that a captain can outlive his ship. Gregory, I can only wonder what is to become of you and I hope you will succeed where I have failed.

Miss Cynthia tells me that if I could walk I would enjoy viewing the collection of valubles that Master Rhydar amassed from the ships of pirates around the world. Upon hearing the tale about Rhydar's childhood, I wondered if the being Epoth were the first pirate Rhydar had prevented from continuing his evil ways at the seas. However, the truth behind Epoth's existence is only—no, I will never know.

January 24th, 1583. I am ready to go home. Kid tells me that winters in Xavier were his favorite time of year, and I cannot agree more. If I could only see Elna City, my adopted homeland once more.

Cynthia and Kid will not let me float out to the ocean and rejoin my mates. They were all honorable men, and although I was unable to bring them back to the ports, they were the only family I had. (Terrence is weeping now, he asked me to write it in.) My brothers, they were. I was only their commander, but they were all brothers. Even you, Kid. All brothers we were, floating along on a house that had sails instead of a foundation. The winds were our destiny, taking us wherever she felt we were needed. Our mother the ocean, both supporting us and disciplining us for our actions. Our road began at Grand Point. It ended on the Nemaris Islands. Cynthia, thank you. That is enough.

January 25th, 1583. I am writing in Terrence Scyhathen's stead today, adding my own entry in his request. His death occurred at dawn today, from his waning health after the destruction of the Nemaris, some distance northwest of here. Although he did not directly say it was his wish, I have entombed him here, with the help of Gregory, in a timeless chamber beyond the archive of Rhydar's collection. Terrence asked me to pass on a message to Rhydar, or his next of kin, as follows. "Although I do not know you personally, I thank you for allowing my crew and myself to visit your lands in peace and hospitality. I regret only failing to identify your unwanted guest, Captain

Epoth, and hope that you can prevent him from ravaging your beautiful home."

Terrence, I and my sisters, Marsha and Acadia, as well as our protector Onell, thank you for sharing your days with us and teaching us the ways of your people. We wish you a safe journey to Mr. Jones and your new home.

Cynthia   January 25th, 1583

Thomas looked at the last page to find a sketch of the waterfall ashore Nemaris Island. It was signed by Mr. Mandalay, and dated November 11th, 1582. Several other pages, including the last portion of an entry describing his crew, were here. The truth about the locations of the missing pages was revealed, and now, the story was complete.

He handed the pages back to Cynthia, who replaced them into the case.

"Does that answer all of your questions, Thomas?" Gregory asked.

Thomas looked at Cynthia before shifting his gaze to Scyhathen, and then back to his father. "If I understand this correctly, then you are Rhydar?"

Cynthia shook her head. "No, but you are close. Think carefully, Thomas. Remember the tiger in the jungle? The voices in the cave? And your uncanny ability to tell stories very well?"

Yes, it all made sense. Ever since his arrival on the islands, Thomas had been experiencing events that were far too unusual to be explained by normal means. Perhaps, just maybe, these events were caused by the only explanation imaginable.

"Rhydar … and I… are …." Thomas began. Did it seem that simple? Could it all be true? His father, Gregory, related to a wizard … a wizard with fantastic powers and skills. Would that mean what he thought it did? And if he was, would he be…?

"Grandfather, and grandson, indirectly," Gregory replied.

The essence of magic and spells began to flow into Thomas's mind as Rhydar's spirit awakened inside the chamber. If he wished it, a flick of his wrist could make a seed blossom into a tree, and a second gesture could incinerate the trunk into a towering *Inferno*, turning it to ashes in moments. He was now as magical as Rhydar had ever been and with training would learn to command the islands with just as much power as the old wizard himself.

Gregory stood and rested a hand on his son's shoulder. "You have inherited the powers that I once possessed. Although mine still exist, they have diminished since my power began flowing to you. Your arrival in this chamber has accelerated the process."

"And that is why you can remain here, or visit your mother, or even see the world in a moment's notice if you desire," Cynthia replied.

Thomas looked at his hands, able to see the magical energy now inside of himself. Before he could really experiment with anything, however, he heard cries of pain coming from the other chamber.

Cynthia gasped. "The crew!"

Greed's Manifest

*M*arshall and his force of pirates had finally arrived at the bottom of the cavern. With the crew holding Marshall's men off as best they could, Janes fought Marshall just outside the room.

"Your head will look good on the bow of the *Inferno*, Janes," Marshall snarled as they locked swords.

"You and I both know that'll never happen, Marshall." Janes pushed him off and they began again.

"Oh! So you can show aggression? Go ahead, show me your skill if you can!" Marshall laughed. They continued fighting with flashing of swords and parries.

Thomas jumped up from the bench and looked toward the treasure chamber. "I must go to help them."

Gregory held up a hand of warning. "Son, you cannot rely on your magical power at this time. You are magical, but unfocused and dangerous. Take your sword. But, do not be afraid to sacrifice it for a better weapon."

Thomas looked at his father. "Sacrifice it? I have no other weapons, except for my knife."

"Then perhaps you will find a better one," Cynthia said.

"Your crew is waiting. Go help them," Gregory said.

Thomas nodded. Then, an odd thought came to him. "Father … will you come with me?"

Gregory shook his head, his expression growing gravely serious. "I cannot help you with my magic now, Thomas. Trust me … as long as there is fear and aggression on the islands, I cannot help you. Please understand me."

Cynthia motioned toward the exit. "Hurry, Thomas! They cannot defeat Marshall without your help."

He was unsure of his father's reasons but confident that the answers would come soon. Quickly, he unsheathed his sword and ran back to the treasure room. As he emerged from the solid wall, he charged toward a nearby pirate and ran him through. Gritzol had been fencing with the man, and was most grateful to see Thomas's arrival.

"Tommy! Excellent timing!" But that was all Gritzol had the time to say, for soon he was slashing at another pirate who had rushed in to take the fallen pirate's place.

Thomas saw the wounded pirate on the ground, the young man's life ending. He had just killed someone....

"Tommy! Over here!" Roberts cried, hoping for another sword.

Perry was fighting off three pirates at the same time, while Benson was spinning and fencing in full melee fashion, taking on his opponents with grace and speed. The rest of the crew was doing as best they could. Thankfully the pirates arrived only a few at a time, preventing the crew of the *Valiant* from being completely overwhelmed.

"Jared, where's the captain?" Thomas called. He helped Roberts hold off his opponent.

"Out front! There's too many; you'll never get through!" Jared dodged a slash to his abdomen.

Thomas looked at the sea of carnage that had been taking place in the treasure trove. Although there had been very little damage caused to the artifacts themselves, the fighting had put them, as well as everyone in the room, in danger. A pirate made a charge toward Thomas. He drove his scimitar through the pirate's leg and let him keep it, before picking up the beech wood staff resting along the wall to his right.

"Fighting me with a stick, boy? Come on, then!" a nearby pirate cried as he lunged at Thomas.

Holding the staff, Thomas became very afraid, upon realizing that a staff wasn't the first weapon he'd normally choose against a swordsman. He pointed it toward the pirate, making the man laugh.

"What're you going to do with that, hm? Tickle me ribs?" the pirate mocked.

"Get out of here!" Thomas cried in anger. The staff did its magic. The pirate vanished from sight, finding himself over the waters of the Centra Sea, far away from any land.

Although not everyone had seen the pirate disappear, the concentration of all the fighters lapsed momentarily. Yet, the battle continued.

"Tommy, do that again!" Jennings called.

"Wait ... this is a staff that can make anything I want to happen, happen...." Thomas waved the staff again. "Take the pirates to the middle of the ocean!" The staff again made its enchantment. All the pirates in the room, including the ones in the outer chambers, vanished and reappeared off the shores of the Sundrop Islands in the center of the Centra Sea.

Marshall and Nyguard were still here, fencing in the cavern outside, but they paused as they suddenly realized Marshall no longer had support from his hired men. Janes seized the opportunity to disarm Marshall and point his silver sword at Marshall's neck. Ward was able to disarm Nyguard, who begged for mercy. Thomas took the time to collect his sword, which he'd left in the leg of a fallen pirate.

"You are beaten, Marshall. Last time I was lenient. This time you may not be so lucky." Janes lifted his swordpoint nearly high enough to give the man a shave.

"Janes, you have me. I am at your mercy," Marshall begged. He dropped to his knees.

"Seriam, how are the others?" Janes asked, his gaze not shifting from Marshall.

"We're fine, captain," Ward replied.

"Bond him," Janes ordered. Benson and Perry tied up Captain Marshall.

"You will spare us, then?" Marshall asked.

"For the moment. Ellis, Gritzol, Jennings...." Janes waved dismissively. "Take these scalawags out of here."

"Aye." They prodded Marshall and Nyguard towards the cave entrance.

"Tommy, what did you do just now?" Benson asked.

"I'm not sure." Thomas eyed the staff in his hand. "This staff enabled me to remove those pirates from this chamber, I think."

Overwhelmingly outnumbered, it had been a dire fight. Ward was relieved it was over. "With good timing, boy."

"What was behind that wall, Tommy? We were starting to worry 'bout you 'fore Marshall showed up," Roberts said.

"Perhaps you'd like to meet someone who can explain." With a wave of his staff, the rock panel slid to the side.

"Tommy, you have a magic touch," Perry said.

"Come, follow me." Thomas led the way to the next chamber.

Everyone was in awe at how the room was lit. No torches lined the walls, as in the treasure trove. Here, the mysterious source of light illuminated the walls from the floor up, rising high between ornate columns.

They crossed the open tomb to the rear, where Cynthia and Gregory had been waiting as before, beside the body of Scyhathen. Janes was aghast at what he saw.

"Who is...?" he asked Thomas, looking at the body.

Immediately, Ward dropped to his knees in reverence. "Captain Scyhathen ... here, all this time...."

Gregory nodded. "He was known as Captain Terrence Scyhathen." He stood and approached Captain Janes. "He is preserved here, gentlemen, and will remain entombed here for all time."

All eyes discovered Cynthia, still sitting on the rear bench.

Mr. Ward rose to his feet. "Greetings, Miss Cynthia."

She inclined her head in greeting. "Mr. Ward."

Janes turned toward Gregory. "Sir, you look an awful lot like young Tommy here...."

Thomas stood between his father and the captain. "Captain, this is my father, Gregory DeLeuit. Father, I present Captain Christopher Janes, captain of the *Valiant*."

"So, Mr. DeLeuit, you've been down here this entire time?" Janes asked.

Gregory shook his head. "Not the entire time. When I learned of your arrival, I opted to come down here and keep my existence a secret. I allowed Thomas to discover this room on his own. I never expected Captain Marshall, although his presence is almost ... uncanny." His speech slowed down as he uttered the last sentence.

"Uncanny? Why?" Thomas asked.

Cynthia quickly climbed into the water in the back chamber. Without as much as a sound, she made her exit.

"Cynthia?" Thomas asked.

"What spooked her?" Ward asked.

"Did we say something wrong?" Benson asked, as Gregory looked worried.

"No, gentlemen. Something doesn't seem right at all," Gregory said. "Father? What is it?" Thomas asked.

"I'm sensing a terrible presence ... one I have never felt before. Come! We must check the archive, quickly." Gregory took off for the treasure room, followed closely by the others.

A Demon in the Den

*E*verything was different when they re-entered the treasure chamber. The artifacts were still intact, but they were piled all the way to the top of the chamber in intricate towers. Larger vases were piled above crystal glasses, towering in ways that defied all laws of physics. The paper money bins were mixed into the coin bins and strewn across the floor, while the jewels were scattered in an ornate pattern on the floor in front of the second bin. Using rubies and dark gems as contrasting colors, it formed a red skull in a dark field.

"Oh, no, no, no, not in the archive," Gregory said anxiously, anticipating what would happen next.

In response to Gregory's distress, Janes rested his hand on his hilt. "Mr. DeLeuit, what is it?"

"Gentlemen ... *he* is coming," Gregory said quietly.

"Who is coming?" Janes looked to the wooden door, but nothing stirred in the near darkness beyond it.

Perry looked toward the ceiling near the entrance of the chamber.

"Perry?" Benson asked, looking at the worried expression on his face.

"Lost souls ... there's thousands of them in here, all around us," Perry said. He could feel spirits swirling together in the alcove near the entrance. Soon everyone could see them, each shaped like men, but faceless and empty.

"Aaugh ... how horrific ... but somehow tranquil," Ward said.

Several spirits brushed past each crewman as they proceeded toward the hallway. The ghosts slowly floated across the room, all the while crying in soft screams of agony. Each spirit's voice was cold and distant, each echoing as if the screams had originated from far away. Their laments could not be understood in words, but the pain in their voices was obvious. The apparitions' presence shook up the entire crew.

"I really, really want to get out of here now," Benson said.

"Aye," Roberts said.

The rest of the men felt the evil assembling at the chamber's front entrance.

"Tommy, Gregory, can you do something about this?" Ward asked, somewhat frantically.

"Silence. You cannot do anything," a deep voice rumbled. The secret doorway to the tomb closed itself, as the rock slid across the opening.

"It's too late now. He's here." Gregory quickly hid behind some bookshelves, hoping to remain out of sight.

"Who said that?" Janes asked Gregory. Even if Gregory had wanted to answer, the deep voice spoke once more.

"The one who calls forth the souls of slain pirates from the abyss of the netherworld." The voice rumbled, sending cold chills down the necks of each crewman. Slow, deliberate footsteps echoed in the cave just outside the wooden door.

The evil spirits took on a man's form, one nearly two meters in height. He was clad in a captain's black coat, elegant and dressy as any that Marshall or Janes might have owned, though the style was very old. The entire outfit resembled that of an ancient pirate captain but more formal, crafted from material that would have been owned by noblemen. The finery was marred by many cuts. His arms were strewn heavily with scars and lesions that had apparently bled immensely at their onset, for dried blood covered the wounds. But they also seeped new blood, as though the marks had never healed. These scars continued over all parts of his body. Here and there, his skin peeked through the tears in his garb. Where it wasn't stained with blood, his flesh appeared lifeless and gray, as though it had first grown pale from lack of light then been stained by years of darkness. They all looked to be old battle scars, but none seemed fully healed. On his hands he wore black leather gloves that matched his coat. In the gap between his gloves and cuffs, there were wrinkles and markings, as though he had been burned by something other than fire. His shadowy black hair was stringy and tangled with traces of dark gray along the edges.

Entering the light, the being's ravaged face came into view. His right eye was completely gone, offering a view of his internal workings behind. The socket was like a crater of pain and turmoil that emanated and traveled outward to his other many scars. His other eye had a single, deep scar underneath it. As with the rest of his scars, it also had never quite healed.

Thick stubble dotted his chin. Beneath his terror-inducing sneer, a crisp set of teeth had been left undamaged. Unlike the rest of his flesh, the skin that remained on his face seemed normal, as if nothing had happened to it. In the eyes of his onlookers, the man's face was warm and alive.

He carried a long sword, hanging unsheathed on his belt. It was just the right length for a man of his height, and had a razor-thin edge. A black basket hilt decorated the handle, with leather covering the grip. Adorning the pommel was a large red skull. The skull wore a snarled grin, almost laughing to itself as the man's thick black boots carried him into the room.

The ravaged man sniffed the air several times. He took a calm look at his surroundings, never once gazing directly at any of the men present. "There be a wizard in this room," he uttered in a low voice.

Gregory spoke to Thomas telepathically. "Did you use that staff?"

Thomas heard the voice in his head and worried about what he may have done. Although he was only thinking to himself, he responded to his father in the same manner. "Yes."

"I feared this would happen...." Gregory thought to himself, hoping not to alarm Thomas any further.

The man turned and looked at Janes. "You are not Scyhathen, yet you wear a captain's coat."

Janes nodded. "Scyhathen is dead. And who are you to speak of him?"

The man paced in a circle before turning his gaze toward Janes once more.

"You do not know of the ways of demons, mortal. But I can see that you carry a blade of many battles, with the initials of many fallen opponents." He gestured to his own weapon. "Mine has few upon it, but they are the ones who are forever living in turmoil, tortured by devils with every heartbeat ... unable to live, unable to die, trapped for all eternity...." He continued to circle around the room. There was neither remorse nor satisfaction in the man's voice.

"The treasure, sir, is that why you come?" Benson asked.

The man sneered at him, making Benson fall to the ground to escape the view of his evil eye socket.

"I know a wizard has amassed this treasure ... yet, you are not him. Should the wizard step forward, you can keep your little collection. For

I no longer need such a waste of metal and rubbish ... they are nothing compared to my idea of a prize."

"Then, you seek a wizard? There are no wizards here, good sir," Janes replied.

The man seemed to ignore Janes's response, again sending his gaze around the room another time. "I sense you are all fair swordsmen. But, are you all excellent wizards? No, I do not think so, for there can only be one of those."

Ward spoke out. "Are you Captain Nepotherden?"

With a flash of his blade, the man pounced on Ward, holding him three feet above the floor against the wall. "That man is neither living nor dead, lost in an endless circle between this world and the next. Speak that name again and you will join him."

Roberts had heard enough and wasn't about to stand by as this thing attacked his mate. He drew his sword and charged the demon but could not even approach him. For his efforts, he was kicked in the chest by the villain and sent flying backward toward the artifacts in the room. Had Benson not been between him and the collection, Jared would've easily flown all the way to the wall through several piles of relics.

"Jared, you all right?" Benson asked. They climbed off one another.

"Y-yeah ... what a bad idea that was," he muttered.

The demon let Ward drop several feet to the ground and continued to hold his neck. Although he seemed to posses the strength to crush Ward's neck with ease, he chose not to.

Perry readied his weapon, glaring at the fiend.

The demon stared back at Perry, and shook his head. "You are not a wizard, either. Should you wish to battle, I will not hold back ... are you prepared to suffer endlessly?"

Perry took a swing, but the demon parried and caught the massive blade in his free hand. Perry then backed away, about to charge barehanded.

Standing between Perry and the demon, Janes held out an arm and stopped his crewman. "I will not have you attacking my crew." With a nimble flourish, Janes unbuttoned his coat and let it slip to the ground behind him. Then he drew his sword.

The man looked at Janes with his head tilted slightly to his right, allowing some light to enter his eye socket. Blood and brains lay behind, just as charred and injured as the rest of his body. The sight of it all made Janes feel ill, but he kept his composure as best he could.

The demon dropped the Kah Lunaseif, its heavy bulk clanging to the ground. Then he readied his own sword, the skull pommel glowing with red, blazing eyes. "I have no quarrel with your men, Captain. But in this room there is a wizard. If he shall not step forward … then I will kill you one by one!" His voice grew angrier and more powerful with each word.

"Who are you?!" Ward cried. Benson and Roberts began inching toward the door.

"Epoth," Thomas and Gregory both said.

A fire grew inside of the demon's eye. It was the flame of a thousand sorrows—the flame that lit a fear among every sailor that had met their end by the Blade of Demons Epoth wielded. It sought out its creator … and had finally found its target. The flame only lasted a second, but it was enough for Epoth to guess who the wizard in the room might be.

"Epoth, I am the only wizard here," Janes said, standing up to the demon.

Gregory felt the wall next to him to find the doorway into the timeless chamber, but even as he found it the wall had become solid, probably because of Epoth's presence. There was no escape in that direction.

Epoth grunted. "I had already ruled you out as a candidate. But if you wish to suffer, I will grant you your wish!" Epoth charged at Janes.

Janes parried and quickly realized he had met a swordsman with superior skill. Soon he was fighting hard for his life. As Epoth had been fencing since before the time of Scyhathen, he had not only encountered swordsmen of fantastic skill, but also improved his ability to detect and exploit his opponent's shortcomings.

Epoth repeatedly pushed Janes into corners, forcing him to continually adapt to tight locations. While dodging and parrying, he also had to contend with protruding weapons among the intricate piles of treasure, which showed no sign of tumbling with the unfolding battle.

Though Thomas continued watching with hopes that Janes would prevail, the expression on his captain's face displayed quite the opposite.

The crew could only watch and keep out of their way as the two captains fought. Although the swordplay was epic as each swordsman displayed his best moves, it was clear that the outcome had been decided from the outset. Even so, it turned out to be a long battle, lasting some ten minutes, but the end soon proved to be most disappointing. After a terrible blow from Epoth, Janes's silver sword clanged as it hit the ground and skidded across the room. Then, Epoth slashed the captain's chest to ribbons, his lifeless body falling to the ground without even a final gasp.

Thomas cringed.... Captain Janes, the man who had displayed his superior technique every chance he got, was no match for the demon. Surely Epoth would eventually find him.

"Who's next!?" Epoth bellowed. Benson and Roberts fled for the doorway. Epoth watched them go as he looked to Ward.

There would not be time for anyone to mourn the captain ... and Seriam knew this well. He was now the commanding officer.... and if they were indeed going to die one by one, he would have to do his best to prevent it.

Perry stood up and collected his sword from the ground. But before he could approach, Epoth turned and glared at Perry with his evil eye.

"Sir, allow me!" Perry cried.

"Go to the surface, Perry...." Ward began, gripping his sword tightly.

"Sir!" Perry cried.

"Go!" Ward ordered.

Epoth glared at Perry again, before Perry fled for the door. He then returned his gaze around the room, again sniffing the air as he turned.

Thomas gasped again, hushing his voice. Even Perry, the largest man on the crew, was no match for Epoth. The time had come, Thomas decided, for him to put an end to it.

"Your allies are deserting you, wizard ... show yourself!" Epoth demanded.

Ward drew his sword and faced the demon. "Captain ... I do not possess your skill, but I cannot allow you to walk after defeating my best friend."

"Then you can join him." Epoth quietly raised his sword.

"No!" Thomas cried as he rushed out from behind the shelves and raised the staff over his head. Sparks shot out from the end as Epoth turned to glare ominously at Thomas.

"Boy ... you have grown a day since our last encounter?" Epoth ignored Ward as he turned to face Thomas.

Thomas was very confused. He had obviously never encountered such a fiend before. "We've never met."

"Perhaps you are not the same as that first boy ... but you I remember. You are the same to my eye as he was," Epoth said, tapping the skin below his good eye. He then growled and began walking toward Thomas. Ward took a slash toward Epoth from the side. Epoth blocked it with his own blade, disarming Ward without even shifting his gaze from Thomas. Ward was about to reach for his blade again, when Gregory called to him.

"Mate, check on your captain," Gregory whispered. Ward headed over to Janes's side, taking Gregory's advice.

"From day one I have anticipated this moment. My creator shall experience what I have ... in an endless struggle ... for centuries...." With a smile, Epoth slashed toward Thomas.

Instinctively, Thomas raised his staff. Although the fragile wood should've been cut easily by the force of Epoth's blade, the staff stopped the blow as a shield would. It remained perfectly smooth, without as much as a mark.

"Grrr...." Epoth raised his sword and tried to slash Thomas's other side, but Thomas again blocked his attack.

Thomas tried to think of a way out, but he could only think of the body of Captain Janes. He had been Thomas's closest ally, and he could no longer help him. Captain Epoth had dispatched Janes with quick work ... perhaps what Thomas needed was another captain.

Gregory sensed Thomas's ideas, and came up with a diversion. He cast a spell to make himself invisible. Since Epoth could follow the trail of magic emanating from Rhydar, or any of his kin, the plan could not fail.

Epoth turned to see where Gregory had been hiding.

"Another? What trick do you have now?" Epoth began.

Thomas used the power of the staff to fully open the outlined door behind him. While Gregory stood in silence and away from the blade of Epoth, Thomas made a dash for the opening. Epoth began to chase.

"Your tricks will not work on me this time, boy!" he bellowed. Epoth rushed behind Thomas, gaining quickly. As Thomas reached the timeless chamber, Epoth caught up to Thomas and slashed toward his back. As the sword made contact, it sent shockwaves through Epoth. The power of Thomas's magic traveled back to Epoth and caused him great pain.

Thomas felt along his back, finding that he was uninjured. His clothing had not even been damaged.

Howling, Epoth raised his sword again, ready go down with his creator. He slashed at Thomas, knocking him against the wall. Thomas did not feel pain at all when Epoth's blade struck him. Again, Epoth hurt himself in the process.

Thomas marveled how he hadn't even been cut, although he quickly realized that the next hit might not have the same results. With his free hand, he raised his own sword. Epoth managed to block his first two cuts easily. On the third strike, Thomas's sword was cloven into two as he attempted to parry a blow.

"No magic? You may have hit me once, but now your defenses are gone!" Epoth raised his sword again.

Thomas abandoned the cloven scimitar and reached for the Spirit of the Sea, collecting the long sword and holding it ready with both hands. Its weight was perfectly balanced, and while it would normally be too much for him, Thomas was able to wield it expertly. Epoth stopped his swing, seeing Scyhathen.

"Well, Captain, it seems you have friends in high places, and enemies in low ones," Epoth muttered to the dead corpse.

"This chamber is timeless, Epoth. His body hasn't aged a day, and neither has his sword!" Thomas said.

"A wizard with a sword?" He scoffed. "You must be joking! Come then, take me." Raising his own sword, Epoth began a swing, and Thomas blocked it with the elegant long sword as he spun left and slashed at Epoth, striking the demon's side. Epoth growled in pain again.

"So ... you wish to fight uninhibited? Beware, for I shall not hold back either," Epoth growled.

With every exchange of blows, Thomas became faster. He did not have time to think about how or why it was possible; he just accepted it. As they fenced back and forth between the first chamber and Scyhathen's chamber, Thomas's skill grew with every hit while Epoth's strength began to wane.

"Unngh ... perhaps you have some skill. But swords will not defeat me, boy ... you know this!"

Epoth managed to score hits on Thomas, but as long as they were in the timeless chamber, it was Epoth who suffered damage instead. The sword swipes passed through Thomas as if he were made of light not flesh, but as the battle wore on that light was fading.

Thomas relied on his training and previous experience to aid him. Despite this, however, Epoth proved too powerful a match for him. With each passing earned blow, the demon grew weak but did not slow down.

The battle raged on for what seemed an eternity. Both contestants exchanged blows, dodging and parrying in an endless melee. When a hit could not be scored, a parry was made, and this went on and on. Thomas was starting to feel pain, but not in the same way he would have before Rhydar's spirit had been awakened in him.

The fighting continued into the front of the chamber. After a swift blow found Thomas, he felt his own warm blood gush out and fell to his knees. Thomas managed to keep the long sword in his right hand as Epoth stood over him.

"My crewmates shall be avenged today...." Epoth raised his sword, ready to end Thomas. In desperation, Thomas hastily slashed with Scyhathen's blade, cutting into Epoth's chest before the demon could deliver the final blow. Thomas cut so deep that he could not pull the blade free. Despite the injury, there was no blood flowing from Epoth's wound. The man probably had no blood left to bleed.

Epoth fell back against the chamber wall, breathing deeply. The fire in his right eye grew stronger. He pulled the longsword out of his chest, threw it to the floor and reached again for his own.

Thomas was now defenseless as a black stain spread across the shining blade of Scyhathen's long sword.

"Well met, boy ... but no matter your skill, no sword can defeat me. Not after what happened when we first met ... I shall arise ... and you shall feel my pain for all eternity." Epoth began to rise from the wall.

Suddenly, flashes of light flooded the room as the ornate designs along the wall came to life. Epoth was disoriented.

"Thomas! Finish him!" an ethereal voice spoke.

As suddenly as the light had appeared, words came to Thomas's head as a mental script unfurled in glowing letters before his eyes. Quickly, he chanted these words aloud.

"Klutara ... minactarea ... beynafecta ... zuhara...." Although he did not know their meaning, Thomas felt the power in them and trusted the wisdom of the voice that had revealed them.

"You ... will ... not...." Epoth strained to get up from the wall. Recognizing the chant, he reached for his sword once more.

"Rhetera ... krettera ... yettera ... zettrha ... *na!!!*" Thomas cried in his loudest voice. A magical burst of white light shot toward Epoth's only remaining eye. The sound of Thomas's voice traveled quickly throughout the cavern and beyond, emanating into the sky above as the incantation was completed. As the spell took effect, it spread through Epoth's entire soulless body, filling the dry blood vessels with a magical energy and gathering light at the center of his chest wound. As Epoth cried out in pain, the light overtook the demon. Then, with a final burst, the light completely eradicated him, dissipating in a blinding flash. His agony echoed through the entire cavern to the surface then grew silent.

As the sound passed through the treasure trove, Ward and the other men dove for cover. Cold winds emerged, forcing their way through the cavern and to the skies above.

Ward opened his eyes, wearily looking around the room. There were no fallen pirates, no jewels on the floor, and no signs of unrest. Everything was back in its original condition. Everything, it would seem, except for the body of Captain Janes.

Thomas kneeled and caught his breath. He then checked the status of Scyhathen's blade. It no longer bore any signs of the battle, nor was it tarnished in any way. The edge had not even dulled. Solemnly he returned the blade to Scyhathen's sheath.

"Forgive me," Thomas said, resting his hand on the man's chest. Somehow, he could tell that Scyhathen was thankful.

Taking the staff, Thomas reopened the sealed door, and returned to the treasure chamber. What he found was not good. Although the treasures and artifacts had been righted, all back to their original locations, the wound in Captain Janes's chest had not.

"Christopher...." Ward said. While Epoth chased Thomas, Ward had not left his captain's side. Sadly, the captain had been long since been dead.

Kneeling beside the first mate, Thomas offered him the only meaningful comfort he could. "Mr. Ward, Epoth is no more."

Ward remained silent.

"Your captain is the same," Gregory observed gravely.

Thomas looked at Janes's lifeless face. He looked at the treasures and then looked back toward Captain Scyhathen in the other chamber. He stood and readied his staff.

"Thomas, that staff cannot do everything. Its power is limited," Gregory said, standing as well.

As Thomas focused on the staff, he sensed its diminished power. This staff would not be usable for some time. Like the staff, he felt tired, but at least he had the time to think about all that had happened to him that day. He began to wonder about the journey that had taken him to this point. Even though his adventure had nearly come to an end, there was so much more to come. Perhaps, Thomas decided, the journey for Captain Janes had begun too.

Holding the staff on its end, he knelt toward his fallen captain, feeling his death. Letting his new instincts flow through him, Thomas concluded there must be another way. Looking around the treasure trove, his eyes were drawn to the blue staff.

Gregory nodded. "Yes, that is the life staff. You must use it immediately."

Fetching the blue staff, Thomas raised it over the captain. A small orb of magical power illuminated the top of the staff and soon expanded to include Janes's body. The wounds across the captain's chest magically healed, and even his clothes were mended. The warmth of life breathed back into the captain. Although he was alive, he remained in a state of fatigue, apparently unaware of the last several moments.

"Thomas?" Janes murmured quietly. Ward supported the captain's head.

"Sir, how do you feel?" Thomas asked.

"I saw a strange place ... wondrous, but strange...." With each breath, Janes seemed to regain some vigor. "It looked like the shoreline near our beach on Nemaris Island." He held up two fingers. "There was a pair of men, one fishing and one walking. The first was fishing with a net, like we did to remain alive. The other man was walking along the surf further down." Shaking his head, Janes frowned. "He seemed familiar, but I could not tell his identity. I thought I had seen a long, gilded sword from his belt ... but I wasn't certain. Turning back to the first man, I struck up a conversation and asked if he had good tidings today. He nodded and handed me a clam shell." Janes looked down at his hand as though expecting to see it there still. "I never saw his face, but he had a beard and was smoking a pipe ... and before I could ask any more questions, the clam opened its shell and I saw a blinding light, then I opened my eyes...." He looked at Thomas. "... and saw you."

Unsure what to make of his captain's tale, Thomas smiled. "Epoth is no more, Captain. The Spirit of the Sea, the blade of Scyhathen, helped make it happen."

"Scyhathen ... Epoth? How?" Janes asked, as he managed to sit up. Although Janes had been to the timeless chamber before, his encounter with Epoth seemed to have wiped his memory.

Ward picked up on this and gestured to the hidden chamber. "Perhaps a reminder is necessary, Captain. Scyhathen is back here."

Although Ward offered to help his captain stand, Janes shook his head and got up under his own power. He stood for a moment, then fell into Ward's arms.

Shifting his captain so he could wrap a supporting arm around his back, Ward huffed. "Chris, you're still a little woozy, come on."

Their progression was slow and careful at first, but soon Janes was walking on his own. He marveled at the glowing markings on the walls, but it was the timeless chamber that amazed him.

Thomas gestured toward the reclining figure. "Captain Terrence Karwen Scyhathen, of the honorable ship *Nemaris*."

"He hasn't aged a day … is he asleep?" Janes asked.

"No, he has lain here since his death in 1583. This chamber has caused him to remain just as he was as he breathed his final breath that day," Thomas said.

Janes looked at the long sword that rested at his side, but Ward wouldn't allow him to touch it.

"It has never left the man's side," Ward began.

Thomas raised a finger. "Except once, to defeat Epoth, the demon that destroyed his crew."

Ward smiled. "Aye."

A moment of silence passed. Janes could see a small amount of the blade exposed from the sheath. There was an "E" inscribed there. "Tommy, if it never left his side, how did that initial get there?"

"An E?" Thomas moved around him to look.

"I felt it was necessary," a voice said.

Everyone looked at Gregory. "I didn't say anything."

From behind them, in the large chamber, an elderly man walked forward. He carried a plain, wooden cane. He had literally appeared out of nowhere, yet apparently had been there the entire time. A magical portal could be seen along the wall behind him, revealing a vessel that had been placed upside down to make a house. Blue skies, green fields, and endless oceans dotted the landscape beyond. The man himself was wearing a white robe that emitted a magical glow. He had a long white beard that extended to his chest. Although it was clear he was old, he had very few wrinkles and a kind gentle face.

An exact match of Acadia and Cynthia's descriptions of Rhydar.

"Such is the tradition of swordsman to initial their blades after a victory," the bearded man said.

"Rhydar?" Gregory asked.

Thomas didn't need to ask—he knew. "Master Rhydar, but how?"

Janes bowed to the spirit.

"I come to thank you for allowing my spirit to rest, now that Epoth is defeated. Never did I complete the spell you chanted, Thomas. That is how he was created," Rhydar replied.

Finally Thomas had access to the man with all the answers! "But where did all that information come from? The spell, knowledge of the staff … everything? I had no such knowledge before we entered the cave."

"I do understand you have questions." Rhydar gestured to Gregory. "Speak to your father. But Thomas, know that the knowledge was always there, inside of you, waiting for this very moment."

"Always there … Father?" Thomas turned to Gregory. With a smile, Gregory nodded.

"I thank you for allowing my men to visit your islands in peace, good sir," Janes said with a bow.

"No, my thanks are with you, Captain Janes. I thank you for bringing Thomas to me, after so many years of turmoil. With my islands in his hands, I shall be able to rest peacefully," Rhydar said.

"Wait, I don't understand, what do you mean?" Thomas asked again.

"You have awakened, Thomas. You are now the wizard of these islands, not I, not your father. This chamber contains the source of my magical essence, and with it came your strength. You wonder why Epoth couldn't hurt you? Because your essence is stronger than darkness … and it was that which saved you. Treasure this gift always, Thomas … and you shall be prosperous forever. Farewell." With a bow, Rhydar turned away.

As he approached the stone wall, his form faded. The portal and landscape beyond also faded, vanishing as quickly as they had appeared.

"Rhydar! Wait," Thomas said, but he was there no longer. Gregory, along with Janes and Ward, turned to Thomas.

"Thomas, you are the wizard of these lands now." Gregory put his arm around his son.

"A wonderful gift, Thomas," Janes replied.

"Aye, lad, ye did good." Ward gave him a pat on his back. "Come on, I want to see if they've got Marshall under control." He started for the surface.

Just then, Benson and Roberts came into the first chamber.

"Is everything all right in here?" Benson asked as they entered.

"Captain ... you're all right?" Roberts asked, awestruck.

Seeing his men safe, Janes couldn't help grinning like a fool. "Yes, Jared. Never better."

Ward nodded. "Aye, things are quite fine. Let's head up." He ushered them toward the surface.

"Aye, coming sir," Roberts said. He and Benson followed behind.

"Is Perry with you?" Janes asked.

"He went ahead," Benson replied.

Gregory raised a hand and followed after them. "Wait, I'll show you a quicker route."

Still not completely steady on his feet, Janes put his hand on Thomas's shoulder and gazed around the pin-neat treasure chamber. "Tell me, Thomas, I must know. Did Epoth defeat me?" There was no evidence anyone had fought there, let alone died.

Thomas found Epoth's blade on the floor in the corner of the adjacent chamber. He picked it up and showed it to Janes; it had no initials on it. "No sir, he only knocked you out."

Janes smiled. "Aye then ... see you at the surface."

Thomas took the black sword to the rear of the treasure trove and placed it in the center of the weapons rack. The eyes of the skull pommel were lifeless and dim.

After everyone had exited the cave, they met briefly before joining the group that guarded Marshall and Nyguard.

Janes took the point toward the jungle. "I think they're over here, lads." He went ahead.

Before anyone could follow, Ward stopped them. "Gentlemen, a moment."

"Sir?" Benson asked.

"All of us know what happened down there ... but there's no need to tell the others. Especially, that the captain may have been killed just now," Ward said.

Roberts nodded. "Aye, and let's keep it that way. No sense in letting Marshall know."

"Aye, agreed," Perry said.

Everyone else seemed to have the same sentiment.

"Right. Now then." Ward grinned his wicked grin. "Let's see how Marshall and Nyguard are doing."

The Wizard of Nemaris

Barry Gritzol and the others had secured Marshall and Nyguard in the jungle just east of the cliff overlooking the Cove, where the two paths intersected. Although it was still cloudy and dark, the rain had stopped.

"Captain!" A huge grin split Gritzol's face. "We were getting worried."

Ellis eyed them uncertainly. "Heard some awful noise down there ... you fellows all right?"

"We're quite well, gentlemen. Any more pirates?" Janes asked.

Jennings shook his head. "No, not a one."

Noticing Gregory, Gritzol's face grew wary. "I say, who might you be?"

"Father, I should introduce you to my mates." Thomas was still getting used to having a father, but was more than willing to adjust.

While the crew stared in astonishment, Gregory smiled politely. "Please do."

"This is *the* Gregory DeLeuit, then?" Jennings asked.

Thomas gestured to each man in turn. "Father, let me introduce Mr. Barry Gritzol, Mr. Harvey Jennings, Mr. Roland Benson, Mr. Jared Roberts, Mr. Horatio Ellis, Mr. Perry ... I don't know his last name, and Mr. Seriam Ward."

As though the thought had only just occurred to him, Jennings turned to his crewmate. "Aye, Perry, what is your last name?"

"Cap'n knows," Perry said.

"Mr. Perry Dekhaezbik," Janes said.

Perry nodded with a big smile.

With a wave to his father, Thomas gave a little bow. "Gentlemen, I present Mr. Gregory DeLeuit."

Gregory shook hands with everyone.

"What about me?" Marshall whined.

"Captain Archibald L. Marshall, and Mr. Leo Nyguard," Thomas said quietly.

"About time I got some proper recognition," Marshall spat.

"You can ignore him if ye like," added Gritzol.

Janes gave his captives a stern look. "We'll deal with ye soon enough, Marshall, you just wait your turn. Perry, watch them."

"Mr. DeLeuit, where have ye been all this time?" Ward asked.

"Living in a cave ashore Opole Island. It's very well hidden. Not even Cynthia knows about it. I went to the Siren Island cavern before you all arrived, hoping Thomas would find me there." He shrugged. "It's a long story."

"But, then, what if he didn't ever find these islands?" Roberts asked.

Gregory smiled slyly. "Well, I should apologize, gentlemen. That storm that directed you here? I had a hand in it."

"And Fallon, our former cabin boy?" Gritzol asked.

"A very temporary illness, I assure you. All I did was make it so his voice would quiver. He should be quite well within several months."

Jennings made a unyielding glare. "Anything else you care to claim responsibility for?"

The captain gave his crewman a stern look, but Gregory nodded politely. "There is much to apologize for, in a manner of speaking, Mr. Jennings. Let's see... the wheat patch that grew to maturity every two days, the trees with fruit that grew daily and remained ripe until you picked them ... oh yes, and the wind storm that allowed you to leave. Am I missing anything?"

Jennings quietly kicked some dirt beneath his boots. "No sir."

Thomas turned to his father. "I don't understand ... if you wanted me to stay, why allow us to leave?"

Gregory sighed. "I was hoping Marshall would let you alone, but I did not count on his greed and ambition. By allowing you to leave, I not only lured him back, but Epoth as well."

"Epoth?" Ellis asked.

"Again, long story. Epoth fed on those ill fearful and aggressive feelings, as well as magic." He looked around the crewmen. "I suppose we may all have had a hand in it."

"Epoth is a what now?" Gritzol asked. Much of the conversation rolled over him like a rogue wave.

Ward cleared his throat. "I'll tell you gentlemen all about it after a bit, aye?"

The rest of the men who hadn't been around for the demon's entrance nonchalantly agreed. Those who had were not anxious to hear it again. Thankfully, there would be time for explanations later.

Janes patted Mr. DeLeuit's back. "Certainly, you were hoping to bring Thomas here … and to do so without revealing yourself."

Gregory nodded. "I'm pleased that you understand, Captain."

Ellis grumbled as he set up the cook set. "And waterfalls just fall out of the sky, humph."

Thomas laughed.

"My apologies, but it was necessary for Thomas to discover who he was," Gregory said. He tapped a wand hanging from his belt.

"What's that?" Jennings asked.

"My transport wand. That's how we got to the surface so fast," Gregory said.

"Fancy that," Jennings said.

"Aye," Gritzol agreed.

"Cap'n, if there was an Epoth fellow, whatever happened to him?" Jennings asked.

"Well, he…." Ward began.

"Nothing but a specter. I trust he was just a passing spirit," Thomas said. Ward nodded with a wink.

"Aye, indeed," Gregory said.

"I see," Benson replied.

"Well, let's rest up before heading back to the ship." Janes took a seat on a log as Ellis began preparing some food.

Gregory walked toward the cliff overlooking the cove. Thomas followed.

"Thomas, how's your mother?" Gregory asked, staring into the narrow strait.

"She has been well, Father. Always baking and renting our extra room to passing sailors who are in need of a warm bed," Thomas replied.

"Has she found anyone to keep her company?" Gregory asked.

"No, nobody. She is good friends with Mrs. Denchfield, but other than that just takes each day at a time." Thomas shrugged. "She always has."

"Marianne knew that I had left, but may have imagined that I was defeated at sea. Did she ever voice that possibility?" Gregory asked.

Thomas thought back to his life in Harper's Bay. "Mother never spoke of you much, but sometimes I would come home and find her crying for no apparent reason. Then, she'd hug me and tell me to go play outside."

Gregory sighed. "I never wanted to involve her in these matters. Your mother is a good and hard-working individual, too innocent for the likes of Epoth and his demons. That's why I left, to protect her from him. Rhydar would've done the same had he a family, I am sure."

"Do you miss Mother?" Thomas asked.

"I didn't want to leave without meeting your crew, but I plan to return to Harper's Bay and spend my remaining days with her." Looking across the water, he smiled to himself. "I not only owe it to her, but myself as well."

"I don't understand … after Scyhathen passed away, how did you ever get back to Harper's Bay? By using that wand?" Thomas asked.

Gregory shook his head. "This wand is only good for transporting a few people or items at once, but I hadn't found that out just yet. I managed to board Epoth's ship, several years after Scyhathen's death. The ship was barely seaworthy. I took it to Teraske before returning with a newer one for transporting everything back to Harper's Bay. It barely made the voyage, turning to dust just as I entered Teraske harbor."

"The *Nemaris*, Father … could you tell me about it?" Thomas asked.

"A nearly total loss. Only the cargo hold and barracks were intact … and luckily, that is also where all of the salvageable items were kept. Even Mandalay's portrait of Cynthia, which was still pristine even though it was partially submerged in sea water. Using this wand, I was able to carry things back quickly … and a good thing too, because the shipwreck vanished from the surface only a year later."

"I had heard that it had vanished, but I don't understand," Thomas said.

"The sea just swallowed it up." Gregory shrugged. "The nearby shoals now are deep below the surface. The ship could still exsist, I suppose."

Thomas nodded. "And these islands? What of them?"

"Rhydar knows his treasure is safe from the likes of Epoth, but not from those like Captain Marshall." Gregory placed a hand on his son's shoulder. "That is why one of us must stay here."

Thomas looked up at him. "On these islands?"

"Someone must look after the collection. There are many charms and secrets that keep these islands safe, but without our presence here they will fade. If we are gone for too long, everything will be vulnerable."

"So, that is why you had to stay to guard the islands," Thomas said.

Gregory nodded. "Rhydar had hoped to return the items to their rightful owners, but he grew old before that could happen. I myself have lost the adventuring spirit … chasing waves and dodging swords. The quiet life at home … at Marianne's side, is where I want to be."

"You don't seem that old, Father … after all, didn't Rhydar himself live a long time?"

"I never inherited that part of his existence." He smiled. "Who knows? Maybe you have."

Thomas knew right away what he was suggesting. After all, he would've wanted to live here with Acadia if the option presented itself.

"What do you know about Cynthia, Father?" Thomas asked.

"She has been a good friend of mine, someone as wise as Rhydar but as gentle and easy to talk to as your mother. Always have I sought her advice when a matter could not be resolved on my own," Gregory said.

"How long has she been living on these islands?"

Gregory thought a moment. "You may not realize it, but Cynthia has been here almost as long as Rhydar himself. Mermaids age very slowly, appearing young until they are of venerable age. She has been here since before I was born, actually."

"That is true, then … but…." Thomas began.

"Thomas, she is 179 years old," Gregory said.

Thomas was surprised to learn her age. Cynthia appeared younger than his mother.

"Of those years, she has spent nearly all of them here."

Thomas thought a moment. "How old would that make Acadia, do you suppose?"

"Acadia was often kept away from me, perhaps by Marsha. She is the youngest, though. If I recall, she was summoned here shortly before Rhydar's mortal life ended," Gregory explained.

"Rhydar died before Scyhathen arrived, yes?" Thomas asked.

"Yes, he did. I think it was several years before, perhaps…." Gregory began.

Shaking his head, Thomas held up a hand. "No, do not tell me. I do not wish to know Acadia's age."

Gregory nodded. "As you wish. Have you any more questions at the moment? I know that my absence had been hard on you."

Thomas shook his head, smiling. "I understand your reasons, Father. Thank you for telling me."

"I'm glad I was finally able to, son. I've been wanting this for a long time."

Ellis called. "Grub's here if ye want it!"

"Come on, son. You've had a long day."

Together they went to dish up.

As Gregory and Thomas returned to camp, Janes was telling the crew of his first encounter with Marshall.

"So then the men fenced ferociously, and...." Grinning, he faced his fellow captain. "Well, maybe you could tell it best."

Marshall's eyes narrowed in vexation. "Scuff off ye barnacle."

"All right then." With a shrug, Janes turned back to his men. "His fencing nearly cut my best swordsmen through. The situation was looking grim, but a solution came to me in the most unusual of forms. I found a reading lens on the deck. To this day I know not how it got there, but I tossed it to another man in between opponents—wasn't it you, Gritzol?"

"Might've been, Cap'n. It was awhile ago," Gritzol replied.

"And whoever that man was took it and, using the bright sunlight, started burning the sails." Holding up his hands, he spread them slowly to emphasize the spread of the fire. "They all caught one by one. Somehow we were able to get back to the *Valiant* and sail away while their men fought the fires."

"Ye want a trophy, Janes?" Marshall muttered.

"I take it you don't want any stew, Marshall?" Ward said.

"May I?" Nyguard asked.

"Certainly." Ellis handed Nyguard a bowl, leaving Marshall on his own. It was difficult for Nyguard to eat with his wrists bound, but he managed and seemed to appreciate it.

"That reminds me ... how dare you! A cook, prancing around as a captain!" Marshall said to Ellis, beginning to rant.

Janes sighed. "Perry, would you please?"

"Aye Cap'n." Perry took some cotton wadding and stuffed it in Marshall's mouth, stopping the flow of vulgarities from the source.

Jennings saluted with his spoon. "Much better."

Marshall made some muffled noises as the men continued to eat.

As soon as camp was cleaned up, the entourage started walking back to the ships. Since the other rowboats were near the cove, there was only one rowboat present.

Marshall had begun to free himself from his bonds. He mumbled through his gag, convinced that Janes' two rowboats had drifted away.

"Sir, the rowboats?" Benson asked.

"Aye, yes, the rowboats." After fighting a spirit and returning from death, such practical details had slipped the captain's minds. "I asked Acadia to bring them to the other side of the cove, didn't I … at least this boat should be enough to get us to the cove. Let's not bother her right now. Jennings, Perry, would you go to the cove and collect our boats?"

"I can get them, shall I?" Gregory asked.

Shaking his head, Janes raised a hand to stop Gregory. "Not necessary, you don't need to use your magic, Mr. DeLeuit. Thank you."

"Magic?" Marshall muttered to himself.

"Where are the boats, Cap'n?" Jennings asked.

"Just to the east of this island, in a narrow strait," Ward said.

"I know where, Cap'n," Perry said.

"All right then." Janes settled himself on a rock along the shore. "Take your time. We are in no hurry."

With a chorused "Aye," the two men set off in the *Inferno*'s rowboat.

"Mr. Janes, uh, Captain, sir … what about our ship?" Nyguard asked.

"Your ship?" There were so many details for the captain to consider now the ordeal was over. "Well … I suppose you won't be needing it no more, hmm…."

Marshall had no intentions of giving up his ship. He mumbled angrily as he tried to lower the gag, spitting as he struggled with the bonds.

"What's that? You saying something?" Benson asked, lowering the gag.

"You'll never take my ship while I still breathe!" Marshall cried. He went after Benson, climbing to his feet. He escaped from the bonds on his feet, kicked Benson in the side, and charged after Thomas, who had been knocked aside as well.

With a cry from Thomas, Gregory came to his son's side and gave Nyguard a swift jab across the face before holding him.

"Get him!" Ward cried as Janes and Gritzol did their best to ensure Marshall was secured by each arm. Nyguard also was held, but he was not as anxious to attempt an escape as his captain.

"Good one, boss. Now they'll kill us both," Nyguard muttered. Marshall sneered back.

"What say you? I'll have your family's heads on a pike if I ever get out of this...." Marshall began.

"Your family?" Janes faced his other captive. "Nyguard?" Everyone shifted their focus to the *Inferno*'s first mate.

"He's bluffing...." Lowering his gaze, Nyguard shook his head. "My family left me after I spoke ill of the king of Cimmordia and his court ... Marshall gave me a way out. For my family's safety, I sold my life to Marshall, who would take their lives and sour our family name, until...."

"What are you going to do, Leo? Seek help from these ... wizards, and whisk your family away, or make yourself the king of Cimmordia? Or conjure up some strange mystical power to save you all? Just you wait, Janes! As soon as my legions of followers discover this place, they'll be upon it like flies on honey ... and you shall all be hunted down like dogs!" Marshall cried.

Marshall shrugged off his captors, advancing on Thomas once more.

Janes and the crew scrambled to their feet as Marshall drew a knife from his belt. He raised the blade and advanced toward Thomas's side.

A silent form emerged from the water. A spear tipped with coral flew through the air and struck Marshall through his chest, killing him instantly. Both his body and blade fell, lifeless and limp.

The group was stunned into silence, except for Nyguard who gasped in shock. "Captain!" Their attention focused on Marshall and Thomas, the silent form had gone unnoticed. Everyone wondered where the weapon had come from.

Janes shook off the shock first. "Hold him!" Ellis and Benson grabbed Nyguard's arms while their captain drew his sword in case Nyguard attempted anything.

The attention turned back to Marshall's fallen body. "That was ... unexpected," Mr. Gritzol said flatly.

Janes turned to his cabin boy. "Thomas, did that come from one of your friends?"

Behind the captain, a man surfaced from the water. Apparently sensing the presence, Janes turned to stare at the man with the rest of his crew. He appeared to be in his twenties. Despite his young appearance, however, there was no question of his experience, for he held a knife similar to the spear that had killed Marshall. Although only half of him was above water, the man wore nothing more than a few necklaces and bracelets, so it was easy to see he was well built. The light brown hair atop his head was neatly kept, clean cut to his shoulders.

Stepping out from behind Thomas, Gregory raised a hand in greeting. "Onell, your timing is excellent as always."

"I remember this one." The merman lifted his chin to indicate Marshall. "I'd heard about him from Cynthia only two days ago. He did not deserve to live."

"A good shot, I must say," Ward commented.

With a regal nod, Onell acknowledged the compliment. "Thank you."

"You are the fourth member of the mercreatures at these isles, then?" Roberts asked.

Onell nodded and turned to Thomas. "I am honored to finally meet you, young Thomas. I have been watching you for a long time, and I am pleased to see you are becoming a young man at last."

"Yes...." Thomas remembered Acadia saying Onell was often away from the islands. "Have you really been watching me in Harper's Bay?"

Onell nodded again. "I have been following Master Rhydar's orders as instructed. Now, I shall await your next orders."

"Then...that was...." Thomas thought aloud. He had not forgotten the large splash in the water that same day he joined the crew of the *Valiant*.

"Excuse me." Benson raised a hand. "But Gregory, I understood that you were the next Rhydar?"

Gritzol nodded in agreement. "Aye, that's what I got from t'all."

"Actually, I'm not in command anymore. Son?" Gregory looked to Thomas.

Onell faced Thomas at full attention.

It took Thomas only a moment's consideration to know what to do. "Return to guard duty on these shores, Mr. Onell."

"As you wish." The merman bowed and gestured to his spear. "I shall need my spear for that duty. Please." Pulling it from Marshall's body, Ward returned the weapon. Onell bowed again and returned to the ocean below, flipping his pale green tailfin as he dove.

"Well Tommy, seems you're the captain of these shores now," Janes said.

Nyguard cleared his throat. "Excuse me, what about me?"

"Yes ... to Cimmordia with you, I suppose," Janes muttered.

Right about then, Perry and Jennings returned from the cove with the two rowboats.

"And the ship?" Nyguard asked again.

"Yes, as I was saying before ..." Pausing, Janes turned to Gregory. "Actually, Mr. DeLeuit, what were your plans?"

"To spend my days with my wife." He smiled. "I owe it to her."

"Anyone left aboard your ship, Nyguard?" Janes asked.

The sailor shrugged. "No one I know of; we left the cabin boy at Sundrop."

Janes lifted his hat to Gregory. "You may do with her as you wish, Captain DeLeuit."

"Aye sir!" He shook Janes's hand. "That's very good of you."

"Wait, wait!" Nyguard raised his bound hands. "Can't I get my things first?"

"I'll allow it." Gregory nodded, climbing into the rowboat. He was ready to get settled. Perry pushed their captive toward the *Inferno*'s rowboat.

"Captain?" Ward motioned toward Marshall's lifeless body. "What about him?"

Janes turned toward Nyguard as he rode with Perry toward the *Inferno*. "We'll need someone to tell the people of Cimmordia that their formal naval commander was lost at sea."

"Captain, I wonder if the castle would like to know about their formal admiral's headquarters, as well? There would be many crimes of the sea solved," Benson suggested.

Janes nodded. "Another story that Nyguard may be willing to divulge."

"Before he is imprisoned for the murder of James Lewinston, of course," Ward replied.

"Of course." He turned toward the body. "I dread the thought of leaving Marshall in these pristine waters, however. A pyre, perhaps?"

"I'll get some wood, Cap'n," Benson said.

Roberts pulled a tinderbox from his pocket. "And I some kindling, Cap'n."

Janes wiped his forehead. "The man may have been a codfish ... but he's surely earning his just rewards."

The midday sun was met by a plume of ash and smoke as the dreaded commander of the Sundrop Cult was committed to the sky. Nobody said a word, and no tears were shed in his memory.

By evening, the site was cleared and the crew was ready to return to the *Valiant*. Janes rubbed his hands together. "Guess we should get on our way as well."

As everyone started piling gear back into the *Valiant*'s rowboats, Ward patted his cabin boy's back. "Tommy, what do you want to do?"

"I'll come with you for tonight. I need some rest." Thomas gestured at the rowboat bound for the *Inferno*. "But can you send a man with my father to help? I mean, I trust my father is a good sailor, but he'll need a crew for a ship of that size." Collecting his own sack of possessions, Thomas climbed in next to Janes.

Without a second thought, Janes nodded. "I see your point. Roberts, would you like to join Thomas and Perry tomorrow?"

Jared grinned. "I'd be glad to, sir. Give me a chance to stay here another day, or as long as they need."

"Aye then. You'll want to double check your things, Tommy. Yours too, Jared." Janes glanced at the other rowboat. "Perry can get his belongings later tonight. We'll want to leave before noon tomorrow."

"Will we be meeting in Harper's Bay, then?" Jared asked.

The captain nodded. "After dropping off Nyguard, aye."

"I'll finish packing once we arrive, sir, but first I need to talk to someone," Thomas said.

"Whatever you need." Janes patted his soon to be ex-cabin boy on the shoulder. "Tommy, let me tell ye something. You're always welcome on my ship, anytime. You're a good buccaneer, and at home on the sea. You just need to get some years on ye, aye?"

"Thank you sir, I've enjoyed serving with you," Thomas said as they approached the *Valiant*.

"You'll do all right."

Once the men boarded the *Valiant*, Thomas took the rowboat and worked his way into the Cove. After tying up the rowboat he blew the shell whistle to summon Acadia. Cynthia surfaced instead.

"Hello Thomas."

"Cynthia … it's nice to see you, but I had expected Acadia."

"She asked me to come. Something is on her mind lately...." Seeing Thomas's expression, she raised a reassuring hand. "Do not worry, she is well. I have informed her of your new situation. Tell me ... are you leaving with Gregory and the others?"

Thomas nodded. "I think I will ... I wish to see my mother again, Cynthia ... but tell me this. Why didn't you ever tell me that my father was here? Or the details about everything?"

"For the same reason that Gregory chose to wait inside the cavern. You had to seek him, Thomas. Not the other way around. If I had simply told you, there would be no guarantee that you would accept your role. You had to clearly, and fully, understand your role on these islands." She smiled. "And, now that you have, your purpose is clear, yes?"

"Yes, I suppose so. It's all a little sudden ... but I am glad to have my father back," Thomas replied.

"I must apologize, Thomas ... for putting you at risk."

"Apologize? Why?"

She lifted a hand to her chest. "I wrongly believed that Captain Nepotherden and Epoth were different beings. I had assumed that Epoth had long since departed this world ... and that you would be safe."

"Cynthia, only Rhydar could've foreseen that." He smiled. "You told me what I needed to know."

Cynthia nodded. "All that remains now ... is for you to one day learn and understand your new skills."

"And with my father's guidance, I am certain I will meet your expectations."

"I trust you will return shortly, once your affairs are in order at home."

Thomas nodded.

"You have an amazing road before you, Thomas, and I wish you well. I will tell Acadia you had hoped to see her once more."

"Thank you ... and take care until I return."

Cynthia answered with a warm smile, probably the friendliest smile Thomas had ever seen from her. "Thank you."

"You are most welcome. Good eve," Thomas said.

"Good eve, Thomas. Be strong, trust your instincts, and return safely." With a wave, Cynthia dove underwater. Thomas untied the rowboat, and quietly returned to the *Valiant*.

That night, Thomas, Perry, and Jared moved their belongings to the empty crew quarters of the *Inferno*. Their first priority would be cleaning the ship, and clearing out any pirate garbage. As for the collection that Marshall had in his cabin, that would be Gregory's to either keep or sell as he wished.

In the morning, Janes and the rest of the remaining crew aboard the *Valiant* gave their final farewells to Mr. DeLeuit, Thomas, Roberts, and Perry. The *Valiant* then headed east to return Nyguard to the city of Cimmordia. There he would have to find another way to live his life.

Thomas took leave of the *Inferno* momentarily and returned to the treasure trove beneath Siren Island. He first checked on Captain Scyhathen's body before taking the bracelet key off of the exterior door. Next he had plans to seal the chamber in the way his father showed him, but stopped when he discovered that he was not alone.

Acadia had emerged from the water inside the timeless chamber and crawled into the treasure trove. Thomas spotted her while looking at the artifacts.

"Acadia? How'd you find your way here?" Thomas knelt next to her.

"Cynthia told me about the tunnel … I never knew Rhydar had such wonderful things." She looked at all the artifacts in awe.

Thomas shrugged. "Most of this wasn't his. I hope someday to fulfill his vision of returning each piece to its rightful place."

"How does it make you feel, being Rhydar's successor? I never would've guessed you were the one," Acadia said with a smile.

Thomas took a deep sigh. "I know a few more things than I did before, but I feel the same as you. I'll have to do my best to make Rhydar proud of me, just like I did with my father."

Acadia laughed. "Oh yes, I met your father before I came here. He looks just like you."

"He's everything I expected, and more," Thomas replied. He stood up and looked over the collection.

"What does that one do?" She was looking at the ordinary staff that made twenty-five pirates vanish.

"Oh, this? I am not entirely sure, but it is certainly powerful. I have yet to discover its limits."

"See if you can make that vase float," Acadia asked, hoping for a show.

"Well ... okay," Thomas said, holding it toward the terra-cotta vase. Using the staff for the purpose of telekinesis, the vase lifted into the air as Thomas raised the staff. Then, he lowered it gently in the same manner.

"Wow, that was wonderful!" Acadia said, clapping.

Thomas thought a moment. Remembering some of the previous conversations he had shared with Acadia, he came up with an amazing proposition.

"Acadia, do you remember how we always talked about what it was to enjoy life on land?" Thomas asked. He leaned on the staff next to her.

"Of course. But, even if you said it could be possible, I'm not sure I'd want to go through with it," Acadia said, turning away slightly.

"No, Acadia. Think hard about it. With this staff, it could happen." Thomas didn't know how he knew it, but he was certain it could be done.

Acadia thought a moment, albeit nervously. "Maybe for a short time, not forever."

"Do you wish it?" Thomas asked.

"Could I? For a day?"

"A human for a day," Thomas said, directing the staff at Acadia. As magical energy surged into her, the scales on her tail began to sparkle. One by one, from the fins to her waist, the sparkles grew into a blue glow that soon covered her entire tail. A matter of moments later, the light faded, as a pair of human legs appeared in their place. She was wearing a dress that extended to her knees, colored the same cerulean blue as her fishtail had been before.

The bright glow switched to her face as she lit up with excitement. "Thomas ... I can't believe ... this is so wonderful!" Acadia cried. Thomas helped her to her feet. After a slight balance adjustment, she stood on her own, just a bit shorter than him. She needed shoes, but otherwise was fully clothed and very lovely—for a human; she was just as lovely as before.

"Try walking," Thomas said with a smile.

Acadia watched her feet as she took a tiny step, and another. With a third step, she stumbled slightly before falling into Thomas's arms. As with all humans, one must stand before she can walk.

"I've got you!" Thomas said.

"Thank you ... this is strange ... but amazing!" Acadia replied.

"You're doing very well! A little practice will help ... come on; try it again," Thomas said, as he taught Acadia how to walk.

Meanwhile, Gregory and his new crew were preparing the *Inferno* for departure.

"Are the sails in good order, Jared?" Gregory called to Roberts.

"Quite good, Cap'n! All we need is a good wind and clear skies," Jared called back.

"And the rest, Perry?" Gregory asked.

"Only a mess in the galley, but otherwise good, Cap'n."

"I guess I can start on that. Good work, then." Gregory went below deck to survey the galley.

Jared dropped from the rigging to the deck. "I'll go help."

"Aye," Perry said.

Thomas had led Acadia to the mainland of Nemaris Island using the *Inferno*'s rowboat. She wanted to view the island from the land and walk upon the bridge.

"Okay, just as before, one step after another," Thomas said as she held his hand.

"One, after another," Acadia said to herself as she walked across the bridge. After reaching the halfway point, she stopped a moment to look toward the waterfall.

"What is it?"

"The waterfall...." She seemed to be in awe. "Even from only a few feet above the water, it is so different."

"Is it a good experience?" Thomas asked.

She nodded with a smile. "I never knew it would be like this."

"As you also know, I never thought you could be like this," Thomas replied.

Acadia turned to him. "You once told me that I should always keep an open mind, and you were correct, Thomas."

She took a step toward the other end of the bridge, only to feel a sharp pain as a splinter punctured her left foot.

"Ooch! What is this?" she asked, sitting down to inspect her foot. Thomas knelt and pulled the splinter out carefully. A trace of blood seeped from the wound.

"Just hold it a moment." He took a handkerchief from his vest pocket and went to the creek below. After rinsing it in the water, he used the damp handkerchief to clean the wound. Applying pressure, soon the bleeding stopped.

"Mmm ... it feels better now, Thomas," Acadia said.

"And this should help too." To protect the wound, he wrapped the handkerchief around her foot tightly.

"Thank you," she said.

"I believe you need some shoes, Acadia. Either that, or a few calluses," Thomas replied as an afterthought.

"Calluses?" she asked.

"Your skin is delicate and has not been conditioned yet ... well, it is difficult to explain, I'm afraid." Thomas shrugged. "Either way, I shall have to bring you back a good pair of shoes for our next walk."

"Do you have any on the ship?"

"I do not believe so. And it is a few days to the nearest port that can make some," Thomas replied.

"Will your father have any ideas?" Acadia asked.

"He may. Come on; we'll go back and find out." Thomas helped her up, and they headed to the rowboat and returned to the *Inferno*.

The *Valiant* had already gained a day toward South Cimmordia. As the crew tended the riggings, Mr. Ward and Captain Janes were in his cabin quietly chatting.

"As usual, Mr. Ellis's tea is both soothing and relaxing." Janes helped himself to a big sip from his favorite cup, which had survived being carted to and from Siren Island without so much as a chip.

Ward was gazing out the starboard windows of the captain's cabin. "Correct me if I'm wrong, but a few weeks ago were we not talking about an adventurous voyage someday?"

Janes chuckled. "Yes, we were, but I dare say we've scratched that itch. And it was all because of that map that was drawn by the late Mr. Mandalay."

"Agreed, but where does our path go now?" Ward turned to his captain. "The cargo hold is empty."

"I suppose we have two choices. Either we prepare a standard cargo trade or...." He gave an airy twirl of his free hand. "We begin seeking out what has not been sought."

"And in doing so, we may end up like Scyhathen did," Ward replied.

Janes took a sip of his tea. "Such is the life of explorers, Seriam. What does not kill you only prolongs the inevitable, I suppose."

"A fair view, Christopher." Their plans were all well and good, but both believed that the crew should really be comfortable with their arraingement. "There seems to be talk of returning to the normal life of a trade cog's crew."

Janes sighed deeply. "Ever since reading of the adventurous ways of Captain Scyhathen, there has been a part of me that wishes to break away from the ordinary and plot a course into the unknown. To simply pick a star in the night sky and chase it until you find its secrets, be they fantasy or mystery."

"There is an old bard's tale of a man who was able to see every port on every island of every sea." Ward turned back to the windows. "Once he had seen every last one, he turned to the night sky and began sailing that sea. Now he lives amongst the stars."

"Aye." Janes sipped his tea. "I'm rather fond of that story."

Ward drank from his mug as well. "What shall I tell the men?"

"Maybe, after Mr. Nyguard is sent on his way, we can start following the coast north. Or maybe we can head south, toward Phrynn like Scyhathen always wanted to. Wherever the wind hopes to take us, I know not. What say you?"

Ward nodded. "I shall inform them once we stop for the night."

"Aye then."

"I see … well, there may be a few problems, I'm afraid," Gregory replied after Thomas explained their plans to him.

"Like what?" Acadia asked. She sat on a chair in the *Inferno*'s captain's quarters.

"Well, for one, the sudden occurrence of a young woman along with us. I do not wish to give your mother a shock more surprising than my unexpected arrival, Thomas."

"I can remain on the boat," Acadia offered.

"And then there's your natural form," Gregory said.

"The staff can be used repeatedly, yes?" Thomas asked.

His father waggled his hands in an ambiguous manner. "Not exactly."

Thomas looked at Acadia nervously.

"So... how far is it to Harper's Bay?" Acadia asked.

"Six days, with a good breeze," Gregory replied.

Thomas looked at Acadia apprehensively. "What about only one use per day? Or a longer time for her to be human, perhaps?"

Gregory shook his head. "Let me explain it in simpler terms, son. Even if you only meant for her to be a human for a day, she'll remain a human until a counter spell is applied."

"And I can be changed back into myself when we return," Acadia concluded.

Thomas nodded, now realizing how simple the process was.

"I'll have to spend some time with you, Thomas; there is much you need to learn about these tools. Anyway, we can head back to Harper's Bay and take as much time as we need. We'll make a stop in Vesper for shoes. I once knew an excellent cobbler there," Gregory continued.

There was a knock at the door. "Yes?" Gregory asked.

It was Mr. Perry. "Cap'n, forgive the intrusion."

"Go ahead, Perry," Gregory said.

"A man is here, off starboard," he replied.

"Onell?" Gregory asked.

"That's what he called himself, Cap'n," Perry replied.

"I'll go, Father," Thomas said. Acadia and Gregory followed behind.

The merman was waiting just off the hull.

"Onell, what is it?" Thomas asked.

"Acadia, are you there?" he asked.

"Here, yes." She leaned over the railing and waved.

Onell smiled. "Cynthia was wondering about you. Are ... are you human?"

She nodded.

"I see ... well, I hope you're enjoying that new experience. Master Thomas, may I come aboard to chat?" Onell asked.

"Yes, please do."

With amazing acrobatics, Onell climbed the hull and flipped his green tail over the rail, landing on the deck just next to it.

"Am I correct to assume you are going with your father to Harper's Bay? You haven't set up any permanent home yet," Onell asked.

Thomas nodded. "I had planned to at least once. I need to see my mother, Onell. Also, if Acadia wishes to spend time with me, I'll have to get her some footwear, you understand."

"Yes...." Onell noticed her bandage as she sat next to him. "Oh my, are you hurt?"

"Thomas helped me. I'll be okay," she said as he inspected it.

"A splinter on the bridge, nothing serious. It was partly my fault, not warning her," Thomas said.

Onell nodded. "All good things heal, Acadia." He turned to Gregory. "Master, if your son has now taken Rhydar's place, what of you? Will you be returning?"

Gregory shook his head. "I do not plan to ... at least not on a permanent basis."

"Master Gregory? You are leaving for good?" Onell seemed startled.

He nodded. "I too, wish to see my wife. I will visit, of course. Thomas will now enjoy life on the islands."

"In the meantime, can you keep watch?" Thomas asked.

Onell nodded confidently. "Of course, always." He turned to his sister. "Acadia, you will be safe here, yes?"

She smiled. "While you were away, Thomas and his crew did me many favors; I feel very safe with him."

"Onell, where were you this entire time?" Thomas asked.

"I had thought you might wonder about that. Ever since you left Harper's Bay, Thomas, I have been near the islands. Cynthia and I agreed it would be best ... I have been at the wreck of the *Nemaris*, in fact. Several leagues northeast of here."

"The *Nemaris*? Father ... you said it vanished?" Thomas asked.

Gregory shook his head. "Beneath the sea. I am sorry if I wasn't clear."

Thomas nodded. It was a good feeling, knowing that the *Nemaris* was still somewhere in the world, even if as a shipwreck.

"You did keep an eye on the ship, then ... yet Epoth still found us," Gregory replied.

"His spirit was too strong to contain, even with my power, sir," Onell said.

"Wait, Onell ... you were that close all along?" Acadia asked.

"Yes, but I saw there was no need for me to visit. You had grown into a lovely mermaid, Acadia. My presence wouldn't change that any. That, and I took the care to protect the islands with one of Gregory's...." At this Onell frowned. "Well, it is a complicated story, which I will not go into at this time."

Perry approached the group. "Captain, forgive the intrusion, but the wind is about right ... I feel the time for our departure has come."

The merman turned back to his sister. "Acadia, are you traveling with Master Thomas?"

Acadia nodded. "I had hoped to see his home, Onell. I'm looking forward to it."

"It is a wonderful thing to see the world. Just be sure to keep your true self a secret, and you'll be fine." Onell smiled as if he knew what it was like.

"We probably shouldn't tell anyone where she's from, Onell. How about ... if we say she's from Crystal Bay?" Gregory asked.

Onell nodded. "Perfect. But, before you go, we should decide on a signal ... so we know that it is you rather than a pillager."

"Good idea," Gregory replied.

"Hmm ... I wonder what...." Thomas had forgotten the solution was inside of his pocket.

"Thomas, the shell?" Acadia asked.

"Oh, yes!" He pulled it out.

Onell noticed it for the first time. "A signal conch? I had lost mine long ago ... I'm glad you have found it, Thomas."

"I found it several years ago, and I gave it to him so I'd know when it was safe to come up to talk," Acadia explained.

"I shall have to craft another one, then." He turned to Thomas. "Three quick signals should be used to inform me of your return, then."

Thomas nodded. "Three signals. We shouldn't be gone more than a few weeks."

"Very well. I await your return," Onell climbed the railing and dove off. As soon as the ripples were gone, Jared came on deck. "Something going on out here? A man can't sleep with all this noise."

Gregory grinned and went to his cabin. "Nothing too complex, Jared."

"When shall we depart, Cap'n?" Jared asked, not yet noticing Acadia.

"As soon as you feel a good breeze, Jared," Gregory said, going inside.

"Aye sir."

"Jared?" Acadia asked, standing up.

He spoke as he started to turn. "Yes, Miss Acadia … huh?" He jumped and bumped into the rail behind him. Jared's jaw hung so far open it would've dropped to his knees had it been long enough.

"Did you have a good nap?" she asked with a smile.

Jared rubbed his eyes in disbelief. "I say I must be dreamin' to be seeing this, aye. I've been dreaming all this time."

Perry gave Jared a soft tap in the back, which from him was enough to propel Roberts forward several feet.

"Ooph … I say, Perry, you may recall a pinch being more traditional, aye?" Jared said as he regained his footing.

"I felt a good breeze," Perry replied with a big grin on his face.

Jared rubbed his back at the place where Perry had hit him.

Acadia giggled at their antics. "Aye, yes … Tommy, I mean, sir, I think you're the mate now, aren't ye?"

Thomas thought a moment about Jared's statement. Yes, he decided he was.

"Let's see … we'll need to raise the anchor, unfurl the mainsail … someone needs to man the wheel…." Thomas said.

"Thomas, what can I do to help?" Acadia asked.

"No, that's okay, Acadia … we can handle it."

Acadia smiled. "You're a hand short. Please, where should I be?"

Jared leaned close to Thomas. "Tommy … you can't ask her to do anything she's not familiar with … climbing ropes, for example."

"I think you're right. She can take command for now," Thomas said, turning to her.

Acadia looked back at him. "Command?"

"Give the order to depart," Thomas said with a smile.

Acadia whispered into Thomas's ear. "What do I say?"

"Bring us underway." He fell into line with Perry and Roberts.

"Uh, bring us … underway, men," she said.

Coming close again, Thomas whispered in her ear. "Say it louder, and from behind that wheel over there."

Acadia walked up to the ship's wheel and cleared her throat as the wind caught her long hair. "Bring us underway!"

"Aye ma'am!" Jared replied happily as he and Thomas worked the sails. Mr. Perry hoisted the anchor, and the *Inferno* sailed away from the Nemaris Islands.

As they left, Cynthia, Onell, and Marsha surfaced and waved. Gregory opened a cabin window and waved once. "Goodbye, my friends!"

Marsha had tears in her eyes, while Onell stood at attention. Cynthia smiled politely, with a wave of confidence that he would return.

Gregory sighed solemnly as they faded into the distance.

Triumphant Return

*I*t took the *Inferno* six days to reach Vesper. Upon mooring, Gregory took Thomas and Acadia to where his cobbler friend used to live and work. As she was wearing the dress that had appeared when the magic of the staff took effect, no one looked twice at the barefoot girl except to admire her lovely hair.

"Why ... this is the Bennedict's, yes?" Thomas asked.

Gregory knocked on the farmhouse door. "How'd you know that?"

Miranda answered the door. It seemed so long ago when Thomas had met her. "Thomas?" She smiled then noticed his father and Acadia. "And ... some others?"

"Hello, child. Is your father about?" Gregory asked.

"Um, yes. Please, come in." She seemed a little confused by Acadia's presence.

"Father! Company!" She left them in the sitting room to fetch Bo from the kitchen.

Seeing Gregory, Bo spread his lips into a wide grin. "Well, well well ... if it isn't my old friend Greg! I thought you were lost at sea or something!" The men shook hands firmly, and Bo gestured for them to sit.

"Looking fine as always, Bo. Where's Sherry?" Gregory asked.

"Sher?" Shaking his head, Bo settled into a chair. "Sorry, Greg, she's been dead for quite a few seasons ... She was lost during a nasty wind storm, I'm sorry to say."

"Oh no...." Being apart from his wife was difficult enough, but Gregory had always known she was safe. "I'm so sorry to have brought it up."

"Where you been all this time? Thought you were lost off of Kalis Island ... And Tommy...." He offered his hand to the boy. "It's good to see you again, young man."

"Oh, been on adventures. Going here and there." Gregory sat next to Thomas on a bench. "Met up with my boy, here, in Crystal Village. This is a good friend of ours, Acadia."

"Hello." Acadia smiled shyly next to Thomas.

"She's a bit bashful," he explained.

"Where're your shoes, sweetheart? Have you been walking barefoot all this time?" Bo asked, noticing her dusty feet.

"Maybe she cannot afford shoes, Father?" His daughter's tone suggested a hint of rudeness.

"Miranda, get these folks some of your tea."

"Yes Father."

Gregory nodded to Acadia. "Actually, she is the reason why we made a stop. I told her, and Thomas, that you were one of the best cobbler's on the Centra Sea."

Bo took a deep sigh. "Much has changed since I saw ye last, Greg. Never could make much money making boots ... these days Miss Mennings is really the expert when it comes to boots and lady shoes in this town. I's mostly doing farm work now, although I've got a few cows. They're all too healthy for making boots out of, though."

Miranda brought tea in for everyone.

"Thank you," Acadia said. Miranda responded with a forced smile.

"Tell ye what. Since I've no materials around, I'll introduce you to Miss Mennings." Bo turned his focus to the barefoot girl. "She'll sell ye a pair of good comfortable lady shoes, Acadia, she'll fix you right up."

Acadia nodded happily. "Thank you, sir."

"Come on, then. While she gets her shoes, you and I can hit the tavern and catch up some, what d'ye say?" Bo asked Gregory.

"Haven't had a good drink in a long while. Sure, why not." Gregory and Bo started outside.

Acadia went to follow, as Miranda stopped Thomas. "Where did you find her?"

"I met her a while ago. I felt sorry for her, having no shoes and all. You'd think she just learned how to walk." Thomas chuckled.

Miranda lightened up. "I had thought ... it was an infatuation ... I hoped we might spend more time together, get to know one another ...."

"Miranda, I don't understand love ... and we really only just met. Can we move on and just be friends?" Thomas asked.

Miranda nodded. "Tell Acadia that I apologize for my rudeness."

"Sure thing," Thomas said.

Acadia came back inside. "Thomas, are you coming?"

"Just finishing my tea, Acadia." He put down the half-full cup on the table.

"A pleasure meeting you," Miranda said with a reluctant smile.

"Yes, you too," Acadia replied.

"Thank you for the tea." Thomas left with Acadia.

She stared at the teacups a long time, finally washing them carefully and putting them away.

By early evening, Acadia had two pairs of shoes, one for normal wear and one pair of low heels, which she was almost certain she'd never be able to wear comfortably. As Marshall had plenty of money stowed on board that he would surely not need, they used it. Acadia purchased blouses and other clothes that she could wear during her stay on land. She even got a deal on a wonderful dress to wear. Since they were buying so much, Mrs. Mennings added the shoes at a discount.

After dining with the Bennedicts, everyone returned to the *Inferno*. They rested for the night before heading north the next day.

They sailed through the day, and as evening approached the lighthouse marking the rocky shoals of Bard's Point came into view. As the *Inferno* made her way to the docks, the crew spotted a familiar vessel was moored there, the *Valiant*.

"Well, looky there," Jared said. He lowered the sails while Perry weighed the anchor. Ward helped to tie them to the pier.

"Ahoy!" Ward cried.

"Long time no see!" Gregory helped him set up the gangplank. Moments later, they shook hands.

"The captain is visiting with your misses, Captain DeLeuit. Since we saw you comin', I figured ye might like a hand," Ward said.

"Thank you, Seriam. Lend me a hand?" Gregory led him to get some trunks.

"Good to see you, sir," Jared said.

Behind Ward came Benson who clapped Thomas on the shoulder in greeting.

"Did you folks come here right away?" Thomas asked.

Benson shook his head. "We made a quick stop at Grand Point before Cimmordia. Made a visit with Ward's mapmaker friend."

"Map … maker?" Thomas asked.

Ward came out from the cabin door, overhearing their conversation. "Yep, met up with ol' Lou. Best mapmaker around. Said a bunch of his maps had been stolen a few months ago … but nothing to worry 'bout, Tommy."

"Stolen maps … I wonder," Thomas began.

Acadia then came out and watched the lighthouse beacon rotate.

Suddenly, Ward noticed her and his jaw dropped. "Is that … Miss Acadia?"

"It sure is." Grabbing a handle, Thomas helped him haul a trunk down the gangplank.

When they came back up, Acadia turned to smile at them as Thomas headed for his cabin.

"Well, well, look at you!" Ward said.

"Good evening, sir," Acadia said, curtseying politely.

"Acadia, dear, you are too polite," Ward replied with a smile.

Thomas joined them, wearing his dress coat that had yet to be worn since he discovered it in his attic long ago. "Acadia, can you wait here tonight? Father and I are going to see Mother."

"Certainly, I wouldn't want to be in the way," Acadia replied.

Sensing her trepidation, he came to her and held her hand. "Well, I'm not sure you'd be in the way … but, you'll meet her tomorrow. Okay?"

Acadia nodded. "I'll be here when you get back."

"We'll make sure your ship's secured good, Tommy." Ward waved at the gangplank. "Go on, yer mother's waiting."

Gregory came out dressed in one of Marshall's fancier dress coats, this one a rich blue similar to that of the cabin's décor.

"Looking fine, Father," Thomas said.

"You too, son. Come on."

Together, they made their way home.

As the two walked through town, Gregory began to draw a fair amount of attention. People couldn't believe their eyes.

"Mr. DeLeuit?"

"Gregory, is that you?"

"I must be seeing things."

Gregory turned to Thomas. "I didn't expect this much attention."

Thomas shrugged. "Apparently, the people missed you, Father. Just like Mother and I have."

"Town hasn't changed too much since I left. But, it's nice to be back at last." He and Thomas continued the walk up the hill toward their house on the north edge of town.

"Your son has been doing an excellent job as cabin boy, Marianne." With a contented hum, Janes enjoyed Mrs. DeLeuit's special tea.

Marianne nodded. "I wonder what he meant by that letter, though."

"What did he say?"

"I've been going over it a few times since it arrived. Some locals?" She shook her head. "To my knowledge, you thought those islands were uninhabited."

Janes sipped his tea before responding. "It becomes a bit fanciful at that point of the story, Marianne. Not sure you'd believe me."

She chuckled. "Of all the stories you've told me, I think I can be at least willing to listen."

"All right." Janes set down his cup and gave her his undivided attention. "I suspect you know about mermaids, right?"

Marianne looked at him with anticipation. "Do they … exist?"

Janes nodded.

"That is pretty farfetched, Christopher."

Behind her, he saw Thomas and Gregory quietly enter the house. "I suppose one has the right not to believe me once in awhile."

"Maybe she would believe me," Gregory said. He stepped around the captain and came into the light.

Marianne stood up. "Gregory … is that you?"

"Marianne … you're as beautiful as ever." Removing his hat, Gregory slowly approached his wife with open arms.

"As it said, there were some locals, but I don't believe Thomas wrote about your husband," Janes said with a smile.

It took a moment before Marianne could find her voice. "Oh my goodness…." She and Gregory hugged each other tightly then pulled back to share a passionate kiss. The long separated lovers had to restrain themselves; after all, Thomas and Janes were both watching.

"Mother, we're home," Thomas said.

Marianne went to Thomas and gave him a motherly, but no less emotional hug. She then reached out and hugged both Thomas and Gregory, as the family was reunited at last.

"There's something you should know about us, dear," Gregory replied.

Marianne wiped a tear from her cheek. "There's more?"

"You may want to sit down, Marianne," Janes suggested.

Although she settled down in a chair by the fire, she couldn't bring herself to let go of her husband's hand just yet. She looked up at him with an uncertain smile. "And where have you been these fourteen years, Gregory?"

"Living on Nemaris Island. Protecting the treasures of my adopted father, Rhydar the Wizard," Gregory said slowly.

"Rhydar the Wizard?" Marianne blinked at him as though he'd just spoken in a foreign tongue.

"A wizard that recovered treasures from those who took of them unjustly," Thomas said.

With a nod, her eyes lit with recognition. "I have read the name before, yes ... then, does this mean...?"

Gregory nodded, sitting down next to her. "Yes, Thomas and myself can cast spells and use magical tools as Rhydar once did. That is why I didn't tell you everything. In fact, prior to the shipwreck, I had been going back and forth from those islands, returning treasures that had been collected there. I worked here, at the Dancing Dragon, and loved you the day we met." With a warm smile, he covered her hand with his. "After Thomas was conceived, I knew I would have to keep watch over the islands until Thomas would be able to continue the process."

"So you see, Mother, Father left to defend the treasure from pirates who would greedily take it as their own. We just now returned here after one of them brought a group of his men along." Thomas nodded to the window overlooking the harbor. "Father and I arrived in his ship."

Janes lifted his tea in salute. "You would have been proud of your son, Marianne ... he defended himself admirably."

Marianne looked at Thomas. "Thomas ... you learned to duel?"

Thomas puffed up a little. "A few of Captain Janes's men taught me during our visit to the islands. I am nowhere near as good as he is, but I was able to defend myself."

"He got a few cuts, but nothing serious," Janes added to reassure her.

"So that explains the shipwreck, then." She turned back to her husband. "Darling, what would you have done if I had remarried?"

Gregory smiled sheepishly. "I had expected that, actually. I would have just lived my life on the islands, then ... but, I'd always rather have spent it here, at your side." Lifting her hand in his, he kissed it fondly.

Frowning, she shook her head. "I would've come with you ... to Nemaris Islands if it meant being with you ... Gregory, I'd go anywhere with you. I was so heartbroken when I heard news of the wreck." Tears began to sparkle in her eyes.

"There would've been nobody to bake for, Mother. There are no ports on the islands," Thomas replied.

Shaking off her reverie, she raised a hand for emphasis. "I could always bake for you two."

Janes whispered to Thomas. "She could've baked for your friends, too."

"Aye," Thomas whispered back.

Janes finished his cup of tea and stood. "I suppose you have much to catch up on, and many stories to tell. But it has grown late, so I'll take my leave of you."

"Sir, will you be staying another day?" Thomas asked.

"We've nowhere to rush off to, Tommy." Janes nodded with a wink. "I think we can arrange that."

"Good eve, Captain," Marianne said.

"Thanks for the tea." Donning his hat, he bowed to his hostess and left.

"So what was it like on the ship?" Marianne asked Thomas.

"Exciting! We saw a host of new places, and once we recovered Captain Marshall's treasure map everything took off!" Thomas began.

"A treasure map? Please, do tell." Marianne gestured for her son to sit near her at the foot of the hearth.

"Well, it was in South Cimmordia, where Jared, my best friend of the crew, and I went ashore to visit the town, and we went to the marketplace where...." Thomas explained as both parents listened, sharing tea and tales of adventure.

They told stories late into the night, until all three were too tired to do more. Marianne mentioned that Thomas had inherited his uncle's style of storytelling and was very impressed. Instead of return to the *Inferno*, everyone slept in their respective beds, as a true family would in any other house in any other town.

Although he was home, he laid awake for a short time that evening, wondering how long he would enjoy such a tranquil existence. He had not forgotten that he would have to return to the islands soon.

The next day, Thomas and Acadia toured the village, seeing all the buildings and the lighthouse on Bard's Point. They visited Diamond Falls, the marketplace, and east to the edge of the coastal ridges. Their journey brought them to Elder Harrion's house. Although they both looked forward to introducing Acadia to Marianne, the old lighthouse was between the docks and Thomas's home and only a short jog out of the way.

"Bobby, are you home?" Thomas asked, knocking on the door.

Elder Harrion answered. "Thomas DeLeuit. Bobby is in Davenport visiting my brother. Haven't seen you in a long time." He turned to the young lady on his left. "I do not believe we have met."

"This is Acadia, sir. I know you have the best collection of maps and nautical equipment in town, and I was wondering if I could show them to her," Thomas asked.

Harrion cleared his throat. "Bobby must've dragged you up there one day...."

"No sir, I've known it for some time now. Everyone talks about it." Thomas wasn't about to give away his friend.

"Is that so?" He stroked his chin. "Well then, perhaps I should make it more public. You know, boy, if I had the money and a building suitable, I could make a library with all the articles I've made. I'm too old for such dreams though, and with Bobby away for the summer, he may never appreciate what I've done for him." With a sigh, Harrion gestured for them to come in and head up the stairs. "Go on up, then. All I ask is that you be respectful of the collection."

"Yes sir, we will," Thomas said.

Harrion raised a hand as though to catch a passing thought. "Say ... did I hear that your father was in town, young man?"

Thomas smiled. "Yes sir."

Harrion nodded, mumbling to himself. "I've still got his things; you remind him when you see him, hm?"

"I'll do that, sir," Thomas replied.

"Where do you hail from, dear?" he asked Acadia.

"Crystal Village, sir," Acadia replied.

"Ahh, I've been through that port once long ago. Quiet little town." Harrion went off to his chambers, finally letting Thomas and Acadia climb the stairs, to where his collection of maps and artifacts were stored.

"Thank you, sir," Acadia called.

Thomas held up a chart. "Here, this one, this is where we are." He showed her a chart of Harper's Bay and the Diamond Range to the east.

But Acadia was not looking at the chart. Instead, on an easel in the corner, she noticed the painting.

"Cynthia?" Acadia asked.

"Aye, it is. Probably Mr. Mandalay's only surviving work," Thomas said as Harrion came up.

"Mandalay? Young man, where did you learn that name?" Harrion asked.

"I ... read about him in Captain Scyhathen's journal, that my father had," Thomas replied.

"Yes ... perhaps that explains the initials on the corner." He pointed out the "N.M." in the corner. "The work is unsigned otherwise."

"He served on Scyhathen's ship as navigator and cartographer, sir," Thomas replied.

"Then ... can you explain this, boy?" Harrion removed a small scrap of paper from inside a velvet envelope.

The paper matched the thickness of the paper used in the journal, and shared ruffled edges on the left side and the yellowed look of years of wear. On it was a sketch of four small islands, as well as the same initials.

"The ... Nemaris Islands," Acadia replied.

"Young lady ... you certainly know your charts," Harrion said.

"Mr. Mandalay spent some six months there, before perishing on the return route ... that would've been January 19th, 1583," Thomas replied.

Harrion put the sketch away and pulled up a chair. "Mr. DeLeuit, I must ask you to excuse me for today ... you have inspired me." He turned and patted Acadia's hand. "You too, my dear ... if there is to be a library in Harper's Bay one day, I shall have to label them so whomever takes possession of them—be it young Bobby or another, maybe your father, perhaps, now that he has finally returned alive—these artifacts should be identified and accessible for the young people of generations to come."

"Of course sir, I would enjoy seeing a library here," Thomas replied.

After chatting with Harrion for a while, it was time to go. Once everything was put back, they headed back downstairs.

Thomas waved. "Good-bye, sir. Please give Bobby my regards."

"Good-bye, sir." Acadia gave him a sunny smile that flustered the old man.

"Good day, and thank you." With a big grin, Harrion waved as Thomas and Acadia made their way back to town.

As they made their way to the path that would lead to Thomas's home, Acadia stopped in the street.

"Acadia? What is it?"

She turned to Thomas. "Thomas, I'm sure your home is very grand, but I think I wish to return my home. I miss the islands."

Thomas nodded. "I understand. I suppose … I have to return too, but there's just one problem."

She gave him a little frown. "And what that would be?"

"My family is here … but I also must fulfill my duty to Rhydar," Thomas replied.

Acadia patted Thomas's back. "Ask your father for help. I'm sure he will know what to do."

Thomas nodded. Together, they walked back to his home along the northern shore of the bay.

After hearing about the situation from Thomas, Gregory and Captain Janes, who had been over for afternoon tea, both knew the only option.

Janes patted his shoulder. "Tommy, there's always a place for you on the *Valiant*."

"I thank you for that, sir," Thomas replied.

Gregory looked at Janes. "You were planning to set sail tomorrow, then?"

"Yes, that was the plan."

Marianne came in from the other room with a basket. "I was hoping to get the chance to do your laundry before you left … must you leave so suddenly?"

Thomas got up and hugged his mother tightly. "I don't want to, mother ... but someone must defend Rhydar's treasure."

Gregory cleared his throat. "I have kept my wand with me, Thomas. Once you're settled, I will make the trip and begin your training. For the first three months, I'll help you get familiar with life on the islands. How to cook for yourself, produce food ... everything that I learned, you will be taught. Then, from then on, twice a week I will visit and give you education on the magical equipment, as well as information about what all is in the trove." He turned to his wife. "Marianne, would you like to come along?"

Her eyes rounded at the prospect. "Oh yes, I would love to!"

"It's settled then." Janes stood and gave him a sympathetic smile. "Thomas, it sounds like fate has offered you a very special thing. Lonely, perhaps, but special."

"Captain, I am sorry, but you are mistaken. Thomas will not be lonely." Acadia drew close and took Thomas's hand.

Janes laughed. "Yes, I believe's you're right, Acadia, you're right."

Marianne looked the girl up and down. "I'm sorry, I do not believe we've met properly."

"I'm Acadia." She smiled a bit shyly.

"Marianne DeLeuit. You know Thomas well, then?" Marianne asked.

"You have a wonderful son, Marianne. I am pleased to have met him," Acadia replied.

Marianne nodded. "I feel strange asking this, but ... how did you meet?"

"We met late at night, in the lagoon," Acadia began.

Gregory leaned up to his wife with a smile. "Honey, there'll be time to answer all of your questions later, I promise. It is late."

Marianne nodded. "Nice to meet you ... and thank you for keeping an eye on my son."

"A pleasure to meet you as well, especially after all the remarkable things I've heard about you," Acadia replied.

"Come on, dear." He helped her see Janes to the door. "Goodnight, Captain."

Janes tipped it at the ladies as he left. "Good eve."

Marianne leaned close to her husband. "Gregory, dear ... is she from the islands? Is she what I think...?"

Gregory smiled. "Come dear. I have much to tell you."

While Janes returned to the *Valiant* for the night, Acadia found lodging in the DeLeuit's guest room. In the morning, Thomas and family found themselves again at the docks.

"When will you return, Father?"

"We'll need a few days to set our affairs in order. Then, Marianne and I will meet you on the islands. I expect you won't be alone for more than a day," Gregory replied.

Thomas nodded. "How will you get out that far?"

"Oh, don't worry about that. We'll arrive in a quiet fashion, I assure you." He gave a wink of confidence.

Marianne gave her boy a hug. "But remember this, Thomas. Take care of yourself, and remember that you can always come here if you are homesick."

"Thank you, Mother, I'll look into your orb whenever that happens and keep your offer in mind."

With another hug and a kiss, Thomas boarded the deck of the *Valiant*. Perry and Ward picked up the gangplank and prepared to weigh anchor.

A well-built sailor came running onto the pier, carrying a sack as he ran.

"Wait! Please, wait a moment!" the man cried.

Janes looked at the sailor. Mr. Gretty?

"Mr. Gretty? What an unexpected...." Janes began.

"Captain, do you need another hand?" Gretty asked.

"Why, yes, I do, but ... I thought you had a family in Vesper?" Janes asked.

Gretty nodded happily. "Aye, but they's doing well. My boy's a father, and my wife's a grandmother. I be a grandfather, too, Cap'n! They are well, and I told them that you needed an extra hand. Knowing you're the one responsible for my freedom, they let me go provided I write!"

"And that was their idea?" Janes asked.

"They know I'm a sailor, Cap'n! My Laura's been saying so ever since I left!" Gretty cried happily.

"Gretty! What're you wait'n fer! Come aboard!" Jennings said, looking for another friend on deck.

Janes laughed. "Well then, I'm not one to argue! Come on, before the ship leaves."

Gretty threw his sack on deck, climbed aboard and manned the riggings as they left port.

With a wave from his parents, who were holding each other tight, Thomas looked back with a smile. He then helped Jared with some ropes.

With a wave of Thomas's magic staff, Acadia was returned to her mermaid self shortly after they arrived offshore of Siren Island a week later. Thomas's things had been unpacked in the cave beneath the waterfall on Nemaris Island. Janes and Ellis left Thomas with cooking supplies and all the tools he'd need to survive, at least until his father taught him how a wizard managed such concerns.

"Tommy, I feel strange leaving you here alone to the elements," Jared commented.

"I'm sure that in time I'll adjust to it, Jared. After all, I now have these islands to call home. Magic and wonder surrounds me. Someday the magical skills I learn will allow me to sail to all the ports in the world, and all of this was given to me by a man I have only just met," Thomas explained.

"You'll be needing a crew when you go, won't ye?" Jared asked.

"Aye, Jared, and you'll be my first mate, unless Mr. Ward volunteers," Thomas replied.

Perry, who had been putting a cot together, stood up. "You'll have my help, Tommy."

Thomas shook hands with Perry. "It wouldn't be the same without you, Perry."

Just then, Gretty came into the cave. "Thomas, Acadia is waiting for you in the lagoon," Gretty announced.

Thomas nodded, heading toward the exit. "Thank you."

Acadia had been waiting for him on the bridge, with her tail dangling over the edge.

"Acadia, what is it?" Thomas asked.

She was looking away. "Are they going to be leaving soon?"

"I think they wish to leave tomorrow...." Thomas sat down beside her. "They have other ports to sail to. I've told the captain that he's welcome anytime, and hopefully we'll see him again."

"It'll be so quiet around here without them," Acadia said.

Jared walked onto the bridge. "May I interrupt?" Jared sat on Acadia's other side.

"Certainly." Acadia smiled.

"Turns out that the captain's ready to leave. He just wanted to make certain you had everything ye needed," Jared replied.

"Oh, I understood you'd be leaving tomorrow...." Thomas reviewed everything in his mind. "Yes, I think I'm all set; give him my thanks."

"Will he come by before he leaves?" Acadia asked.

"He plans to. You'll be able to thank him in person. I just wanted to give ye this before I returned to the ship." Jared took an object out of his vest pocket. It was a long wooden flute, one that was played horizontally similar to Jared's fife.

"Oh my ... is that for me?" Acadia asked, taking it and looking it over.

"Hold it like this, and blow through here," Jared took her hands and put them into the correct positions.

Acadia blew through the flute and drew back before blowing again. With just a few stray notes, she began playing the melody that Jared had taught her so long ago. Once the song was complete, she put the flute on her lap with one hand and kissed Jared on the cheek. "Thank you very much. I shall have to play it for you next time."

"I thought it be the only proper thing to do, since you found mine. Think of it as a friendship present," Jared said.

"I wish I had something for you ... of course, here," Acadia said, taking the small shell charm from around her left wrist. It was a pair of scallop shells with a shiny gem in the middle.

"This is too precious, I cannot...." Jared began.

"It is okay, I have a few of these, as Cynthia showed me how to make them. It has the power of good luck for good friends." She put the charm into his hand.

Jared slipped it onto his vest pocket and gave it a little pat. "I shall keep it by me always, then."

"You both shall have to play together sometime," Thomas said.

"Say … that reminds me of something. Acadia, when we were first approaching this island, I heard a strange voice … would you know anything about that?" Jared asked.

Acadia smiled, but did not respond.

Jared laughed. "I should've known!"

"I hope you'll be able to remember this place, Jared. Please do not forget," Acadia replied.

"Forget? Acadia, I'll never forget this place. Ever. Even without the charm, I will always remember you," Jared replied, as he patted her shoulder. She leaned close to him, and as he leaned closer, accepted a small kiss on the cheek.

"Thank ye, miss," Jared said, blushing.

"I look forward to hearing from you, Jared." Thomas shook his hand.

"I as well. I should be going, so as not to keep the cap'n waiting. Take care."

"Farewell." Acadia waved. Jared stood up and left for the *Valiant*. Thomas gave a deep sigh and returned his gaze to the southern coast, near where the ship was anchored.

"I do not wish to see them leave, but I suppose that is the way of things." Acadia sighed.

"Perhaps I am not willing either, but they have their journey to complete. We shall have to stay here," Thomas said with a sigh.

"Your family will be here, Thomas." She waved a hand around as if pointing out each person in turn. "You, me … my sisters Marsha and Cynthia, my brother Onell … and your father and mother will visit. Yes?"

Thomas nodded, a shy smile crossing his face. "Even if not all the time … yes, I believe you are correct."

Captain Janes and Mr. Ward arrived a moment later.

"Tommy, Mr. Ward and I thought we should bid farewell before we left."

Thomas stood to greet them, and Acadia turned around so she could see them better, flipping her tail onto the bridge.

"Sir," Thomas replied.

Ward laughed. "You don't have to be at attention, Thomas." He sat on the bridge next to Acadia.

Thomas nodded. "Sorry, it's an instinct, sir."

"Someday I'll be doing that to you, I'm sure." Chuckling, Janes also sat. "Do you have everything you are going to need?"

"I think I am set. My father will be here, and whatever I need to learn I will learn from him," Thomas replied.

"The common word is we feel strange leaving ye here, Tommy." Ward shrugged. "But I guess as time goes on we'll understand."

"Yes, I feel the same way, and I have plans to go sailing again. Until that time comes, you can find me here." Thomas gestured at the beauty around them. "You shouldn't have any reason to worry."

Acadia smiled. "We appreciate your concern, and you are free to visit at any time ... right, Thomas?"

Thomas nodded. "Any time you wish."

"It's good to see you're confident in yourself, then." The captain removed his hat to mop his brow. "Tell me, Tommy, did you ever expect to find yourself on such a voyage?"

Thomas thought a moment, and then gave his reply. "Captain, I cannot think of an appropriate response, other than this. I found my father, friends, and myself. I am very glad that all of us found each other."

Ward nodded in agreement. "I think ye'll do all right, Tommy. You'll do all right." He started to get up.

"Excuse me, but what is your first name, Mr. Ward?" Acadia asked.

"Huh? All this time, miss, and you're only askin' now what my name is?" Ward asked.

"I was just curious, is all."

"Seriam. Named after a great admiral of the seven seas," Ward replied.

"I like that name," Acadia replied.

"Likes yours too, Acadia." Ward stood and patted Janes on the back. "I suppose we've got places to go to, eh Captain?"

"I'll meet up with ye in a minute." Janes also stood up.

"Where are you headed now, sir?" Thomas asked as Ward walked away.

"Well Tommy, I can't really tell ye. Seeing how we've been enjoying this adventure with ye, despite a few losses." The captain spread his hands wide. "Our only plan is to have no plan. Let the sail go limp and catch the next wind, no matter where it goes. Chart some new lands, maybe find a sack of gold or two, and once the adventuring spirit gets sleepy, we'll head back the way we came. I assure ye this much, we'll be back to see ye before ye know it."

Acadia raised a hand for attention. "Christopher, before you go, there's one thing I must say. If I have not done so before, I would like to thank you formally for rescuing me and saving my life."

"You've done much for us, Acadia, my thanks to you as well. And Tommy...." He turned to his ex-cabin boy. "Thomas, when you're all grown up and have younglings of yer own, make sure ye pass on these stories of yours. Someday they'll become legends, and they'll all be because of you." Janes extended his hand.

Thomas shook Janes's hand firmly. He held it a few moments before letting go.

"Madam." Janes removed his hat and bowed to Acadia.

Acadia smiled and leaned forward so she could kiss Janes on the cheek before he stood back up. "I wish only good sailing weather for you, Captain."

"You'll be in our thoughts, miss." Returning his hat to his head with a jaunty flourish, Janes turned around and left.

The *Valiant* returned to the seas that day and journeyed into the unknown, ready to make more stories and adventures.

A few days passed. Gregory and Marianne arrived at the Nemaris Islands, and Thomas's education on how to survive on his own began. Among other things, Gregory gave Thomas a blank journal, saying it was something he'd regretted not having. That same evening, Thomas sat down inside his new home and took a quill pen and some ink, and began to write. His first words were as follows:

Although I've never kept a journal before, I have been inspired over these past few months by the penmanship of a venerable and well-respected buccaneer named Captain Terrence Scyhathen. His correspondence about his adventures to the islands he named the Nemaris Islands were the basis for my own adventures. Since I am hardly a buccaneer or seaman, I shall have to tell his story as it was for me, a viewer from the outside of a window looking in, taking one page at a time. For it was with great anticipation I read about the

*good captain, even imagining myself sword to sword with his nemesis, Epoth.
How was I to know my journey would mirror that of such a great man as
Scyhathen?*

*Later in this book you will learn the truth about Epoth and his former
existence as Captain Nepotherden. To find the correct page you will have to
bear with me, for although it is already written in the mists of the past, it
has yet to be written on these pages. The dates may not be entirely accurate,
and I do not expect a reader like yourself, whom I have not yet met, to fully
understand what has transpired on the Nemaris Islands.*

*These stories are all true, as are the characters associated with them. They
are as real as the book you are holding before you. Should you believe these
words as I write them, then you may read on. I invite you to learn more about
these adventures, involving the Buccaneer of Nemaris, those who have come
after him, those who have lived before him, and those who have yet to live.*

Thomas Arthur DeLeuit, June 21st, 1623.

The End

Epilogue

$\mathcal{J}$t is late afternoon, and the winds are growing faint. Birds are chirping, and the waves are subsiding. All is calm as a man strides casually through the surf, a gilded long sword sheathed at his side.

Captain Scyhathen takes in the view along a quiet beach during low tide.

He sees a man fishing along the shores with a net and a bucket. The man wears a hat that flops into his eyes, and there is a pipe in his mouth, which is surrounded by stubble. A bottle of rum is half sunk in the sand at his feet. He has never met this man before, yet Scyhathen feels compelled to talk to him ... and he senses he could do so as if he has known this stranger all his life.

"Good afternoon. May I join you?"

Removing his pipe, the man uses it to gesture to a nearby log. "Sit yerself down. I welcome the company."

Scyhathen takes a seat. "Is the fishing favorable today?"

"Some days you'll fish the ocean dry, other days they need to replenish their population." The man's gaze never leaves the waters.

"Which one is today?" Scyhathen asked.

"Neither. I've both taken fish out and put them back in."

Scyhathen chuckles in his confusion. "How could that be neither? I would call it both."

The man turns to look at him at last. "Ahh, but it is always both regardless. If I take out one fish here, there is another fish being hatched out there. If I let the fish swim free, another man may catch a similar fish at his own beach like this one we stand upon."

"You know your ocean well." Scyhathen nods in understanding.

As he speaks with the man, it soon becomes clear Scyhathen has indeed known the man all of his life. It is as if they are old shipmates who once met in some distant harbor.

"It is not all my ocean, but of this little amount, yes, thank you." With a nod, the man lifts his hat to Scyhathen, revealing his face. Although the captain has never met this man, he would recognize him anywhere.

Removing his own hat, Scyhathen stands to shake the man's hand. "To meet you at last is a true honor, Captain Jones."

"You as well, Buccaneer of Nemaris."

The Buccaneer of Nemaris
Of Forests and Friends

*I*n ancient times Cimmordia was unified by a vast stretch of trees known as the Everbloom Forest. An untamed wilderness of endless wonder and ethereal beauty, it was governed by a family of unicorns, led by the magnificent Mastaphin. They had defended their lands with peace and understanding since the earliest days of Crellan, and families of unicorns roamed the mountains freely with none to invade their territory.

Those were wonderful times—before men came.

Explorers discovered the fertile lands of Cimmordia and the first port cities were built. Ships brought hundreds of hard-working, determined men, and mighty fortresses took shape. The three great nations of Cimmordia, Dieteria, and Xavier, each in their infancy, grew larger by the day.

With endless resources for the humans to claim as their own, mankind's borders grew ever closer to Mastapin's sacred lands. Hunters invaded the forest, and the unicorns grieved to see their closest friends slain by arrows. The majestic elk, the timid rabbit, even the birds were not spared from the slaughter. Overwhelmed and outnumbered, the unicorns began to leave in search of safer regions, and the animals left with them. Slowly their magical protection across many parts of the forest faded.

Hunting parties began to find game scarce, and although the king of Cimmordia protected his kingdom's forests from hunters, it was too late. While the animals and wildlife eventually returned, the unicorns did not.

Divided throughout the continent, isolated and disconnected from each other, the unicorns became so few that their future grew uncertain. In a desperate move to save his people, Mastaphin decreed that any unicorn who found another that was not of the same blood line, they would be required to bear offspring. Separated from his own family, Mastaphin's hopes to travel across Cimmordia in search of his children was brutally ended by his death at the cursed hands of a mysterious outsider.

Of course that was long ago, and the world is now ruled by men, save for the few tiny pockets of wilderness where traces of magic remain.

One such place resides in mighty Ernell Cape on the farthest eastern reaches of Cimmordia. Bordered by rugged shorelines and impassable mountains, the cape's peace is untainted by an otherwise hostile world. Known for its abundant farmlands and orchards, the true treasures of the region are not valued in soil or gold, but as a place ripe with enchanted beauty. Upon the rocky cliffs of the cape's shoreline, a ring of trees surround sun-soaked burrows that house the Lavender Forest, the last known remnant of the great Everbloom Forest. Although a mystical presence seems to linger there, stories of Mastaphin and his kind have faded into the mists of time. Only academics, bards, and charlatan healers concern themselves with talk of unicorns. But all that will change when a young woman searching for her father enters a world only heard of in legends.

Future titles

Look for these other titles from J.D.Delzer:

The Buccaneer of Nemaris: Of Forests and Friends
The Buccaneer of Nemaris: Of Scimitars and Sands
The Buccaneer of Nemaris: Of Sapphires and Sirens
The Buccaneer of Nemaris: Of Tabia and Terrors
The Buccaneer of Nemaris: Of Damsels and Dragons
The Buccaneer of Nemaris: Of Masters and Slaves